D1616849

The Battle
Of Verril

Joseph R. Lallo

Security Public Library
715 Aspen Drive
Colorado Springs, CO 80911

Copyright © 2011 Joseph Lallo

All rights reserved.

ISBN: 1477684751

ISBN-13: 978-1477684757

DEDICATION

This book is dedicated...

To Gary, who inspired me to start writing the books.
To Sean, who encouraged me to keep writing the books.
To Cary, who convinced me to finish writing the books.
To Mom and Dad, who are the reason there is a me to begin with.

ACKNOWLEDGMENTS

I would like to acknowledge the hard work and contributions made by the following people, without whom this book would probably never have made it into your hands:

Nick Deligaris
For the magnificent artwork.

Anna Genoese
For the help in polishing my lackluster grammar.

My fans, bloggers, and friends:
For giving me the help, confidence, and exposure to come this far.

Chronicling the tale of the Chosen is a monumental task, and one that cannot and must not remain half done. If you have read the volumes already written, then you know well the trials that heroes must face. Already, there have been triumphs and there have been tragedies. Friends and allies have been pulled from the jaws of doom, while others have not been so fortunate. Despite these adventures, the truest tests of the Chosen still remain to be told. With these final pages, I shall set that right.

To do so, I must begin where my last account ended. Myranda, a young and dedicated wizard, had returned. Believed dead by the other Chosen, she swept in to snatch her friends from defeat. When all had been brought to safety, and for a moment things seemed calm, she agreed to share the events of her absence. They began where the others believed that Myranda's life had ended, in the lowest level of the personal menagerie of Demont, a general of the Northern Alliance. The devilish structure, filled with nightmarish creatures, was quickly consuming itself in out of control flames. She held the burning fort together with the strength of her will until she felt her friends escape, then relented, ready for the whole of the structure to collapse upon her, ready for fate to claim her. Fate, it seemed, had other plans.

#

The boards beneath Myranda's feet gave way just as the remaining ceiling over her head did the same. She dropped down into some sort of recess into the floor. Scrambling backward away from the very fort that was coming down on top of her, Myranda's desperate hands found their way to a metal handle. It was attached to a low door, seemingly carved into the stone of the ground. With only moments to spare, she pulled it open and dragged herself into the blackness beyond. The roar of the structure collapsing on itself rumbled all around her, as she clawed her way down the pitch-black tunnel. As she did, the rumble became more muffled, debris settling in above her. She pushed aside the thought that it was burying her alive. So too she ignored the concerns of what this place was and what she might find here.

The only thought on her mind was survival--get away from the fire, from the collapse. The rest could wait.

The fire had taken a greater toll on her legs than she had realized, as several attempts to stand failed. The sound of buckling stone behind her convinced her that it was better to crawl now than to die trying to walk. The smoke from the smoldering debris that had tumbled in behind her continued to burn at her lungs. She crept every inch of distance her body could offer before collapsing. The rumble and roar drifted away as Myranda's body finally reached its limit.

Perhaps hours, perhaps days later, Myranda's eyes opened to the blackness. The smoke no longer stung at her, but the air was stifling and stale. She coughed and sputtered as she rolled to her back. A sharp pain prompted her to pull something free that was jabbing her in the shoulder blade. As wakefulness fully returned to her, the stillness permitted the concerns she'd brushed away to rush back in. What was this place? If the monstrous creations she'd seen inside the fort were any indication, she shuddered to think of what kind of beasts might be kept in the catacombs beneath. In darkness such as this, her eyes may as well have been closed. Desperate for some form of information, she listened. Nothing. The silence was eerie, oppressive, and complete. Her nose and tongue told only of the acrid residue left from the burning wood, so she was left with touch alone. What it told her confused her.

The floor was . . . tile. A complex pattern of it, she felt, and skillfully made. She rolled to her stomach again and felt for the wall. It too was of the same intricate tile. Then her fingers came to something smooth, like a strip of metal or glass along the wall. As she ran her fingers against it, there was a white-blue ember of light that silently faded in, terrifying her at first. But as the soft glow of it spread along the strip, splitting and winding across what revealed itself to be an arched ceiling, she realized that she sensed nothing powerful, threatening, or purposeful behind the light. It must have been added simply to illuminate the walkway. Bathed in the glow of the curling ribbon of light that swept and wound its way down the tunnel, she caught her first glimpse of what she'd been feeling.

It was a mosaic, one that sprawled across every surface of the tunnel, spreading backward as far as the caved-in ceiling behind her, and onward into the depths of the tunnel, further than her dry red eyes could see. Irregularly-shaped pieces of white and black tile gathered together into forms. Some forms seemed to be composed of the black tiles, others of the white, such that every inch of the masterpiece was some part of a creature, interlocked and entwined like pieces of a puzzle, locked in some struggle or dance. The beasts depicted varied greatly, from horses, birds, dragons, and other creatures she knew, to beasts that had no eyes, no legs, nothing that she knew a creature should have. Yet, she knew it *was* a beast, that somewhere this completely alien form lived.

With considerable effort, she raised herself to her badly burned legs. Next to where she had been laying, the object that had jabbed her in the back was revealed to be the broken head of her staff. The rest was nowhere in sight. She scooped it up, immediately wishing it was whole again, as she badly needed something to lean on--for now, the wall would have to suffice.

As she moved painfully down the tunnel, the images of the mosaic began to seem more familiar. The creatures that had been borrowed for Demont's purposes appeared again and again, changing slightly each time. The dragon she had seen where she awoke began as white and, as she moved on, it appeared again and again--each time with more black mixed in, each time more twisted. Finally, the dragoyle was all that remained. Worse, the shape of a man began to recur, slowly making its way toward the nearmen that she had fought so often. The images chilled her to the bone. To see something she knew corrupted so was one thing; the truly disturbing thing about it was that each successive form was so subtly changed, she might not have noticed the shift at all if she hadn't seen them so close together.

Dark concerns about the same thing happening in the world around her began to emerge in her mind. There were so many nearmen, fiendish creations that masqueraded as humans. By now, surely the bulk of the army was composed of them. Yet she had only learned of their existence so recently. Did the other soldiers not realize? Did they not care? What other parts of her world were being twisted before her eyes so gradually that she was blind to the change? What were these other creatures?

Before long the burning in her mind was as unbearable as the burning in her legs. Ahead was a door; she hurried as best she could toward it.

When she reached the door, Myranda paused. It bore no lock, no markings. Nothing secured it at all. It was not the way of the D'karon, her enemy, to be so careless. Something was on the other side of the door, something secret enough to bury it deep underground. Surely there was some measure in place to protect it. Of course, none of that mattered. The way behind was blocked. The only choice was to go forward.

Carefully, cautiously, Myranda pushed the door open. The instant that she did, all of the light behind her vanished. A warmer, orange-yellow light, like that of a torch, took its place. The room before her became illuminated. It took no more than a glance to guess who owned this place. Just as in the laboratory that had fallen behind her, the room was immaculately kept. Thin, leather-bound books lined shelves along the wall in neat little rows. Sketches of this creature and that were pinned to boards and hung with care. A cabinet stood, filled with vials labeled in a placeless language. Everywhere, sheets of paper, neatly lettered with the same unnatural runes, sat in meticulous piles or organized files. If the fort above had been the laboratory of General Demont, craftsman of the horrid creatures, then this must have been his study.

If it were another time, she might have been fascinated by it all, but she was weary, wounded, and certain that if she remained in this place, she would be discovered. The room was not a large one, and there was but one other door. Best of all, a telltale draft whistling beneath it told her that beyond it lie the outside. Without the wall to support her, Myranda had difficulty navigating the room. She paused briefly to attempt a spell to heal at least some of her injuries. It was a futile gesture. The strength she'd spent holding the fort together long enough for her friends to escape would take days, perhaps weeks to recover, and this was no place to rest. The best she could hope for was to reach her friends. With them by her side, she could at least rest knowing that she would not face the next threat alone. If she was to join them again, she would have to hurry.

When she reached the door, again she found no security to speak of. She sensed no magic protecting it, though her recent ordeal had dulled her mind at least as much as it had her other senses. She pulled open the door and stepped outside, into the icy wind and biting cold of the north. Out of the corner of her eye, she saw a flash of light as she crossed the threshold. The door jerked shut behind her. She threw herself against it, hoping to stop it from shutting tight, but the force of the slam threw her to the ground. She placed her hands on the frozen ground and tried to stand.

A clicking sound on either side of the door that had ejected her drew her attention. Two alcoves, one on each side of the door, slid open. From each recess strode a beast that could only have come from Demont's twisted mind.

The creatures were long and lithe, their bodies not unlike that of a panther. The head, though, looked at best like a collection of cutlery grafted onto the beast. Two pairs of great serrated mandibles clacked together menacingly in the place where a face should have been. A jagged, blade-like horn jutted from the "forehead" of the creature, though the lack of eyes, ears, or anything else that a creature should have robbed the area of any resemblance to a head. Cutting edges ran like stripes along the creature's hide. The beasts could not truly *look* at her, but each most certainly had its formidable weaponry pointed in her direction.

Desperation and fear momentarily allowed her to ignore the state of her legs, and she lunged aside as the first beast dove at her. The second galloped off, away from the door. As Myranda rolled to her knees and tried to stand once more, the beast quickly recovered from its missed attack. The two creatures moved as quickly and surely as the cats their form had been cruelly adapted from, and it was mere moments before the first creature was ready for a second attack. The second creature had put a fair amount of distance between them, and now turned, bursting quickly into a full sprint.

Myranda gathered together the frayed remains of her mind and threw up a meager defense. A pulse of mystic energy fazed the nearest creature only slightly as she sidled over to the door and heaved herself against it. It would not budge. She turned her eyes to the nameless beast that faced her. Jagged, unnatural blades clacked expectantly. She raised her broken staff, but it was a futile gesture. Her spirit was drained. Defeat was at hand. What little strength her aching body could offer was poised to make the victory a costly one. The hair on the back of her neck stood up. Her heart pounded in her ears. As it had so often before in the heat of battle, time seemed to slow to a crawl. Her mind was burning with fear. Her skin tingled. With each passing heartbeat, the sensation grew. This was not fear. This was not anticipation. This was something more.

With a sound like the very fabric of reality tearing, a slash of light split the air above her, like a bolt of lightning that stopped in midair. Then another, and another. The slashes widened as feathery cracks began to spread out from them, each splitting into finer and finer cracks. In mere moments, what hung above her was like a thorny wreath of pure white light. She closed her eyes against the brightness. A distant cry grew suddenly louder. Even with her eyes shut tight, Myranda could see the brilliant pattern in the air.

With a tumultuous crash, the light suddenly vanished. Myranda opened her eyes. Before her, in a heap, was a young man with unkempt brown hair in a gray tunic. Beneath him were the twitching remains of a now-destroyed creature. The inexplicable newcomer groaned in pain, and slowly recognition forced its way through shock, fear, and confusion. She knew this man. He was a young wizard she'd met in a place called Entwell. It was a place of learning, tucked away on the other side of a treacherous cave. She'd spent time there, what seemed like a lifetime ago, learning the ways of magic. He had been her teacher, her mentor--and, above all, her friend--but she'd had to leave him behind in that paradise. His name was Deacon.

She'd reflected upon their time together more times than she could count in the eternity since she'd left. Now, with no explanation, he had returned, and his appearance had crushed the beast that had been threatening her.

A thousand questions and a dozen emotions fought for Myranda's attention, but one pressing matter defeated them all: the other creature. Before she could draw breath to shout a warning, a second gash in the sky opened and a small white bag came tumbling out. It landed with a force far too great for its size, directly atop the beast that was only steps away from bringing the unexpected reunion to an all-too-swift end. Thus, in the most unlikely of ways, the crisis was ended.

Myranda looked down upon her ailing friend. The fall, and more so what he had fallen upon, had taken a rather severe toll on him. He groaned again and rolled to the ground, rising to his hands and knees, then finally, unsteadily, to his feet. Suddenly, his clenched eyes shot open.

"Myranda!" he cried, as though he had just remembered the name.

The wizard's eyes darted around; finally, he found Myranda. He rushed to her.

"Myranda! Heavens above. It is a miracle! Are you well?" he asked, crouching at her side, his own injuries instantly forgotten. "No, no, you are not well at all! My crystal! Where is it?"

"Deacon . . . Deacon. *Deacon!*" Myranda called, finally with enough of her wits about her to appreciate the appearance of her old friend.

"Here, yes," Deacon said, scooping up his crystal and rushing to her side. "What requires healing most urgently!?"

His voice was insistent and desperate.

"Please, Deacon calm down. Thanks to you the danger is gone. Now, where did you come from? How did you get here?" Myranda asked.

"From Entwell, directly," he said, calling to mind his long neglected white magic teachings and beginning to restore Myranda's ailing legs.

"But how? It is so far. When did you leave? How did you find me?" she asked.

"I left a few moments ago. I've been watching you as best I could. It has been . . . well, part of a recent change in focus for me," he said.

"A few moments ago?" Myranda said, confused.

"Yes. Instantaneous travel. Transportation. It flirts with a number of techniques we have forbidden, but the principles were there. It just took some digging. Some innovation. A few weeks," he said, finishing up on the injuries he could see before beginning on his own.

In Entwell, Deacon had been the resident master of a field of the mystic arts known as gray magic. It was a catchall, dealing with anything that did not explicitly heal or hurt, and was not based on the elements. He'd devoted the whole of his life, since before he could speak, to mastering these arts, and thus they were second nature to him, an afterthought that he understood so thoroughly he often forgot that there were those who did not.

"How could you have been watching me?" she asked, trying to stand on her restored legs.

"Well, distance seeing is actually rather low magic. Penetrating the obscuring effect of the mountains required that you be exerting yourself mystically, but that was hardly a rarity for you. It took a bit of diligence, but I was able to pinpoint you rather frequently," he answered, his voice beginning to waver as he began trembling.

"Is something the matter?" she asked.

"Nothing at all . . . I am just . . . Is it always this cold?" he said.

Myranda realized that he was in no way dressed for the northern weather. The same light gray tunic he had worn in Entwell was all he wore now. It was scarcely enough to ward off the freezing wind.

"Good heavens! Why didn't you wear something warmer?" she asked.

"I-I haven't been thinking very clearly of late. Not s-since . . . Never mind. I have some things in my b-b-bag which might h-h-help," he said.

Shakily, he made his way to the crater that contained his bag and the remains of the second creature. When he spotted it, he jumped back.

"W-w-what is th-this?" he said, clearly having just noticed the beasts he had saved Myranda from.

"I don't know, they just came out from the walls. Something Demont dreamed up, I'm sure," Myranda answered.

"Demont . . ." he mused, as though somehow he knew the name. "F-fascinating. I've not seen something crafted in s-s-such a way."

"You can study it later. You need to warm up," Myranda reminded him.

"Indeed," he said.

Deacon grasped the cinched-closed end of the bag and tugged at it, but it barely moved.

"B-b-b-blast it. I was afraid something like this would happen. The transportation damaged the enchantments," he said. "Won't t-t-t-take a moment to fix."

He held his crystal unsteadily over the bag. A pulse of light and a flex of will later, and the bag seemed to rise up, as though it was no longer heavy enough to compress the broken creature beneath it. Sure enough, Deacon grasped the bag once more, this time lifting it as though it were empty, which it indeed seemed to be. He began to paw through it clumsily. As he did, the sound of much clinking and jostling could be heard from within.

"Sh-sh-sh-should have organized this better," he said, suddenly beginning to cough a dry, hollow cough as the bite of the cold finally got the better of his lungs. When the fit subsided, he cast a harried eye to the door behind them. "Is it warmer inside, p-p-perhaps?"

"I wouldn't risk it. There was some spell on the door that released those creatures," she said.

"If it was placed there, it can be removed," he said, gathering the bag closed and rushing to the door.

Myranda watched anxiously as he inspected the door. He looked it over, even without his crystal at work, seeming to follow lines and patterns that weren't there, until his eyes settled upon the door sill.

"Here. R-r-runes. I don't recognize them . . . but . . . it would seem they are spent. If we can manage to p-p-p-pry the door, the spell will not activate again," he stated with certainty.

With that he heaved a shoulder at the door, bouncing off painfully. He then raised his crystal. Another pulse of light and the door burst open so forcefully that it was nearly torn from its hinges. He rushed inside. When the door did not slam shut again, and no more creatures appeared, Myranda followed, shutting the door behind her. Deacon was beating his arms and looking desperately for some source of heat. Finding none, he raised his crystal once more and released it. The immaculately clear, egg-shaped focus stone took on a warm orange glow, and almost immediately the room's temperature rose to a comfortable one. He settled against the wall, sighed with relief, and slid to the floor.

"We need to move on from here as quickly as possible. This is Demont's workshop, I believe. I do not wish to be here if he returns," Myranda warned, nervously scanning the room once more.

"Duly noted. A wise decision," he agreed, as he rummaged through his bag once more.

The satchel was by no means large. Stuffed to capacity, it looked as though it might be able to hold a tightly-balled blanket, and it was hanging quite loose. Yet he pulled one full-length white cloak, and then another from it. Dropping the bag on the ground, he hurriedly put the cloak on. It was not ideally suited for the northern cold either, but perhaps in addition to the tunic he wore it would be enough. He then presented the other cloak to Myranda and helped her to put it on.

"How did you fit those inside that small bag?" she asked.

"It is quite large inside. A little trick traveling wizards use. I could make one for you, if you like, but it would take a bit of time," he said, showing her the bag.

When he opened the top of the bag wide, the inside looked to be mounded with vials, books, tools--indeed, the entire contents of Deacon's hut. They had not become any smaller, either. Looking into the bag was like staring into the mouth of a deep pit.

"That is quite all right. Deacon . . . I . . ." Myranda began, fumbling for the right words. "How long will you be out of Entwell?"

She wanted desperately to tell him how often her thoughts had turned to him, to tell him how much she valued their time together, but the words wouldn't come. It was as though it had been so long since she'd had someone like him in her life that she had simply lost her ability to express herself adequately.

"For quite a while . . . quite a while," he said. "My actions prior to my escape have soured attitudes toward me. I'm not certain I would be welcome."

"What did you do?" she asked.

"It doesn't matter," he said, his eyes beginning to wander to the contents of the workshop. "The important thing is that I managed to reach you in time. You say that this workshop belongs to Demont. He is . . . one of the generals, yes?"

"He is," Myranda said.

"Then . . . I think anything we might do to delay him is useful to the cause," Deacon remarked distractedly.

"I suppose," Myranda replied.

"To that end . . . I think it prudent that I take samples . . . remove pieces of his puzzle, as it were," he said, beginning to pour over the shelves and tables.

"If you must, but do it quickly. We need to rejoin the others. And be careful," she relented.

Like a child given permission to raid the shelves of a candy store, Deacon began greedily plucking up artifacts, sheets, and vials. After a cursory glance that somehow assured him that it was safe to do so, each was dropped into his seemingly bottomless bag. There was a case filled with crystals that he dropped in its entirety inside, and book after book followed it. Finally, he pulled down a large map that had been affixed to one wall, folded it, and tucked it inside.

When he was done, the shelves were near bare, and the bag did not even bulge. Myranda smiled at the utter enthusiasm in Deacon's face as he shuffled the things inside his bag, reaching down into it nearly to his shoulder to pull up things he was interested in looking at first and positioning them at the top. When he was satisfied, he cinched the bag shut and hung it effortlessly from the tie of the tunic beneath the robe.

"Well, I suppose that I am prepared to brave the weather again. Are you certain you are well? It has been some time since I last practiced the healer's art. I may have missed an injury," he said, suddenly realizing he had been ignoring her.

"I am well enough. Let us go, quickly. There is no telling how far the others have gone," she said.

"Then by all means," he said, bracing himself for the cold before opening the door.

The instant that the harsh wind touched him, he knew that the thin cloak was not nearly enough. After briefly considering coping with the cold, he decided that further action was required.

"Just a moment more," he said, shedding the cloak and clutching it in one hand as he held his crystal in the other.

He closed his eyes briefly, as if remembering, and then cast a spell. In addition to the swift, clean pulse of light from the crystal that signified his spells, a wave of light swept up the cloak from bottom to top. A glow trailed behind it, lingering briefly before fading. He stepped into the wind again, this time seemingly unaffected by it.

"What did you do?" Myranda asked.

"I imbued the fabric of the cloak with an enchantment that counteracts the cold by preventing any of my own heat from--" he began.

"An enchantment against the cold. That was answer enough for me," she said.

"Of course," he replied, clearly a bit disappointed at his explanation being cut short.

"Is it really so simple to cast an enchantment?" she asked as she stepped out into the cold, her layers of protection and years of experience making a similar treatment unnecessary.

"Well, normally no. The strength and complexity of an enchantment that a garment or other object will hold is . . . We make our cloaks specifically to ease enchantment," he said, catching himself.

"Thank you," Myranda said with a chuckle.

The pair stepped outside. The terror of Myranda's previous venture through the doors had been so overwhelming, she'd scarcely noticed where the door had led her. They were on the edge of a steep, icy slope. The weak glow of the morning sky cast light on a sparsely-treed countryside. The memory of their trip was faded by her ordeal, but she was certain that she was nowhere near where she had entered the fort with the other Chosen.

Nothing her eyes told her gave her any indication of where she might be. After a few moments of straining her eyes, trying to find something unique about the countryside, all she knew for certain was that the fort was somewhere to the southwest. An endless column of black smoke stretching high into the gray sky betrayed that.

"Where do we go?" Deacon asked, marveling at the sheer size of the countryside. He had no memories of any place but Entwell. Tiny and perfect as it was, it was his world. The rolling hills and mountains of white, the scattered, snow-capped trees, the tiny flickering hints of far-off fires . . . it all had a scope that was dizzying and disorienting to him.

"We have to find the others. They were headed south, for the Tressor. I . . . I don't know which way they are, or how far they've gone. Can you find them?" she asked.

"I can't, but I can help you to do so. I've only truly met Lain, and I certainly do not know enough of his soul to pinpoint it, but I could empower your own search," he explained.

"Very well," she said, immediately closing her eyes and raising her broken staff, weakly spreading her mind.

A moment later, she felt Deacon's warm fingers close about her hand. Instantly a cool, steady clarity swept over her mind, like that brought by a focusing stone, but far more substantial. She began to reach out, but as she did, his hands left hers and the steadiness withdrew from her mind as quickly as it had come. She opened her eyes to see a nervousness on Deacon's face.

"You must never do that. At a time like this, it is the worst thing you could do," Deacon warned.

"What?" she asked.

"Cast your mind far and wide," he said.

Myranda blinked. "I know of no other way that I might find them. What danger is there?"

"To do so is to send up a beacon for all to see. You may find who you seek, but those who seek you will most certainly find you," he explained.

"Then what shall I do?" she asked.

"I will demonstrate," he said.

He took her hand and both returned to their concentration. Deacon spoke, his voice as clear in her mind as in her ears. He told of the very same means he had used to find her. It was more direct, more targeted, and virtually undetectable. Before long, she felt the presence of the minds of the others, as clearly and as strongly as if she were standing beside them.

"I feel them. I know where they are," she said. "Ivy . . . she is . . . I can feel her sorrow. She thinks I am dead."

"She will know the truth soon enough," Deacon said.

"No . . . you do not understand. Her sadness is as much a hardship for the others as it is for her. I need to let her know I am alive," Myranda explained.

"It would not be possible with the others--they have minds far too strong to permit a message to be delivered against their will--but at the moment it would seem that . . . Ivy . . . is susceptible. I will link you," Deacon said.

She felt a flex of his will and suddenly the physical form of Ivy seemed to manifest itself in Myranda's mind. The malthrope, a half-human/half-fox creature, stood before her, seemingly real enough to touch. Her stark white fur and muzzle, her inquisitive pink eyes, her pointed ears and tail--they all seemed vivid as life.

"M . . . Myranda!?" Ivy cried joyfully.

"Ivy, I am glad to know that you are all right," Myranda said.

"You are glad!? I thought you died. The fort fell! You were inside!" Ivy gushed tearfully.

With their minds linked, the emotion was like an earthquake. Myranda had to fight to remain connected.

"Listen, Ivy. I just want you to know that I will be with you soon. Tell the others. And be careful," Myranda said.

"I will, Myranda," Ivy said, another surge of joy finally shaking the bond that connected them.

Slowly, Myranda allowed her concentration to wane, the cold whistling of the wind returning to her ears. Deacon's grasp lingered for a moment before he lowered his crystal.

"That was remarkable," Myranda said. "Is that how you searched for me?"

"Each and every moment of my waking days. With those blasted mountains between us, it took a measure more effort, but I found you, so it was all worth it," he said, his eyes staring at the hand that had touched hers. As his gaze wandered up and locked briefly with her own, he tried to continue. "I-I knew that I had to help you. Your cause, it--it is far too important. Are you confident that you know where the others are? Can we reach them soon?"

"I know where they are, but I still am not certain where *we* are," she said.

"Navigation . . . navigation spells. I . . . never truly pursued them. They exist, but in a place like Entwell, there is just no need. Foolish of me. All spells have importance. One moment; I will turn one up," he said, scolding himself under his breath as he rummaged through the bag again.

"The map," Myranda reminded him.

"Yes, yes. I am certain I can create a map, I just require a few words to refresh my memory. The primer. Where is my primer?" he replied.

"No, Deacon, you took a map from inside. We can use that," Myranda explained.

"Oh . . . oh, yes, yes. Of course. Where is my head?" the wizard replied, quickly drawing the neatly folded sheet form the bag.

The instant it was removed, the wind tried to tear it from his grasp, but with a gesture, the wind parted around them. Myranda marveled for a moment at the effortless, casual way in which Deacon incorporated magic into everything he did. He used it as one might use one's hand to brush away a hair or tighten a knot while the mind was busy with other things.

She turned to the map. It was drawn with the same exacting detail as everything that Demont had put his hand to. The labels were in the mysterious language that she had seen throughout his laboratory and workshop. Not a word or symbol of it had any meaning for her, but that was of little concern. Here was the place she knew the fort to be. There was the thin line of the tunnel she'd trudged through. And here was the workshop they'd just left. The place that she'd felt the others to be was a considerable distance away. Either Lain and the others had moved very quickly, or she'd been unconscious for some time. Likely both. Regardless, they would not be able to catch up on foot.

"They are here. Heading toward the mountains, or there already. I don't know why they are going there. They had been heading south before," she said.

"What is our course of action?" Deacon asked eagerly.

"They are much faster than us, and there is much distance between us," Myranda mused out loud. "Is it possible for you to bring us to him in the same way that you brought yourself here?"

"No. No, certainly not. The spell is too rough. Too dangerous. I have neither the strength nor the focus necessary to transport even one of us safely," he stated firmly.

"Then how did you come here?" she asked.

"I required a great deal of aid from Azriel, as well as more than a little manipulation of likelihood," he said.

"Then we shall have to reach this town. With any luck, there will be horses there. While we walk, you must explain to me what you mean by 'manipulation of likelihood,'" she said.

When the map was folded and stowed, and the wind was permitted to resume its preferred course, the pair headed off toward the town indicated on the map. As they traveled, Deacon spoke at length about the methods he had used to find her and to reach her. He twisted confusing analogies, likening the fabric of reality to folded paper with a hole pierced through one moment, the next to a many-sided die weighted to fall as one requires. He claimed that the spell he used was not strong enough to allow him to be certain he would be transported unless an endless string of factors turned out in his favor, and he hadn't the strength or knowledge to manipulate those factors. Instead, he had diverted his strength to twisting and pulling at the rules that governed reality, turning probability on its head until some spectacularly unlikely circumstance, whatever it might be, produced the needed effect at the needed time.

Apparently, the three lightning bolts she had seen had been the impossible coincidence he needed. It all seemed like madness, but he spoke about it plainly, as though it was the utmost in simplicity.

When his lecture was complete, he prompted--indeed, pleaded--Myranda to offer up the tale of her journey since she had left his home. He had seen only precious, fleeting glimpses, and though there were scattered moments when he caught a whisper of her thoughts, his mind ached to know every last detail. Myranda agreed. Instantly, the thick tome that had been perpetually in his hands when they were in Entwell emerged from the bag. He recorded her words studiously, now and again requesting details and hastily sketching the sights she had seen.

His enthusiasm at each new piece of information mercifully distracted his mind from the cold. Increasingly, as the short northern day progressed, he took his hands from the stylus and book to wring some feeling back into them. Rather than stop his careful record for even a moment, the book and pen drifted dutifully before him as he did so, continuing to record Myranda's words on their own until he was finished.

Myranda, indifferent to the cold, was driven to continue, despite the weariness that cut her to the core. Her "sleep" in the tunnel had been anything but refreshing, and though Deacon had spared her of her injuries, he had done nothing to restore her strength--of body *or* mind. By the time the light began to fail, it was clear that the town would not be reached before her body gave out completely. Her eyes fixed themselves on a small, tight stand of trees that would shelter them--at least from searching eyes, if not from the wind or cold.

When Myranda settled down on the ground, leaning against a tree, Deacon did the same, across from her. He looked anxious, as though there was something he or someone else had forgotten.

"Is something wrong?" Myranda asked.

"We . . . we will be spending the night here," he half asked, half stated.

"I'm afraid so," she said.

"Oh, not a problem. It is just that the weather is harsh and I was not certain that sleeping unsheltered was in our . . . never mind. A fire? Should I start a fire?" he stumbled.

"There doesn't seem to be much dry wood about," she said.

"Not to worry," he said.

A gesture later and a flame danced a few inches from the ground with little regard for the fact that there was no wood to fuel it.

"Will that last until morning?" Myranda asked, smiling at the latest impossible feat Deacon had performed. Technically, she could do the same--but for him it seemed effortless.

"It will last for the rest of the week if I don't dismiss it," he said.

"Wonderful! I don't suppose you have any food in that bag of yours?" Myranda said.

"I . . . I hadn't thought to include any . . . Oh! I believe I brought a few of your apples!" he said, quickly rummaging through. "Had I been thinking, I would have brought food enough for an army. And something to sleep on! Blast it all, where was my mind?"

Finally, he produced four glossy, red apples, tossing one to Myranda.

"It does seem odd," said Myranda, taking in the scent of the fresh fruit before taking her first hungry bite.

"I was focused primarily on what I thought would be the more difficult task of *reaching* the outside world. The thought of what to do if I actually succeeded barely brushed my mind. I suppose I didn't think it likely enough to plan for," he explained.

"You shouldn't have taken so great a risk," Myranda scolded.

"I cannot bear to imagine what might have happened if I didn't. You *would* have been killed. I had to try. All I had to risk was my life. I mean nothing in the grand scheme," he said.

"You mean a lot to me," she said.

For a time, Deacon and Myranda were silent.

"I . . . you mean a . . . a great deal to me as well," Deacon struggled to say.

He fidgeted a bit, looking as though he would crawl out of his skin if he could.

"And to the world," he added uncomfortably, flinching as he said the words, as though he regretted them leaving his lips.

He crunched nervously at an apple and sheepishly avoided eye contact. After a few more moments, Myranda broke the silence.

"So, if you failed to bring the necessities, what *did* you bring?" she offered, sensing a change of subject would be the best thing right now.

"I, um, I brought a great deal. In fact, I really should have given them to you sooner," he said, beginning to rummage through his bag again. "There was the cloak, of course, but aside from that, I have a bow and set of arrows. A few daggers . . . Here is my spell primer . . . A few healing potions . . . Where is it? Ah! Here."

He drew from the bag a jewel every bit as pure as the one he perpetually held.

"The day you became a full master, our craftsmen set to work refining a crystal befitting your skill, and a similarly fine staff to mount it in. You left before either was even nearly completed, but work continued. The staff is still incomplete, but this was finished just days ago. I managed to . . . acquire it. I felt it would do more good in your hands than on the shelf awaiting your return," he said, presenting her with it.

He touched the head of her shattered staff. The wood that held the crystal in place uncoiled like a living tendril, accepting the replacement and wrapping back into place. He dropped the old crystal, barely more than a bundle of cracks and shards after the trials it had endured, into his bag.

Myranda felt the effects of the superior gem wash over her. Holding it lessened the haze that addled her weary mind, as though the staff had taken a portion of the stress of her mind upon itself.

"Like night and day, isn't it," Deacon said. "It was not so long ago that I received my full mastery crystal. Just a few years. Wait until morning, when you've more of your strength about you. Things that were impossible to you before are well within reach, and things that were simple are effortless."

"It is remarkable," Myranda said with a yawn.

She finished the rest of her apple.

"Deacon, tomorrow we should reach the town. Perchance, did you bring any gold with you?" she asked.

His expression was answer enough.

"Don't worry about it. We will work something out," she said, leaning back and closing her eyes.

As Myranda drifted off to sleep, Deacon watched. His mind scolded him relentlessly for dozens of missed opportunities and mistakes. Not only things that he had failed to bring, plans he had failed to make, but things he had failed to say, and things that should have been left unsaid. Even now, the confounding state of mind that had plagued him since that fateful day when she disappeared from Entwell burned at him.

He cast a quick spell to end some aches that had been nagging him from his fall. His left hand tingled slightly, a bit numb from the cold. He flexed it a few times until the feeling passed. Carefully, he began to assemble words in his head. Care must be taken. Things must be right. Tomorrow he would make up for his foolishness. Tomorrow . . .

The morning sun was still hours away when Myranda stirred. Deacon's eyes had never closed. Each ate the remaining apple allotted to them before the fire was dismissed. Myranda shouldered her quiver of arrows and bow, equipping herself with the other items Deacon had brought for her, and they set off once more. She sensed that something had changed as they continued on their way. Deacon was quiet, and the book and stylus remained in the bag. He was rolling the crystal in one hand, his eyes distant and pensive.

"Is something wrong, Deacon?" she asked.

"There is . . . there is something," he replied hesitantly.

"What is it?" she asked, concern in her voice.

Deacon stopped walking; Myranda stopped and turned to him.

"I am not sure that this is the time for it, but . . . in the days since I met you . . . I have done a great number of things that I don't understand. Things that didn't make sense to me. Things that I shouldn't do. I knew that they were wrong, foolish, impossible things, but I could not help myself. I was not sure what was happening. You know that my choice of gray magic has led me to have few friends among the wizards in Entwell. Indeed, I have lived there all of my life, yet there were only a handful of individuals in whom I might confide. I spoke at length to them about this sickness. This affliction of the mind. Some would not listen. Only Calypso seemed to have any insight, but she was vague about it. She seemed to think that I would not accept her advice if she was direct. She was right. It doesn't matter though . . ." Deacon began, cryptically.

His words had a measured, rehearsed quality, yet it seemed that it took all of his strength to say them. As he spoke, he fiddled with his crystal more and more, shifting it to the other hand, slipping it in the bag to wring his fingers, then pulling it out again.

"Logic had always ruled my life. Spells followed a graceful order. One thing followed another, and always with a specific cause. Whatever was happening to me was different. It had no cause. My mentor, Gilliam, had spoken to me early in my apprenticeship, warning that there was one thing in the world that followed no rules, obeyed no laws. That thing, he said, was the most powerful force in the world. He never did explain what it was he was talking about, what force he spoke of. I know now. Myranda . . ." he said, sweat rolling down his brow in spite of the cold.

The crystal dropped to the ground. Myranda stooped to retrieve it for him. He reached out to stop her. When he did, she gasped and recoiled.

"Your hand!" she cried.

"Never mind it, I must finish," he pleaded.

"Deacon, your hand!" she repeated, grasping his wrist and raising his left hand.

"Myranda, I . . . that's . . . curious," he said, now realizing the source of her concern.

His hand was partially missing. It had faded to nearly nothing, like a weak reflection. He tried to grasp it with the other hand, but it passed through, as though his left hand was not there at all. Quickly, he pulled back his sleeve to find that the change was steadily creeping up his arm. Myranda, panicked, grabbed the crystal from the ground and placed it in his other hand. She made use of her own upgraded staff to try to determine what the source of this horrific occurrence was, but nothing presented itself. Mystically, it was as though all was as it should be. As though whatever was happening was natural.

"What is happening? What should I do?" she asked.

"I am not certain yet," he replied.

There was naught but calm in his voice, and naught but fascination in his eyes. He closed them, gathering his mind into a spell. The affliction began to slow, and then recede. Just as solidity returned to his palm, however, he cried out, his fingers twitching into an agonized claw and shifting to some sort of pitch-black stone.

"It would seem--" He grimaced in pain. "--that the bag was not the only thing damaged by the incomplete spell."

"Tell me what to do!" Myranda pleaded helplessly.

"I am . . . not certain," he said.

His hand suddenly returned from the petrified, blackened form, and instead sprouted extra fingers. Deacon sighed with relief.

"The pain is gone. This is . . . this is chaos," he said, suddenly realizing the answer. "Chaos. Of course. Chaos magic is the one field that Entwell has never had a master for. The manipulation of probability must fall into that realm. Naturally it would!"

"Can you stop this?" she asked.

The spare fingers vanished and the hand made it partway to some other form before rebounding back to normal. When it did, he thrust the crystal into the hand. Instantly, a sharp glow arose in the heart of the crystal. A moment passed, then another. The hand remained normal.

"What did you do?" she asked.

"I am . . . manually enforcing normality. The manipulation of likelihood, it would seem, has fundamentally altered my hand. It appears that it no longer behaves as logic would dictate. It is bounding from one side of improbable to the other on its own. It is unpredictable by nature now," he explained.

"How could you have come to that conclusion so quickly?" she asked, confused by the degree of detail and certainty with which he spoke.

"I . . . had determined that this was one possible outcome of such a spell," he answered.

"*And you still did it?* Why would you *do* such a thing!" she cried.

"It was the only way to--" Deacon began.

"Don't tell me that! We both know that all you needed was time! You are brilliant! You risked your life and did this to yourself for what? Because you were impatient? Because you weren't thinking? Because--" Myranda raved.

"Because I love you!" he cried out.

Myranda sunk into a stunned silence.

"That is why I couldn't think clearly! That is the sickness that Calypso had spoken of, the force that Gilliam had spoken of! All I could think of was you! I had to be with you. Nothing else mattered then, and nothing else matters now!" he ranted.

The words came out with a pressure long waiting to be released. Myranda looked into his eyes. They were alive with emotions--and, most of all, relief.

"If I were not a fool, I would have realized it sooner. I would have told you before you left. I would have gone with you. But it wasn't clear to me then. Now it is," he confessed.

"Deacon . . . I feel the same way. Of course I do. I have longed all of my life to even know someone like you. I had convinced myself that such a person did not exist. The time I spent with you in Entwell was like paradise. To be with someone caring, intelligent . . . everything I had always hoped for. I suppose I didn't realize it either, or I would have stayed," she said.

"No. You had to go. This is the way things had to be. I do not regret my decision for a moment, and nor should you," he said.

Myranda stepped forward and embraced him. He warmly returned the gesture. They held each other for a long moment, before finally they separated, the task at hand unwilling to wait any longer.

"Can you cure your hand?" she asked.

"Well, certainly not in the same way that it was altered. As you might imagine, it is in the nature of chaos magic to be unpredictable. There is very likely a cure, but for now I will have to settle for something a bit more temporary," he said, reaching down into the bag. "Another enchantment should serve the purpose well enough. I just need something . . . something I won't have to hold onto, or mistakenly leave behind."

"One moment . . . perhaps it is time to give this new crystal a test," Myranda said.

Pulling free an arrow and a dagger, she cut the lashing that held the sharp tip in place. Then she brandished her staff and released the arrowhead. It hung in front of her with scarcely a thought. Drawing to mind some of the other teachings she'd brought with her from Deacon's home, she quickly raised the temperature of the piece until it was little more than a floating blob of white-hot metal. A few more thoughts and it twisted and turned itself into a ring, a simple design embellishing the surface as what little metal was unneeded swirled off into a simpler, more delicate band. A final thought cooled the pair of rings and dropped them into her hand.

"Brilliant. And masterful," Deacon said, admiring the piece he was handed. "Worthy of being an exam back in Entwell, I would say. You would have made a fine teacher."

"Is it sufficient? Will it hold the enchantment?" she asked.

"A normal arrowhead might not have been, but those we make in Entwell will be quite sufficient," he said.

Deacon thought for a moment before casting the appropriate enchantment upon the ring. He slipped it onto his finger and slowly transferred the crystal to the other hand. Even without his constant counter influence, the afflicted limb remained normal. Both heaved a sigh of relief. Myranda began to slip her own ring on.

"No. Wait a moment," he said, taking it from her. "You have given me a gift. The least I can do is return the favor."

He cast a second enchantment, then took her hand in his. He slipped it onto her finger with all of the respect and reverence that such an act warranted.

"There. An ancient spell of protection, one of the most fundamental in Entwell's history. The very same enchantment adorned a pendant around Azriel's neck when she found the land of my birth. May it bring you the same luck and fortune as it brought her," he said.

When they finally continued on their way, it was with spirits higher than they'd been in years. Suddenly, the cold seemed to be gone. The blackness of night was no longer oppressive. The countryside was as icy and unforgiving as it had been minutes before, but there was now no place that they would rather be. The conversation flowed easily, as though the months that they had been apart had never happened.

Deacon was filled with a sense of wonder at these, his first steps into a vast world entirely new to him. He marveled over the size and isolation, hearing tales of the sights he was sure to see. He looked forward with great anticipation to their arrival in the town.

Now and again, the map was consulted, but not to find their way. The initial glimpse of it had been more than enough to restore Myranda's well-practiced sense of direction. It was not the towns on the map that drew their interest, but the other markings. Deacon looked with fascination at the shapes and symbols. It was that rarest of things, a language he knew nothing of. The very same writing covered the books and notes from Demont's study, occasionally accompanied by familiar words and terms. He launched himself headlong into the task of deciphering these new runes.

"They differ fundamentally in structure from any other language I've seen," he said, an array of different notes and books scattered in the air before him, the folded map at their center. "It is used for place names, terminology, spells . . . yes. This is definitely a spell. I think that this may be the true purpose for the symbols. Remarkable . . . a language defined for spells first and communication second."

"How is that possible?" Myranda asked.

"Well, these runes here have unmistakable mystic power. These others are different. Weak . . . it is . . . it is as if this is not one language, but several. Five . . . a dozen . . . more than that. A patchwork of languages, none familiar to me. What do we know of this race, the D'karon?" he asked.

D'karon was the name applied to those they fought. Even before she learned she was one of the Chosen, the D'karon were her foes. They constructed creatures, commanded armies, and wove twisted and cruel magics. Indeed, of the five generals of her homeland, the Northern Alliance, all but one seemed to be a member of the dark race. Despite their unmistakable influence, and her repeated confrontations, their origins and their nature remained shrouded, save one small notion.

"Nothing beyond the fact that they are not of this world," she said.

"I dare say they are not from any single world. The way these words collide into uneven, ill-fitting phrases implies some fusion of different cultures. Amazing," he posited.

"You can tell all of that from their writing?" she remarked.

"There is nothing so telling as the language of a people. One moment . . . Yes. Patterns are emerging. See? Here. This is a spell book, it must be, and all of the pages end with this symbol or some variation of it. This other book--it looks to be notes--does not bear the mark anywhere. It is unique to the spells. Like some activation phrase. It is possible that this mark, when accompanying any phrase written in this language, will bring about some sort of mystic effect," he thought aloud.

"What is this?" Myranda asked, pointing to a shape with some runes beneath it on the map, located deep within a mountain range.

"I am not certain. Why?" he replied.

"I don't know of anything there. No town. No fort. Nothing. And it looks the same as this other mark, here in these mountains. That was where I found Ivy. And the same mark here, where we just left," she said.

"The D'karon forts!" he said, unfolding the map fully.

The sight they beheld was chilling. They were everywhere. Like black stains on the map, every valley, every mountain, every place far from prying eyes was marred by one of the marks. Several forts she knew of, Northern Alliance forts, bore the mark. Worst of all, the black mark rested on the capital itself. There was even one far to the north of it, at the very edge of the map.

The fort that they had just toppled had nearly taken her life, and now there were dozens more.

The unfortunate revelation put a renewed urgency in their minds. Deacon had been lucky until now. He'd not yet faced one of the generals, and had had only the merest brush with their creations--but Myranda knew all too well the things that they were capable of, and to know that their roots were so deep was terrifying to her. She fairly ran, her mind only on securing the means to catch up with the others. Deacon kept pace, stumbling now and again as he tried to keep one eye on the ground and one on the mound of indecipherable notes.

Aside from the assortment of sheets and artifacts orbiting before him, there were a handful of other items he had draped over his shoulders and tucked under his arms, each featuring familiar symbols alongside foreign ones. These might prove the key to unlocking the secrets of the language, offering some manner of common ground between the languages.

The dull light of day came and went, with the last of its glow lingering at the edge of the western sky as they approached a tiny town. One needed scarcely a glance at the town from afar to see that the destruction of the fort, a fort that may well have been a mystery to them until the black smoke rose from the field the day before, had put the town into an uproar. The place was far too small to have soldiers patrolling it, but the streets were alive with the sturdiest townsfolk serving as a makeshift town guard. It was clear to Myranda that this was not the time to come walking in from a field looking as she did, even if she wasn't an increasingly well-known enemy of the state. Worse, there didn't appear to be much in the way of a stable. Likely the horses of the town were the property of the residents and visitors. To deprive a person in a town as small as this of their horse, be it through sale or theft, would be to maroon them here.

Myranda stood for a few moments, contemplating what to do. Deacon, at first, took the opportunity to devote his full attentions to the latest in the stack of Demont's notes, but quickly became aware of Myranda's look of concern. At his prompting, she explained the situation to him. The source of the difficulty clashed repeatedly with the life he was accustomed to in Entwell. There, if someone needed something, they merely asked for it. Indeed, even that was seldom necessary. All was provided. He similarly was not certain why they would be distrusted for arriving on foot, looking as though they had been through the ordeal that, indeed, they had. Above all others, one confusion could not be cleared.

"But you are Chosen. You are trying to return to the other Chosen Ones and return to the task of saving the world. Surely the townspeople would gladly offer you anything you need," he said.

"The prophecy is something of a child's tale here," Myranda explained.

"I . . . see," Deacon said, attempting to process the statement. "Well, nonetheless. This should not be a concern for you. If you cannot risk showing your face in the town, then I shall do what needs to be done. Tell me what you require and it shall be attained."

"Deacon, I am not certain that you are ready for this. We will just need to find a different town," Myranda said, her mind working hard at the problem.

Deacon looked Myranda in her eyes and spoke earnestly. "Myranda, I came here to be useful to you and I mean to do so. Tell me what you need and tell me where to meet you. You can trust me."

Myranda hesitated, but relented.

"Be careful, and put the crystal away. There are very few wizards about. Don't use any magic if you can help it," she warned before listing what was needed.

A few moments later, Deacon was on his way to the town, stuffing items into his bag. He knew that he needed at least one horse, preferably two, and enough food to last a week. He had no clue how he would attain them--but, for him, that was beside the point. Myranda watched nervously as she skirted around the edge of town to the other side. Deacon was every bit a capable person, but he was well out of his element. She set her mind to the dual task of escaping whatever mob was sure to come sprinting behind Deacon and reaching the others quickly.

#

Deacon approached the nearest entrance to the city. Standing guard was a frail-looking older man. He looked as though he could have been a grandfather, gray hair peeking out from beneath a war-scarred helmet that had no doubt served him well in his youth. The rest of his armor fit poorly, a relic from an earlier life in the military. He bore no proper weapon, brandishing instead a recently sharpened shovel. He looked haggard, as though he had been at his post for far too long without relief. As Deacon drew near, he straightened up.

"Halt. What is your business here?" he demanded in a very official tone.

He squinted a bit, trying to get a good look at the curious sight before him. Deacon had neglected to stow the materials he'd hung on his shoulders for further study, and without magic to lend an extra hand, he was having difficulty keeping them together.

"I am in need of supplies," Deacon said, simply.

"Where is your horse?" he demanded suspiciously.

"A horse is among my required supplies," Deacon answered.

"Where are you coming from without a horse?" the makeshift guard growled.

"That direction. I'm not certain of the name of the place. One moment," he said, burrowing into his bag, attempting to reveal the map.

One of the artifacts that had yet to be stowed, a strap of leather with a rather ornate medallion on it, stubbornly refused to stay in place on his shoulder. It dropped for a second time as Deacon tried to keep from dropping the papers under his arm.

"I am terribly sorry. Would you hold this for just a moment?" he asked, snatching it from the ground and holding it up to the soldier.

"Get that out of my . . ." the soldier sneered, trailing off when his failing vision finally focused on the seal on the strap.

He took the strap and looked it over. It was a general's seal. One of only five. This one bore the name Demont. He remembered it, even from his youth. Soldiers seldom met face to face with the generals. He'd gone from recruitment to retirement without seeing even one. Could this young man be Demont? Either he was or he was skilled enough to kill or steal from him. It didn't matter. Regardless, this was not a person to be trifled with.

"Th-this way, please," he stammered.

"Oh, thank you," Deacon said, having only just managed to stow the loose papers.

He took back the strap and looked it over as he was led to what must have been the general store for the town. Slowly, he realized what was happening. The misunderstanding was greatly in his favor, but it was dishonest to allow them to believe that he was someone that he was not.

From the youngest age, he'd been taught that dishonesty was the first step down a road that ended very poorly for deceitful wizards. Magic users tended to attract the attentions of, and occasionally draw strength from, the spirits around them. Deceit was one of many things that twisted the soul, and a twisted soul attracted twisted spirits. After a short, one-sided debate in his head, Deacon conceded that he would allow the misunderstanding, but he would not foster it.

The weathered soldier opened the door and held it as he entered the store. After a harshly whispered exchange, the woman minding the store looked nervously to Deacon.

"I can get anything you need right away," she offered shakily.

"Provisions for two people for seven days," Deacon requested in an even tone.

As the storekeeper hurried off, gathering armful after armful of provisions, the soldier turned to him.

"Why might the general favor us with a visit today?" he asked, nervously.

Deacon silently thanked fate for the awkward phrasing.

"A fort of great value was destroyed in the field I came from. I am pursuing the individuals responsible," he replied. It had been destroyed, and he was indeed seeking those responsible. No word a lie.

The answer was quite enough for the soldier, now certain that it was the general he stood beside. Pride welled inside of him at being graced by his presence. Deacon, on the other hand, was simultaneously berating himself for allowing this disgrace to continue and fighting heroically to keep the nervousness and shame from his face. In less time than he would have thought possible, the shopkeeper dropped not only food, but blankets, bandages, and a dozen other things on the table.

"We have no horses for sale, I am afraid, but, ah, I would be honored to donate my own steed," the shopkeeper offered nervously.

"If that is what you wish," Deacon said.

"I too would like to provide you with my steed. A fine, sturdy animal it is, too," the soldier chimed in.

"That would be most appreciated," Deacon said gratefully.

#

Myranda crouched behind a drift of snow near the top of a hill, the rising wind whipping at her, anxiously watching the rear exit of the city. She had only been there for a few minutes, not yet settled upon what manner of action she would take in response to whatever trouble Deacon managed to cause, when she saw him lead a pair of heavily-laden horses out of the town and onto the road. When he circled around the hill, out of sight of the town, she ran to him. He had everything they needed and far more, but his expression was one of utter shame.

"This is remarkable!" she said, hugging him. "What did you do?"

He handed her the medallion.

"This is . . . Demont's seal, isn't it?" she said.

"I suppose the man is a recluse. At least enough that his own people would mistake him for me," he said.

"You managed to convince them that you were a general?" Myranda said, eyebrows raised in genuine surprise.

"They managed to convince themselves . . ." he said.

Myranda was quickly able to surmise the source of his turmoil.

"Deacon," she said, mounting one of the horses, "I don't mean to make light of the situation, but there are a great many things that may need to be done before our task is complete. Some will be difficult. Some will fly in the face of your morals and beliefs. Just know that, if it truly had to be done, then doing it was the right thing."

"I suppose," he said, scarcely consoled.

He twice tried and failed to pull himself onto the horse's back as he'd seen her do. A third try landed him unsteadily in the saddle.

Myranda looked at him flatly. "You don't know how to ride a horse, do you?"

"In truth, this is the first time I've even seen a horse. They don't fair very well in caves, I understand, so they have never made their way to Entwell," he said, apologetically.

What followed would have been an endearing experience if not for the tremendous rush that they were in. Myranda coached him along, teaching him the ins and outs of horseback riding as they tried to make their way toward the others. Fortunately, and not surprisingly, he was a swift learner, and before long they were breezing along fairly swiftly.

A few days passed, traveling a route far from main roads. As day after day passed without so much as a glimpse of another traveler, Myranda became more and more aware of how empty the war had left her homeland. The conflict with the massive southern country of Tressor had been raging off and on for well over a century, and the years of bloodshed had taken their toll. The north was nothing more than a handful of roads connecting a handful of dying towns. All of the rest was vast ice field after forbidding forest after rocky mountain.

There should have been life. There should have been some hint of the people of the land. Instead, the people gathered into smaller and smaller groups, ever more remote and isolated.

For a moment, at least, that isolation was in her favor, a fact of which she repeatedly reminded herself. It seemed that luck had momentarily begun to favor them.

In her ongoing efforts to bring the Perpetual War to an end, Myranda had been branded a murderer and traitor by the five generals. She was still not certain of the degree to which the Northern Army had managed to spread her infamy, so any situation that kept them from prying eyes without the need for stealth was quite helpful indeed.

Deacon, when his mind was in need of distraction from his slow progress on the translation of the D'karon language, resumed his instruction in the ways of the gray arts. A variety of useful spells were taught and even practiced without the fear of being noticed. Nightly, Myranda sought the others with her mind. She felt herself drawing nearer. This road seemed to be ideal.

That notion did not last very long. After the sunset on yet another day without so much as a trace of the others, it became clear that the most direct path on the map was not necessarily the swiftest. Long disused roads had eroded to little more than patches of loose gravel for the horses to lose their footing on. That, coupled with narrow passes made all but unusable by years of uncleared snowfall, made the going painfully slow. Before long, it was not clear if the ample supplies that they had managed to secure would be enough, particularly when there was little food about for the horses.

Fortunately, before much longer, the roads they came upon began to show the telltale signs of upkeep. Soon after, they reached a road with fresh hoofprints. Further ahead, the smell of burning wood signaled the presence of a town. Hope began to rise. This must have been where the others had been headed. Gradually, though, Myranda's heart sank. Perhaps they had been here, but were not any longer. Any attempts to detect them assured her that they were nowhere near. Worse, it seemed that they were no longer together. They now were far below, perhaps already off of the mountain. She wanted badly to join them, but the horses--and, truth be told, she and Deacon--needed shelter, food, and sleep.

When they finally reached the town, it was a tiny mining community called Verneste, a place Myranda had passed through before. This was good news. She'd raised little stir during her last visit, and there was an assayer who would likely give them gold in exchange for some of the more unique contents of Deacon's bag.

The gray wizard, rather than relying upon the general's seal to provide him with free provisions, sold a few of the smaller shards of Myranda's broken crystal. In addition, one of the bottles of healing potion brought a very high price indeed, as it was revealed that the alchemists and wizards who normally crafted them had been warned, under penalty of death, to provide them only to the military. This was ostensibly to ensure that the military had a plentiful supply, but most knew it to be simply another way of keeping the general populus in check.

The money was enough to resupply, stable the horses, and spend a night with a roof over their heads and pillows beneath them. Myranda was mercifully able to reach their accommodations without drawing any attention. The room had but one bed, and thus it was shared. If this were another time, that night might have been--and, by all rights, should have been--something truly special. Alas, the weariness of travel and the heaviness of the task on their shoulders brought little more than sleep.

The next day, the first in some time that saw both Deacon and Myranda fully refreshed, was spent desperately trying to catch up with the nearest of the Chosen, but the fear and duty that had driven the others along put far too much space between them. By the time flat land was reached and real progress could be made on horseback, the three Chosen they sought had already converged, and were in the presence of two generals.

The two wizards arrived in time to narrowly ward off both of the generals and escape without losing a single hero.

#

"And that brings the tale full circle," Myranda said.

With the last words of her story told, Myranda fell silent. Deacon put his hand on her shoulder, trying to comfort her. The telling of the tale had done little to dull the edge of the sorrow she felt. In her desperation to end the devastation of the general named Epidime, and to save the lives of her friends, she'd crossed a line she had promised herself that she would never cross. She'd killed a man, a fellow human.

At the time, she'd believed him to be Epidime himself, and that taking this one life would save countless others. In the end, she'd discovered that the man she killed was but a pawn, and Epidime was not a man at all, but a presence, a possessing spirit associated with the halberd he always bore. His body destroyed, he merely selected a new one and escaped, leaving Myranda emotionally shattered, blood on her hands and a death on her conscience.

Now she sat with the others, hidden by a small glade of trees and licking their wounds from a fight that destroyed half of a city and nearly claimed their lives.

"That was a somewhat more mundane explanation than I had anticipated. For a moment, I had thought you were almost worthy of your place among us," Ether stated.

The lack of compassion was typical for this Chosen One. She was a shapeshifter, able to assume virtually any form, physical or elemental. She'd existed since the dawn of time, but seemingly had spent the whole of her life convincing herself of her own superiority, and that emotions were little more than poison for the soul.

"Are you *mad!?*" came a voice of protest.

All eyes turned to Ivy. The young hero had been sleeping, recovering from near death since the recent battle ended. Now she was sitting up and fully awake. If ever there was a beast that could be considered wholly Ether's opposite, it was Ivy. The very same malthrope who Myranda had contacted, she was an enigma. Her own history was unknown even to her, though it seemed likely that she owed her current form to the machinations of General Demont. She was childish, enthusiastic, caring, and dangerously emotional. When her feelings ran strong enough, she became something else entirely. A berserker, surging with rage or fear, she seldom left behind anything but rubble, and often found herself helplessly drained when the smoke cleared. If not for the intervention of the wizards, she would have bled to death from her wounds--or, worse, she would have been left in the hands of the generals.

"I heard the whole thing. I didn't want to interrupt you," Ivy said to Myranda before turning to Ether. "This man *fell* from the *sky* to save her life! What about that is mundane!?"

She turned to Deacon and approached him, arms extended. He offered a hand for a shake, but she pushed it aside and embraced him.

"You saved Myranda's life. That makes you my friend, and friends don't shake hands," Ivy asserted.

When she was through, she released him from her embrace and turned to Myranda.

"It is so good to see you! I told them that you were alive, but they didn't believe me. At least, *she* didn't. I'm not so sure about Lain, but *I* knew for *sure,*" Ivy said.

Ivy threw her arms around Myranda and hugged her tightly. The joy was quite literally infectious, as a golden glow spread weakly out from the ecstatic creature. Deacon's eyes widened in wonder at the phenomenon he'd only heard described before. A feeling of warmth and joy filled him-- and, to varying degrees, the others as well. Any nagging ailments melted away. It was another peculiar effect of her emotions. They tended to spill over into others, and just as rage brought strength and fear brought speed, joy brought relief and recovery, easily the match for a spell of healing.

"It . . . it is remarkable. Emotion radiates from you!" Deacon proclaimed.

"What?" Ivy asked, turning from Myranda.

"I've never seen anything like it. It is like some sort of mystically fostered empathetic symbiosis!" Deacon blurted.

Ivy blinked.

"Oh, never mind. I am just . . . it is a dream come true to meet you. All of you. It is an honor and a privilege of which I am truly unworthy," Deacon said.

Ether raised her eyebrows.

"I would not have expected a human to be so keenly aware of the degree of his lack of worth," she said.

"Don't listen to her. What is your name again?" Ivy asked.

"Deacon," he said. "And she is quite right. You are all Chosen, the warriors selected by the gods to protect your world. You have a purpose greater than any other. The world rests in your able hands. By comparison, I am nothing at all."

Ivy turned to Myranda again.

"Your friend is very strange," she said.

"He means well," Myranda replied.

"That I most certainly do. I mean to be as useful to you as I can. If there is anything at all that you wish or require of me, I would be honored to do all that I can. I am a capable wizard and an able fighter. Do not hesitate to ask anything," he offered eagerly, looking to each of the Chosen. "Lain? Ether? Ivy? Anything at all."

Lain showed no reaction. He seldom did. A malthrope, like Ivy, his life had forged him into a vicious warrior and a feared assassin. The hatred shared by his race and the hardships it had brought had burned away at him until all that was left was a shell of a being, nothing but iron resolve and an absolute dedication to his purpose. Currently, that purpose was to see to it that Ivy would be safe from harm. She was the only other malthrope he'd met in ages, and judging by the life he was living, she would soon be the last. She must survive, whatever the cost. If something did not contribute to this goal, it did not concern him.

Seeing that the silent hero required nothing of him, Deacon looked to the others.

"There is nothing that you could offer that I could require," Ether rejected.

"Umm . . ." Ivy thought aloud. "I really don't think I need anything."

"Just get some sleep. When we have rested, we will share what we have found. There is much more to be done than we had suspected," Myranda said.

"I will make every attempt to sleep, but in the light of our current company, it will be difficult to do so," Deacon said.

Myranda settled with her back to a tree, Deacon to one side and Ivy to the other, her head rested dreamily on the girl's shoulder as she drifted happily back to sleep. Myranda's own slumber was slow to follow, and the dreams it brought were painful. Her battle with Epidime haunted her. A bolt of lightning tearing from the sky by Myranda's will. His body blackening to stillness. Then, impossibly, the halberd rising and flitting to the hand of a child. The young boy's face taking on the look of terrible intellect and detachment.

The images were repeated constantly in her mind.

#

Far away, three figures settled down at a table. The room was dark; the only light came from the cherry-red embers of a pipe, the weak, blue glow of a gem-embedded halberd, and a handful of similar gems that shifted about organically before settling against the wall amid much clattering. The room in which they had gathered was located within a seldom used wing of the residence of the king of the Northern Alliance, a castle on the north end of Northern Capital.

There was an uneasy silence as the man at the head of the table drew a long breath through his pipe. The man was Bagu, one of the four remaining generals of the Alliance Army, and the most senior among them. He had stark, handsome features, marred only by a scattering of scars. The well-dressed man held himself with a regal bearing and, at the moment, barely-contained fury. He pulled the pipe from his mouth, breathing out the smoke.

"Demont, report," Bagu ordered, frustrated anger adding an edge to an already forceful demand. "I feel I have waited too long to hear your explanation as to why you came rushing to us with your tail between your legs."

"There are three Chosen together now. That is more than I cared to face unprepared," explained Demont.

The man who spoke was shorter, dressed in clothing less suited for a nobleman, and bearing features sharper and less immaculate. His was the air of a scholar forced into a business he considered beneath him, and little was done to disguise the sentiment.

"Unprepared? That was your testing facility, was it not? That put a veritable army at your fingertips," Bagu growled.

"They were being tested because they were incomplete!" Demont fumed. "Those Chosen came to my facility unprovoked, with no time on my part to adequately fortify, and I still nearly destroyed them. If I'd had a force the size I have been supplying to Epidime every time you have a tantrum and decide to send him to kill them, *in complete opposition to the plan,* I would have brought them back barely alive."

"Yes, yes. A well-formed excuse," Bagu jabbed. "Do you have anything useful to add?"

"They aren't acting like heroes. They destroyed the fort. They fight viciously. I do not believe that we will be able to count on them reining themselves in for the sake of honor," Demont warned.

"One of them will," interjected a small, confident, but utterly out of place voice. It was that of a young boy, the body currently occupied by the general called Epidime. "Myranda is strongly principled."

"If that is the human, she is neither Chosen, nor among the living," Demont reminded him.

"Wrong on both counts. Whether she was or was not a Chosen before, she most certainly is one now. And she is quite alive. Worse, she is quickly becoming a force to be reckoned with, particularly with the partner she brought along," Epidime countered.

"You say she has a partner with her?" Bagu asked urgently.

"Not a Chosen!" Epidime explained. "A male, another human. Certainly not Chosen, but remarkably skilled. I'll have to learn more about him, but the spells he was hurling were unique, and quite effective."

"Never mind learning about him. If he is not Chosen, then kill him--as soon as possible," Bagu instructed. "Unless . . . Trigorah was with you. Was she present when . . ."

"No. I had her removed prior to Myranda's arrival. Conditions for the convergence were not ideal," replied Epidime. "She was not pleased."

"Yes. She was quite vocal in her complaints," Bagu recalled.

They spoke of Trigorah Teloran. A spectacularly skilled tracker and military commander, she was the least senior of the generals, despite her elfin heritage. She'd become increasingly displeased with Bagu's decision to keep her from the front, the place she felt her skills would be best used, leading the others to keep her on a still-tighter leash.

"There is a problem," Epidime continued.

Bagu's fingers pressed to his temple as a look of anger surged briefly in his expression.

"What?" he growled through clenched teeth.

"Lain is trying to deliver Demont's pet to someone in Tressor for protection. If we expect to be rid of the Chosen with any finality, we need the convergence to occur, and that will not happen with Ivy in the south," he reminded.

"Agreed. This situation is threatening to escape our grasp. Demont, despite your consistent and damaging failure, I am giving you another chance. Any resource you need is yours. I want something that they can't beat. Epidime, they are working too well together. Fix that, but do not forget that we need them all in the same place at the same time," Bagu dictated.

"Intriguing. If I interpret your commands correctly, you wish for me to destroy their unity without compromising their proximity," Epidime said.

"Do it," he hissed.

The orders thus laid out, the trio parted company. Bagu lingered in the now-pitch-black room, drawing in another puff on the pipe before marching off after them.

#

Deacon tried desperately to drift off, but he could not push from his mind the fact that so many figures of legend, beings anticipated even before their own births, were in his presence.

Ether, apparently satisfied with the degree of her recovery, stepped from the fire and assumed her human form.

"A second human. This is just a replacement for that lizard she lost," Ether said with disgust, referring to the young dragon named Myn, who had been a valued companion to Myranda until a battle took the creature's life. "Her stubborn reliance on lesser beings is sickening, and a threat to us all. How much will this one slow us before it is destroyed?"

"I will do everything in my power to be a benefit to you," Deacon said, opening his eyes from the latest failed attempt at sleep. "And I would respectfully request you not blame Myranda for any delays or troubles I may cause. She does care deeply for others, and though I can scarcely imagine why you find this a fault, I assure you that, in this instance, the choice to accompany her was my own."

"You are in no position to make requests, human," Ether said, not even remotely apologetic.

"Certainly not," Deacon said, hesitantly adding, "but as a firsthand observer of the speed that Myranda has shown in her development, and the skill she has shown in her execution, I do not believe that it is fair or right for her to be viewed as anything other than an asset. She is a truly remarkable person."

"And what of you? What do you add to our cause besides your refreshingly well-adjusted sense of worth?" Ether asked.

"Well, my mystical skill would normally be that which I consider my most valuable asset, but in the presence of a being such as you, I feel it pales. However, I *have* unlocked a number of the secrets of the D'karon language, and more than a bit about their peculiar style of magic that I think may be of great use," Deacon offered.

"Doubtful," Ether replied.

"The map," Lain stated.

"Yes, of course," Deacon said, quickly retrieving the rugged piece of parchment.

It was unfurled before Lain and his eyes pored over it.

"These marks are D'karon forts. I am certain of it now. The other makings, here, are some sort of ranking system, a priority or value, and these others have something to do with classification. I haven't fully determined their meanings. This mark is an identifier, not a name, but some sort of designation. I've been able to determine that the D'karon consider the Northern Capital to be a key stronghold, but it is second in importance to something a fair distance north of it," he explained.

Lain's finger traced downward along the map. In his mind, he counted off the days, weighing the roughness of the terrain against the likelihood of their discovery. In his years of traversing the land unseen, he remembered encountering many of these forts marked on the map. Alone, he'd seldom had to give them a second glance, but with the others . . . and while they were being actively sought . . . It was unlikely that he could risk straying near to any of them. What was left was a razor- thin path that was midway between cities and forts, at times dangerously close to each.

Deacon could not help but notice the route he was planning; he had been told of Lain's desire to take Ivy to safety by bringing her to the far south, past the battlefront--and, he hoped, out of the reach of the D'karon.

"I know you worry about Ivy. If she truly is Chosen, then her place is by your side. You cannot leave her behind and expect to succeed. You must trust in fate," Deacon urged.

"Fate has done quite enough for my kind," Lain stated.

"Leave him. You say that you have determined something about their magic. What is it that you believe that you have learned?" the shapeshifter asked.

"Oh, yes," he said, sitting down on the ground and rummaging through his bag. "I've spoken to Myranda about this. These crystals, they have the peculiar property of drawing in any source of mana--the souls of the living, even ambient elemental sources. Once filled, they can be treated, so that when broken they consume the energy while bringing about a desired effect. Conversely, they can be coaxed to release their stolen power, either through a conduit engraved with their runes, or another crystal, or even one of Demont's creations. It would appear from the notes he has taken concerning their creation that--"

"Yes, yes. The beasts almost universally draw their power from the crystals. I am quite familiar with his creations," Ether said, losing interest.

"But the most disturbing thing about their magic, as opposed to ours, is that our spells merely re-purpose existing forces, eventually returning all magic from whence it came. The D'karon spells actually consume it, convert the mana completely into the effect, never to return again. Any spell upsets the balance, however slightly. If such spells were rare, then time could repair the damage, but if they are allowed to continue . . ." Deacon explained.

As Ether listened, her expression grew more grave.

"And you are certain of this?" she asked.

"Most certain," Deacon assured her.

Ether became visibly angered.

"There is no end to the abominations that they unleash upon this world," she hissed. "What more did you learn from Demont's workshop? What more did you take?"

Deacon began to slowly empty the contents of his bag out for Ether to inspect. Most repulsed her, but one item drew her attention. It was a case filled with vials. The slender glass containers were tiny and many. Each was labeled with a word or two of the D'karon language. She opened the case and removed a vial, opening it and looking over the liquid within.

"Blood," she said, "of a lion."

Each vial was a small sample of the blood of another creature, except for the cases of some of the smaller creatures, when the entire creature was stored in the vial. Ether systematically sampled each. The usefulness of having a sample of so many beasts could not be overstated, as each sample was another form she could swiftly assume, another weapon in her arsenal. None of the other things interested her.

When contact had been made with most of the samples, Ether returned them to the case and returned the case to Deacon. When it was stowed, he removed his book and stylus and eagerly began to ask Ether questions regarding the nature and extent of her powers. Perhaps out of the desire for more of his endless praise for her, she indulged him, but her patience for such things was short, and before long she ordered him to be silent. Deacon thanked her and began to expand upon the notes he'd taken on her answers. Perhaps an hour passed without a sound, aside from the hushed rustle of the northern night and the scratch of Deacon's stylus.

"Deacon," Lain said, breaking the silence.

The young wizard's head snapped up instantly.

"Yes," he said, scrambling to his feet.

"Armories. Barracks. Have you identified which marks might indicate them?" he asked. It would be more important to avoid such places on their path south than mere fortified buildings.

"Not with any certainty. I believe that I am close to determining that. Might I ask why you wish to know?" Deacon said, glancing over the words on the map once more.

"This. This is an armory. I have seen it," he said, pointing to one of the black marks.

"Ah . . . so this . . . and here. They have the same marks. Perhaps armories as well. And . . ." Deacon began.

"I believe that troops are trained here," Lain said, indicating another fort.

For several minutes, Deacon combined Lain's observations with his own, and it became clearer and clearer what each mark meant. Before too long, Ivy awoke and groggily approached them. She'd been in the healing sleep for much of the last day and could not sleep any longer.

"What are you doing?" she asked, curious as to why the pair was hunched over a map.

"Well, the D'karon have a very strange language. We are hoping to determine what the markings on this map might--" Deacon began to explain.

"Troop production. Troop production. Research. Prisoner retention. Research. Prisoner retention . . ." Ivy began to recite, pointing to various marks on the map.

Deacon stared at her in disbelief.

"You can read this!?" he asked in wonder.

"Uh-huh . . . you can't?" Ivy asked, tilting her head.

"Teach me," Deacon said, pulling out his book and setting one of the more cryptic sheets before her.

"Let's see. 'The energy requirements of' . . . uh . . . well, this word sort of means poison and acid . . . and disease, all at the same time . . . I'll just say poison acid . . . 'poison acid production are . . . very high. A second' . . . this isn't a word that translates. It is just what they call those crystals. Thir," Ivy said, uncertainly at first.

"Fine, excellent. Continue, please," Deacon said, almost overflowing with enthusiasm.

Ivy smiled. Happy to be helping, she continued. "'A second thir crystal will . . . help spread the load . . . but will . . . make for a single point of failure . . .'"

When Myranda finally could not bring herself to endure the nightmares any longer, she awoke to Ivy merrily filling in the gaps in Deacon's knowledge.

"No, they aren't numbers. Well, they are like numbers. But they are like measures of . . . distance? It isn't distance, but it is." Ivy struggled to explain, indicating another component of the labels for the forts.

"What is going on?" Myranda asked.

"Ivy can read their language! The D'karon language. I think that I almost understand it now," Deacon said.

"How can you read D'karon?" Myranda asked.

"I don't know . . . I just know it. I don't think they taught me. But I know I didn't know it until they started teaching me," Ivy tried to explain. "But I've been helping! Look!"

Myranda looked over the nearly fully-translated map.

"It looks as though your newest lapdog is not completely without merit," Ether said.

Myranda's eyes widened at the near compliment coming from so unlikely a source.

"Enough," Lain said. "We need to move."

The loose papers and gems were quickly gathered, horses were mounted, and the group moved off. One horse bore Deacon, the other Ivy and Myranda. Lain and Ether traveled by foot. The latter, for reasons hardly inscrutable, took the form of a snow fox. Lain stayed a dozen paces ahead, straining his senses to be sure that they were not followed. Once again, the emptiness of the north was in their favor, and travel, though slow and cautious, was uneventful.

Deacon, with the language he'd been grappling with all but unraveled, found himself with his mind unoccupied, a rare occasion that he sought to avoid. His eyes turned to Ivy.

She was riding behind Myranda, arms wrapped around her to steady herself. She could not have looked more out of place among the solemn group of warriors. Her eyes were lively and excited. A smile was on her face; she was clearly thrilled to be with the people who cared about her. He only truly knew what he had been told about her, and precious little of that.

He reached down into his bag. There was more to be learned, though he hesitated to do so. It was Demont's workshop he had liberated these notes from, after all. He was her creator. Surely she was mentioned. It wasn't long before the bundle of pages devoted to her emerged.

Now that the symbols had meaning, the coldness of the process became clear. Notes were carefully taken, speaking of vastly different earlier revisions. Flaws were noted, addressed. The variations from the basis--in this case, Lain--were outlined and recorded. It was every bit a recipe, a procedure. Later pages skewed toward art, dealing with nuances and coloring, clearly still left to be done when she'd been liberated. The details of the connection between mind and soul were listed, with potential difficulties. Finally, there was a series of sketches of the various stages of development. The nearest that the notes came to discussing her as an individual came in the description of the "extractor" that contained "Epidime's contribution."

It was her soul. No name. No history. Just another component in the final product. There was nothing describing her as a person, because, to him, she was never anything but a concoction. The last few lines he'd scribed spoke of the level of development when the "vessel" would be "sufficient." This final word, it would seem, assumed all of the wonder and splendor of life. A body that was completed, able to support the evanescent spark that was the spirit, was "sufficient."

As a student, always eager for knowledge, particularly of a mystic nature, he had never turned away from anything. This made him recoil. These things Epidime had done were the tasks of gods, and yet he spoke of them with sterility and detachment.

A motion out of the corner of his eye distracted him. Ivy had slipped off of the back of Myranda's horse and was jogging over to his. He quickly began to stow the papers, but the last was still in his hands as she hopped onto the back of his horse. She noticed it and reached around to snatch it from his fingers.

"Is this . . . is this me?" she asked.

"I-I believe so," he said, anxiously eying the page that she held. It fortunately bore only a handful of markings, nothing that might upset her. Mostly measurements.

"It looks like me. Why am I standing like that, with my arms held out? Did you draw this?" she asked.

"I didn't," he said. "Would you like me to?"

"I'll do it! I am very good!" Ivy twittered eagerly.

He fetched his book and the stylus and she quickly set to work. He nearly led the horse off course trying to watch her, prompting her to scold him to keep it steady. Before long, she was finished and she presented it proudly.

"I made some mistakes. I don't look at myself very often," she said.

The work was truly exquisite. She'd managed to capture every ounce of the playfulness and innocence he'd been admiring earlier. More telling, perhaps, was the pair of scribbled out errors. Each was a barely roughed-out form. It was difficult to determine what they were, but they were not malthropes.

"I must say, it is far better than I could do. How did you learn to do such fine work?" he asked.

"I don't know, I just can. You should hear me play . . . oh . . . *no!*" Ivy pouted. "My violin. I left it. I . . . we have to go back."

Myranda cast a sympathetic glance that at once soothed Ivy and made it clear that it could not be.

"I really am very good at that, too," she said dejectedly.

"Well, the least you can do is sign your work," he said, offering the book and stylus to her again.

She nodded, hesitating briefly before making a large, stylized I and V.

"It would have been better if I wasn't on horseback. Can I draw some more when we stop for the day?" she asked.

"Well, of course," Deacon said.

With the exception of a brief retreat to the nearest cover as a black carriage crept along ahead of them and out of sight, the rest of the night's journey went by without incident. Their path took a fairly sharp westward turn, and they found themselves at the foot of the mountain that ran the length of the north. They were on the western edge of the Low Lands. If the sun had been up, Ravenwood would be visible to the south. As it was, a shallow cave would serve as shelter for the night, with food supplied by Lain's remarkable hunting skill. Ether started a fire and vanished into it as she always did.

"Do you feel any better?" Deacon asked, concerned for Myranda, who still seemed distant, the act of taking a life still heavy on her mind.

After a long pause, Myranda answered, "I will be all right . . . I just. I can't . . . What if I do it again?"

"Myranda, listen to me. You know yourself better than I. Do you honestly believe that you will let that happen? You didn't know that Arden was not to blame, that he was not Epidime, and now that you know, you will not make that mistake again. You just have to trust yourself," Deacon said. "I cannot even imagine you taking the lives of the innocent unless there was no other choice."

"I . . . I don't want to be the sort of person who to whom this sort of thing comes easily," Myranda muttered, tears in her eyes threatening to roll down her cheeks.

"Do not fool yourself," Lain said.

All eyes turned to him.

"It never becomes easy. It takes tremendous effort to bring yourself to take a life. The only change that comes is a keener sense of when it has to be done. It makes the decision a quicker one to make, not an easier one," he instructed.

Of all the heroes in attendance, Lain was the one most experienced in the matter. He was, after all, an assassin. From time to time, Myranda had wondered what type of a man could do such a thing. Did he have a heart at all? Did he feel any guilt, any pain when he took a life? This was the first glimpse she'd been given. As the words began to sink in, Ether stepped from the flames and spoke. As usual, it was anything but helpful.

"Besides. The fact of the next death on your hands is already established," Ether said, assuming her human form once more.

Deacon, Myranda, and Ivy all turned their heads and cast the same look of anger.

"Ether, when are you going to learn that you should never, ever talk?" Ivy asked irately.

"Ignore it if you must, but any creature that curls in Myranda's lap without bearing the Mark is doomed. The lizard was first and now Deacon," Ether tossed off casually.

"Don't you *dare* wish death upon him!" Myranda raged, rushing forward at Ether.

Ivy found herself in the uncommon role of trying to hold Myranda back.

"Calm down. It is all right. You know she is too stupid to know what she is saying," Ivy said.

Ether scoffed and made ready to retort when Deacon spoke up.

"Ether is probably right," Deacon said.

Ivy looked to him with confusion.

"You know you don't *have* to agree with everything she says," Ivy huffed.

"The prophecy never explicitly says that the mortals who aid you will die, but the phrase 'tasks which no mortal could survive' is not an uncommon one. Indeed, most interpretations of the prophecy predict that even one of the Chosen will not survive the journey. I harbor no illusions that I am anything more than a mortal, and as such I must accept the very real possibility of my own death," he explained.

"I won't let that happen. I don't care what we face. I will not let you die!" Myranda declared.

"This is--" Ether began.

"You shut your mouth before he agrees with you again! And Deacon! Not another word! Everyone just be quiet for a while!" Ivy ordered authoritatively.

Ether crossed her arms and turned to Lain.

"Surely you agree with--" she attempted.

"Silence," he interjected.

When Ether reluctantly complied, Ivy crossed her arms and huffed again triumphantly. For once, she was the one reining in the emotions of others. Tensions were slow to ease, a fact that Ivy decided needed work as well. She borrowed Deacon's book and stylus and directed him to sit beside Myranda.

"I want to show you what a good artist I am, so help me out by putting a smile on. This will look much better if the two of you are happy," she said, carefully positioning them, placing Deacon's arm across Myranda's shoulder.

"I didn't know you were an artist, Ivy," Myranda remarked.

"Oh, yes, an excellent one. You should see what she--" Deacon eagerly offered.

"Shush. And look at me. This won't take long and you two can take a look at what I can do when I'm not bopping around on a horse's back," Ivy said.

After a few minutes, and number of minor adjustments and instructions, Ivy was finished. The rendering was astonishing, even ignoring the fact that it was done in virtually no time. It had a tremendous amount of detail, while still having a definite style to it. This was a portrait intended to describe not just what the pair looked like, but who they were, and it did a remarkable job. She marked the portrait with her name and then turned to Lain and Ether.

"We may as well capture the other two lovebirds," Ivy said, plopping down before them and quickly setting to work.

"Lovebirds?" Myranda questioned.

"Oh, you didn't know? Ether is in love with Lain," Ivy said with a smirk as she worked.

"The little beast doesn't know what she is talking about," Ether retorted.

"She gave Lain permission to love her instead of me," Ivy snorted.

"I was offering Lain an alternative to being distracted by you," Ether hissed.

"Well he didn't take you up on it, did he." She giggled again.

"Ivy, it isn't nice to make fun," Myranda scolded, all the while trying to keep from laughing herself.

Truthfully, this glimpse into the way Ether truly felt made Myranda respect her much more. They were not so different after all. By the time the second sketch was through, the mood had lightened greatly. Ether was, of course, silently furious, but the remarks she had made were nearly forgotten. The drawing of the other Chosen was, if anything, even more remarkable than the one that preceded it. The quiet dignity and nobility of Lain came through, and somehow Ether's aloofness and transitory nature seemed to leap out at the viewer.

"Do you mind if I keep drawing?" Ivy asked after showing off her latest work.

"Don't fill up Deacon's book," Myranda said.

"Oh, I assure you she can't do that. Watch," Deacon said, taking the book and riffling through the blank pages.

After a few seconds, it became clear that the stack of fresh pages was not getting any smaller. He then flipped a few pages back and the artwork that should have been buried in hundreds of blank pages revealed itself.

"It will never run out. Every note I have ever written is still in this book, and I have a second that features every last page of our library, but it is no larger than this. I used to do much of my research at night, and the library was off limits at that time, so I received special permission to create a book that would link to it all. For some reason, the spells that deal with the books and my stylus are virtually the only ones that will work through that confounded mountainside without any difficulty," he explained.

Ivy blinked again.

"So does that mean I can?" Ivy asked.

"Later, when we are into Ravenwood. For now, rest," Lain said.

"Oh. All right," Ivy said reluctantly.

That day passed quickly, rest finally coming easily to all. When they mounted and set off the next day, it was with renewed speed. As before, the denseness and size of Ravenwood would make tracking them difficult, and discovering them all but impossible. It had been just less than an hour away when they had sought shelter the night before, so in almost no time, they were among the trees. As the thicket closed behind them, a tenseness was lifted. The nagging feeling of fear, that any corner hid eyes that might betray them to their enemies, quickly faded away.

When Myranda had first set foot in this place, it had been with fear. The forest itself had held the dangers that she shrunk away from. Now it was a savior.

Ivy seemed excited by the new surroundings. For her, there was much more to experience. There was a symphony of sounds and a banquet of smells that was lost to Myranda and Deacon. This was the first she'd seen of a true forest. She was a bundle of energy, switching between riding with Myranda and riding with Deacon, and even occasionally running up to be with Lain from time to time. Lain tended to ignore her. He was far too engaged with his diligent watch for anything that might threaten them. Ether, however, was quite the opposite. She typically took her human form when the young creature drew near and delivered a short but scalding string of threats and insults to chase her away.

There was certainly something to that talk about her affection for Lain. She'd become downright possessive of him. She had even taken to remaining among the flames only as long as necessary so that she might sit beside him during the times that the others rested. He would drift into his warrior's sleep and she would stare at him with eyes that, despite her considerable efforts, betrayed the tiniest hint of longing.

It was late in the second day's travel in Ravenwood when Myranda began to feel uneasy. There was something she recognized about this place. It was madness to suppose that she was able to recognize the trees and stones, and yet this stretch of the woods seemed familiar. Soon, she knew why. Four swords stood, mostly buried in the snow. Three still bore helmets, a fourth with one nearby. She'd spent a night here. She'd found Myn here, ages ago. It had been during her first brush with mystic training. The dragon had run off from the tower where the girl was being taught. Despite the urging of her teacher, she'd gone after the little creature, and found her near death in this very stretch of forest. She'd managed to save the creature that day, but only just.

A shudder went through her. It did not go unnoticed by Deacon.

"Wolloff is near here," Myranda said, hoping to deflect the question that would surely come.

"Wolloff . . . the white wizard. The gentleman who gave you your introduction to magic," Deacon recalled.

"I wouldn't call him a gentleman, but yes, that is him," she said.

Deacon raised his eyebrows, remarking, "I do wish we weren't in such a hurry. It might be interesting to visit with a fellow spellcaster. At the very least he deserves congratulations for starting you off so well."

"He isn't the type to welcome visitors," she said.

"That's just fine with me. I like having this time alone with my family," Ivy said, as she finished off another sketch and returned Deacon's book to him.

"Family?" Myranda asked with a grin.

"Well, what would you call it?" Ivy said. "We travel together, we help each other, and if we are all Chosen, then that means that all of us can trace ourselves back to the gods. So that means we are all related, sort of. Except Deacon."

"I never thought of it that way," Myranda quipped.

"And nor should you. The gods *created* me. I was not born. Thus I have no parents, no siblings, no family. I am unique," Ether objected.

"You just don't want to admit that you and I have something in common," Ivy said tauntingly.

"We share nothing but a common purpose," Ether growled.

Ivy rolled her eyes. As she opened her mouth to retort, Lain raised his hand to silence her. He began to stalk slowly into the woods, motioning for the others to follow. Minutes passed before the others noticed anything out of the ordinary. First came the tracks. Fresh. A pair of horses. Then, emerging from the darkness as they approached it, a tree with a sheet of paper nailed to it.

Lain approached it. As his eyes scanned over it, a visible fury came over him. He tore the paper from the tree and threw it to the ground, rushing ahead. The others followed. There was another paper, and another. Before long, every tree in sight had a page affixed. Lain was shaking with anger, his clawed fingers scoring deep gashes in the tree as he tore away another page. Myranda tore down a page of her own and read it.

"What is it?" Deacon asked.

"Names. Nothing but names," she replied.

"Do you recognize them?" he asked, removing a page as well.

"None of them," she said.

Lain drew in a long, slow breath and turned to something in the distance. He removed his sword, sheath and all, from his belt and handed it to Myranda.

"Do not follow," he warned.

Lain rushed into the darkness. His motion was less measured than usual. His footfalls, normally silent, betrayed his path with each pounding, crunching step. They retreated quickly into the trees until they could no longer be heard. What followed was a long silence. It was broken by a horrible noise, like the roar of a beast mixed with a glimmer of voice. It came again, the second time accompanied by a cry that was vaguely human. Then more silence.

When the crunching footsteps returned, they were slower, less driven. Lain emerged from the darkness. The anger was still clear in his eyes, but he seemed more composed. He approached. His hands were coated with black, and more of it stained his mouth, chin, and chest. He spat something on the ground.

"Where is the nearest fort?" he asked, prompting Deacon to swiftly begin digging for his map.

"What did you do?" Myranda asked nervously.

"What had to be done," he replied, taking his sword back.

"The nearest fort is northwest of here. It is one of twelve forts labeled 'Final Reserve.' It seems to be a rather poorly guarded one," he said.

Lain looked over the map and set off quickly, the others having to scramble to avoid losing sight of him.

"What has gotten into him?" Deacon called over the sound of the pounding hooves.

"I don't know!" Myranda replied, trying unsuccessfully to look at the flapping paper without guiding her horse into a tree.

She caught a glimpse of a name here and there. What could make Lain completely reverse his decision? What about these names could make him change his mind about taking Ivy to the south? Perhaps . . .

"All of the names are Tresson," she called to Deacon.

"I fail to see the relevance," he replied.

"Well . . . we were heading to Tressor. We were trying to find people that he trusted," she said.

"Are you suggesting . . . these are the names of those people?" he asked.

"What else would explain it?" Myranda asked.

"No . . . no, that must be it . . . but there are so many!" he said. "Lain doesn't strike me as the sort to make so many friends!"

"I don't think they are friends . . . I think they owe him," Myranda said.

"It doesn't matter, right? If they know about them, then I won't be safe there, right? I won't be safe anywhere, right?" Ivy said enthusiastically.

She was happy, so much so that the faint telltale yellow aura began to appear. It was not the sort of realization that should prompt such a reaction, but it meant something very different to her than it did to the others.

"And that means there is nowhere you can leave me! I *have* to stay with you!" she almost sang.

"*No!*" Ether cried.

She shifted to her wind form and soared to Lain's side.

"Tell them they are wrong! Tell them you've simply found a faster way to take her there! Tell them you've found a better place to leave her! *Tell them!*" she demanded.

Lain kept his eyes resolutely ahead, offering nothing in reply but his deep, rhythmic breaths.

"No. *No!* I will take her! Entwell will be safe! Damn the waterfall, I can get her there! I will take her over the blasted *mountains* and down the *cliff* if I must. That *thing* must not be allowed to fight beside us! She is a liability! She is a *threat! She does not deserve to be near you!*" the gusting form cried in a mixed plea and demand.

"If you could have done so . . . You would have by now," Lain said, the strain of the sprint beginning to show. "I can only keep her safe . . . if she is by my side. She will only be safe . . . from the D'karon forever . . . if the D'karon are gone . . . forever."

Ether continued her begging, growing almost desperate, but Lain was silent. He led the others farther in those last few hours than they had gone in the entire previous day.

They were heading toward a pass in the mountains just to the south. Oddly, the map indicated that it led to a large and vital road that ran the length of the mountain range. Myranda had lived all of her life in the north, and she had neither seen nor heard of this road even once. Even having seen it on the map was not enough to convince her. The cost and effort to keep a road through the mountains maintained made it an act of idiocy to even propose such a thing.

When the group finally settled down to a long overdue rest at the mouth of the pass, Lain forewent the hunt, entering his trance and leaving the others to pick at the meager provisions and leftovers they had managed to set aside beside an equally meager fire. Typically, Ether would take advantage of the flames. Instead, she sat sullenly beside Lain, her furious gaze locked on Ivy, who had pranced over and sat beside Lain, resting her head on his shoulder. Myranda was settling down for sleep when she noticed Deacon was leafing through a book rather than doing the same.

"Deacon, that can wait. You will need your rest," Myranda advised.

"I know, but . . . I just can't put this down. It is so . . . new . . . so different," he said, trying briefly to set it aside before turning his eyes eagerly back to the pages.

"What do you mean?" she asked.

"Now that Ivy has filled most of the gaps in my understanding of this language, I can read the spell book. I've . . . never seen anything that has even approached the subject matter that this book covers," he said.

"How can that be? I thought your colleagues were the best in their fields. How can there be something you've never seen?" she wonders.

"Well, as you know, there are a number of practices that my fellow wizards at Entwell frown upon. I happen to be the foremost authority in . . . well, all of them. However, there are two that we are explicitly forbidden to perform, or even pursue beyond theory," he said. "The first is any act that can interfere in any way with past events--time travel and the like. The second is any act that contacts another physical realm--summoning creatures, opening gateways, even communicating with creatures on another plane. These D'karon . . . they have based their entire practice around the latter of these forbidden arts. There is a fragment of a spell for opening a path to some other world that is presented with solemn reverence. It is almost a prayer to them."

"Why would such practices be forbidden to you?" Myranda asked.

"It has been known to the elders of Entwell that the threat that the Chosen were to face would come from outside of this world. They believed that such a threat could be at least delayed and at best prevented if it was assured that no contact with other realms was ever made. Clearly, fate would not be so easily denied," he said. "And now I am left with no knowledge of how to combat such a tactic. Though I can determine the spell to open such a gateway from what is written here, I cannot determine how to close one. It is possible . . . that there *is* no way to close one . . ."

"There must be a way," Myranda said.

"I am not so certain. Do you remember when Epidime escaped in the town? He opened a portal. It closed behind him and sent out a shock wave. I don't believe that is an intended effect of the spell. It felt like a backlash, as through the will of the spell was pulled from it before it had time to complete. That was merely the remaining magic spilling off in a raw form," he said.

"I don't understand," Myranda replied.

"Neither do I, not entirely, but . . . once a portal is allowed to fully open, I don't think that even *they* would know how to close it," he said anxiously.

"Do you suppose that such a portal already exists?" Myranda asked.

"Well, it looks from Demont's notes that the nearmen, the dragoyles--everything that we've faced thus far--were designed and produced in this world . . . but the generals themselves must have gotten here somehow," he stated gravely.

It was that chilling thought that would accompany Myranda to sleep that night. It was not enough to overcome her exhaustion, however.

As the haziness of sleep drew over her, she found herself in a familiar place. A dark field. No sky, no trees. There was a cold wind rustling past her. Far in the distance was a vague, flickering light. She pulled her cloak closer and hurried toward it. The ground became rocky and increasingly entangled with black, thorny vines. After what seemed like hours, she came to the source of the light. There was a vast, tarnished metal structure. It was hopelessly entwined in the vines, and here and there embedded with broken glass. Inside, a flame barely clung to an oily piece of cloth.

She stepped back and looked over the hulking metal device. It was twisted, almost unrecognizable, but slowly it too became familiar. It was a lantern. Massive, misshapen, but unmistakable. The cold grew more intense. She stepped closer, trying to draw some warmth from the flame. Suddenly, there was a creaking sound. The vines began to creep over the form, drawing it tighter. She pulled at them. Something told her that she could not allow this to happen. This source of light could not be allowed to remain in their grip. The thorns tore at her hands and would not relent. The flame inside fizzled and sputtered, finally sparking. An ember touched a vine and fire swept over it. The others shuddered and peeled away. Inside, the fire flared, the light suddenly blinding, filling the field.

Myranda's eyes opened. She was with the others once more. The dream had been intense and vivid. The dark field had crept into her dreams before, but she hadn't had to suffer the terrible visions of it for some time. She quietly hoped she wouldn't have to see them again anytime soon. The chilling imagery made the icy forest around her seem warm and safe by comparison. Lain was finishing a freshly-caught meal. Ivy was leaning against a tree, enthusiastically finishing her own share. Ether was finally in her usual place in the fire. Deacon had not moved. Pages were scattered all around him, his eyes rimmed with red. It was clear he had not slept.

"Deacon. Have you been at that all night?" Myranda asked.

"Hmm? Oh, you are awake. Well, it was day, not night, but yes," he replied.

"Have you found anything?" she asked.

"Very little. I . . . I have been able to determine that if counterspells do exist, they are not a part of their practices. They . . . do not undo their own work. They design spells to perform an action and complete. If an end is not implicit to the spell, the spell does not end. I've never seen anything like it," he said.

"There is no way to stop it?" Myranda said.

"There are ways. The spell can be deprived of its source of power. It can be rendered incomplete. Perhaps . . . perhaps a counter can be developed, but it will need to be developed from nothing. And it will have to be cast with at least equal power to the original spell. Unless it is poorly crafted, which it quite likely will be. In that case it will require much, much more," he said.

His voice was shaky, nervous. It was as though his own words terrified him.

"If that is what it takes, then that is what shall be done," she said.

"But the power it takes to open a portal for one is considerable. I *may* be able to muster it alone. If the portal is much larger, perhaps, *perhaps,* Ivy, Ether, you, and I might be able to work as one to close it. Much larger than that . . ." He shuddered.

Myranda placed a hand on his shoulder.

"Deacon. When the time comes, we will do what we can. Fate will have to handle the rest," she said.

"Eat. We need to move soon," Lain interrupted, dropping their share in front of them.

It was a snow rabbit, and it had been roasted already.

"Try it! Lain let me cook it! I think I did a very good job!" Ivy chirped.

Myranda and Deacon ate their share. It was nearly raw, but edible. Nevertheless, both claimed that it was exquisite. Deacon's own praise was carefully worded to avoid outright lying, but his diplomacy was greeted by a warm glow and warmer smile. Lain prepared himself and the others mounted, but before they could move out, Ivy turned to the south.

"Do you smell that?" she said.

Lain turned.

"Stay here . . . join me where the pass opens to the road . . . use your best judgment and tell me what you learn. Ivy, Ether. Follow," Lain said.

Without further explanation, he took Ivy by the hand and led her quickly into the pass.

"Wait, what's going on?" Ivy objected.

"Just go with Lain. We will follow in a moment," Myranda said.

Reluctantly, Ivy did so, with Ether whisking windily behind.

"What do we do now?" Deacon asked.

"Wait," she replied.

It was not a long wait. The distant sound of hoofbeats could soon be heard. There were quite a few. Possibly a dozen. Myranda waited tensely. The first of the strangers came into view. Myranda took her staff into her hand and took in a slow breath. As they drew nearer to the yet-to-be-extinguished fire, Myranda heaved the breath out as a sigh of relief.

"Caya!" she called out.

"Myranda?" came the reply.

Indeed it was she, the wild-eyed, wild-spirited leader of a rebel group known as the Undermine. The outlaws, as one of the few groups of northerners opposed to the war, had crossed paths with Myranda many times, and they tended to be of great help to one another. She leapt from the back of her mount to grasp Myranda's hand in a firm shake and give her a slap on the back. The others with her approached into the light. Among them was Tus, Caya's second-in-command who had the physique, disposition, and verbal prowess of a bull elephant.

The others with them were new to her. They looked as one might expect, a mismatched group of men and women too old, too young, or too infirm to do battle. They were those who had not already been snatched up by the Alliance Army, and every last one of them had lost too much to the war to stand by and let it continue. Curiously, despite the fact she'd not seen a single one of them before, they all seemed to recognize Myranda immediately.

"It *is* you. I should have known you wouldn't have gone into hiding. Not the biggest thorn in the side of the Alliance in the history of the war," Caya said proudly. "Are you being followed?"

"Well, very likely, actually," Myranda answered.

This prompted a cheer from the others.

"I knew it! Tus, you were right to demand this woman as your wife," she said with a smile.

Deacon's expression changed to a confused and slightly anxious one.

"What brings you to my neck of the woods?" Caya asked.

"If only I had the time to tell you," Myranda said.

"In a rush? Anything we might lend a hand with?" Caya asked with a wink.

"No doubt we could use it, but the others I'm working with are slow to accept others," Myranda said.

"Assassins are like that," Caya said, nodding knowingly.

This time Myranda's expression changed as well. How could she know about Lain?

"What . . . what did you say?" Myranda asked

"I suppose you haven't seen them yet. Tus, dig out one of the posters," Caya ordered.

Tus revealed a large poster, dominated by a sketch of herself, Lain, Ivy, and Ether's human form. Each was accompanied by a brief description. A price was offered for the capture of each, with the stipulation that they be brought in alive. It was similarly made abundantly clear that they all were of the highest of risk, and nothing should be held back in the pursuit of disabling them. Myranda's eyes lingered on the entry for Ivy. There was a sentence or two of additional information, which wasn't surprising. What was surprising was the nature of the information. It spoke of her history . . .

"These are showing up in every town and on every sign post," Caya said, interrupting her thoughts. "I've never seen anything like it. Naturally, we are trying to eliminate them. The last thing you need is people knowing that you are working with the Red Shadow, but even with half of the Undermine working on it, they are going up more quickly than we can take them down. They started showing up just a few days ago."

Myranda gravely handed it back, but Caya pushed it away.

"Keep it. We've got over a hundred of them. These fine recruits were able to capture a black carriage filled with them. Though I notice this fellow isn't featured," Caya said, indicating Deacon. "A new addition to Myranda's Militia? Or are you a hostage?"

"I am with them, most assuredly. The name is Deacon," Deacon quickly answered, folding the proclamation poster and slipping it into his bag.

"Well, Deacon, good to have you on our side. If Myranda would choose you to fight the good fight beside her, then I am sure that you will be an asset. Speaking of assets, while I appreciate that you may be better off without us for the time being, I am afraid that the same cannot be said for us," Caya said. "We've only just managed to relocate Wolloff."

"How did you manage that?" Myranda asked.

"Several weeks of convincing, and several more of lugging books. At any rate, it will be months before we can have another mystic healer, and there is a limit to the work our traditional clerics can do," Caya said.

"Caya, I--" Myranda began.

"I know that you've got yourself tangled up in something a bit more important, but I think you can spare a few moments to deal with the soldiers in attendance. And, while you are at it, perhaps we can partake of a sample or two of our current treatments," Caya said, pulling a flask from her belt.

Myranda nodded.

"I think I can spare a few minutes," Myranda said with a reluctant grin.

A few small groups of scout units were gathered, bringing the number of soldiers to twenty-three. Not a single one of them was in what Myranda would call good health. Arms that should have been in splints and slings. Ankles that could scarcely support any weight. Broken bones. Infected lacerations. The telltale signs of many battles gone badly.

"How has all of this been happening?" Myranda asked as she willed another rib into place.

"Even with you and yours distracting most of the attentions of the soldiers behind the front, this is a very dirty business," Caya said. "You've been very deep in this. Perhaps too deep to see or hear what has been happening. Not surprising. It has been rather discreet. Supply lines are being choked off, severed."

"I suppose you should be very proud," Myranda said.

"Not *to* the AA--*by* the AA," she said. "Supply lines vital to the survival of *many* large cities are being re-routed. The situation is getting serious."

"Why would they be doing that?" Myranda asked.

"We've intercepted dozens of messages ordering it. None with a motivation, none with a destination for the rerouted supplies. Have some, would you?" Caya said, sloshing the flask in front of Myranda.

"I doubt that would help my focus," Myranda said.

"I can handle the rest. Enjoy," Deacon said.

Myranda looked at Caya.

"Don't make me force you," she said with a grin.

Myranda reluctantly took a sip. Caya tipped the edge of the flask up, turning it into a sputtering gulp. It felt like fire running down her throat.

"There. That's much more like it," Caya said. "A little bit of liquid courage never did any harm. And this reunion, however brief, is one worth celebrating."

Myranda coughed a bit more.

"You and I have a different idea of what constitutes a celebration," Myranda gagged.

"Perhaps. So . . . you really trust the Red Shadow?" Caya asked.

The Red Shadow was another name for Lain. More accurately, it was the name of a legend he'd constructed to obscure the truth. Every assassination he'd performed, along with no doubt hundreds that he hadn't, were attributed to the mythic Red Shadow. Some saw him as a champion, striking down the wealthy and corrupt. Others saw him as a terrible menace. All feared him.

"I do trust him. With my life," Myranda said.

"Just what is on the horizon for you?" she prodded further.

"I don't know for certain. But he has finally agreed that this war must end," Myranda said.

"Mmm. Funny. The Alliance made a few token gestures to stop him when he was a murderer on an unprecedented scale, but now that he has turned his efforts squarely against the war, they plaster his face everywhere they can manage. It certainly makes it clear what their priorities are," Caya said with a sneer, taking another swig.

She turned to look at Deacon with her men.

"He certainly doesn't take his time. Just finishing up. Well, I won't keep you from your task. I only have one more thing to ask of you," Caya said.

"You know I will do what I can," Myranda said.

"If this doesn't work, whatever it is--if you find yourself without an ally and the war is still raging--come to us. You are too valuable a person to be squandered on a single attempt," Caya requested earnestly.

"I intend to give all I have to this cause. There won't be anything left if it fails," Myranda said.

Caya smiled.

"Here's to giving all you have! May it always be enough!" Caya said, raising her flask.

The others joined in and a long toast was tipped back.

She dug through her saddle bag and produced a bottle, sloppily refilling her flask.

"Here," she said, tossing the engraved silver canister to Myranda. "I may not be with you at the moment of triumph, but at least I can make sure you celebrate it properly. Now go. I'll tend to the fire. Best not to keep the other enemies of the state waiting."

Myranda and Deacon bid farewell and mounted their steeds to a cheer from the Undermine soldiers they left behind. When they were far enough into the mouth of the pass that he felt that they would not be heard, Deacon spoke.

"That large gentleman, Tus . . . he proposed to you?" Deacon asked.

"I wouldn't call it a proposal. More statement that I would be his wife," she said.

"Has . . . has that happened before?" Deacon asked.

"No. Why the sudden interest?" Myranda asked.

"Well, I . . . When you first came to Entwell, it was hard for me to imagine what you'd come from. What you'd left behind. You may as well have been born that day. I suppose it is only natural that I am not the only man to realize what a wonderful person you are," Deacon said.

"It wasn't like that at all, Deacon. I'd just helped him escape from a prison," she said, trying to set his mind at ease.

"I see . . . but. There *have* been others. I mean . . ." Deacon began.

"I've had a few associates, but seldom for very long. When I was still with my uncle, I could barely get past learning a boy's name, and since he died, well, I really haven't been in one place long enough to get to know someone. What about you?" Myranda said.

"No one. As I've said, I have known all of the people in Entwell since I was born. They are like an extended family. The thought of romance never even came to mind," he said.

"Really . . . I . . . never imagined I could have that effect on someone," she said, blushing.

"Well, I . . . ahem . . ." Deacon attempted. "Er . . . I didn't mean to make you feel uncomfortable. I just--"

Myranda shook her head and smiled.

"It is all right . . . Deacon," she said, her face turning serious. "Did you look at the proclamation poster?"

"I didn't. I was curious, though. There are descriptions. Are they accurate?" he asked as he retrieved it.

"See for yourself," she said.

"Myranda. Known murderer and Tresson sympathizer. Possesses training in the mystic arts, in violation of Alliance law. Guilty of treason. The Red Shadow. Infamous mass murderer, notorious assassin. Skilled warrior. Ether. Extremely powerful mystic. Shapeshifter. Indifferent to mortal life. IV. Highly volatile. Artistic prodigy. Student of . . . Lucia Celeste," he said. "Was . . . was that?"

"My mother," Myranda said.

"It can't be true," Deacon assured here.

"Can't it? The rest is true . . . or, at least, it is now. We know that she was something before they changed her. And if she is a prodigy, then she is one of the original Chosen. Clearly they want us captured. There is no reason why they would have felt differently then. Look at what happened back there where we found Lain and the others. They fairly destroyed that city trying to capture us . . . and she was in Kenvard, all of those years ago. They did it then, too. It was because of her, Deacon . . ." She struggled to say, a lump in her throat. "They *destroyed Kenvard . . . to get her!*"

The tears broke through as she fought to keep from sobbing.

"Myranda, please . . . Don't do this to yourself," Deacon pleaded.

"He knew just what to say. That line about my mother. It does no good to anyone. No one who reads it will remember her. No one will even know she was from Kenvard. But he knew I would see it," she said with a wavering voice.

"Who?" Deacon asked.

"Epidime. He was in my head. He knew just what it would take. He knew I would make the connection and only I could," she hissed. "The other names. The ones from Lain's book. They were his idea, too. I feel it. His fingers. Manipulating all of this. I can almost feel him in my head, even now."

"What good does it do him to lead you to this?" Deacon asked.

"Ivy . . . is the reason my family is dead!" she replied.

"It wasn't her--" Deacon began.

"I know, I know!" she interrupted. "It wasn't her fault. She didn't know they were coming. She couldn't have done anything to stop it. She didn't make the decision to stay. Do you really think any of that matters? Do you think knowing that will let me face her without feeling the pain all over again? How can I fight beside her when I know, in my heart, that if it weren't for her, everyone I love would still be alive? My life would not have been cast away, all of those thousands of lives would not have been trampled. When she was born . . . she doomed them all!"

"Myranda, this is just what Epidime wants to happen! You can't let him control you like this!" Deacon urged.

"What do you know!? *How could you even imagine how I feel?* All of my life, I have been torn apart. Adrift. I spent years blaming the soldiers who swept over us. The soldiers who failed to turn them away, but none of it made any sense. It was too quick, too big. Somehow, after so long, I'd almost been able to get past it. Now to have it re-awakened! To have the pain come back! And to have a *face* put on it! The face of a *friend!* Do you really believe that I can just put it *behind* me?" she cried.

"Myranda. I left all of the people that I ever cared about behind when I came here. I know they aren't dead, but they may as well be. I'll never see them again. Worse, I know that those who do remember me will remember me in disgrace. But I did it. I left them forever. And I do not regret it. Because I know that coming here had a greater meaning. I knew that finding you would make me whole, and helping you would save the world. That is what the people gave their lives for. They aren't victims; they are martyrs of this war. You must remember that," he said.

Myranda's gaze hung low, her eyes too clouded with tears to see. After a moment, she looked up. There was an opening ahead. The others would meet them soon. She wiped the tears from her eyes, the icy breeze freezing them to the rough cloth of the cloak.

A few more minutes in the whipping wind and blown snow brought the two wizards to that which Myranda never would have believed could have existed. It was a road. Narrow, to be sure, but better maintained than most she'd seen even in the days before this mad quest. It was unlike anything she'd ever seen. Most roads through the mountains hugged the mountainside or conformed to valleys between, but this one was almost perfectly straight, and nearly level. As the mountains rose up around it, it bored down into them until it was a tunnel disappearing into the inky blackness. From the looks of it, most of the road would be made up of such tunnels.

The road itself was made of gravel, and the fact that it was not embedded in a solid mass of ice betrayed the fact that great efforts must have been made to keep this path safe for travel. The one prevalent feature was the pair of ruts that ran in parallel along the ground, just the right distance apart to be wagon tracks, and deep enough to have been the result of continuous traffic.

"What was that all about?" Ivy blurted as they came into view. "Lain said that there were some friends of yours that would be meeting you. Why couldn't I meet them, too?"

Lain looked at her sternly.

"It isn't good, Lain. Show him," she stated with measured calmness.

Deacon pulled out the proclamation and handed it to him. The anger inside of him boiled just below the surface, but it was all too clear to the others.

"The Undermine is trying to take them down, but they are showing up everywhere," she explained.

"What? Let me see!" Ivy said, standing on tip toe to look over Lain's shoulder. "There's a picture of me there! Ugh. It looks like it was drawn by the same person who drew that picture of me that Deacon had. They all do. Except Ether."

Myranda looked about. The shapeshifter was missing.

"Where is she?" Myranda asked.

"She went to get food. We aren't going to be able to hunt in the tunnel and she didn't want to be alone with me while Lain went to get food, so she went," Ivy said, with the air of a tattletale.

"That . . . may not turn out well," Deacon remarked. "She doesn't strike me as the sort that is terribly concerned with exactly what it is that we eat, or the proper way to get it."

"I wonder how she will bring the food back," Ivy mused absentmindedly. "You don't think she is stupid enough to carry it along with her in the wind, do you?"

Lain was through looking at the poster. He crumpled it and threw it down.

"Hey!" Ivy said, snatching it up and carefully unfolding it. "I'm not done looking at that."

"This changes nothing," Lain growled.

"When this is all over, it might be difficult to go back to being an assassin if everyone knows what you look like," Myranda said.

"What happens after this is over doesn't matter," he replied.

"This must be an old picture of you, Myranda. And you, too, Lain. Look at the hair. Myranda's is shorter. And Lain's is long and tied back," Ivy noticed. "I've never seen either of you look like this. Did Lain ever . . ."

She looked up to see Myranda's eyes locked resolutely on some indistinct spot on the far wall of the valley. Despite her best efforts, Myranda could not hide the fact that she was not so much looking at something as *not* looking at Ivy.

"Is there something wrong, Myranda?" Ivy asked, concerned.

Deacon placed his hand on her shoulder and gently turned her aside.

"Myranda learned something when you went ahead. Something she wishes she hadn't. She will be fine, but for now she needs to have some time to think," Deacon explained. "Is that all right?"

"I . . . guess so," Ivy said, looking to Myranda briefly before turning back to Deacon. "Are you all right? Can I talk to you?"

"Of course," he replied.

"Well, these pictures. Demont drew them, I know it. I saw that paper you had. It was Demont's. He drew me the same way as this," she said.

"Are you sure?" he asked, looking over the drawings.

"Can't you tell? Look at how it was shaded. The light is always here, the shadow always here. And the way these lines run together. The pictures of Myranda, Lain, and me were drawn by Demont. This one of Ether is different. Why would they do that? Why would they have Demont only draw three of them?" she asked.

Deacon looked over the drawings yet again. As he did, it became more and more clear to him. What is more, the drawing of Ivy was not precisely accurate. It was identical to one of the design sketches of her. Possibly the very same image copied. What did that mean for the others? If he recalled correctly, both Myranda and Lain had had reasonably long imprisonments with the D'karon, while Ether hadn't. If Demont was the one responsible for crafting Ivy as she was now, and he had taken the time to sketch the others, could that mean that . . .

His thoughts were interrupted by both Ivy and Lain suddenly shifting their attentions to the mouth of the pass. They didn't seem concerned, merely interested. Moments later, the stout gray form of a large wolf stalked into view, a pair of gray bags slung around its neck. As it approached them, its form slowly changed; by the time it reached them, it was Ether who stood before them, the bags over her shoulders, and a gray fur cloak on her back.

"What did you get?" Ivy asked, as she greedily pulled one of the filled-to-bursting bags from her shoulder.

"As though it would make any difference to you. You would swallow anything I put before you," she replied, lowering the other bag to the ground.

"Fruit . . . and vegetables . . . fresh!" Ivy said, pulling out various fine samples as proof.

"And this bag is filled with cured meats? How did you manage all of this?" Deacon asked.

"Unencumbered by mortals, I can travel quite far in a very short time," she replied.

"The ones in the middle are still warm from the sun!" Ivy said as she pulled a large and decidedly tropical-looking fruit from the bag.

"Um . . . unless I've missed my guess, those do not grow anywhere *near* any of the Northern Alliance kingdoms," Deacon said.

"Show off," Ivy said. "You didn't run these all the way from wherever they grew as a wolf, did you? I was right, you *did* fly through the air with these."

"I was not seen," she replied.

"No, but I bet the fruit was," Ivy said.

Deacon snickered.

"What is it, human? Do you intend to mock me for my superiority as well?" she sneered.

"No . . . It is just that . . . I imagined the poor fellow who saw you in transit and is trying to convince his friend that he saw a migratory coconut," he struggled to say without laughing as he held up the fruit in question.

"Laugh all you wish. The simple fact of the matter is that not even Lain could have provided the provisions I have in the time I have," she said.

"It is time," Lain said, ignoring the squabble.

The group set off, taking their nourishment as they went. Myranda eagerly partook of the fruits and vegetables. Ivy and Lain didn't seem to mind subsisting on meat alone, but in the days that she'd been relying upon the game he was able to capture, Myranda had begun to feel an all too familiar sense of weakness. Neither human had ever tasted the fruits offered before, and Ivy was eager to give them a try as well. All told the bag of meat was untouched, while the well-stocked bag of produce was reduced by half.

By the time the meal was complete, the travelers had reached the point where the road entered the mountain. It was immediately clear, as the walls of the tunnel rose up around them, that this was not the work of Myranda's fellow northerners. The sole purpose of this tunnel, it would seem, was to remain straight and level. Not a turn or dip was made, despite the fact that the stone of the walls was of such strength that not a beam or timber was needed to keep the mountain from falling in on them. As for size, it was quite small. Wide enough, perhaps, for three horses to ride side by side, and perhaps tall enough to allow a coach through. The ruts that had worn their way into the road could clearly be seen here as well, each nearly touching the wall on either side. It was as though the tunnel had been designed around whatever carriage it was that was so frequently taking this route.

Scarcely a dozen paces into the tunnel, darkness prevailed. Myranda summoned a light from her crystal, as did Deacon. The walls were smooth. There were no torches, nor were there even holders to place them. This path had been created with no intention of ever being lit. Total blackness around her, combined with the echoing footsteps, gave Myranda unwelcome recollections of her trip to Entwell. Now, as then, she was not sure what she would find when her journey was through, but at least this time there was no fear of being lost. There was but one path.

The even, well-maintained ground would have allowed for a far faster rate of travel than before, but Lain maintained only a brisk walk. Perhaps it was the seclusion the tunnel permitted, or perhaps his need for revenge had been dulled somewhat, but for now he set a pace that barely put the horses at a trot. Despite this, the opening behind them retreated quickly from view, leaving only blackness ahead and behind. Ivy, who had been on foot with Lain and Ether, strayed closer and closer to the wizards, and the comforting pool of light they provided. Finally, she hopped onto the back of Myranda's horse and wrapped her arms around the wizard's waist.

"I don't like it here," Ivy whispered.

She was clearly anxious, though the lack of a blue aura betraying this fact indicated that it was either not a very great fear or she'd managed a degree of control over herself. Either was a good sign. As she calmed down a bit, she noticed that Myranda was sitting very rigidly, and had been ever since she'd joined her.

"Are you still upset, Myranda?" she asked, sheepishly.

Myranda gave no answer.

"Is . . . Is it something I did?" she asked.

"Ivy, perhaps you should join me instead," Deacon offered.

"But . . . Myranda, I don't know what I did, but it must have been very bad. You wouldn't be like this if it wasn't. Is there anything I can do to make you feel better?" Ivy begged. "I'll do anything."

Myranda took a deep breath and spoke. Despite her best efforts, the words wavered with emotion.

"It is something that happened long ago. Can . . ." Myranda began, a lump in her throat choking off her words for a moment. "Can you remember anything at all before your time with the teachers?"

"I can't. I tried. I don't like to think about that," Ivy said, shutting her eyes and shaking her head.

"Ivy . . . I need to you try again. Don't try to remember anything specific. Just . . . try to take yourself back . . . and tell me what you see," Myranda said.

"All right. For you, I'll try," she said, shutting her eyes.

For a few minutes, she was silent. When she did begin to speak, it was in spurts, and accompanied with flares of blue light and tightly-shut eyes.

"I remember . . . the cage . . . being inside of it . . . there were teachers. So many . . . I remember when I first opened my eyes . . . like they hadn't been open for a long time . . . I remember . . . seeing her . . . in the cage. The white beast. And the crystal. That horrible crystal . . . it is so dim," she murmured.

"You have to try. Go further," Myranda urged.

"Just blackness . . . for so long . . . nothing but my own thoughts. They were slipping away. I couldn't hold onto them . . . wait. I remember . . . a fountain. There were three trumpets . . . I remember the walls. It was a city . . . so big . . . home. They were there. Then . . . the gates . . . so many soldiers . . ." she muttered.

As she spoke, she sank deeper and deeper into her mind. The visions were in control now. Myranda listened to the images as they were described. They became more and more familiar with each step back. And with each step back, the doubt in her mind slipped further away. Tears began to trickle down her face.

#

Far away, a young boy reclined in his chair. Lightly clutched between the fingers of his right hand was the shaft of a halberd, the cracked crystal set in the blade flickering and pulsing. He was alone in a large room filled with books and maps. On his face was a look of deep contentment. There came a knock on the door. It was ignored, as had been the dozens that had come with ever-increasing insistence before it. Finally, the door was flung open.

"I demand to know what you think you are doing!" cried Trigorah as she charged in.

Her immaculate and graceful features were twisted in fury.

"Quiet," he hushed lightly. "Do you feel it?"

"What?" came the impatient reply.

"Anguish. Sweet as a summer wine. I couldn't feel them before. The girl has become quite proficient at masking herself. All she needed was the tiniest nudge to set her mind on fire, though. Now two of them are inflamed with decades of pent-up anguish. It is ringing out, strong and clear. Exquisite," he said. "It never fails. The old wounds cut deepest."

"Where are they?" Trigorah asked.

"I said quiet! This is a moment to be enjoyed," he replied, leaning his head back and stirring the air with his fingers as though he were conducting a symphony.

"Stop wasting my time," Trigorah demanded. "Tell me where they are and let me do my duty!"

With a frustrated sigh, he opened his eyes.

"In the tunnel, heading for the compost heap. I'll tell Bagu in a moment. I'm sure he'll want to send someone down to greet them. Did you find that friend of yours I'd asked you to locate?" he asked.

"I did. He is barely alive," she replied, suddenly disgusted by her words.

"See to it that he is strong enough to stand; that is all that I require. Entertaining as it is to see you all unsettled by having to deal with a child, once I am able to take *him* as a vessel, we shall close this chapter of the prophecy once and for all. Until then, leave me to savor the fruits of a few well-planted seeds," he proclaimed.

He then closed his eyes again and returned to his delighted reverie. Trigorah stood for a few moments, watching Epidime as he harvested the sorrow of the heroes far away. It was clear no more progress would be made here. She turned and stalked off to the dungeons again.

#

Back in the darkness of the tunnel, Ivy's tone had grown more distressed.

". . . that horrible, horrible crystal . . . the spike," Ivy continued, clutching her chest with her last words. "No. NO! WHY!"

She began to struggle against hands that were holding her down.

"Open your eyes!" Myranda commanded.

Ivy's eyes shot open and darted about. She was no longer on the horse's back. They had all stopped. Myranda was holding her by the shoulders; Deacon holding his glowing crystal near. The whole of the tunnel was bathed in a bright blue light that sharply faded as she realized that it was all in her mind. Behind Myranda, now almost invisible among the shadows, was Lain. Beside him was Ether, casting her scornful gaze.

"They stabbed me! In the chest! It was a spike. Like Demont used on Ether when we were in his fort. It was him *then,* too. The soldiers killed the rest. Everyone died. My mother, my father . . . me! He . . . he killed *me!* How can I be alive!? What *am* I? What did they *do* to me!?" she cried, tears pouring down her eyes. "Why did you make me remember!?"

Ivy beat her hands on Myranda's chest weakly as the girl cried as well. It was not Ivy's curse, forcing her emotions upon others. This pain she felt was genuine. Immersed in the same sorrow, the pair embraced, their bodies shaking with the force of their sobs.

"There were flames. I saw them . . . I heard the screaming . . . It was all I could hear . . . even after they were dead. I . . ." she sobbed.

"I'm sorry. I didn't mean to make you relive it," Myranda forced through the tears. "I just needed to know if it was true. I needed you to remember who you really were."

"But . . . I don't . . . I don't even remember my name . . . or the names of my parents . . . my family. All I remember is that horrible day . . . And I remember . . . just for an instant . . . seeing me, this me, from the outside . . . . like it was someone else. I . . . I wasn't always what I am now . . . but I can't remember what I was," she managed to speak between sobs.

Ether watched the outpouring of emotion with disgust. Deacon placed his hand on Myranda's shoulder and offered what little consolation he could. The shapeshifter turned to Lain, who stood emotionless as ever, his eyes locked on Ivy.

"Well? Aren't you going to coddle the beast?" she grumbled.

Lain turned away, his gaze shifting to the darkness that lay behind them. He twitched his ears and tried to listen over the slowly subsiding sobs of his fellow travelers. Nothing revealed itself, but something did not feel right. He stepped a few more paces into the darkness. Ether joined him.

"You aren't suited for this, Lain. And neither am I. We are Chosen. We are not meant to be babying the weak of mind. I was at first pleased by your sudden dedication to our cause, but it swiftly became clear that it was not the desire to do that which is your birthright that motivated you, but revenge. Revenge is a petty thing, Lain. And, worse, revenge for what? Denying the beast a safe haven?" she judged.

"I do not seek your approval," Lain replied simply.

"Nor should you. I know that I have behaved in a way that was . . . overt in my attempts to direct your heart's desire to where it rightfully should reside. I realize that such behavior was inappropriate, and quite unnecessary. Whether you accept it or not, you are an original Chosen, and so am I. The two of us are the only beings, created of the will of the gods expressly for the purpose of turning back the tide of darkness, that have managed to remain untainted and whole. This affection you place with Ivy is misguided, and you will see that, just as you will see that there can be only one who is worthy of it. All that is required is time. Fortunately, the two of us have an abundance of that. So I shall wait for your senses to return to you," Ether proclaimed.

Lain drew in a slow, deliberate breath.

"I do, however, offer a word of advice," she continued.

"What is it?" he growled, patience at an end.

"I had believed that there were no more Chosen to be found, even prior to our discovery of the beast. The fact that she, technically, remains a valid Chosen suggests that there may yet be a fifth yet to be discovered. I realize that Myranda claims that the Great Convergence has already occurred, and that somewhere, a creature we have already met stands as the fifth and final of our own. This is absurd. However, if there is even a remote possibility of it, it is of paramount importance that the actual final Chosen be found. Even if it means locking that . . . thing . . . into her place among us. When your thirst for revenge is sated by the decimation of this meaningless fort, I suggest we devote our full efforts to searching for our final ally until we are certain that such an ally no longer exists," she advised.

Lain remained silent and turned his attentions fully to the darkness behind them once more. There was something in the air that he didn't like.

Deacon, helplessly watching the others pour out years of anguish at once, tried his best to comfort them.

"It is all right. It is all in the past. What's done is done," he fruitlessly offered.

"What was that place? The place I saw?" Ivy begged Myranda. "Tell me you know it!"

"It was Kenvard. It was my . . . our home," she replied, wiping tears away.

"That was Kenvard . . . the massacre you talked about, that killed everyone but you and your uncle . . . I was there? But you said that it was years ago . . . My head . . ." Ivy said, wincing in pain and covering her eyes. "I guess this is what sadness does to me. Makes me weak . . . and opens old wounds. Kind of poetic, huh?"

She was quite right about the old wounds. The deep gash in her arm that had nearly cost Ivy her life a short time ago was trickling blood again. Myranda closed the wound and helped her to her feet.

"So . . . if that was Kenvard, did you know me?" Ivy asked.

"Perhaps. I was very young. My memories of that time are vague at best. But I'm sure my mother did. Lucia. Her name is on the proclamation," Myranda said.

"Lucia . . . I remember the name now. She was . . . a teacher. But not a bad one like Demont and them. I think I had a lot of teachers then. But I can't . . . I can't remember. Why! Why are the bad memories the only ones left?" she cried.

"You remembered this. The rest will come," Myranda said.

"Quiet," Lain ordered in a whisper.

Everyone turned to face him. He closed his eyes and focused on what was silence to all, even Ivy. After a moment, he opened his eyes. Now it was certain.

"Someone has entered the tunnel behind us," he said. "At least a horse. We need to keep moving. Keep the light low."

The group hastily returned to horseback and continued. The sound of the horses' steps echoed infuriatingly, wiping out any hint of the sound of the follower and making it all the more likely that they would be found. The group could travel more silently on foot, but leaving the horses now would give away their presence when they were found, and the speed they provided just might keep them ahead.

Time had passed slowly before, but now each passing moment was an eternity. It was clear that Ivy was doing all she could to keep the fear she was feeling from showing. Tension only grew as the horses began to falter. They'd had little to eat or drink. Provisions had run out for them shortly before they had entered the mountains, and here in the tunnel there was no source of water and not even a single blade of grass for them to eat. Their purposely slow pace grew gradually slower, until there could be little doubt that the mysterious followers would be gaining.

As they progressed, the tension grew thicker. A long section of the otherwise completely featureless tunnel was stained with two shades of blood, and shortly after that, a pile of unrecognizable remains came into view. Time had rendered it a dried-up husk, and the same ruts that had remained constant throughout the journey ran right through it. It filled the tunnel with the smell of death. Not long after that, Lain signaled for the light to be doused entirely.

Many believe that they know true darkness, but until it has been experienced, it cannot be imagined. Without even a flicker of light, the mind begins to play tricks. There is the constant feeling that there is a wall before you, that you must stop. The eyes open as wide as they can, hungry for light. The only thing that helps is to shut them tight. The horses' eyes were covered and they were led along. Ivy's arms were wrapped tightly about Myranda's waist, her head pressed hard against Myranda's shoulder, shakily breathing in the girl's ear. She was practically whimpering, but with the exception of a flare of blue occasionally, she was doing a heroic job of suppressing her fear.

In the darkness, it was impossible to tell how far they had traveled, and hours and minutes bled together. Even Myranda could hear something in the echoes now, something near. She pulled in a breath of the stale air in the tunnel. It still reeked of death. If anything, it had grown stronger. How could that be? Surely that . . . thing was miles behind them by now. Then Myranda felt something she had been waiting for. It was the tiniest puff of cold air on her skin. She opened her eyes. Far ahead was the silver light of the moon falling on snow. It was barely there, but after so long in the darkness, it may as well have been a beacon.

What followed was maddening. The end of the tunnel was tantalizingly near, but they had to maintain speed, lest they be heard over the hoofbeats of their pursuers. The opening ahead crept closer. The breeze from outside became steady, until the air in the tunnel took on the frigidness they had become accustomed to in the mountains. Until then, it had not been obvious just how much warmer the inside of the tunnel was without the wind bearing down on them.

Myranda took another deep breath, anxious for just a whiff of the fresh air that was so near, but what she drew in was anything but fresh. The stench was horrific, worse than she'd ever smelled. It was the scent of death magnified. It caught in her throat. She could taste it in her mouth. Her lungs urged her to cough it out, but she could not risk the sound.

Another eternity passed, and finally it was over. The group emerged from the tunnel. It emptied into a valley. The mountains towered around them. Great circular platforms had been carved like steps around the irregular floor of the place, providing flat areas for the same structure repeated exactly on every spare inch of space. Each was a vast building with no windows and a single wide door. They were stone, a few stories tall, each topped with a tall, sloped roof. At each peak was a crystal, the very same type that accompanied everything the D'karon put their hands to, with identical ones at each corner.

There were dozens of the buildings, perhaps a hundred, arranged in ring after ring. Only the center of the valley and the road leading to it was free from one of the structures. The center of the valley bore a wide stone platform, stained black by a thick and seemingly ancient coat of grime. Despite the staggering amount of architecture, it seemed that Deacon's translation had been accurate insofar as the degree to which it was guarded. There was not a soul to be seen.

The heroes hid themselves in an alcove beside the tunnel entrance and waited. They attempted to remain silent, but it soon became clear that the odor that permeated the tunnel had come from this place. The air was thick with the smell of death. Myranda managed to keep from gagging, but only just. She felt sorry for Lain and Ivy. Their sensitive noses could only compound the torture. The horses were visibly uneasy as well. Only Ether seemed unaffected, no doubt owing to her ability to forgo the senses as she saw fit.

The sound of echoing hoofbeats grew louder until, finally, their pursuers exited the tunnel. It was a vehicle all too familiar to Myranda: the wretched black carriage. She'd been unlucky enough to spend some time in one before, as a prisoner of the Alliance Army. The windowless sides of the carriage made identifying the unfortunate occupant impossible. A pair of horses pulled the carriage, guided by a single driver.

Myranda heard something drop to the ground beside her and looked to see that Lain had deposited his sword there. In a flash, he was streaking across the ground toward the carriage. He dove at the driver, tearing him from the seat and throwing him to the ground. As he opened his mouth, revealing his vicious teeth, Myranda turned away, covering Ivy's eyes.

A few moments later and Lain was beside them once more, a familiar black stain upon his mouth. He wiped it off with some snow and retrieved his weapon. The body of the driver, clearly a nearman, lay twitching on the ground, blood running from beneath its mask. Normally, the mockeries of humanity turned to dust when they died. That this one remained suggested that Lain had left him alive, suffering.

"Why didn't he use his sword?" Ivy asked as they followed him to the carriage.

"I am not certain I want to know," Myranda said.

The remains of the nearman finally collapsed into empty armor and dust as they approached. Myranda leapt from the saddle and rushed to the doors of the carriage. She undid the latches and pulled them open, only to recoil in horror.

"What is it? Oh . . . oh . . ." Ivy said, turning away.

The carriage was filled with soldiers. Dead. They were stacked like a cord of wood, blue-armored soldiers of the north and red-armored soldiers of the south alike.

Myranda closed the doors. She'd heard tales of this. That the dead were being loaded up off of the fields. She had more than her share of memories of funerals for the fallen soldiers of the many villages she'd drifted through after Kenvard was destroyed. Seldom was there a body to grieve over. It was believed that there simply was no one to spare to return the dead to their homes, but there were those who said that the black carriages hauled them off of the battlefield.

"What is this place?" Myranda asked.

"If I understand correctly, the map labels it 'Final Reserve,'" Deacon said.

"What could that mean? There is no one here! Why would they bring the dead to this place?" she asked.

"Maybe the reserves are in those buildings," Deacon offered.

"Trust me. There is nothing *alive* here but us," Ivy coughed.

"Do you feel any magic about?" Myranda asked.

Deacon grasped his crystal tightly and slowly scanned the area.

"Nothing active," he replied. "Those crystals have something potent in them, but I can't quite place what . . . wait . . . there is something more."

He raised his finger to the night sky. A black form against the faded gray clouds emerged a moment later, bursting from the clouds where he had indicated. It seemed close, judging from the size, but as the seconds ticked on, the bat-like form took up more and more of the sky. By the time the flapping of the wings could be heard, a horrifyingly large section of the sky was blocked out by them.

It was a dragoyle--or, at least, that was what it most closely resembled. The size was at least triple that of the largest such beast they'd yet faced, and it seemed far stouter overall. The neck was slightly shorter and much thicker, as were the legs. The tail was covered with spines that grew longer and broader along its length, until they ended in a near morning star. Its head bore similar armor-plating, and in place of the cruel beak that normally adorned such beasts, this one seemed to have a jagged, tooth-like serration. At the sight of the creature, the horses bolted, vanishing into the tunnel.

Lain readied his steel. Ether shifted to her flame form. Both wizards held their casting stones at the ready. Ivy stared in open-mouthed awe, not having gotten a firm enough hold on her wits to be afraid yet.

The monster descended into the valley. The wind from the massive wings was a constant gale. When it touched down, it did so with enough force to shake free much of the snow that had clung to the steep slopes of the surrounding mountainside. Instantly, the tunnel behind them was hidden in a cascade of rocky ice and snow. All were prepared for a monumental struggle. Oddly, once it landed, the massive creature held its ground, each foot planted just outside the stone platform, not making the slightest motion of hostility. Slowly, it lowered its head. As it opened its mouth, the heroes scattered, expecting a torrent of the wretched miasma the similar beasts had spewed--but none came. Instead, what looked to be a wooden treasure chest fell to the ground. Slowly, the chest opened.

"Steady, everyone. Some sort of spell is activating. A weak one," Deacon warned.

A pale blue mist stirred from within the chest. Slowly, it coalesced into the form of a man. Ivy and Myranda stiffened at the sight, and Ether's fiery hide flared. They had encountered this man before. It was the most senior of the generals, Bagu. He appeared to be reclining in a chair that had not fully appeared along with him. As the mist took on the appropriate hues of his flesh, he stood.

"You kept me waiting. This beast has been circling over the clouds for some time," he stated.

"Who is that?" Deacon asked, fascinated by the act of magic he was witnessing.

"General Bagu," he replied. "You must be the newest thorn in my side. The human foolish enough to associate with the Chosen."

"Incredible! An illusion coupled with communication . . . brilliant," he admired.

"Listen, Chosen. I am certain you know a great deal about me--but, I assure you, I know a great deal more about you. I have been gathering information on some of you since before your births," he said. "I was concerned that you were functioning too well as a unit, but I realize now that I could not have been more wrong. You all fight for a single cause, perhaps, but your motivations are your own. I am the focus of your fury because you believe that my defeat will provide you with the goal you crave. You are mistaken. I do not stand between you and your desires-- your own foolish beliefs do. I am the only one that can offer you all what you seek. And all I request in return is for you to lower your weapons and allow me to finish my work--or, if you prefer, join me and see it to as bloodless an end as you like."

"Don't listen to him!" Myranda cried.

"The wizard . . . What is it that you want? An end to this war, and perhaps a taste of revenge in exchange for the price your homeland had to pay. Do you really believe that this war will end simply by killing me? There will be others to take my place, I assure you, and others to replace them. You blame the D'karon for keeping this war alive, but it is your own people, and the people of Tressor, that will allow it to continue. Join me, and I promise you this war will end tomorrow. I will issue the order to cease hostilities. Negotiations can begin. If you join me, the next drop of blood could be the last," Bagu said.

"You would never do such a thing," Myranda replied.

"Are you so certain? Certain enough to allow another few generations to be cut short rather than risk trusting me? Or have you let the assassin's pathological distrust poison your mind?"

Myranda was silent. Bagu turned to Lain.

"And you, assassin. You don't even care about this war, do you? You want us dead because we threaten that precious little experiment behind you. Again, your blame belongs elsewhere. We did not kill your kind. It was the humans, the elves, everyone who saw them as inferior, as dangerous. If you kill every last D'karon, the murderers who took your people will still remain, and so will the threat to your precious race. You have accepted Ivy as one of your own, and she was not even complete. We created her, giving your kind another breath, and you seek to destroy us for it? Do as I say and I will have Demont resurrect your race. There will be hundreds, thousands of your kind again," Bagu offered.

"You didn't create me! I don't remember everything, but I know I wasn't always this way," Ivy retorted, a flare of red surging around her. "Someone give me a weapon. I'll show him!"

"The experiment. Your motivations are more difficult to determine. Do you seek revenge for being altered? Or do you simply wish to remain with the others because you have nowhere else to go? Regardless, you have nothing to gain by our defeat, and everything to lose. Everyone who knew you as you were is dead. If you seek answers, you need only return to our fold. We and only we can provide them," Bagu reasoned.

Ivy tried to reply, but her mind was suddenly awash with conflicting thoughts.

"And what would you offer me, fiend? I have no motivation, only a purpose, and that purpose is to rid this world of you and your kind," Ether interjected.

"Yes, yes. The protector. Existing from the dawn of creation for one purpose alone, to fend off the threat to your world. And if you succeed? What then? If we are well and truly defeated, you are left with nothing. An eternity of hollow, meaningless existence. You can be more. This world is not the first we have sought. It will not be the last. As we pierce the veil, sweeping from realm to realm, you could have a new purpose by our side. You could be a conqueror. Or, if you must defend, why defend just one world? Join us, and when this world is ours, it will be yours to defend once more, and a thousand others besides. You are not our only enemies. There will be an eternity of meaning for you with us," the general offered.

"It doesn't matter what you offer. Fate is not so flimsy as to even allow the heroes of this world to be corrupted," Deacon proclaimed. "The Mark will strike down any divine warrior that would betray its cause."

Bagu turned his gaze to the young wizard. "The scholar of the group, are we? Listen, human. We have been at this game for a very long time. We are familiar with the rules, more so than you could ever be, and we are equally aware of their exceptions. It is well within our power to accept you safely into our ranks. It has been done before."

"And what will you do if we refuse? Kill us? There are only four Chosen here. Without the five of us united, even if you *could* kill us, it would only delay our cause. New Chosen would arise. You are afraid of us. That is why you came to bargain with us. You are so afraid you wouldn't even come in person," Myranda said, gambling that the general did not know what she did--that the convergence had already occurred.

"Afraid! You insignificant piece of flotsam! How *dare* you even *think* that you could instill anything but contempt in me? I have seen thousands more powerful than you crushed. You are *nothing!"* Bagu raged, before adding in a smoldering tone, "And as for not killing you? It is true we need you alive for now . . . but life is more loosely defined than you might realize . . ."

The image of the general vanished. In a swift and sudden motion, the massive beast burst into the air. Astoundingly and mercifully, the dragoyle did not instantly bear down on them. It managed to heft its ponderous girth into the sky, spiraling higher and higher until its inky form merged with the equally inky clouds. For a few moments, where seconds ago it seemed certain there would be a titanic clash, there now was only an eerie stillness. The only hint that the unusual standoff had happened at all was the still-open chest in the center of the valley. Myranda cautiously approached it.

"Careful!" Ivy urged.

Myranda, staff at the ready, peered inside. There were a few crystals, now dull and lifeless. No doubt they had enabled the message to be delivered. The only other things in the chest were an assortment of gold ornaments. There were two oddly-shaped metal plates, a gauntlet, and a headband. She leaned closer. There was something familiar about them. The gauntlet in particular. She was about to pluck it out of the chest when she heard Deacon shout a warning.

"Those spells are waking up," he called out.

Myranda looked up. One by one, the gems on each of the roofs were winking to life. In the space of a few seconds, the dim light of the cloud-obscured moon was replaced by the pale blue-white light of the gems.

"Did you hear that?" Ivy gasped, as Lain turned to the source of the noise unheard by the others.

A moment later, it came again, louder. A low rumble, like the long, slow slide of heavy stone.

"It can't be. They wouldn't," Deacon spoke in a deathly hushed tone.

The irregular rumble began to grow and it mixed with a stirring from within all of the dozens of structures. A few of the doors rattled, shaking free their sheaths of ice and straining against the mounded snow that had gathered at the base of each. More doors followed. Soon the cacophony of countless doors threatening to tear themselves from their hinges was deafening.

Lain stood resolute. He'd come here to destroy it, to take away whatever it was that the D'karon hoped to hide here. To punish them. Ivy's breathing was growing faster, her thus-far-heroic grip on her emotion showing the first signs of slipping. As she backed toward the carriage, the only hint of shelter in the whole of the chaotic valley, she stumbled over the remains of the ruined soldier. There on its belt, was its unused sword. She scrambled to it, pulling it free and clutching it shakily.

Finally, one of the doors gave way. There was a rush of stale, pungent air, and a stir of choking dust and fumes. When the cloud settled, what it revealed was horrifying beyond all measure. The dead. Hundreds of them, some surely a hundred years gone, or more. The cold, dry air had reduced them to little more than bone and leathery sinew, but still they shambled forward. Most still wore some shred of the armor they had fallen in, the heavy plates of metal tugging at rotten straps. Noses and ears, if they remained, hung loosely from skulls, eyes long ago rotted away. Yet, somehow, each sensed the intruders and trudged their way.

"By the gods . . ." Myranda said.

"The gods have nothing to do with this abomination," Ether growled.

Instantly, she rushed at the shambling legion. They took eagerly to flame, their ancient flesh little more than kindling now for the flames of the shapeshifter's form. Ether continued inside the crypt. With a rush of hot air, the mixed roar of a thousand unholy wails, and the surge of a thousand flames, every last lumbering corpse inside took to flame.

Myranda pulled what she knew of flame magic to mind, ready to unleash it on the next door that gave way, but from the glow of the crucible Ether had created, forms continued to flow. In flames, the undead continued. Even when the flesh fell entirely from the bones, the skeletons of the fallen continued their march. A second and third door crumbled away, unleashing hundreds more into the valley, a single one of them yet to be defeated.

"Deacon. Do you know anything about this? The undead? Can you dispel this?" Myranda called.

"Necromancers were few and far between in Entwell. I'll try what I know," he offered.

He raised his gem and mumbled a few words, thrusting the crystal outward with the last of them. A thread of light swept out from the casting stone. As the twisting filament struck the burning revenants that had already grown dangerously near, they dropped to the ground. It was as though whatever will had given them life had been pushed away, leaving them to crumble into misshapen piles of remains. A smile and a glimmer of hope flashed across his face as he prepared to unleash another volley, but just as suddenly as the half-dozen or so that had been struck down fell, they rose again.

"Blast it! Something is fueling the curse. It doesn't take a genius to determine what," he said, looking to the gleaming gems that adorned the roofs. "There is no reason to assume that this spell is any different from their others. Interrupt the source, eliminate the spell."

"Then we have to destroy the gems," Myranda said.

That was all Lain needed to hear.

"Keep Ivy safe," he ordered, sweeping into action.

Instantly, he was a blur. Not bothering to evade the thickening hoard of the undead, his blade sliced through the ancient flesh like dry reeds, clearing a path that quickly closed behind him.

"Ivy, stay close," Myranda said, looking back to make certain she was not in danger. She was gone.

Myranda turned back to see Ivy bounding after Lain. Was she afraid? She was terrified.

Fear coursed through her mind until it seemed to flow through her very veins. It burned at every part of her. The aura that accompanied it was blinding. She'd never been so aware of the change, so deep into it without losing herself, but she couldn't let it happen. Her friends needed her. Not some mindless monster. Not some shivering little girl. They needed *her*. As she came to the first of the monsters that had once been men, she swung the weapon she held. Distant memories--her own, yet not her own--barked orders to her body. Hold the weapon this way. Place your feet that way. It was training, some residue of what the teachers had forced into her mind. Her muscles moved of their own accord. The blade cut deep and true. The head of one of the corpses rolled from its shoulders.

Deep in her mind, there was a surge of encouragement. Something urged her on. She swung again. Again. More of the creatures fell. She felt something grow stronger, the desire to strike at these foes growing like a mad hunger that needed to be sated. More of the lumbering bodies closed in around her, but she hacked and sliced on. The fear was slipping away. Everything was. With each swing, she felt the desire to grow stronger. It was growing into a need.

The leading edge of the horde of living dead was reaching Myranda now. The fire Ether had sparked among them was spreading, resulting in the far greater threat of mindless monsters swinging and clawing indiscriminately while consumed in flame. Ivy was now deep among them, some manner of frenzy they'd never seen before blinding her to the fact that there was no end to the foes she faced. All the while the flames leapt from corpse to corpse, drawing nearer to her. That sword would do her no good if she was surrounded by fire.

There was a rush of flame and a radiant form burst out from the crypt once more. Ether hung for a moment, high over the valley. For the first time, she could see that she'd done no good. Lain had destroyed a few. Even Ivy had. But the creatures she'd attacked still stood. A look of focus came to Ether's eyes. These creatures would fall. She tightened her fiery fists and gathered her mind. The flames began to rise. The light from them grew to an almost blinding level. She shook with exertion, but still the forms below stood.

Great torrents of energy flowed out of her, fueling flames that burst high into the sky in great spires. The scorched stone of the crypt she'd set alight now began to glow around the edges. She cried out and funneled even more into the inferno. Fine cracks climbed like vines up the walls, crumbling the mortar and letting the white-hot glow of the flames within through. Finally, the crypt collapsed, and so did Ether. The flames died down with no supernatural will to fuel them.

A great swath of the valley was blackened, the bodies that had been crawling along it were little more than jagged broken bones and ash. The shapeshifter crashed down in the center of the patch of scorched earth and, with great effort, managed to shift to her stone form.

Lain reached the top of the nearest crypt. The doors of this one had not yet opened, but the fiery rage of Ether had melted much of the snow that blocked them. It would not be long before the creatures within were loose. He slashed at the large central gem. There was a flash of light and a crackle of energy and his sword leapt back, the gem untouched. A second and third strike were similarly repelled. He sheathed his sword and thrust his heel at the stone stalk the crystal was mounted on. It chipped. Another cracked the icy stone, and finally a third blow broke the short spire free. It plummeted to the hard earth. He ventured to the edge and peered over. The gem had fractured and gone dim, and a handful of the undead that were clawing their way up the walls to reach him grew still and dropped to the ground, but there were more to replace them. Quickly, he rushed to a corner of the roof, ready to bash another free.

The constant wail of the resurrected soldiers was growing to deafening levels as door after door was bashed to pieces by the relentless foes. Myranda waded into the mob, pulsing out waves of magic to scatter the legion enough to manage a few more steps. She had to reach Ivy. Deacon rushed in behind her. When he reached her side, he pulled the twin-bladed weapon from his bag. Though he'd brandished it when Ivy was last rescued, he'd not yet made use of it. At first glance, it was not clear how he intended to do so now. The blades were barely a hand-length each, curving slightly in opposite directions off of the ends of the weapon.

"What good is that going to do?" Myranda asked, managing to hoist one of the undead into the air with a spell and launch it forward, clearing a few more steps toward Ivy.

"A little trick Gilliam taught me," Deacon explained.

He released the blade. It hung in midair, now revealing a network of arcane designs on its grip. Suddenly, it began to spin, in moments accelerating until the air hummed with its speed. He swept his hand forward and the whirling blade launched itself in a similar arc. The rotten flesh of the risen dead offered little resistance. By the time the blade finished its swing, every creature it made contact with was reduced to a writhing pile of limbs.

"You will have to teach me that," Myranda said, thrusting another corpse backward to clear the path behind them.

"Surely," he replied, casting the weapon out for a second sweep.

As the pair made their way forward in that manner, Ether trudged toward the next crypt. Her stone form, for the moment, was weathering the constant attacks of the swarm of undead that shambled in to replace those she'd incinerated. A heavy swing of her stone arm bashed apart the creatures, but their numbers were wearing on her. She'd seen Lain on the rooftop, dislodging another of the crystals, and similarly noticed the effect it had had on their foes. When she reached the crypt, she thrust her claw-like stone fingers into the wall and began to scale it, her ponderous gait only slightly faster than that of the horde that followed her.

Lain finally broke free the last of the crystals, returning a few scattered clusters of the undead to lifelessness. The doors of a handful more crypts had failed, leaving the valley more flooded with the walking dead than before. They were rapidly losing ground. Worse, the writhing mob of living dead below had made it to the roof, climbing over one another to reach him. He hacked and sliced at the creatures, but as quickly as they were struck down, more replaced them. There was no safe way down the wall.

His gaze shifted to the roof of the next crypt, then down to the crowded alley below. There was no other choice. He sheathed his sword, kicked a revenant out of his way, and launched himself off of the roof. He collided with the wall of his next target about halfway down, managing to just barely find a grip. He scrambled up to the top, the tide of living dead already shifting toward him.

Below, the cost of Ivy's frenzy was beginning to show. The jagged, bony fingers and broken teeth of the wretches she hacked at had found their way to her flesh more than once, and she was taking less and less notice of it. Her own safety was being washed away by this strengthening compulsion to strike down these undead soldiers. As the whirring blade of Deacon swept around her, eliminating the threats nearest to her, she turned instead to hacking the still-twitching remains below her to pieces. Anything to sink the weapon into her enemy.

Myranda and Deacon called for her to stop, but their voices were distant. As they drew closer, she turned to them. Her mind saw them as friends, but this madness saw them as something else. She didn't know it, but what she felt now was the same programming that drove the nearmen, forced upon her while she was still in the clutches of the D'karon. And now it demanded that these wizards taste the blade. The malthrope lunged at them. Midway through the attack, the dim realization that she was attacking her friends finally broke through to the surface. She managed to halt the weapon a hairsbreadth away from Myranda and recoiled, dropping the weapon. Deacon took the task of keeping back the constant push of undead entirely upon himself as Myranda looked after Ivy.

"What was that? Are you all right?" Myranda asked, looking her over for injuries and quickly healing those she found.

"I . . . I couldn't control it. Those blasted teachers . . . I think that is how they trained me to fight," Ivy said. "I don't like it."

"Are you in control now?" Myranda asked.

Ivy nodded vigorously.

"Good. I want you to follow me. There must be someplace in this valley that the undead can't reach. Once you are there, I want you to stay there while we take care of--" Myranda explained.

"No! I am one of you. I am part of this team. I am going to help," Ivy demanded.

One of the walking corpses lashed at Deacon, its attack grazing his arm. There was no time to argue.

"Fine. Take the sword, we've got to--" Myranda relented.

"No! I don't like myself with a sword in my hand. Just tell me what we need to do, I'll manage," Ivy said.

"Fine. Do you see those crystals? We need to break every last one of them," Myranda said.

Ivy looked to the roofs, then to the field of lumbering undead between them. A dozen fears tugged for her mind's attention, but she shook them away and heaved herself forward. Instantly, instincts took over, but these were more familiar, more welcome. Her steps took on a certain fluidity and rhythm. She twisted and turned, slipping through the slightest gap in the line of foes. The density of the creatures became greater, and her maneuvers became increasingly acrobatic. Tumbles, handsprings, and rolls finally took her to the base of a crypt.

With a speed and deft precision that more than rivaled Lain's, she made her way to the roof. Once there, alas, her grace vanished, as she began to pound and bash at the stone spires that bore the crystals with her bare hands. Though lacking the finesse of her ascent, it was nonetheless effective, as her deceptively strong blows steadily weakened the supports of the spires.

A few buildings away, Ether finally finished her laborious climb. Approaching the crystal, she heaved a heavy backhand at it, shattering it in one blow, but staggering backward. A sharp pain ran up her arm. It was the crystal. The spell protecting it was no concern, but the accursed crystal itself pulled hungrily at her own strength when she touched it. She turned angrily to the next spire and stalked toward it. One of the undead pulled itself onto the roof ahead of her. Ether grasped the rotting creature by the throat and hurled it at the spire, ruining the creature and dislodging the crystal in one blow. She dispatched the next three foes and the next three crystals in the same manner. When her work on this roof was done, she stepped to the edge and dove off, bringing those corpses below her to a rather messy end as well.

Meanwhile, Deacon's blade was taking longer and longer to clear a swath through the ever-thickening throng of creatures, and they had yet to reach a crypt.

"This isn't working. We need to keep these things from escaping. You do something to brace the doors that haven't broken free. I'll try to stop the ghouls that have already escaped," Myranda said.

Deacon nodded and recalled his blade. He raised his crystal and focused on the nearest door that had not yet given way. The gap between the doors began to glow. As the glow faded away, so did the gap, leaving a solid stone wall where there had once been a door. Myranda swept together as much of the melted slush and snow that had resulted from Ether's earlier onslaught as she could, and cast it over as many of the undead as she could manage. When she could not drench any more of them, she set her mind to summoning an intense wind and bone-chilling cold and directed it at the mob. Gradually, their plodding movements slowed, until the creatures she had managed to douse were frozen solid. Now safe from the attackers, Myranda wove between them as quickly as she could to help Deacon.

Deeper in the valley, far from the patch of living dead immobilized by the wizards, Ether had yet to make it to the next crypt. The undead had formed a solid wall in front of her, and no amount of hacking, shoving, and bashing afforded her a single additional step. Worse, the shambling mass began to crawl upon one another like insects, mounding up on her and attacking from all sides. Finally, she gave up on her stone form. Gathering what little strength she hadn't already squandered, Ether turned her mind to the long list of creatures that she'd sampled from the case Deacon had pilfered. Selecting one, she set about taking on the form. The undulating pile of undead that had crept over her began to heave and bulge upward, and then she finally burst from the pile, soaring skyward. Now in the form of a griffin, she swept quickly back and plucked up a pair of the undead and spiraled high into the air, dropping them with deadly accuracy, shattering two of the crystals before diving to fetch two more.

Ivy finished shattering the crystals in the roof and rushed to the edge to climb down, only to be suddenly and intensely reminded of her fear of heights. Try as she might, she could not push this fear aside as she had the others. She retreated to the peak of the roof, the undead swarm beginning to creep over the edge and close in on her. She backed to the shattered remains of the topmost spire as the creeping terror drew nearer.

"H-help," she whimpered meekly, reluctant to turn to the others.

The spire she leaned on gave way, nearly taking her with it as it plummeted to the ground below.

"HELP!" she cried, her hesitation gone.

A moment later, she felt a sharp tug and was yanked into the air by her waist. She released an earsplitting scream as she watched the rooftop drop away beneath her.

"Cease that screaming, beast!" Ether warned.

"I DON'T CARE! PUT ME DOWN! I'LL TAKE MY CHANCES WITH THE DEAD PEOPLE!" she shrieked, her eyes clamped shut.

Ether dipped and deposited Ivy on a roof on the far side of the valley.

Ivy, opening her eyes reluctantly, suddenly cried out. "No, no! On the ground! ON THE GROUND!"

Ether ignored the pleas. Ivy kicked the nearest spire, dislodging it with a single blow, the dash of anger giving her a surge of strength. She stomped over to the next spire and tugged at it, snapping its base and dragging it with her as she continued her tantrum. She grumbled loudly, punctuating her complaints by smashing additional spires with the makeshift club.

"What sort of a stupid *idiot* takes someone who is afraid of *heights* and drops them on a *roof!*" she cried, destroying the other spires.

Now once again trapped on the roof with nothing more to do, she swung the crumbling remains of the makeshift club in a few circles and hurled it. It soared in a high arc, smashing into the stone platform in the center of the valley.

Deacon rushed through the narrow walkways between the structures, finding it harder and harder to find one that did not already have the undead pouring from it. Myranda followed just behind, conjuring up freezing winds, tangling vines, and anything else she could think of to slow the flood of creatures. Finally, Deacon came to a stop, trying desperately to catch his breath.

"It is no good . . . There are too many loose already," he panted. "I need to get to a roof. I might be able to figure something out about these crystals."

After an abortive attempt to levitate himself to the roof, he willed a portion of a shattered door into a makeshift ladder. With his crystal floating faithfully beside him as he ascended, he made his way to the roof, destroying the ladder when Myranda was safely beside him.

"If those things start to climb, do what you can to keep them off of me, if you would," Deacon requested.

Myranda nodded. The wail of ruined voices and the shuffle of withered feet was constant. Picking out which was closest or what might be a threat was nearly impossible. Deacon, on the other hand, filtered it all out, committing the whole of his considerable attention to the largest of the radiant crystals. He held his own crystal up to the larger one and furrowed his brow, eyes darting occasionally, almost as though he were reading. Without the pair of them below actively slowing the progress of the undead swarm, it was not long before they began to work their way up the sides of the crypt.

On a distant roof of his own, Lain was just finishing the final spire. Most of the crypts were near enough to one another for him to leap directly from roof to roof. The undead were too slow to reach him before he moved onto the next roof, and too mindless to climb onto adjacent roofs, rendering them a non-issue for him. As he chose his next target, he saw Ivy, far in the distance, hesitantly approaching the edge of a roof before retreating amid a splash of blue. His eyes swept across the roofs. Most around him were littered with the sinewy remains of those unlucky enough to be chosen by Ether as projectiles, not a spire remaining. Breaking into a sprint, he bounded from roof to roof when they were near enough, and down to the ground when he needed to. His blade made a path through the legion of undead who, despite the considerable efforts of he and his allies, only seemed to be growing thicker.

In moments, Lain had carved a path to Ivy, bursting up to the roof where she stood. She was first startled, then relieved by his appearance. He took her by the hand and led her to the edge of the roof. She reluctantly allowed herself to be pulled along, but as the ground came into view, she pulled back again, drawing in a sharp breath and trying hard to push down the rising fear.

"You can do this," he insisted.

"No. No, I can't, Lain," Ivy stammered, crouching and covering her eyes.

"Ivy. Listen to me. Listen!" he ordered, jerking her hands away from her face.

She locked her tear-moistened eyes on his gaze.

"Stand up. Do you see that roof there?" he said, pointing to the next crypt.

"I don't want to--" she began.

"Look! Do you see it?" he repeated forcefully.

She nodded.

"I want you to jump to that roof. Don't look down. Just look to the roof. You can make it," he instructed.

She took a shaky breath as he led her back for the running start. Her eyes were on the far roof. Lain held her hand and took his first steps forward. She forced herself forward, charging down the slope of the roof a half-step behind him. When she reached the edge, she shut her eyes tight and jumped. A moment later, she crashed down, sliding first up, then down an icy surface. She splayed out, digging her claws into the ice and clenching her teeth against the fear. When she slid to a stop, she felt a sharp nudge at her shoulder. Cautiously opening her eyes, she found that she was clutching the shingles on the opposite side of the peak of the roof she'd been aiming for. She'd cleared nearly the entire crypt.

"I . . . I did it!" she cried, springing to her feet and bouncing about happily.

Lain nodded before dropping from the roof and climbing to another. Ivy took a few more moments to savor her achievement before setting once more to the task of destroying the crystals.

Overhead, fatigue was beginning to get the better of Ether. Locked entirely into the form of a griffin to limit the parasitic effect of the crystals, she found herself subject the weaknesses of the form as well as the strengths. Settling her massive shape down on one of the roofs furthest from the others, the shapeshifter took a moment to catch her breath and survey her progress. Perhaps a third of the crypts were rid of their spires, as mound after mound of once-again-motionless dead would attest to. Curiously, it seemed that those they had defeated had been completely replaced with more to spare.

Deacon continued to stare at the crystal, occasionally shouting out an observation to Myranda, oblivious to how quickly she was losing ground to the undead that dragged themselves in ever-increasing numbers onto the roof. She quickly learned that, now as near to the magic-absorbing crystals as she was, it was best to resort to more traditional means of dispatching the horde. The bow was removed from her shoulder, and arrows were carefully aimed. The sinewy walking dead offered little resistance to the arrows. Her shafts passed right through them, and often through the creature behind as well. The mindless beasts were soon being struck down three to an arrow, and still the roof grew more dangerous.

"Hurry!" Myranda called out, finally resorting to blasts of wind to knock the swarm from the roof. Sure enough, the nearest crystals took on a far brighter glow and a handful of the fallen dead rose once more.

"There are three spells. One shielding the crystal, one supporting these creatures, and . . . I cannot quite determine the last one," he said, finally deciding he was out of time.

He stepped back and flexed his mind. Steadily, his influence spread. One by one, the surrounding crystals took on a brighter and brighter glow as they drew in the strength that was pouring out of him. More and more of the corpses that had been deprived of the unholy force that was fueling them stirred and rose from the ground.

"What are you doing?" Myranda cried.

"Just a moment more . . ." he muttered.

Finally, every last one of the surviving crystals was glowing brightly. There was a brief flash in the heart of each one, and finally he relented, nearly losing his footing as the vast mental effort came to an end.

"There. The shield spell. It was the only one I could break," he said.

Myranda drew back an arrow and let it fly at a crystal on a nearby roof. It shattered easily.

"The crystals are vulnerable. Shatter them directly!" Myranda cried.

Lain put blade to crystal again. This time, the brittle gem shattered. Ivy fetched up a rock and did the same. Myranda launched arrow after arrow. Deacon guided his deadly blade. The undead dropped by the dozen with each crystal broken. In mere minutes, the whole of the valley was stripped of every last gem. The heroes gathered on a single roof to survey the aftermath. Every last patch of ground was piled high with the remains of the horde.

"That was an ordeal," Deacon said, wiping beads of sweat from his brow.

Myranda looked over the horrid sight with revulsion. As stomach-turning as the landscape was, littered with the dead, a thought entered her mind that she could not shake.

"It isn't enough," Myranda said.

"I'd say it is plenty enough!" Ivy said, inching cautiously to the edge of the roof before pulling back. "I really don't like it up here."

"No. I mean. This war has been going on for more than a century. If the fallen of each battle have all been brought here, there should be more," she said.

"You give the D'karon more credit than they deserve. They couldn't possibly account for every last casualty," Ether offered.

"Even so . . ." Myranda said distantly.

Lain closed his eyes. Ivy did the same.

"Uh-oh," Ivy said. "Do you hear that?"

Lain nodded, adding, "Underground."

"What do you mean, underground?" Deacon asked.

"Look!" Myranda called, pointing to the stone platform in the center of the valley.

The spire Ivy had hurled at it was gone. In its place was a hole. Beyond it, darkness. Myranda made her way down to the ground, trying to push from her mind the fact that the mounds she trudged over had at one time been human beings. Deacon and Lain followed. Ether, still in the griffin form, glided from the roof, leaving Ivy behind.

"Hey!" she cried angrily. "Don't leave me up here!"

Ether landed beside the others, just at the edge of the platform. A few paces ahead, the hole made it clear that it was not a platform at all, but a roof. Beyond it was darkness, and the distinct sound of shuffling feet and voiceless moans came from inside.

"The whole floor of the valley must be riddled with tunnels and chambers," Myranda surmised.

"With their own crystals, no doubt," Deacon added.

"Bah. Leave them. If our purpose here was to damage the cause of the D'karon in some inane punishment for threatening Lain's precious little pet, then it has been done," Ether dismissed.

"What would happen if we did leave them?" Myranda asked Deacon.

"Well . . . provided the undead didn't escape the valley, the crystals would likely run down and they would cease to live," Deacon offered.

"And if they did escape the valley?" she asked.

"I can't be sure, but it was clear that the curse that raised these soldiers was meant to be spread. If even a single afflicted corpse were to make it to the outside, the curse could conceivably be spread without limit," he replied.

Myranda thought silently for a moment.

"The crystals that are down there, would they have been stripped of their protection as well?" Myranda asked.

"I poured a fair amount more effort into that spell. I would say any object on this mountain with a similar protection has been deprived of it," Deacon answered.

"So any crystals that are down there are as brittle as glass," Myranda continued.

"Roughly," he replied.

"Good. I have an idea, but I think I am going to need your help. You as well, Ether," Myranda stated.

"If you are even considering going down there, you can be sure I will be of no help to you. Such a foolish endeavor is undeserving of my aid," the shapeshifter stated categorically.

Myranda calmly stated her plan. In her present form, a look of disgust was a near impossibility, but Ether succeeded admirably before reluctantly nodding. Lain set off for his part immediately, whisking to the rooftop that held Ivy and, amid considerable protest from her, bringing her to the ground. The pair then found the safest route to the rim of the valley and waited. With them in place, Ether took to the air, circling just overhead.

Myranda crouched on one knee, Deacon assuming a similar posture. She placed the tip of her broken staff into the icy earth just beyond the edge of the stone platform. He flattened his hand against the same earth. Both entered a deep state of concentration. Slowly, a soft but undeniable rhythm began to emanate from the ground where they touched it. It was erratic at first, but as it grew stronger, it grew more steady. The rhythm grew into a rumble, then a roar. Bricks fell from damaged buildings. The hole in the roof widened.

The pair of wizards worked at the spell, building it to the limits of their strength. Cracks split the earth. Whole sections of the valley floor fell away, bringing with them the mounds of fallen soldiers they had supported. Still the shaking grew. Snow, ice, and stone from the walls of the valley slid in great flows to the quaking floor. One by one, the floor beneath the stone crypts gave way, swallowing them up. Finally, whatever earth had been left to support the valley floor crumbled away. The roofs of untold many tunnels fell in a single, earth shattering collapse.

As the very patch of ground that held the wizards turned to rubble beneath them, Ether swept in and snatched them up, pulling them safely into the sky. She deposited them beside Lain and Ivy and landed, quickly assuming her human form. All eyes, save Ivy's, watched as the tunnel-weakened valley floor swallowed itself in a churning chaos of stone and snow. For minutes, the relentless crash of stone upon stone continued as more and more vast unseen vaults caved in.

Finally, the deafening rumble subsided, and there was peace.

"Is it done?" Ivy asked, venturing a peek that she swiftly regretted.

The valley was much steeper now, little more than a sheer drop down into a vast field of jagged rock.

"I would like to remain here until I am sure of that," Myranda stated.

"But . . . you destroyed the whole valley!" Ivy protested, finding the thought of spending any more time than she had to beside that dizzying drop far from pleasant.

"If there is even one chance in a million that one of those things could claw its way to the surface and find its way to the outside, then I want to be ready to stop it," she said.

"It has been a rather long time since we've had a proper rest, and likewise a proper meal," Deacon added, though few required a reminder of that.

"How remarkable that you would speak in favor of Myranda's proposal," Ether remarked, her more expressive form peppering her words with the understated look of condescension she lacked as a griffin. "And what if that massive creature returns while we are still defenselessly atop this mountain?"

"I rather doubt we will fare any better if we are trudging along one of the passes below if it comes," Myranda said.

After a few moments unmarred by objection, it was decided. The team moved to a somewhat more sheltered cranny of the valley edge, and Lain swept off to attempt to scrape some semblance of a meal from the wind-scoured mountainside.

"Wait, I thought we had two big bags of food!" Ivy cried out from well away from the edge of the valley where the others sat.

"Yes . . . I would imagine they are now buried in a stratum of debris and human remains, along with the horses, unless they made it through the tunnel before it was blocked," Deacon said.

"Aw!" she replied, edging closer to the others, as though the edge of the precipice would drop into the valley below if she made a false move. "Well, couldn't Ether just get more?"

"Feh. It was folly to have fetched it in the first place. I see no sense in aiding you in such a way if you treat my bounty so carelessly," the shapeshifter sneered.

Ivy sneered back, before turning and declaring, "Did you notice? I didn't change! Not once!"

There was pride in her voice that was matched on her face. It was well deserved. In quite a short time, she had gone from not believing that she and her violent transformations were one and the same to being able to consciously delay or even ward them off.

Myranda turned to give her praise, but was cut off by Ether.

"Yes. So I have noticed. You have made great strides toward completely wiping out the only thing that made you the least bit useful on the battlefield," she stated, instantly wiping the joyous look from Ivy's face.

"Ether, please!" Myranda scolded.

"No, it's fine. Let her talk. She's just jealous anyway," Ivy said matter-of-factly, "because I'm getting better and better and she's making all the same stupid mistakes."

"You have no idea what--" Ether scoffed before being cut off.

"Enough. We are all tired. I think it would be best if you kept your daggers to yourself until we've had a chance to recover from this battle," Myranda said.

Ether remained silent for a moment.

"Human," she said flatly.

"What?" Myranda asked, frustration in her voice.

"Not you, the human that actually seems to understand my superiority and treat me with the appropriate degree of reverence," Ether remarked.

"Yes?" Deacon asked, his excitement over being addressed directly by Ether quickly washing away any sting the remark might have held.

"Build a fire, a large one, and quickly," she ordered.

"I shall do my best," he said, springing to his feet and scanning the ice, snow, and rock around them for some semblance of fuel.

Finding none, he rummaged through his bag and retrieved one of the vials from Demont's workshop. He opened it, retrieved one of several acorns, and forced it into the ground. He held his crystal above and instantly it sprouted. Within a few minutes, it was nearly fully grown.

"If I recall correctly, it took me more than an hour to do that, and you said it was remarkable," Myranda remarked, having been asked to cast that very spell as part of her training.

"For a first try, it is beyond remarkable. I've had a bit more practice. There, that ought to provide a fair amount of fuel, and a bit less effort than feeding the flames myself," he said, ushering the oak tree to full maturity.

A few limbs were trimmed and took to flame far more quickly than such fresh wood should have, no doubt due to a silently cast spell or two. Regardless, there now was a fire to be warmed by, and to refresh Ether, who stepped quickly into it. Deacon reached up and plucked a new acorn to replace the old one from the vial. As the others settled around the warming flames, Lain arrived with the meager find from the mountainside. With a frustrated sigh, Ether stepped out of the flames long enough for the meat to be cooked, rather than be used as a tool for the purpose.

Ivy partook of her meal raw, as did Lain. The humans made short work of a portion that was barely adequate. Myranda quickly resumed her post at the valley's edge. Deacon sat beside her and lent his eyes to the task, sweeping the darkness below for movement. Over the course of a few minutes, Ivy edged closer and closer. Finally, she was beside the others, albeit with her eyes dutifully turned away from the rather steep drop that theirs were turned dutifully toward.

"How long are we going to stay here?" Ivy asked.

"Until morning," Myranda said.

"Ugh. I don't like it up here," she huffed.

"You climbed up here. You weren't afraid then," Myranda pointed out.

"Climbing is different. You are on the ground the whole time, and you don't have to look down," she said. "But that's not the only reason I don't like it up here. There is nothing to do here."

"I suggest you get some sleep," Myranda suggested. "We still have a long trip ahead of us."

"I'm not even tired. Not even a little . . . I need something to do," Ivy said, restlessly.

"I could give you my pad again, if you would like to do more sketches," Deacon offered.

"No. I'm not in the mood. Myranda, your hair is a mess. Could I braid it?" she asked.

"I suppose so," Myranda said with a chuckle.

Ivy squealed with delight and edged behind Myranda, her eyes carefully focused on Myranda's hair lest she catch a glimpse of the dizzying fall.

"Deacon?" she said as she set to work.

"Yes?" he replied.

"You really like Myranda, huh?" she said.

"I love her with all of my heart and soul," he replied.

"Wow . . ." Ivy said. "How . . . how did you know?"

"I suppose if I'd just opened my mind to it I would have known the moment I met her, but as it was, I didn't really realize until . . . well, until I found my way to her again," he replied.

"And, Myranda, do you love him back?" Ivy asked.

"Of course," she replied.

"And how did *you* know?" Ivy asked.

"Well . . . I suppose I realized when my thoughts turned to him so frequently after I left him. Why the interest?" Myranda asked.

"I don't know. It's just nice to know . . . to know that that sort of thing exists," she said, fumbling for the words to express an elusive feeling. "I can't remember very much. And what I do remember is all bad, until I met all of you. I just . . . I'm glad that there are still good things, even if I don't know about them."

She finished braiding Myranda's hair.

"It is very nice, Ivy," Myranda complimented, admiring the intricate braid.

"Thanks. I don't remember being taught it . . ." she said, shaking her head as the terrible feeling of uncertainty began to buzz about it again. "I--I need something else to do. I need to keep busy. My head doesn't feel right."

"I'm sure I can find something that will interest you," Deacon said, pulling his bag in front of him and beginning to pull items from it.

Pile after pile of papers were shuffled out of the bag. Ivy glanced uninterestedly at them before putting them aside. The wind sometimes caught them, but the pages obediently halted and returned to the bag when casually requested to do so. When it became clear that the writings held little interest for her, Deacon instead withdrew some of the other artifacts liberated from Demont's workshop. Ivy's eyes brightened at the sight of the colorful gems that he produced. The gems began to take on a faint glow.

"What is doing that?" Ivy asked.

She tried to pick one up, but recoiled.

"Ow. They're hot," she gasped.

"Get those wretched things away from me, you fool!" Ether scolded from her place in the fire.

"Oh, you hush, they're just little things," Ivy replied. "Except that one. Is it broken?"

She indicated a fairly large, irregularly-shaped piece of crystal.

"It looks to be. That's odd. I seem to remember this being perfectly clear. Now there's a cloudy black bit in the middle," Deacon remarked, plucking the crystal from the ground.

He inspected it carefully, turning it about in the light of the fire. The hazy blackness within was not an imperfection, but a slowly shifting stain, like a drop of ink in a glass of water.

"Curious," he said, offering it to Ivy to hold.

She did not reach for it. Indeed, she simply stared blankly at him as he held it forth. There was no hint of emotion, interest, or even *life* on her face. He moved the crystal back and forth slightly, her blank stare slowly shifting to follow it.

"Ivy?" he said with concern.

"What is wrong?" Myranda asked, turning away from the valley.

"She . . . she just went blank," he said, placing the crystal on the ground.

Ivy's eyes suddenly sparked back to life, a look of confusion coming over her.

"What the . . . didn't you just pick that up?" she asked.

"Ivy, what just happened to you?" Myranda asked.

"What do you mean what just happened to me? He reached to pick the crystal up, then he wasn't holding it any more. Ask what happened to him!" she said.

Lain was by her side now.

"Pick up the crystal again," he ordered.

"Are you certain?" Deacon asked.

"For heaven's sake, I'll pick it up," Ivy said, leaning forward.

Deacon quickly snatched it up before she could. The blankness took over again.

"Ivy?" he asked again.

She remained silent.

"Give her an order," Lain said.

"An order? Very well . . . Ivy, stand up," Deacon said.

Ivy slowly and deliberately obeyed.

"Ivy, what is your name," he asked.

"I have no name," she replied lifelessly.

"What is this?" Deacon asked Lain.

"Demont had a crystal like that. While he held it, Ivy did everything that he told her to do. She even saw what she was told to see," Lain said.

"Really . . . I must look into this further," Deacon said, placing the crystal on the ground.

Instantly, Ivy was back.

"What? It happened again? And why am I standing up? What's going on?" she asked, a swirl of fear and anger sweeping over her.

"Oh. Eh . . . It was a bit of magic I hadn't tried before. Sorry to startle you," Deacon explained, once again relying upon evasive honesty in hopes of avoiding a lie.

"Oh . . . well, ask next time," she scolded.

"I am very sorry. I will," he said, pinching the crystal with the hem of his cloak to avoid touching it as he returned it to the bag.

The other crystals were scooped up to follow it, the last of them knocking against something else within, producing an odd sound that seized Ivy's attention.

"What was that?" she asked excitedly.

"I don't know," Deacon said, reaching into the bag.

What he withdrew from the bag brought a look of utter ecstasy to Ivy's face and a look of deep confusion to Deacon's.

"My violin!" she squealed, snatching it from his hand.

Ivy joyfully plucked at the strings.

"Do you have the bow?" she chirped.

A second dip into the bag revealed that he did indeed. She grabbed it and drew out a long, clear note from the instrument.

"I never thought I'd get my hands on one of these again, and it is the very one that I left behind when Trigorah and the D'karon caught me. How did you know to get it?" Ivy asked, the yellow glimmer of happiness pouring from her.

"I . . . I didn't," Deacon said, confusion mixing with a dash of concern.

"Don't be silly. How else would you have it? Oh, never mind. Myranda! You weren't there the last time I played. I was so sad that you couldn't be there," the excited creature rambled. "Lain! Please say I can play for her, just a little while, just so she can hear me play!"

Lain looked at the eager eyes staring into his. They were at the edge of a valley in the middle of a mountain range, far from any prying ear. They were as well hidden as they were ever likely to be. Besides, the D'karon had made it clear with their timely visit in the valley just minutes before that there was not a place in the world that was beyond their reach. He nodded once. No sooner had he started the motion than Ivy put the bow to the strings.

The melody was bright and lively, and utterly flawless. Her fingers danced across the strings with a master's skill, and the joy she felt to her core was obvious. The whole of the group was bathed in a golden glow, and pain, weariness, and other ailments were washed away from all but Ether, who rigidly resisted the wondrous effects. Ivy's eyes were shut as she focused deeply on the intricacies of the increasingly complex song. As she played, Deacon discreetly sifted through the contents of the bag, withdrawing a few select papers and looking with distant concern over the other contents. When it seemed likely that Ivy was several minutes away from a break in her playing, he quietly pulled Myranda aside.

"Isn't it astounding? She is phenomenal!" Myranda whispered to him.

"Yes. Remarkable . . . Listen, Myranda. The crystal? It is mentioned here. Ivy's soul was held in a crystal for decades while they determined how best to put it to use, according to these notes. The soul was released by fracturing its vessel when she was placed in this new body. The crystal Demont wore, along with this crystal, must be the remains of that vessel. It would appear that the gem is still tightly linked with her soul," he explained in an almost silent whisper.

"So it would seem," Myranda said, still distracted by the truly astonishing performance that Ivy was putting on. "When did you place that violin in your bag?"

"That is the other thing . . . I didn't. I am certain that I never placed that instrument in this bag. There is no point that one might have been placed there without my knowledge. Certainly not the very one she claims to have left behind," he said nervously.

"But . . . what would that mean?" Myranda asked, puzzled.

"I don't know," he said solemnly. "And that concerns me greatly."

Any reply she might have had was interrupted as the rousing tune reached its epic finale. It was an almost dizzying sequence of notes and chords. When she was through, she opened her eyes, a triumphant smile on her face. Myranda applauded her and lavished praise.

"Where did you learn to play like that?" she asked, hugging Ivy.

"I just know!" she said. "Deacon, did you bring the case for the violin?"

I sincerely hope not, he thought, as he reached once more into the bag. "I'm afraid not."

"No matter. I really don't want to put it down anyway," she said, plucking a light melody to busy herself.

With the graceful notes of the instrument softly lilting in the background, the hours passed quickly. As the short day came and went, there was nothing in the way of motion from the ruined valley below. Deacon cast a spell or two to be absolutely certain that there was no longer any danger, and as the moon rose dimly behind the clouds, the group marched on. The infectious joy Ivy had felt had done more for them than a night of sleep ever could, so there was no need for further delay. The mood was considerably brighter now. Forgoing the bow as she walked, Ivy plucked the strings merrily, a smile on her face.

The path they followed twisted into the mountains, nestled deep in a narrow pass. The going was slow, with ice and snow tumbling into cascades with nearly every step. It left the path unsteady, and constantly shifting, but they made their way as best they could. Ether, for reasons she kept to herself, chose to remain in her human form, slipping and stumbling with the others rather than becoming something more surefooted. When the pass widened a bit and leveled out, Deacon took advantage of the more forgiving terrain to spend a few moments scratching at a sore spot on his arm.

"What is it?" Myranda asked.

"Nothing to worry about. What direction are we heading?" he asked, adjusting his sleeve once more.

"North, roughly," she said.

"Have we decided upon our next goal?" he asked.

"The capital," Lain answered, a few steps ahead of the rest.

"The capital. Do you really feel that is wise?" Ether asked. "We are incomplete. The fifth Chosen must be located before we attempt the final confrontation lest we risk failure."

"I do not care what fate has intended to happen. My intention is not to fulfill my role in history, it is to find and kill the beings responsible for continuing this war. When they are dead, the structure of the northern army will collapse. The war will end. I will be able to find a place for Ivy, and I will be able to turn back to my earlier cause," he said.

"And if the war does not end with these few assassinations?" Ether asked.

"Then I will continue to cut the threads that bind the war until it unravels," he said.

His words carried an air of finality, making it clear that further questions would be unanswered. The group continued with as much speed as they could manage until the constant wind that whipped at them rose to painful levels. The ice and snow it hurled at them was mixed with fresh flakes from above. A long overdue blizzard surged up with little warning, driving them into the shelter of a cramped cave with an uneven floor, high up a rather steep slope. The driving wind continued to howl harder and harder outside the mouth. Ivy had carefully protected the violin against the worsening weather until they reached shelter, but before long the whistling outside was enough to drown out even her loudest notes.

The temperature inside the cave, numbingly cold to begin with, dropped steadily. Myranda shivered, casting one spell after another in an attempt to keep feeling in her extremities. Deacon managed to repeat the enchantment he'd placed on his own cloak on hers, but it only managed to take the bite from the cold. As time passed, the storm only grew stronger. The opening began to fill with snow, so much so that Lain and Ether had to clear it every few minutes, lest they be trapped within.

Hours passed. The wind and snow did not relent. Soon the cold was joined by an equally serious concern: hunger. The meal they had eaten the previous day had been a meager one, and easily a day had passed since then. Before long, Myranda's mind began to drift back to that horrible day all those months ago, starving and lost, freezing in the middle of a field. The day she found the sword. The day this all began for her.

Ivy plucked at her violin, the sound lost in the wail of the wind, but as she did so, she seemed increasingly flustered.

"I can't . . . I can't quite . . ." she called out, attempting something that she seemingly couldn't complete.

"What's wrong?" Myranda replied, maneuvering closer to Ivy to avoid yelling quite so loud to be heard.

"I keep making mistakes. I don't know why," she said.

"It is the cold, Ivy, it is getting into your hands," Myranda said, clasping them between hers. "You are cold as death, Ivy!"

"No. No I'm not. I don't feel cold," Ivy said, lowering the violin to clasp Myranda's hands back. "And . . . you don't feel cold either. And you don't feel warm. I can hardly feel you at all."

"Your hands are numb. You've got to warm up!" Myranda said, pulling her staff free and conjuring up a flame. "I don't know how long I can keep it going, everyone, so gather around."

Ivy did as she was told, with Deacon joining her. He lent a bit of his own mind to the flame, to ease the burden on Myranda. It didn't help much. The heat was a godsend, though. For the first time since the wind began to pick up, Myranda stopped shaking.

"I really don't feel the warmth. Or the cold," Ivy said, holding her hands to the fire so closely they threatened to singe. "What I feel mostly is hungry."

"I know the hunger seems bad, but right now we have to worry most about the cold. Give the fire time to warm you," Myranda said. Her unfortunate life had made her something of an expert at prioritizing such things.

More time passed, and Ivy's condition began to worsen. The breath of all others within the cave left as great foggy clouds, but her breath was weak and wispy. She seemed distant, her head drifting and jerking suddenly, as though she would collapse at any moment.

"Ivy. Stay focused. Why don't you play the violin some more?" Myranda offered as she edged in for a closer inspection.

Ivy picked up the violin, but nearly dropped it into the fire, her fingers refusing to close around the neck. Myranda gathered to mind what she'd been taught about healing. What she sensed was worse than she could have imagined. Ivy was failing. Her heart was weak. Her breathing was weak. Even her soul was a flickering ember of what it should have been.

"What is wrong?" Lain demanded, an intensity in his eyes, and for the first time, fear in his voice.

"I don't know. She is beyond weak. I can't explain it," she said. "We need to do something to get her strength up."

"Will food help?" he asked, almost begging.

"It may, but I'm not sure it will be enough," she said.

Deacon rubbed his eyes and held his crystal out, the glow within it flickering to life as he tried to lend a hand in the diagnosis. Lain rushed out of the mouth of the cave and into the deadly weather outside. Ether watched him go, glancing back to the others briefly before rushing after him.

"Keep her talking," Deacon said, shaking his head before returning to the task of finding the source of the weakness.

"Ivy. Ivy, listen to me. I want you to think back," Myranda said.

"No . . . no thinking back," she almost moaned, her voice barely audible against the whipping wind.

"Not to the bad times. To the good times. The times after we found you. Please, just say anything. Anything you remember," Myranda urged.

"Uh . . . I remember when everything fell," she said.

"Good, good, what else?" Myranda prodded.

"Things. Things are always falling. The valley. The town. The fort. All of the forts. Everywhere I go, things are falling down," Ivy said.

"Yes, what else?" Myranda said.

"Uh. The horses never last . . . the supplies, too . . . we always end up on our feet, the sky over our heads, hunting for food," Ivy muttered. "Myranda . . . am I . . . dying?"

"No! No, Ivy, you are not dying!" Myranda urged.

"It is all right . . . As long as you are here . . . I don't mind . . . thank you . . . I'm sorry I couldn't . . ." Ivy slurred before slipping into unconsciousness.

"Ivy!? Ivy!" Myranda called out, shaking her.

"Leave her rest. I know what it is," Deacon said, slumping back.

"What? How do we help her?" Myranda cried desperately.

"She was hurt by the undead. You closed the wounds, remember?" he replied rummaging in his bag.

"Are you saying she is infected? Cursed?" Myranda gasped.

Deacon withdrew Ivy's crystal. The wisp of black was now a thick, inky cloudiness, and it was slowly but surely growing.

"It is the curse. It has wrapped itself around her soul. She's got time, but not much," he said.

"Why didn't I detect it?" Myranda asked.

"It is a disease of the soul, not of the body," he said.

"What do we do?" she asked.

Deacon dug into his bag and pulled out a slim, leather-bound book, different from the one he constantly took notes in. As he flipped through the pages, vastly different script and illustration swept by, as though he was riffling past whole volumes without getting any closer to the end of the book. When he found what he was looking for, he pulled his other book out and scribbled some hasty notes on a clean page. As he did, he muttered to himself, closing his eyes and tilting his head back from time to time before launching on a new search.

"There is no *single* spell like it. Soul Blight . . . similar. And Reanimate," he mumbled.

"What are you saying?" Myranda asked, anxiously glancing at Ivy's barely breathing form.

"The black magic and necromancy practitioners in Entwell do not speak of a spell exactly like this one. It seems like a combination of two of them, with something else added. Soul Blight is a spell that feeds off of the target's soul until it is too weak to recover. Reanimate restores motion to a soulless husk, but it requires an outside will to support it. This spell is a masterful union of the two. It feeds off of the victim's soul, then uses the strength it sapped away to sustain a spell of reanimation. Something I've never seen before allows it to spread itself by breaking the skin of a new host. It is a work of dark genius," he said.

"Is there a cure?" Myranda urged.

"The only way to cure reanimation is to dispel the controlling will, the source of power. But her own soul is the source of power, so we must act before she is fully reanimated. But that would require that we cure the Soul Blight aspect of the spell and . . . well, it is black magic. It is intended to be irreversible, a way to kill a wizard that might otherwise be able to raise himself from the dead," he said.

"You're saying that there is no saving her?" Myranda said solemnly.

"The spell has to be changed," he said, the sound of realization in his voice.

"How can we change a spell that has already been cast?" Myranda asked.

"*You* can't, but *I* may be able to. There is no time to lose, if this has a chance to work, it must be done *now,*" he declared, throwing aside his books.

He crawled to her, raising her to a sitting position and propping her against the freezing wall. Her head lolled limply. He held her forehead with one hand and steadied himself with his other on her shoulder. His eyes locked on hers; they fluttered ever so slightly to reveal the milky pupils brought by the affliction. The unmistakable look of concentration that came with the most strenuous of spells mixed with a tinge of almost manic desperation as he went to work.

"She . . ." he struggled to say. "She may . . . she will . . . worsen. And quickly. As will I."

"Why? And why will you?" Myranda asked, suddenly fearful for them both.

As she asked, part of the answer became clear. The sleeve had slid back on his raised arm, revealing a day-old scrape, suffered during the battle with the undead. It was minor, but it did not remain so. His skin, already a sickly pale she'd attributed to the cold and hunger, grew paler still around the wound. As the pallor spread, a blackness crept into the wound and then feathered outward slowly along the veins of his arm.

"When did those creatures touch you?" she gasped.

"Never mind . . . me," he said, the focus taking virtually all of his mind. "When I am through . . . keep her safe. And warm. Keep the fire going . . . as long as you can. She will be weak . . . but . . . if she can last just a few hours . . . the curse will be gone."

The blackness that, even as he spoke, brought the look of death over Deacon now began to show itself on Ivy. The snow-white fur began to darken in patches where it was thinnest--around her eyes, the pads of her fingers, her ears. Her claws split, leaving jagged, yellowed shards. The sight was stomach-turning, the rigors of death pouring over her friend and her beloved in a matter of minutes. Slowly, Deacon removed a shaking hand. His fingers were bone-white; his face was gaunt.

Weakly, he reached for the crystal, Ivy's crystal. He held it up to the fire that Myranda had faithfully kept alight and stared. The shifting black stain within halted. A long minute passed as he and Myranda pored over the waving of the cloud. Finally it seemed to slow and pull inward ever so slightly.

"The deed is done," he said, his voice harsh and raspy.

"What did you do?" she asked with urgency. "We need to cure you."

"Not the same way. Too dangerous for you," he said. "There are other possibilities. She was further along than I was. We still have time."

"I don't care how dangerous it is, I will not let you die while we try to find something else when we know that there is a method that works," she assured him.

"We don't know that it works. She has a long night ahead of her. She will need every bit of her strength to fight off the last of the curse," he replied.

"Just tell me," she demanded. "I'll deal with the consequences."

"Absolutely not. Now, the traditional treatment for necromancy is to counter its darkness with--" he began.

"This is madness! Why are you risking your life!?" Myranda protested, tears clouding her eyes.

"--holiness," he continued, raising his voice to compete with her cries. "Holy water, in fact. Anointing the wound has proven effective in some cases."

"You yourself said that there isn't a cure for Soul Blight," she tried to reason.

"But this isn't Soul Blight. It may have a weakness that the true spell lacks," he countered.

Myranda threw her hands up. "Where are we going to get holy water!?"

"That is . . . a valid point," he said, as though the thought hadn't occurred to his increasingly addled mind.

He reached for the slim book again, leafing through the pages.

"Necromancy . . . yes . . . the--ah . . . the blessing of a priest is a powerful tool . . . but we haven't got a priest. Ah . . . there some herbs that can slow the process," he offered.

Myranda looked about helplessly. She pulled the canteen from the provisions she carried with her and scooped some snow from the mouth of the cave.

"What are you doing?" he asked.

"I'm Chosen, right? That means that I am a product of divine will," she said, filling the canteen with snow and willing some of the fire around it.

As the snow melted, she thought. In time, the words came.

"Oh, powers above. The mark on my hand is your sign that I am your tool in this battle. I represent our world. I defend it. I did not ask for this role, but I have done my best to fill it, and I have expected nothing. But now the very forces that I am tasked with turning back are threatening to take the one soul that has touched mine. A being whose life may as well be my own. All I ask is that you give me the power to wash away the blight of the dark ones. All I ask is that you imbue this humble water with some trace of your purity, that it might restore this victim of the darkness," she spoke solemnly.

Myranda waited and watched, her senses aflame, hoping for some sign, any sign, that her prayer had been answered. The flame she maintained flickered, the wind outside wailed, but there was no indication that anything had changed. She drew in a deep breath and motioned for him to uncover the wound. She sprinkled just a few drops upon the blighted flesh.

"It . . . it feels warmer . . . no . . . hot," he said, pain creeping up in his arm.

He cringed as the blackness pulled back, giving way to the red blood and pink flesh that it had replaced. Deacon stifled a cry of pain as the feeling that had been stolen from him returned all at once. In a few moments, his arm seemed almost healthy, and the complexion of his face had improved.

Myranda let out a sigh of relief that turned into a laugh of joy.

"I suppose I was a bit premature in my desperate act a moment ago. And we've discovered a new talent of the Chosen!" he said with a smile, recovering from the pain.

Slowly, the smile faded from his face. He pulled back the sleeve to reveal that the pale, stained flesh was creeping back down. Myranda applied the holy water again, and again, but there was now no effect, as though the spell had somehow tempered itself against it. Before long, any evidence that they had tried anything at all was gone, and no further attempt worked.

"It is . . . remarkable," he said in a wavering voice. He attempted to make a note of the discovery in his book, but his fingers would no longer cooperate.

Myranda grasped his hand and pulled it away from the book.

"Stop praising the spell that is killing you!" she demanded.

"It is a masterwork. And I need to catalog its effects for future study," he said, trying to pull free.

"Stop it, Deacon! It is madness! Just tell me what you did to Ivy and let me do it to you," Myranda cried.

"Myranda, listen to me. I cannot allow you to risk it," he said, suddenly wavering enough to lose his balance.

"But . . . I can't lose you!" Myranda screamed through the tears. "I am the reason you are here. If you die, it is because of me!"

"Myranda, no. It is only because of you that I even lived. Where was I before I met you? A . . . a tiny, unknown corner of the world. I was learning for the sake of knowledge. Perfecting spells that would . . . never be cast. Then you arrived. I had the honor of helping teach you . . . spells

Joseph Lallo

that would be used for the very highest purpose. I . . . became the first being in the history of this world to cast a spell of transportation. I was able to meet the Chosen. Children of legend. And I helped you.

"Myranda, you gave me a place in history. You gave me . . . immortality. Who . . . who . . . could hope for . . . anything . . . more," he struggled to say, his breathing becoming more labored.

The hand he steadied himself with slipped and he nearly fell to the ground, but Myranda caught him.

"No! Deacon, don't let go! Don't give up!" she cried.

Her mind raced as she tried to determine why he would not share with her the means to save his own life. How could she force him to tell her? She cast a desperate look at Ivy. The answer to both questions came at once. She grasped his hand firmly.

"What are you doing?" he asked weakly.

Without a word, she dragged his twisted, jagged fingernails down her arm, opening a long gash.

"No. *No!*" he cried, his eyes opening wide.

"Now you have no choice," she said. "This was why it was too dangerous. You had to *have* the curse."

His mouth moved wordlessly, his clouded mind awash in despair. As quickly as he could, he gathered what was left of his wits.

"Listen. What I tell you now, I tell you so that you can save yourself, *not* me. You must seize control of the spell. As it gnaws . . . at your spirit, some your own control . . . over your stolen will . . . fades in time. That time is . . . the key. You must feed the blight. Force . . . as much of your will in as you can . . . as quickly as you can. The curse . . . will grow like . . . . a weed, but more and more of your will . . . will linger . . . there will come a moment . . . a brief one . . . when the will of the . . . spell is more yours than its own. It . . . is then that you strike . . . turn the affliction's hunger upon . . . itself. If you succeed . . . the blight will leech at itself . . . and waste away. Do you . . . understand?" He struggled, fumbling his hand through his bag.

"I do," she replied.

"Good . . ." he replied, pulling free the blade he'd fought the undead with.

He knew that there was no dissuading her. She cared too much about him to do what he knew was best for the world. There was only one way to be sure she made the right decision. Make it the only decision. With all of the strength he could muster, attempted to thrust one of the curving blades into his heart.

Myranda caught his hand and wrenched the blade away, throwing it far from his reach and pushing the bag away.

96

"You must . . . save . . . yourself . . ." he begged her before the last of his will failed him.

Quickly she propped him into the position he'd placed Ivy in and placed her hands upon his temples, searching his spirit with hers. In her mind's eye, the sight was even more horrific than it was physically. His soul, once brilliant and pure, was withered and twisted. She searched desperately for the blight, the affliction that she'd not seen in Ivy, but it simply wasn't there. As she sought, she felt a tinge within her own soul. It was unsettling, a foreign influence, tiny, pulling hungrily at her. Despite the fact it was unlike anything she'd ever felt, she knew instantly that it was what she was looking for.

Her searches turned back to Deacon, sifting for the same alien hunger. Having felt it, it was now impossible to miss within him. The nature of the affliction revealed itself, like a clinging vine that wrapped around his soul, ravenous, and drawing away what little power he had left.

She forced her will upon it, and it eagerly devoured. Its poisonous influence drew tightly around his soul, growing stronger with every moment. As it did, the spell within her own soul supped upon the feast of will as well, sprouting and entwining itself about her. The speed with which she was weakening was frightening. She could feel a part of herself flow into the spreading infection and wither away, as though it was being dissolved. She jerked and twisted her mind, prompting an ever so slight imitation in the blight. She needed more.

Without hesitation, she unleashed every last bit of her mind, feeling it slip into the abyss eagerly. The strength poured from her like a torrent, seemingly to no avail. It drank up all that she had without pause. Her view of the spectacle began to fade, her focus quickly wicking away into the darkness. In a few moments, she would have nothing left to give. Dizziness seized her mind, threatening to tear her from her trance. She fought the disorientation, knowing that if she lost focus now, there would not be another chance.

The end was upon her. Her grip was slipping. Just as she was about to lose the last thread of connection to him, she felt a feeling she'd never imagined before . . . like her mind was simultaneously inside of the abyss and out. This was the moment. She turned what little was left of her mind to the almost mechanical workings of the spell that gorged on her power-- and twisted it.

And then the connection was gone. The world faded slowly in around her. She was in darkness, the fire had vanished, but she felt no cold. She felt nothing. As her hands fumbled blindly about the ground, her mind struggled to grasp what had happened. Some small corner of her thoughts tried valiantly to hold her mind together, but it was filled with a deafening static and disorienting stirring. She could not remember what it was that she had done, nor what she was doing. Indeed, she could not even *think*. Her fumbling tipped the canteen she'd placed upon the ground, the contents sloshing onto her fingers.

Instantly, there was a white-hot pain. It was a stinging--definite, solid, and real. It cut through the static and stirring like a knife and she latched onto it. Time was against her. Already it was fading, already she was forgetting what it was that she had so briefly achieved, but she knew she wanted it back. Her fingers closed around the neck of the canteen and she raised it up. The contents spilled out, burning everywhere it touched, giving her an instant of clarity. This was it. Her chance to repeat the miracle. She put the canteen to her lips.

The stream of blessed water burned its way to her core, stabbing at her from the inside. The blight inside of her recoiled from it, losing just a hint of its grip on her. She knew it would not last long. Already she could feel the curse hardening to it. Resisting it. She dove her mind into it entirely, seeking the thread she'd pulled before and flexing what little will she had. Then: darkness.

There was a stillness. The stirring, the static, everything was gone. She sat up, the motion requiring the merest thought, not a whisper of effort, as though effort didn't even exist. Slowly, her surroundings appeared to her-- not as though a light was growing stronger, but as though darkness was peeling itself back.

There was a presence before her. It was Oriech. Once she had believed him to be little more than an aging priest who despised her hatred of the war. He had since revealed himself to be much more, an agent of fate who guided the lives of those with a role to play. Now he stood in one of the few places in the cave tall enough to allow it, his eyes covered by a gray blindfold.

"Myranda," he said, shaking his head slowly.

"Am I . . ." she began.

"Dead? No. But neither are you alive," he stated.

"Why are you here?" she asked.

"The more important question would be 'Why are *you* here?'" he said.

"I don't know what you mean," she replied.

"Don't you?" he asked, turning his unseeing gaze to Deacon.

"I had to save him," she said.

"No, my dear. You did not. You wanted to," he replied.

"I had to. I had to do what was right. If there was even a chance, then I had to take it. Was it worth it? Is he alive?" she asked.

"For now," he replied.

"And am I?" she asked.

"In a sense," he answered.

"Then why speak to me now?" she asked.

"You are an oddity, Myranda. The powers above showed great concern when the fallen swordsman, Rasa, passed his role on to you. He was the intended Chosen One, not you, after all. Since, you have become a favorite among them. You even coaxed them to take direct action to bless the water. And it is not the first time that you have managed to move them so. In your short time as a weapon of the gods, you have cut deeper than any other. It is a testament to the greatness to which the people of this world may rise. In a way, you deserve the honor of the Mark more than any of your fellow Chosen. Until now, your heart and your judgment have done more to bring the others closer to their goal than anything I could have done--but that same heart has also brought you to death's door time and again. It has done so this time in a struggle that you needn't have risked," he said.

"What would you have me do? Shrink from danger? Protect myself at all costs? Are those the actions of a hero?" she asked.

"I would have you do as you always have. Let your heart be your guide, but temper its guidance with the knowledge that it is not always the place of the hero to do what is right. It is the place of a hero to do what must be done," he said. "Know that not everyone can be saved."

His last words faded into echoes as the darkness reclaimed her surroundings. For a time, there was nothing--only blackness and silence. Slowly, the wail of the wind outside found its way to her ears. The icy chill of the water she had spilled stinging at her hands was quick to follow. Her eyes opened, though it made little difference; there was not a hint of light. She felt for her staff, but it soon became clear that she hadn't the strength of will to cast a spell even if she did manage to find it.

She languished in the darkness, her other senses and sensations slowly returning to her. The penetrating cold. The gnawing hunger. The paralyzing fatigue. She'd been tired before, but some aspect of her ordeal had left her with scarcely the strength to breathe properly. All she could manage was to lie still, listen, and think. She thought about the weakness she felt. The fact that it wasn't abating. She thought about the cure. Deacon was not sure that Ivy would make it until the morning. The malthrope was far heartier than either of them. If she didn't survive, there was no hope for them. She thought about Oriech's words. A warning. If there came a choice between victory and the life of someone she cared deeply for . . . could she let them go?

In her mind, the torture of doubt clawed at her for more time than she could comprehend. Outside, the wind died slowly, perhaps over minutes, perhaps hours. In its wake was a stillness that was infinitely worse. The slow, steady beating of her heart filled her ears. Her eyes shifted. The faint gray light of reflected sunlight traced long shadows across the stone ceiling. Daybreak. Suddenly, a sound.

Myranda's heart leapt. A weak cough echoed around her.

"M-Myranda?" came Ivy's harsh voice.

The young wizard tried to answer, but the strength just wasn't there. The sound of clumsy shuffling motion drew nearer to her. Finally, a pair of pink eyes stared into her own.

"Myranda? Are you all right?" she asked, weary anxiety in her eyes.

Her face was gaunt, worn, but alive. The mask of death had retreated. It had taken a toll, perhaps, but it was gone. Her eyes had a heartbreaking mix of fear and urgency.

"Say something, please. Did . . . did something happen? Did I do this!?" she begged, tears falling on Myranda's face.

With great effort, Myranda turned her head. The light of the narrow mouth of the cave fell on her broken staff, just beyond her reach. She locked her eyes on it and released a ragged breath.

"Your staff? You need your staff?" Ivy asked, dragging herself to the fallen tool.

She placed it in Myranda's hand and closed it. A whisper of clarity came to Myranda's mind. She fought a breath into her lungs.

"Deacon," she croaked.

"Deacon," Ivy repeated, pulling herself now to his side. "He's breathing."

Myranda pulled in another breath and heaved it out as a sigh. She wanted to pull herself up, to place an arm upon Ivy's shoulder and set her mind at ease. All she could manage was a weak smile and a profound sense of relief.

Ivy sat, nervous and confused, watching Myranda slowly recover. She thought back to the times she had transformed. This did not begin the same way. It was not a racing heart and a blinding light that she remembered last. Quite the opposite . . . but the ending was the same. Surrounded by the people she cared about, the only people who cared about her, weak and beaten. Could this be some horrible thing she had done? Something that had never happened before? The thought cut into her. The crunching footsteps and familiar scent that beckoned her senses came as a blessing.

"Myranda! Lain is here! He'll take care of us! Don't worry!" she said, a smile fighting its way to her teary face.

As Lain forced enough snow from the entrance to squeeze inside, Ivy dizzily climbed to her feet to greet him gratefully.

The sight that greeted his eyes was a disturbing one. Myranda was on her back, eyes fluttering weakly. Deacon was slumped against the wall, eyes shut. Lain dropped the results of the hunt, a pair of mountain goats, on the ground, but Ivy ignored them, shuffling past and pulling at his arm.

"You have to help them! I don't know what I did, but they're sick!" she cried.

"Stay calm. Are you well?" Lain asked the frantic creature.

"Never mind about me!" she urged, pulling him to Myranda's side.

He crouched beside her, touching her face and listening to her chest and breathing. She was weak, there was no doubt.

"Has she been worsening?" he asked.

"No. No. I think she's been getting better. But not much," Ivy said.

"She needs time," he said.

"Are you sure? What about Deacon? He hasn't gotten any better at all," Ivy asked, now pulling him to the slumped young wizard.

He was considerably worse, colder to the touch, a weaker heartbeat, and managing only the shallowest of breaths. Death was not far off.

"Well? Is he going to be all right?" she begged.

Lain's silence was telling. Ether stepped inside of the cave in her human form, dropping a load of gnarled, dry pieces of wood, no doubt every last bit that was to be had on the mountainside. She surveyed the others with a cold, detached stare.

"What did that foolish girl do?" she asked with a sneer.

"Ether! You need to do something!" Ivy cried.

"What would you have me do?" she replied.

"I don't know! You know magic! Myranda heals people with magic? Can't you!?" the panicked creature cried.

She glanced over the ailing humans. Her eyes saw much that others did not. The sorry state of their faltered spirits was even clearer to her than their worn bodies. Myranda had always had a soul with respectable power, Deacon's perhaps her equal. The amount of effort it would have taken to tax them to this state was considerable, and yet there was no sign of struggle, no sign of anything that could explain it.

"What happened here?" she asked.

"I don't *know!* I just . . . I got tired. I passed out, and when I finally had the strength to stand, this is what I found. Can't anyone do anything?"

A fire was started and some of the meat prepared to the best of the rather limited abilities of those who had any strength. Ivy was starving, as hungry as she'd ever been before, but the concern for her friends robbed her of any appetite she might have. Carefully, she moved Deacon and Myranda together, nearer to the fire, and rested their backs against the wall.

"You've restored them before. The yellow aura," Ether pointed out.

"That happens when I'm happy," Ivy said.

"Well, then the solution is in your hands," Ether stated simply.

"It isn't that easy, Ether. I can't just *be* happy," Ivy replied.

"That is preposterous. Why?" Ether asked.

Ivy shook her head. "It . . . it is an emotion. You wouldn't understand."

Ether bristled with anger. "Don't you *dare* condescend to me! *I* do not understand? I have watched you tossed about by the seas of emotion since we had the misfortune of finding you."

"Stop it!" Ivy barked, the faintest hint of a red flare accompanying her words.

"There. You see. Anger comes quickly enough. As does fear. Why should happiness be any different?" the shapeshifter asked.

"It just is," Ivy said sternly.

"And what of that noisemaker you seem so pleased to tug at? That seems to improve your mood," Ether asked.

"I don't feel like playing. Anything that I might play now would be mournful and sad," Ivy replied.

Ether shook her head. "It is nothing short of remarkable how a being with such considerable potential can manage to be so paralyzingly useless."

Ivy sneered and turned her attentions back to Myranda. After a time, as the fire warmed the cave enough to be livable, Myranda recovered slightly. Her body still seemed uncooperative, her fingers barely able to close and her arms too heavy to lift. Ivy managed to feed her a bit of the cooked food, and give her some water. It was nearly an hour more before Myranda was able to speak without slurring and feed herself, albeit with help. She reluctantly explained what had happened. When she was through, the result was not a surprising one.

"I wish that I could say that this came as a surprise, even a slight one, but really, it is typical behavior for you, isn't it? You endanger your life saving meaningless beings. I had begun to believe that you were on the verge of grasping your role in this world, but now I see that such a revelation is *far* beyond what you can manage. I had thought Ivy was the greatest threat to our cause, but now I see in even that way she is inferior," Ether ranted.

"Even when you are insulting someone else, you insult me too," Ivy growled. "Leave both of us alone. Deacon is a good man. He has helped us, why shouldn't we help him!?"

"No, no. She is right, I--" Myranda began.

"Don't agree with her!" Ivy scolded. "What does she know? You just ignore her and get your strength back so that we can finish making sure that Deacon is healthy, too."

"Listen, beast, I--" Ether began.

"No, *you* listen! Myranda has a good heart and a good mind, and if she decided to do this, then it was the best decision. I don't have to listen to you spray your venom at us every time we show something you consider to be weakness, be it emotion or compassion or anything like that. You just save your breath, because I am not paying any attention to you anymore. When we have to kill something, then you can open your mouth. Until then, just keep it shut! Understand!?" Ivy lectured.

Her heart was racing, and no doubt if she'd more of her strength about her, she might have been fighting off the fiery transformation that anger so frequently pulled from her.

Ether was taken aback, holding her tongue as fury and indignation each fought to have their own words expressed first.

Ivy smiled triumphantly and snatched up her violin. She launched into a spirited melody that managed to perfectly convey her mood. The golden aura soon followed, filling the cave with a warm glow. It was not long before the weariness began to vanish from Myranda's muscles and her mind began to clear. By the time the final jaunty notes of the tune rang out, Myranda was nearly herself, albeit tired, and Deacon was beginning to come around.

Ivy continued to play, though the aura faded to a dim glow as her mood drifted back to normal. Deacon looked about, his eyes turning first to Ivy, then to Myranda, each looking none the worse for the ordeal that they had been through. He then looked himself over. The effects of the spell lingered, it would seem. The scrape that was the site of the infection was far worse than it should have been, and he barely had the force of will to hold his eyes in focus, but the withering feeling eating at him from within was gone.

"How did you manage to cure yourself?" he slurred to Myranda.

"Your method, with a bit of aid from the holy water," she replied.

"You must describe it to me," he said, searching the area around him for his book and stylus.

"Later. For now you need to eat and get some real rest," Myranda said.

"Myranda, I cannot be expected to sleep knowing that doing so might risk the loss of the facts of this momentous occasion. The clarity of our recollection is fading as we speak. To allow information to be lost is the greatest crime I can commit. I . . . ." Deacon rambled, trying to pull himself to where the book had fallen.

"Fine. You eat, I will write," Myranda offered, adding. "Ivy, make sure he eats something. I haven't got the strength to argue with him."

Ivy nodded vigorously.

Reluctantly, he agreed. Myranda began to record all that she could recall.

Deacon asked questions, directed her writings, and generally focused on what was written to such a degree that it was only with the gentle insistence and aid of Ivy that he managed to eat anything at all. Finally, Deacon seemed satisfied with Myranda's record and turned his attention to nourishment. As Myranda flipped through the pages of the book, looking over Ivy's illustrations, she became aware of the fact that not a single word of the volumes that Deacon had written was familiar to her. Her time in Entwell had exposed her to a fair number of languages, both written and spoken, but save for the occasional character or symbol, the book bore little resemblance to any of them.

"What language is this?" she asked, looking over the random assortment of runes with increasing confusion.

"It isn't any *one* language," he replied, eagerly turning away from the food Ivy was offering. "It is shorthand. I record my ideas in the language in which I can state it most tersely. It allows for a very information-dense--"

Ivy interrupted him by shoving the next bite of food into his mouth.

"You, stop asking questions," Ivy ordered Myranda, turning to Deacon to add. "You, stop answering them. You are never going to get better if you don't eat something."

Myranda grinned at how seriously Ivy was taking her new role. When the dutiful creature was satisfied, she made sure that each of those in her care were as comfortable as she could make them, and watched over them until real sleep came--not the exhausted unconsciousness that so frequently took its place. When she was sure that they were resting properly, she eagerly took her meal and her rest as well.

Lain watched as she nestled between them. He scarcely believed it was possible. He'd never had a place in this world. He'd never belonged. All that he had, he had carved for himself. All of the problems that he faced, Ivy faced tenfold. She did not even know her past. Even her form was forced upon her. And yet, here she was. This was her place. These were her people. He turned to Ether. On her face was the look of detached disdain, but behind it there was something else. Something out of place.

Ether watched Lain sit and begin the trance that took the place of sleep. As she did, she smoldered with an emotion she never imagined she would feel. Envy. It was only right that the pitiful creatures of this world envy her, but to envy one of them? Or two or three? They were useless, weak, foolish, and yet . . . they had the respect, even the adoration of Lain. *Lain,* who in Ether had his sole equal, instead squandered his attentions on the blasted facsimile. When he spoke to Ivy, there was affection. When he spoke to Myranda, there was trust. When he spoke to the shapeshifter, there was none of that.

He actually saw her as an annoyance, while the manufactured beast, one who was naught but a liability, was coddled and fawned over. What could the two of them possibly have that she lacked? And the two humans. They found in one another what Ether was denied. It was a sign of weakness to desire this waste of time, this mental illness that they called love. Nevertheless, the yearning for it consumed her mind.

She tried desperately to force the thoughts away. They had led her to betrayal in the past. If she could not master them, there was no telling what they might drive her to. They were a weakness, a weakness she'd convinced herself that she simply lacked. Now, after an eternity to prepare wasted, she was at their whims.

Without sleep as a respite, the thoughts steeped in Ether's mind for a silent few hours. Lain was the first to stir, stepping outside to survey the conditions outside and plan their next steps in the journey. Myranda was second, Ivy waking shortly after.

"Have you recovered from your act of idiocy?" Ether asked with her usual level of contempt.

"I feel as well as I ever have, thanks in no small part to Ivy's excellent care," Myranda said. It was not entirely true, but she was better by far than she had been the day before.

"Oh, it was the least I could do," Ivy said shyly.

"Enough!" Ether shouted, turning away from the spectacle.

"Are you well enough to move on? We have lingered here for too long," Lain said.

"I am," Myranda replied.

"Me, too!" Ivy chimed in.

"Wonderful. That only leaves us with Myranda's latest lost cause," Ether remarked.

"No need to worry about me," Deacon said, groggily.

He managed to stand, but it was clear that the night had not been as kind to him as it had been to the others. There was improvement, to be sure, but he clearly was far from well. Twice he nearly fell as he gathered the scattered books and paraphernalia he'd removed from his bag. When he took his crystal into his hand, it became clear that the weakness went deeper than his body. The light in the crystal flickered dimly as he tried to cast a simple spell to supplement the fading glow of the meager fire. Finally, he gave up on the spell.

"It would appear that without a touch of the divine to keep it at bay, the curse cuts a bit deeper," he surmised.

"Are you certain that we can continue?" Myranda asked.

"I'll manage well enough, but I fear it will be a few more days before I can cast a spell," Deacon replied.

"Tremendous, then you are completely useless to us," Ether stated.

Deacon picked up his bag.

"I shall endeavor to avoid being a burden to you," he promised.

"A lofty goal," the shapeshifter sneered.

"You are meaner than usual . . . and I didn't think that was even possible," Ivy remarked.

Ether silently moved to the mouth of the cave.

"When the lot of you are through wasting precious time, I will be outside," Ether growled, stalking out.

When all had been gathered, and the remains of the previous day's meal choked down as breakfast, the group set off. The long storm had dumped a remarkable amount of snow on the narrow valley. Whereas it had taken a bit of a climb to reach the mouth of the cave when they sought shelter, they were almost able to step right out of the mouth and onto the fresh snow. It was a thick, icy mix. That was a blessing. The lighter snow would have caused them to sink fairly to their hips as they trudged through it. The dense blizzard snow merely swallowed them to their ankles. They would be slowed, but not by much.

They continued north. Lain seemed familiar with the area, knowing without consulting the map that the pass they were making their way through would let out into a wide, deep valley.

Myranda and Ivy stuck close to Deacon, concerned that he might fall behind. Thankfully, once the fresh air got to him, he perked up, making his own way with only slightly more difficulty than the others. Conspicuously absent, though, was his constant note-taking. He'd tried it for the first few minutes, but without his magic to hold the pages flat against the wind and lay out his other materials, it was simply too difficult. He finally put the book away after he finished reading Myranda's entries on the trials they'd survived in the cave.

"I thank you for your thoroughness," he said between gasps of the thin, freezing air. "I look forward to rewriting it."

"Rewriting?" Myranda asked.

"Oh, not to worry. I intend to use your exact words, but I find that I remember things more completely if I write them myself," he replied.

"I don't see how you could possibly manage to write in that shorthand of yours. Honestly, how many languages would one need to know to read it?" Myranda wondered.

Deacon thought for a moment, replying. "All of them, I suppose, though less of some than others. And I suppose the abbreviations I use will complicate matters as well. Well, regardless, there are at least three people back at Entwell who can read it . . . Not that any of them will. I wouldn't be surprised if they've burned my books by now."

"You really believe that?" she asked.

"Well, there may be one or two who might care about what I may write . . . Azriel, but she'd never leave the arena to see it. Calypso, Solomon. I don't know. I've broken nearly every rule that we'd all agreed to live by," he said.

His voice carried regret, as naturally it would, but a dash of realization as well, as though it was just now occurring to him.

"I will not be remembered well," he added.

Myranda placed a hand on his shoulder. He took her hand in his and looked her in the eye. Instantly the regret washed away as he was reminded why he'd done it in the first place.

"But so be it. This is where I need to be," he said. "This is where I belong."

Ivy marched along beside them. She had heard the tale he'd told when they first met. Of what he'd done to get here. Of what he'd left behind. As she turned it over in her head, slowly she came to realize that all that he'd left behind . . . a home, friends, comfort . . . things she could never remember having. The memories of the days before she was rescued came in brief, blurred flashes. Until now, she'd never truly felt that she was missing anything, that these people who had found her were all that she would ever need. But now, she felt the tiniest twinge of longing--or, at least, curiosity. What was it that had been taken from her? Was it something as wonderful as he had given up? She would not trade her new friends for anything, but without so much as a memory of her own name, she felt incomplete.

"Myranda?" Ivy asked.

"Yes?" she replied.

"Do . . . do you think I'll ever remember what it was like before? Who I was, I mean? Any of it?" she asked.

"In time, I'm sure it will come to you," Myranda said.

"With any luck, you won't," Ether remarked.

"Hey!" Ivy objected.

"Have you forgotten what happened last time you remembered? You were on the verge of losing control. Better to avoid pushing your weak mind to its limits," Ether reminded.

"That was because it was something bad I remembered! There will be good things, too!" Ivy asserted.

"And you would like to learn of all of the wonderful things in your life that were destroyed during that tragedy? Do you believe *that* will bring you happiness?" Ether asked.

"I . . . I don't know. I don't care! They are my memories, I want them back!" the confused creature replied with finality.

She crossed her arms. Ether's words had turned her mild yearning into a burning need. It grew quickly into an obsession. She wanted to know now. No--she *needed* to know. To satisfy her own curiosity, to prove Ether wrong, just to know. The reason was eclipsed by the need. A tiny, nagging worry prodded at her, questioning why it could have come to mean so much so quickly. It was ignored. The smoldering hunger for the knowledge grew.

They crossed into the valley, and if Ivy had been in a lighter state of mind, she most certainly would have been struck by the beauty. It was left pure white from the fallen snow and sparkling in the light of the moon, which was peeking through a rare break in the constant clouds. The silvery light revealed a wide, crescent-shaped plateau leading around one edge. It sloped steeply upward a few dozen paces to the east, and dropped sharply down into a low, flat-bottomed valley to the west. Where they stood, it was perfectly level. Down in the valley, a thin river caught the light of the moon, flowing in a lazy curve, west, east, west, and east, like a pair of cresting waves, with a ring of five trees opposite the trough between.

The image stirred a weak memory. It was familiar. As quickly as it had come, though, the notion was gone, a surge of anger sweeping it away, and a thought rushed in to replace it. Ether had existed since the beginning of time, and she'd ended up with no more than any of them, and yet she looked down on them. The thought stuck in her mind. Since the beginning of time . . .

"Wait a minute! *You know!*" Ivy accused. "You know about what I was!"

"Don't be a fool," Ether said.

"No, no, no. You must know. You've been around forever, right? Either you know about me, what I was before, or you are even more worthless than I am," the malthrope said, poking Ether in the chest for emphasis.

All eyes turned to the shapeshifter.

"Myranda, tell this cretin the circumstances of my time in this world in the recent past. You may be able to phrase it in words she might be able to comprehend," Ether fumed.

"Oh, I know. Myranda has told me plenty of stories. You were sort of everywhere, able to look but not touch until Myranda and Deacon and his people brought you back. But you did it to make sure you'd know when Chosen--*like me*--showed up, right? So I say it again: either you know about me, or you couldn't do the *one* job you claimed to be doing for all of that time," Ivy said, a flicker of yellow and red betraying an ounce of triumph mixing with her rising anger.

"Fine . . . I was aware of you, but that was all. You were just a little girl, not worthy of my interest yet," Ether hissed.

"A little girl . . . what was I like? Did I have a big family? Was I human or an elf, or . . ." Ivy asked eagerly.

"It didn't matter; you were too young to have any attention paid. At the time, there were dozens of potential Chosen in the world, each and every one of them more powerful than you. I had my doubts that you were Chosen at all," Ether explained.

"Do you at least know my name?" Ivy begged.

"Names are meaningless. It would have been the last thing I would have sought," Ether replied.

"How do you even know it was me!?" the creature raved.

"You were a prodigy of music, art, all manner of frivolities, but you weren't the only one. Since then, the others have been tainted or killed. You were the only one whose fate I was not certain of," the shapeshifter said.

"I . . . I can't believe it! Even before you knew me, you were looking down on me! And because I just wasn't *interesting* enough for you, you just paid me no mind! You could have known it all, everything! You could have had all of the answers to all of my questions! But you were too small-minded even then to take the time to so much as look in my direction! WHAT ABOUT THE MASSACRE!?" Ivy cried, a flare of red surging as she grasped the shapeshifter's currently-human form by the cloak and pulled her nose to nose. "You didn't think to save anyone, not even me, one of your own *precious* Chosen?"

"GET YOUR FILTHY CLAWS OFF OF ME!" Ether cried, briefly taking the form of wind and slipping from Ivy's grip. "I realize that weak, damaged bit of fluff that you call a mind cannot long grip even the simplest of facts, but you said it yourself in your own painfully simple way. I could 'look but not touch.' There was nothing I *could* do."

Lain stepped between them.

"Enough. There is something wrong," he said.

"Of course something is wrong. This beast's descent into madness is finally complete!" Ether raved.

"No. I can't smell anything. Anything at all," he said.

The others looked nervously about.

"The wind is blowing and I can't hear it," Myranda said, holding up her staff.

She tried to sense something, anything about her surroundings, but there was something preventing it, some sort of force. Slowly, she followed the flow of it. She could feel it grow stronger. As she turned slowly to face its source, Ivy cried out once more.

"Listen to me! She could have prevented it, I know she could have!" the malthrope cried. "Why won't you listen to me!? *I'll force her to tell the truth.*"

The maddened creature hurled herself at the shapeshifter, who again changed to wind to evade her.

"Ivy! Calm down!" Myranda cried, turning from the search.

Lain too tried to get the wild creature under control. At first, she struggled, then turned her hostility to them.

"Why are you helping her? She is a *murderer!*" Ivy screeched, throwing Myranda to the ground.

The instant Myranda struck the ground, Ivy cried out and clutched her chest. The pain dropped away to a look of fear and confusion.

"What am I-I . . ." Ivy stuttered, her look growing more desperate as she seemed to be quickly losing a struggle against something.

"Ether," Myranda called out, climbing to her feet. "Somewhere over there. Something is being concealed. I'll hold off Ivy."

The shapeshifter swept toward the edge of the valley from which they had come. When she reached the exit, she collided with something. The collision sent a ripple through the air, leaving a shimmering veil behind. The veil spread, revealing a full wall leading high into the sky. She pulled back and dropped to the ground, turning to stone and bashing at the wall. It wavered, but would not give.

Behind her, Ivy's frenzy grew stronger. The fiery red aura was threatening to overtake her. Just as Ether was about to rush to the aid of her allies, she heard a sound. It was peculiar, one she had heard before. At the same moment, Ivy's rampage suddenly ended. In place of her frenzied screams for revenge came impassioned pleas.

"Help me, please! You've got to put me to sleep, or tie me down or something, I can't help it! I don't want to hurt you!" the creature cried, fear and desperation in her voice.

There was a second sound, the sharp slice of an arrow through the air. Ether's eyes, locked on the point from which the first sound had come, beheld an arrow streaking into the sky, seemingly from thin air. Instantly, she pounced upon the point of origin. There was the splinter of wood and the sound of someone falling to the ground. The snow depressed under the weight of an unseen foe, and Ether quickly snatched up the enemy. As she did, an engraved metal amulet with a broken chain dropped from mid-air. A moment later, the struggling form that the talisman had concealed faded into view.

"You! What are you doing here! What is this!?" Ether demanded.

In her grip was the throat of Desmeres, Lain's infuriating former partner. He wore ornate armor; a handful of amulets, each glowing brightly, hung from his neck. Ether tore them from his neck as he clutched desperately at her arm, trying to loosen her grip enough to draw in a breath. Instantly ,the effects of the artifacts wore off. The sound of rushing wind, joined by the crackle of mystic energy, rose up all around them. The scent of their foe revealed itself to Lain and Ivy.

"Explain yourself before I squeeze the life out of you," Ether warned, tightening her grip.

Desmeres's left hand held tight to Ether's stony arm, while the fingers of his right crept to one final crystal that dangled from his wrist. As he finally made contact, Ivy's madness surged back, and the helpless creature threw her friends aside, unable to resist the beckoning of the crystal. Ether quickly clutched the crystal with her free hand, halting Ivy, but also cringing in pain as it tore at her. She wrenched it free and threw it aside.

As Ivy struggled to understand what was happening to her, the others recovered and ran to her side.

"You have only a few moments of breath left; I urge you not to waste them," Ether hissed.

"You can kill me . . ." Desmeres croaked. "But if I were you, I'd do something about that arrow."

She turned. At the far end of the valley, the arrow had landed. More of the same accursed crystals were affixed to it. Whatever spell had been assigned to them, it was beginning, and it was one of terrifying intensity. The shapeshifter thrust Desmeres against the shimmering wall behind him and shifted to wind, streaking toward the arrow. She was not the only one to notice, as Myranda was already rushing toward the quickly manifesting spell.

The air burned with the raw power of it. All of the light near the gems seemed to wick away, leaving a midnight-black gash in the valley that began to swirl and churn.

Ether reached it first, but the force of it began to push her back. She fought against the torrent of energy, but began to lose ground. Finally, she turned to stone once more, dropping to the ground and plodding slowly forward. Myranda fought hard, but the energy burned at her viciously. Behind, Lain left Ivy with Deacon and stalked toward his prey. Desmeres was gasping for breath, pulling himself toward the nearest amulet. He had only just seen Lain out of the corner of his eye when he was pulled violently from the ground. The furious assassin's eyes burned with rage as he drew his former partner face to face.

"Lain. I can't say I was looking forward to meeting you under these conditions," he said.

"What is this?" he demanded.

"Business," Desmeres replied.

Deacon steadied Ivy by the shoulders and tried to look her in her wandering eyes. She was dazed, confusion and fear vying for control of her embattled mind.

"Ivy, look at me; focus," he said, shaking her slightly. "I need you to calm down."

"Calm down? Calm down! Deacon, my mind is screaming things that don't make sense! How can I calm down? How can I know what is even *real!*" she cried.

"Listen to me, do you know what is doing this to you?" he asked. "Has this happened before?"

"I don't know what's doing it, but Demont did it to me once. Only it was worse then," she forced through the fear.

That was all he needed to hear. The crystal was to blame, the other half of the one he'd found in the workshop. He turned to search for it. When Ether was dealing with Desmeres, no less than a dozen crystals had been shaken free. Surely it was one of them. As he tried to move toward them, he was pulled back.

"Don't leave me alone!" Ivy begged.

Lain put a blade to Desmeres's throat.

"What did you think would happen, Lain? This had to end sooner or later," he said.

"Tell me what you have done and how to undo it, or it ends *now!*" Lain stated, drawing the blade a few inches, prompting a trickle of blood.

"Well, they were not content to let you come to them, so I had to bring them to you," the elf said with a smile.

As if taking the words as a cue, the building spell chose that moment to reach its peak. A flood of energy burst out, throwing Ether and Myranda back and knocking Ivy and Deacon to the ground. Only Lain and his prey remained standing. Desmeres managed to wrench himself from the grip and raise a blade of his own. Lain swung his sword, but Desmeres's own weapon blocked it.

"It is rare that one of my creations meets one of its brothers," Desmeres said, "but, I can assure you, it is a reunion of equals. A last bit of advice, old friend. Don't waste your time on me. There are larger threats on the horizon."

Lain raised his blade once more, but the sound of thundering hooves drew his attention. Desmeres tried to slip away, but Lain struck. The ornate armor proved no match for the masterfully-honed weapon. The blade found its way to Desmeres's thigh, slicing deep into it before Lain finally rushed to the more pressing task at hand.

He turned to find the once-empty plateau filling rapidly with foes. Where once there had been only the arrow, now there was a great shifting black ring. Outside of it was the valley. Inside, as through he were looking through a window, was a paved courtyard filled with troops and beasts. The army began to flow through the portal.

Dozens of soldiers on horseback and dozens more on foot rushed into the valley, every face hidden by a mask. Six standard dragoyles, and one beast that would have been a dragoyle save for the fact that it was easily three times their size and lacked wings, followed. The formerly silent valley was now filled with a deafening thunder of hooves and feet. Myranda managed to pull herself to her feet, dodging sword and pike long enough to retreat to Ivy and Deacon. Lain soon made his way to them as well, Ether fighting her way in soon after.

The heroes formed a tight circle, the soldiers all around them working their way into formations and holding their ground. A stillness came suddenly, only the odd shuffle of feet breaking the tense silence. All weapons were held at the ready, each side waiting for a move from the other. The only motion came from the portal, as a pair of soldiers on horseback appeared.

The first was Trigorah, her gem-embedded sword held low but ready. The other was not familiar. He wore light armor, with a helmet bearing the same face guard that obscured the twisted features of the nearmen from view. The man's build seemed light, and he seemed far too frail to be on a battlefield. An infamous weapon was strapped to his back, the accursed halberd, dispelling any doubt as to who it might be.

"Attention, Chosen!" Trigorah's voice bellowed with authority. "This, I assure you, will be our final battle. Too long you have evaded us. Too long have you resisted us. If it is your place to end this war, it is my place to see to it that you do so with the Northern Alliance intact. I am going to offer you this last chance to join our ranks. I beg you. Take your place by my side and together we will see this war to an end within the year."

"Look at the abominations you've come to rely upon. How can you be blind to what has become of the north? These are the very beings we are charged with destroying!" Myranda replied.

"Remove your helmets!" Trigorah ordered.

The soldiers obeyed. Myranda's eyes widened, and her heart leapt to her throat. They were no nearmen. Every last one of them was human.

"The nearmen are an unfortunate necessity in these trying times, but they are too weak-minded for this task. Every last face you see is a son of the north. These are your brethren," she replied. "Dare you take their lives and call yourselves heroes?"

Myranda licked her dry lips and swallowed hard.

"It is the place of a hero to do what must be done," she said, resolutely.

"Truer words were never spoken," Trigorah said solemnly. "Men, capture if you can, kill if you must. This ends today."

In a flash, every last soldier was in motion. Myranda crouched low and drove her staff into the ground; an expertly guided tremor knocked the nearest soldiers to the ground, but spared her friends, providing a precious moment of safety. Each of the heroes knew their target--save two. Myranda would face Epidime, Lain would face Trigorah, and Ether would handle the beasts. Ivy's eyes darted about, a sharp blue aura around her.

Deacon tried to gather some manner of spell, but his mind simply had not recovered enough. As he drew the Gray Blade and a dagger from his bag, he silently wished he'd spent a bit more time on the warrior's side of Entwell. As he was about to launch himself into the fray, he felt a hand on his shoulder. He turned to find a familiar pleading look on Ivy's face.

"Is this real? Is this really happening?" she begged.

"I assure you. This is real," he replied.

"Oh, thank heavens," she replied, a look of relief rushing to her face.

With that she charged quickly into the circle of soldiers. One of the men who had been knocked to the ground had lost his sword, and deep in Ivy's mind she heard a call to take it up, but she knew that the instinct was not her own. Her mind had been the plaything of others already today. If she was going to fight, she would do it her own way. For the moment, she was unaffected by emotion. The mob of soldiers simply did not frighten her as much as the manipulation of her mind had. Any speed and strength she had was her own--but, fortunately, that was plenty. When combined with her practiced grace, she was utterly untouchable. The swords of a dozen soldiers were dodged with fluid motions. It was nothing short of a dance, but when the way was closed, when there was nowhere to dodge to, that was when the warrior within came to the surface. A single, well-placed blow was all that it ever took. A soldier would be sent reeling, the force of her attack sending him tumbling backward, scattering those behind him, and creating an opening.

Deacon hurried after Ivy. Without his magic, the Gray Blade was virtually useless, managing to do little more than deflect the odd blow that reached him. He lacked most of the speed and all of the grace of the warrior he followed, but the chaos her motion caused created a wake just barely wide enough for him to slip through. He didn't know where she was heading, what she was planning. In fact, he doubted *she* knew. For the moment, though, she was heading precisely where he needed to be. Before the portal had opened, he'd managed to catch sight of what could only be the crystal that had been controlling her. He rushed toward it, almost invisible in the snow just this side of the wall, knowing full well that if one of the soldiers were to find it first, Ivy would become little more than a weapon.

Ether threw herself at the first of the dragoyles. Despite the fact it was one of the smaller ones, the soldiers gave the clash a wide berth. The shapeshifter, still in her stone form, sidestepped a powerful snap of the beast's jaws and delivered a blow to the creature's head. When it tried to pull back for a second strike, she grabbed a hold and was drawn into the air with it. Once she'd managed a firm hold of the beast's neck, she began to rain blows down upon it unmercifully. In mere moments, cracks were opening in the monster's stony hide, oozing the black blood that flowed beneath. The abomination was well past the breaking point before long, and the soldiers and beasts that had held back until now moved in.

Arrows began to rain down upon her, but her rocky form shrugged them off. Not so for the vicious strikes that the other dragoyles delivered. By the time the third such blow found its target, her own stony hide was showing fractures of its own. Worse, a small contingent of the soldiers who held spears tipped with the blasted crystals that tore at her so effectively had made their way to the battle. Knowing that any one of those spears would do more harm than a dozen of the dragoyle's attacks, Ether decided the time had come to abandon her stone form for one that would not be affected by the crystals. The choice was obvious.

Desmeres grimaced as he rummaged through a pouch at his belt. It was filled with glass ampoules that had held doses of his healing potion. Most had been shattered when he was thrown and had leaked out into the snow, but one small one had mercifully remained intact.

"This is precisely why I do not get my hands dirty," he muttered through pain-clenched teeth. "It is not a one-man job. When this is through, I must find someone to fill Lain's role."

He shattered the appropriate vial and poured it through the jagged hole torn in his armor and into the gaping wound. Instantly, the pain compounded as the imperfect elixir began to do its work. Desmeres stifled a scream and resolved to improve the concoction and produce some more effective armor before attempting something like this again. The agony faded somewhat, leaving an incompletely-healed wound, thanks to the undersized dose. After failing to pull himself to his feet, he scanned the ground desperately.

The battle was raging less than ten paces away, but he had no place in that. Simply by assembling the Chosen here and distracting them long enough to open the portal, he had earned the lion's share of his fee--but it was in his best interest that the battle end in the D'karons' favor. For one, it would no doubt increase the size of his reward. Far more important, though, was the simple fact that if Lain finished this battle on his feet,

Desmeres would not live long enough to collect. His sharp eyes spotted the crystal that would turn the tide and set about dragging himself toward it.

Myranda flexed her mystic knowledge, conjuring gale force winds, tremors, and bursts of force, anything that could occupy or immobilize the soldiers without killing them. Epidime, the only soldier on the battlefield with his face still obscured, stalked slowly toward her. When a final heave of magic scattered the men that surrounded Epidime, Myranda coaxed thick, woody vines from the ground in an interlocking ring around them. The soldiers on the outside of the wall immediately begin hacking at it, trying to break through. It was clear that it wouldn't hold for long.

"End this now, Epidime. I won't hesitate to do whatever it takes to stop you," Myranda said, gathering her mind for an attack.

She unleashed the spell, a potent example of the little training in black magic she'd received, fully expecting it to be deflected. Instead, her foe did not even raise his weapon, the crackling ball of magic connecting and throwing him backward into the wall of vines. His frail body bounced like a rag doll off of the wall, his grip on the halberd loosening. She seized the weapon with her mind, trying desperately to pull it from his grasp, but his spindly fingers tightened around it, the first hint of the unnatural strength that Epidime brought to his hosts beginning to show. Myranda charged in and grasped the shaft of the weapon with her free hand, readying a second attack.

"You chose poorly this time, Epidime. What is the matter? Have you used up all of the able bodies in the Alliance Army?" Myranda taunted, hoping to force him into a misstep.

"I chose this one for sentimental value," came the voice from behind the mask.

Myranda froze at the sound of the voice. There was a chilling familiarity to it. Without thinking, she released the weapon and grasped the helmet. Epidime thrust at her, knocking her backward, but her grip on the helmet held. It was torn from his head. As Myranda scrambled to her feet, the face she saw before her stopped her heart. It was old, but looked worn beyond its years. Gray streaks ran through the once-black hair, but the features, even twisted by Epidime's perpetual look of cold intellect, were unmistakable.

It was her father.

Myranda's mind was aflame with a thousand emotions. Tears came to her eyes. Joy, fear, anger, hate, and love all combined in a paralyzing chorus of voices in her head. A fiendish smile curled her father's lips, followed by a mocking laugh.

"What is the matter, my dear? This should be a joyous reunion, shouldn't it? After all, you sought me for years. Well, here I am," he said, cruelty peppering the voice of Myranda's loved one.

"You . . . aren't my father," Myranda replied, her voice barely a whisper.

"Oh, but I am. You look upon his body, and deep inside, his soul still resides . . . if only you could hear how it cries out for you, Myranda. Truly touching," Epidime said.

Elsewhere, Lain made his way through the soldiers on his way to Trigorah. They did not resist him, pulling back with their shields and weapons held defensively. The first real resistance came when another special contingent, bearing whips, nets, and other tools of entanglement, sifted to the forefront. Lain evaded them effortlessly, reaching Trigorah in moments. When the two warriors met, the surrounding soldiers pulled back. There was no exchange of words. Indeed, there was barely time for a heartbeat. Lain launched himself at the general, still mounted on her horse.

She managed to block the attack, but was knocked to the ground. Instantly, Lain was above her. Before he could manage a killing blow, however, one of the surrounding soldiers lashed at his raised weapon with a whip. He managed to evade the attack, but at the cost of a few moments. It was enough time for Trigorah to deliver a kick to her foe, staggering him. He recovered to find her on her feet. The warriors clashed swords again, again, and again. Each time, the gems that lined the general's blade took on a brighter glow. Soon, the weapon was burning with energy.

Lain was relentless in his attacks. At first, it was all that Trigorah could do to block each one. As the clash progressed, however, the force of her blows increased. Soon, she was knocking back her foe, each time offering a window of opportunity for her men to attack. They hurled nets, lashed with whips, and swung bolos. It was clear that their intention was not to strike Lain, but to separate him from his sword.

A bloodcurdling screech split the air. Where once there was a single massive dragoyle, now there were two. As the titans clashed, the soldiers below scattered. Earthshaking blows were traded, rocking the whole of the valley. Identical in every way, it was impossible to tell which of the beasts was friend and which was foe. The battle raged on, threatening to collapse the whole of the plateau into the valley below, until one beast forced the other to the ground, clamping its jaws on the head of the other and twisting its neck past the breaking point.

For a moment, all motion in the valley came to a halt. The eyes of Chosen and soldier alike turned to the massive beast. The monster moved slowly, taking two plodding steps away from the fallen one. The inky black hollows of its eyes swept over the valley. Suddenly, in a lightning motion, the enormous creature snapped its jaws shut on the nearest dragoyle, shaking it to pieces. Instantly, the remaining dragoyles took to the sky, tearing at their new target as arrows rained down on it from the soldiers.

Ivy's confidence was growing as the soldiers proved unable to lay a hand on her. She'd seen some of them out of the corner of her eye bearing nets, but they were swiftly and easily left behind. She'd managed to knock down quite a few of the soldiers, but she could not bring herself to truly attack them. These were not the teachers. They were only doing what they were told.

"Ivy," Deacon called amid the chaos. "Head for the wall!"

"Sure thing!" Ivy replied, grateful to have a direction for her efforts.

The skillful creature dutifully cleared the way for Deacon, who tried his best to keep his eyes trained on the crystal. As they drew nearer, something which added a measure more urgency to their trek became visible behind the wall of soldiers. Desmeres had nearly reached the crystal. Deacon desperately tried to break free of the cluster of soldiers around them, but each time it was only through the masterful intervention of Ivy that he avoided being struck down. The soldiers were under orders to forgo fatal means when facing the Chosen, but it would seem they were not similarly instructed regarding Deacon.

Amid his attempts to keep the crystal in sight and dodge the constantly swinging swords around him, the wizard dug madly through his bag.

Generally, he managed to keep it in a state of relative order, but in the rather brief time that he'd been too weak to cast any spells that had changed. Keeping track of the contents of a bag that was so much larger on the inside than it was on the outside without the aid of magic was exceptionally difficult, even knowing where things had been before. Doing so while under constant attack was impossible. He glanced up. Desmeres had nearly reached the crystal. Time was running out.

"Hurry!" he urged his protector.

In response, Ivy grabbed the nearest attacker by the wrists, yanked him from his feet, and hurled him at the remaining soldiers who stood in their way. After pausing briefly to marvel at the sudden showing of strength, the pair burst through the opening before them. Deacon sprinted as fast as he could toward Desmeres.

"What do we do now, Deac . . ." Ivy began, but suddenly her voice trailed off, her expression blank.

Desmeres breathed a sigh of relief as the soldiers surrounded Ivy and Deacon. The breath caught in his throat as Deacon managed to slip between them. He clutched the crystal tightly.

"Get him! GET HIM!" he ordered.

Ivy burst into motion, forcing her way through the line of soldiers and quickly closing on Deacon. Suddenly, a net was thrown over her.

"No, no! Let her go!" Desmeres pleaded to the soldiers who, having finally managed to capture her, were not inclined to release their prize.

It was too late. Deacon dove at Desmeres and tore madly at the crystal. As the pair vied desperately for control of the artifact, Ivy's mind was pulled in every direction. She bounced between Desmeres's insistence that she escape and help to defeat Deacon, Deacon's insistence that she escape and save herself, and her own increasingly terrified thoughts.

"Give it up! It is only a matter of time before these *soldiers* realize that they need to *come here and help me!*" Desmeres taunted.

As the ruined body of the final dragoyle dropped to the ground, Ether looked over the battlefield. The creatures had taken a greater toll on her than she had anticipated. Taking the beast's form had left her with precious little strength. She found that the beast's eyes seemed to have a special sensitivity to the crystals she'd taken the form to avoid.

At the far side of the valley, Ivy was tangled in a net with dozens of the crystals knotted into it. There were a number of other such nets scattered among the soldiers. The only other sizable crystals she could see were those adorning the spears of the men who had managed to form a ring around her. If she was to have any hope of returning to one of her fundamental forms safely, she would have to eliminate the bearers of these weapons. Unfortunately, the soldiers quickly proved to be far less dimwitted than the dragoyles, and managed to evade her attempts at trampling them.

As the men continued to bait her and evade her, Ether could feel her strength quickly waning. She'd been trying to avoid using the corrosive breath of her form, lest she risk injuring the others, but now it seemed she had no choice. She opened the massive maw of the creature and began to heave out a great cloud of the miasma, but no sooner had the first wisp of it wafted forth than she felt a sharp pain in her throat. Instantly, all of the strength drained from her. She could feel the stony hide begin to give way, falling to pieces.

As she attempted to abandon the form, she felt the intense sting of a dozen crystals jabbing into her. If she were to change now, what little strength she had would be sapped away by the crystals. She remained in the defeated form, the slow realization of what had transpired dawning upon her. The soldiers had been waiting for her to resort to the beast's breath, hurling a spear into her mouth the instant it had opened. They knew that she would take on that form, and that she would have the same weakness. The dragoyles were easily felled in one blow by a precise strike to the back of the throat, and they had goaded her into revealing this flaw to them. It had been a plan, a trick, and she had fallen for it. Now, she was trapped within this helpless husk, a handful of the mounted soldiers already beginning to drag what was left of her through the portal.

Myranda struggled to restore some measure of clarity. She tried to remind herself that Epidime had brought her father here for precisely this reason, that she was only playing into his trap. It was useless. Half a lifetime of searching and hoping had found their answer at the worst possible time, and her emotions would not relent.

"Don't you have any questions for your dear father, little one?" Epidime asked, Myranda's turmoil obvious to him. "Don't you want to know how he was treated? What kept him alive through those long years of torture and isolation? Do as I say, what I know you want to do. Just come with me. I'll tell you everything. It has been too long, my dear daughter."

The tortured wizard longed to take his offer. She knew that he was only trying to get her to betray the others, but to hear the pleas spoken in her father's own voice burned at her mind. As the first of the soldiers finally broke through, she lowered her staff slightly. The protective wall was torn away, revealing the battlefield that had been hidden. Myranda's eyes turned. Fleeting glimpses of Ivy's tortured struggles and Lain's continuing battle with Trigorah slowly filtered though the haze of emotion.

Epidime approached her as she was surrounded by soldiers. She raised her staff again, her eyes filled with resolve. Epidime's expression grew more sinister.

"You always were a disobedient little whelp," he hissed.

The clash began in earnest between Myranda and Epidime. Nearby, Lain's battle was fairing poorly. On the ground around him were a handful of soldiers unlucky enough to feel the bite of Lain's blade. Others had quickly stepped in to replace them, and they were growing more courageous. If this was not ended soon, it would not end in his favor. As the sword clashed again and again, Lain finally saw an opening. He managed a swift slash, cleaving Trigorah's armor and digging deep into her shoulder. The general lurched backwards. After a swift slice to the soldiers near enough to intervene, Lain moved in for a final attack.

Trigorah swung her sword, despite the fact Lain was not within reach. A ribbon of light arced forth from the blade. The assassin's own blade was able to deflect the spell, but it collided with enough force to hurl Lain backward, knocking the weapon from his hand.

When he landed, he was instantly buried under a pile of soldiers. For a moment, they seemed to have him under control, but suddenly there was the screech of steel on steel and the soldiers scattered to reveal Lain, now holding the sword from a fallen soldier. As he began to carve his way back through the soldiers to get to their leader, Trigorah leveled the point of her sword at Lain and spoke a few arcane words. Lain's pace slowed, his motions suddenly subdued. His legs faltered, forcing him to drop to one knee. A tremendous weariness came over him. Soldiers closed in and restrained him, but he wrenched himself from their grasp, managing one last charge at Trigorah.

The general poured all of the energy stored in her blade into the spell. Without Desmeres's blade to protect him from the magic, he was at its mercy. Finally, his strength failed him, and he collapsed.

Deacon finally tore the crystal from Desmeres's grip and plunged it deep into his bag, shuffling the other contents to be sure it was concealed. Without another will to command her, Ivy's mind was finally her own again. Realizing that she'd been captured, and still reeling from her chaotic ordeal, the blue aura of fear surged up around her. The crystals embedded in the net around her drew hungrily at the power, further terrifying Ivy.

"What do I do!? WHAT DO I DO!?" she begged, trying desperately to escape the net.

The soldiers restraining her were drawing the net tighter and beginning to drag her to the portal through which Ether's remains had been carried. The sight of the swirling form, coupled with the thought that they wanted to drag her through it, pushed her over the edge. Instantly, she was a blaze of blinding blue light. The net held, its crystals glowing brilliantly as they drank in her power, but the men who had been restraining her could not hold her back. As she desperately leapt toward the wall that trapped them in the valley, they were dragged along behind her. She collided with the shimmering wall with incredible force, the dozen or so soldiers yanked along by the net smashing into it a moment later. The mystical barrier rippled violently, but held. She hammered on it with her fists, but fear had granted her more speed than strength.

As the men slowly recovered and attempted to secure the net around her, there was a burst of light. One of the crystals, bathed in more energy than it could contain, had burst, showering soldiers and Ivy alike with gem shards. The already-terrified Ivy's fear doubled as she tried to escape the crystals. The net, still tangled about her upper body, was dragged behind, along with the hapless soldiers who had managed to become entangled as well. Soon, other crystals began to burst, each time startling the creature and sending her in another direction.

A streak of blue zigged and zagged through the valley, parting the soldiers like a boat cutting through the waves. Her frenzied path tore past Trigorah, colliding with her weapon and sending the blade hurdling through the air. It embedded itself in the cliff face high above them.

"Someone stop that beast!" Trigorah ordered.

All available soldiers rushed to the task, leaving Myranda alone with her opponent. She and Epidime had been hurling spells at each other without relenting; hers intent on separating him from his staff, his intent on simply defeating her. The valley was scorched and aflame in some places, deeply frozen in others. Now that there were no soldiers to distract her, Myranda knew that she would not get a better chance. She focused intensely, flexing all she knew of levitation and wrenching Epidime into the air. Holding out a hand to guide her foe into the air, she spread her fingers. Instantly, Epidime's weapon tugged away from him, threatening to escape his withered grasp.

"What do you think you will accomplish with this, my child?" Epidime asked, as he clutched desperately at the halberd with both hands.

"I *will* break your hold over my father," she declared.

"Is that wise? After all, a decade in a dungeon tends to wear on the body," Epidime struggled to say. "Perhaps your father is only alive because of my presence."

Myranda hesitated, but just for a moment.

"I can hear his screams as you threaten to pull his fingers from their sockets, and I can hear his thoughts. The man has a greater will to live than you give him credit for," Epidime said.

As Ivy continued her terror-driven rampage, Deacon rushed to join his friends. He didn't get more than a few steps before a painful blow from behind knocked him to the ground. A pair of the soldiers tossed about by Ivy had managed to get to their feet. When Deacon rolled to his back to face his attacker, a foot was placed on his chest and the tip of a sword held to his throat. Desmeres limped to where the bag had fallen and fetched it. He gazed inside, rolling his eyes at what he found.

"Been to Entwell, have you?" he said. "I sincerely doubt anyone out here could have produced one of these."

He reached into the bag, rummaging through the warehouse worth of contents.

"I don't suppose you will be willing to locate the crystal and stop that creature from killing us all," he said after realizing that finding it on his own was unlikely at best.

"You are siding with the D'karon. How can you dedicate yourself to a cause that threatens the very world you live in?" Deacon replied as they pulled him to his feet and held his arms behind his back.

"Right now, I am primarily dedicated to survival," Desmeres replied.

"What does he mean? Who are the D'karon?" the soldier restraining Deacon asked.

"If you are so curious, ask him . . ." Desmeres said, immediately bashing the wizard with the hilt of his sword, rendering him unconscious.

"When he wakes up. We'll need him to get the crystal back. Take him and the bag through the portal as soon as you can."

Myranda's strength was beginning to flag. So, it seemed, was Epidime's, as his grip grew ever looser, and his intellectual look had become one of desperation.

"You know . . ." he managed to say. "You seemed like a smart girl . . . I was afraid it wouldn't have come to this. And you seemed weak . . . I was afraid you wouldn't have lasted this long . . ."

"What are you talking about?" Myranda asked.

"Don't worry . . . the answer is forthcoming," he replied.

The energy squandered in Ivy's mindless rampage, as well as that stolen by the crystals, began to take its toll. As she slowed, more soldiers were able to grasp the threads of tattered net that streamed from her to slow her more. Finally, a second, then third net were thrown over her. The new crystals finished what the old had started. The last of her surge of strength was wicked away, and the creature collapsed.

Myranda turned to see Lain, Ivy, and Deacon heavily restrained and being led toward the portal. Lain's eyes were weakly open, but it was clear that he lacked both the strength and will to so much as struggle. As she realized that she was the last of the heroes that remained, her eyes turned back to Epidime. The look of desperation was replaced by a satisfied grin. His fingers closed tightly about the halberd and he launched a swift burst of black energy at her. The wizard dove to avoid it, rolling to her feet. Epidime dropped to the ground, not a hint of fatigue or concern on his face. It had all been an act, a distraction to keep her from helping her friends.

In a final, desperate act, Myranda summoned an intense wall of flame. It weaved its way across the valley between Myranda and Epidime, blocking off the rest of the soldiers from those carrying her friends. The soldiers were then lifted into the air and hurled over the flames to join their fellow warriors. Myranda was not sure where strength she burned now was coming from, but she was certain it was the absolute last she had, and it would not last long. She focused on reviving Lain. There was a powerful spell at work on him, one that would not be a simple one to unravel. She set as much of her mind as she could spare to the task. The familiar sound of arrows hissing through the air drew her attention. She raised a hand and they stopped in mid-air, hanging over the fire. Just a few moments more . . .

If Lain could be raised then perhaps there was a chance. She felt Epidime's powerful will pressing against hers, trying to undo all that she was doing. The wizard redoubled her effort. The spells held.

"Myranda!" Trigorah called through the flames.

Myranda looked through the burning wall. A dozen of her men had arrows drawn back and ready to fire at Myranda. The general pointed, and a single soldier trained his bow on . . . Epidime. He motioned for a pair of soldiers to restrain him, and when they had, he released the halberd. A look of confusion, fear, and anger came to his face.

"Trigorah, you traitor! You've seen what the generals have done and you've done nothing to stop it! You've allowed your men, our brethren, to be sent to their deaths on the whims of demons! Fire the arrow quickly, and fire it true, because I will *not* live in the world that your treachery has created," he raved.

Trigorah let fly the arrow. Myranda did not think. She threw aside all other spells. The arrow was all that mattered. She clamped her mind down on it. It halted, stopped dead in its path a mere whisper from her father's chest. Then came the pain. The soldiers, under orders to take Myranda and the others alive, had aimed at the staff she held. One shaft plunged through her arm. As the intense pain swept through her, any hope at focus was lost. Trigorah's men rushed to the fallen heroes. Lain was still under the effects of the spell. Myranda's fading vision locked on the general as she approached the unconscious assassin.

"I have given so many years, and so much of myself to catch you, Lain. First as an assassin, and now as a warrior of legend, your capture has been the one thing standing between me and my rightful place. And now that is over. In your defeat comes your greatest contribution to this world. Presenting you and the others to General Bagu will allow me to command the front once more. This war will finally see its end. The north will finally see victory," the general proclaimed.

Epidime applauded.

"Yes, yes. A life's work completed. Alas, I am afraid Bagu's trust in you is not what it once was. As such, it will be I who must present the Chosen to him. You will await reassignment," he stated.

"What are you saying? I *earned* this," Trigorah replied viciously.

"You could not have achieved it without my help. I should think that would imply we've equal claim to the right to present them, and since I am your superior, it is within my rights to claim the reward. Besides, that wound on your shoulder proves to me you are not as valuable as we had believed," Epidime mocked.

"What difference does the wound make? Victory is still ours," she replied.

"Victory is mine, not ours. Now, if you will, return through the portal," Epidime ordered, impatience mixing with his tone.

"I will not allow you to take this from me, Epidime. And neither will my men," the general said, pulling a dagger from her belt. "Soldiers, restrain General Epidime!"

For a moment, the remaining soldiers hesitated. An impatient tap of Epidime's staff and a surge of its crystal made their minds up. They turned, weapons ready, to Trigorah.

"Well, I would say that it is quite clear where the loyalties of *my* troops lie. As for you? Well, I would count this act of insubordination as treason. Because of your admirable service to the Alliance, I will forgo the death sentence, but I'm afraid I must relieve you of your rank," Epidime said with false compassion.

A look of pure hatred came to Trigorah's face.

"So be it. If this is the way decades of faithful service is repaid, you can have my service band. I don't want it," she proclaimed.

A smile came to Epidime's face as she pulled away the sleeve that had been ruined by Lain's attack. She ignored the pain of her injury, carefully undoing a latch that had remained clamped since before she'd been sworn in as a general. She pulled the engraved gold band away from her flesh for the first time in all of those years and threw it at the general's feet. Immediately, she felt a searing pain where it had been.

There, shining brilliantly with an unnatural light . . . was the Mark. The same mark that each of the Chosen bore. The former general cried out in pain as the burning of the Mark spread, the divine price for betrayal finally free to be paid.

As confusion and fear filled the minds of the soldiers who looked on, Epidime approached Trigorah. His frail fingers closed with unnatural strength around her throat and raised her from the ground.

"So single-minded, so dedicated to your goal, you managed to convince yourself it wasn't there. That the mark you had worn since birth was nothing . . . meaningless. I knew you would. The instant we hid it beneath the band, I knew you'd thought your last thought about it, gleefully hunting down your would be partners. Digging your pit of betrayal deeper and deeper, until the only thing keeping you from the exquisite divine retribution you are feeling was our band. How does it feel?" Epidime asked.

Trigorah struggled, now almost completely consumed in the soul fire.

"You will pay for this, Epidime. I swear by the gods themselves that you shall pay, even if I have to claw my way back from hell!" Trigorah cried in a voice twisted by pain and hatred into a soul-searing screech.

"You will have to," Epidime replied, hurling the burning form into the valley.

After watching intently as the burning ember of her form streaked like a comet into the rocky valley to be dashed apart by its jagged floor, Epidime was satisfied. He turned to savor the look of horror on the faces of the soldiers before ordering them to their tasks. Each of the heroes was gathered up and brought through the portal. Desmeres limped to the portal, turning his gaze to the valley below and casting a long, thoughtful look before stepping through the gateway.

#

For a long time, there was only darkness. When the blurry light of a lamp slowly came into focus, the glow revealed something far worse than the darkness. Deacon shook his head. He was sitting in a chair, his hands secured behind his back. The room was small. Turning his head made the world around him swirl and the knot left by Desmeres's blow throb. The only other things in the room besides himself and the chair he occupied were a table, upon which the lamp and his bag sat surrounded by a large pile of its former contents. The walls were stone, and the door heavy iron, protected on the outside by a pair of guards. They were nearmen, no attempt having been made to conceal their crude, monstrous faces. His motion prompted one of them to disappear down the dark hallway.

The young wizard struggled. Around his neck was a collar identical to the one he'd seen affixed to the flickering image of Myranda that he'd managed to summon to his crystal all of those weeks ago. A brief, painful, failed attempt at a spell affirmed that it served the same purpose. Any attempt at magic would bring horrible pain. At least he knew that he'd recovered from his ordeal enough to cast spells. Even if the skill was currently useless, having it returned to him was a relief. As he plotted his next move, a figure appeared in the doorway. He matched Myranda's description of the general called Demont. Two of the odd weapon creatures hung at his back. His face had a look of weary disinterest.

"Name," he stated.

"Deacon," the wizard replied.

"Well, Deacon. A few words. First, I would like to make it perfectly clear that, unlike the Chosen you've gotten yourself involved with, we have no particular motivation to keep you alive. Second, if you had been hoping you could escape from the collar in the same way the other human did, don't. We learn from our mistakes here. Corrections have been made. Finally, this is not an interrogation, and I am not Epidime. I do not consider this a battle of wills, a game, or anything else. I have very little patience. If I do not get the answers I desire quickly, you die, and I look for them elsewhere. Do we understand each other?" he rattled off.

"Most certainly," Deacon replied.

"Splendid. Now, how is it that the entire contents of my workshop seem to have been wedged into your bag?" Demont asked, irritation in his voice.

"When I arrived to help Myranda, she was just outside the workshop . . ." he began.

"No, no. Not why. How? Through what means can so much fit inside of so small a space?" the general corrected.

"The bag has been enchanted to have a disproportionate interior," he said.

"That is within your capabilities?" Demont replied, intrigued.

"Given the time," Deacon said.

"And is that information contained within this book?" Demont continued, holding up one of the two books that had been within the bag.

"Not in a form that you will find useful . . . You haven't developed that particular enchantment?" Deacon asked.

"Not to the degree that you have. I'd toyed with the idea of creating a beast that would act as a mobile prison, swallowing down detainees, but the size necessary for it to be useful made it a slow, easy target. Incorporating this enchantment would alleviate that, if it could be as significant as you've achieved," Demont said, flipping briefly through the book.

"Interesting. You haven't perfected an age-old enchantment like that, yet your own transportation skills are tremendously ahead of ours. And, frankly, I never would have imagined actually manufacturing a living thing," Deacon remarked, letting his academic side show. "Such are the differing aims of our cultures, I suppose."

"Mmm," Demont replied. "So it would seem."

He reached into the bag and pulled out a violin case.

"So it *was* in there," Deacon remarked.

Demont looked over the case and set it down.

"Would you consider joining us?" Demont asked flatly, as though it was more a formality than an actual request. "As a man of knowledge, the prospect of looking over a few of our more complete spell books should appeal to you, and you seem to be not without usefulness."

"I can't do that," Deacon replied.

"So I suspected. Very well, then. If you would kindly remove my crystal from your bag, we shall be through here," Demont said.

"You haven't found it yet?" Deacon asked.

"As I have said, Deacon, I have very little patience. Emptying the contents of your interminable satchel does not appeal to me. I've found the largest piece. Simply return the other," Demont said.

"I am afraid that it is in the satchel. Occasionally things find their way out of arm's reach. Recalling them to the opening is a bit of a tricky spell," Deacon explained.

"Mmm. One that you will not be casting," Demont replied. "I am not so foolish as to remove that collar so easily."

One of the staff-like creatures dropped from Demont's back, sprouting its insect legs and clattering toward Deacon. The wizard's gaze shifted to it, a mixture of nervousness and fascination on his face.

"Do they have a mind? A soul?" Deacon asked.

"No soul. I can imbue varying degrees of intellect, from primal to superhuman, given the resources . . . You know, for someone who has been made aware of his impending doom, you seem in awfully high spirits. Almost as if you were expecting this," Demont said, suspicion beginning to rise.

"I knew that joining with the Chosen would lead to my death. I'd come to terms with the fact," Deacon explained.

"Still. It makes me wonder if you haven't got some manner of insurance in place. Some secret that will keep that crystal from us if you die . . ." Demont remarked thoughtfully. "This is an occasion when Epidime's talents would be useful. He could extract what we can use from your mind. Perhaps you'd best be kept until he is through with his work elsewhere . . ."

"I think that sounds like a splendid idea," Deacon said.

"I suspected you might. We shall see if you continue to feel that way once Epidime has forced his way into your mind," Demont said, turning to address the nearmen. "In the meantime, I've work to do for Bagu elsewhere. Remove every last item from the bag. If you find a small fragment of a large, refined thir gem, alert me. And if he shows any signs of escape, disable him and alert me."

The nearmen nodded. With that, Demont paced out of the room, shutting the cell door behind him and disappearing down the hallway. The telltale sound of a portal opening and closing signaled his departure. Deacon watched as the nearmen removed an assortment of Demont's items and his own from the bag.

Every so often, they would pull something out of the bag that he was certain he had not placed into it. The first was a bundle of papers. The second was an odd figurine. The third was a vial of some sort, attached to an extremely long, fine linked chain. His mind began to work at how and why his bag had begun to produce objects on its own. What aspect of the flawed transportation spell had brought that about? The thought of the malformed spell reminded him of another side effect of it. He began to struggle to reach one hand with the other.

#

Far away, Myranda's overtaxed mind faded in and out of consciousness for a time. She was vaguely aware of being loaded into the back of one of the black carriages, and later being carried through stone hallways. The only thing that was constant was the blinding pain in her left arm. As her mind slowly recovered, even though her strength didn't, Myranda looked over her surroundings. There were shackles on her wrists and ankles, studded with the blasted crystal that the D'karon seemed to have an endless supply of. These were attached to chains that were similarly studded, leading off into the darkness. Bars that led from the ceiling to the floor surrounded her, forming a small cage with no door. The only light came in a steady glow from the many crystal studs which traced out the path of the chains along the floor as they led to four larger crystals well outside the bars.

With no light from the outside, it was difficult to gauge the passage of time. For hours, perhaps days, Myranda fought to gain any sort of focus--if not enough to cast a spell, at least enough to think. Perhaps then she might be able to work out where she was, and how to get out. It was no use, though. The crystals were a constant draw on her spirit, keeping her weak, and the throbbing of her arm occupied what little of her thoughts remained.

As time crept on, new concerns began to coalesce in her tortured mind. She'd not been fed in all of her time here, a fact her stomach reminded her of frequently. Neither was she given any water. Indeed, the only evidence that there was anyone even aware of her was the rare occasion when someone would step into the dim glow of one of the larger crystals to replace it with a fresh one.

Faint memories of her last detainment drifted to the surface of her murky mind. She'd spared herself the pain of the collar they'd placed on her by forcing her strength down deep. Perhaps that would help here as well. Gathering what little she had, Myranda did so. It was not long before she was sure it was working. The glow of the larger crystal ceased to increase. Her mind cleared a bit, too, though it did little good. Her eyes brought her nothing useful, and what she could hear did little to help her. Mostly, there was the periodic sound of plodding footsteps approaching to check the gems, then retreating again. The only other sounds were distant, muffled noises that sounded like the roars of animals.

With nothing but her thoughts and her pain to occupy her, Myranda began the long, difficult task of sorting though the events that had happened in the valley. The D'karon had known precisely what was needed to defeat each one of the Chosen. Her own refusal to kill humans, Lain's reliance on his sword to defend against magic, Ether's weakness against crystals and her tactics to combat them, and the gem that controlled Ivy.

Everything had been planned out from the start, and each hero had played into the traps perfectly.

Her own manipulation had been masterful. Epidime had managed to make her reunion with her father the most painful moment in her life, instead of the moment of joy it should have been. And Trigorah . . . all of this time, she'd been the last of the original Chosen. All of this time, she'd fought to defeat, to capture, those who should have been her allies, and each success had been another nail in her coffin. Somehow, that band had protected her from the retribution that fell upon the divinely Chosen when their loyalty strayed.

Myranda worked it over in her mind. The swordsman had fallen, Ivy had been transformed, Trigorah had been subverted, and Lain and Ether remained. The intended five were all accounted for.

More time passed. The strength sequestered deep in her soul grew stronger. Her mind grew sharper. She was beginning to administer small doses of magic to the wound on her arm, healing it slowly so as to not be overtaxed. It had only just been reduced to a dull ache when the click of boots on the stone floor approached again, this time coming much closer, and accompanied by the glow of a torch.

The face the torch revealed was anything but a welcome one. It was General Bagu. On his face he wore a look of superiority and triumph.

"Ah. Alive, I see. I was beginning to think you'd been pushed beyond the breaking point," he remarked.

"You would have let me die? I thought you needed us alive," Myranda replied in a hoarse voice.

"Not for much longer. Now that the four of you are in our possession, we've found ways to utilize you to our own ends. A few more weeks of harvest and we shall be prepared to pass the point of no return. After that, your failure will be assured, whether more Chosen arise or not," Bagu explained.

"How?" Myranda asked.

"That is not for you to know," Bagu said. "All you need to know is that your life right now depends upon your ability to fill these crystals. If you prove unable to do so, you shall be disposed of."

"And if I am unwilling?" she asked.

"Your cooperation is not essential. Even if you hold back, you will have to sleep eventually, and when you do, the crystals will drink what there is to be had from you," Bagu informed her. "At this point, there are only three possible outcomes. You can join us, at which point you will be restored to health and given a place among the generals. You may even be made the overseer of this world."

"I've seen what you do to the Chosen who join you," Myranda hissed.

"Trigorah's fall was unfortunate, but necessary. She attempted to turn her back on us, and in doing so shunned our protection from the curse of the Mark," he stated. "But if you will not join us, I suppose you shall simply have to wither away to nothing as we leech away every last bit of your strength."

"And the last option?" Myranda asked.

"Suffice it to say that the final option is mine to choose, not yours," he stated ominously. "Now, since you've been informed of how to cooperate, I shall give you an opportunity to do so. I suggest you take it."

He turned and marched off, leaving her in darkness once more. A short time later, food and water were delivered to her. It was the same watery gruel she'd been served during her last detainment. Myranda considered foregoing the food, letting herself waste away rather than give them the power they wanted. There seemed no way out. Even if she were to release all of the strength she'd been able to keep from them at once, whatever spell she cast would be leeched away to nothing by the overabundance of crystals before it could be of any use.

Myranda was languishing in despair as a form approached her. No light was brought along this time, the presence signaled only by the click of boots upon the floor. Something clattered to the floor just outside of the bars, and a creak followed. Slowly, a bluish light appeared in the heart of a gem that had thus far been hidden. It was affixed in the head of a halberd, and cast its light on the form of her father reclined in a chair that had been placed beside the cage. Once he saw the pained look of recognition come to her face, he let the light drop again.

"So we meet again, my dear," he said.

"Why have you come? Do you plan to make another attempt at my mind?" Myranda asked weakly.

"Tempting, but no. Where is the challenge? Besides, I am still busying myself with your father's mind. We've been using him for quite a while, you know. Most of the nearmen fight using maneuvers plucked from his head. But until recently, the facts of his life were of little interest. Quite the noble soul, your father; did you know that--" Epidime began.

"Stop it!" Myranda cried. "Is this why you've come here, to torment me?"

"Partially. In truth, things have become *painfully* tiresome these past few days. With the Chosen all either dead or in custody and the end in sight, I find myself stricken with ennui. You've always been the most interesting to me, so I decided, while they are busy securing my next target for interrogation, I might have a word with you," he said. "It might interest you to know that Lain has nearly escaped no less than three times since our little encounter in the valley."

Myranda was silent.

"I believe we've worked out a way to keep him in line though . . ." he remarked.

"You know . . . If my end has finally come, there is one good thing about it," Myranda said. "You'll never get the chance to grasp at my mind again. I turned you away once, and you will never be able to redeem yourself. You will simply have to live with the defeat."

"There, you see? Fascinating. The motivations behind such a statement are a delicious little puzzle. Was it simply out of malice? Are you trying to goad me into an attempt, or are you trying to trick me into releasing you?" Epidime replied. "Not that it matters, of course. I sincerely doubt your path ends here. You are the clever sort. That is why I like you. That boy of yours, on the other hand . . ."

"You leave Deacon out of this. He isn't Chosen!" Myranda said.

"I knew that he would get a rise out of you. Demont wants me to take a look through his head. The old beast wrangler seems to think there are some parlor tricks inside that we might use. I suppose I shall get to that. He could be interesting, as well. After all, you seem to have grown rather attached, haven't you," Epidime thought out loud.

"Why! Why do you do this? What do you get from torturing me?" Myranda cried.

"Why, to *know,* Myranda--to know," he replied. "That is all there really is in the end, my dear. Knowledge. There is an awful lot of it, and there is always more to be had. That is why I agreed to come along with these fellows. They could take me elsewhere."

"You aren't one of them? You aren't a D'karon?" Myranda asked.

"Well, naturally I am a D'karon. I wouldn't be here yet if I wasn't. You see, I've noticed this about you and the others. You've incorrectly interpreted that word's meaning. I'll explain it to you one of these days. I'd explain it now, but it might give you some insight into something that it is in our best interests to keep hidden," Epidime said. "But I digress--I do what I do because I wish to know things. Not trivial matters like the names of spies and the movement of troops and the sort of things I dig up for them.

"I live for skills, and techniques, and the nature of things. Look at emotion! I mean, love, happiness, joy. They are not without their allure, but in the end they are a bore. They just lead to more of the same. Things get really interesting when you start to unearth things like anger, jealousy, sorrow, hate, worry, and lust! Once I set one of them churning about in your mind, you start to do things that don't even make sense to *you.* Things you don't *want* to do. Things that you know are *wrong.*

"How can you help but be fascinated in that? It is as though each one of you is not an individual, but a spectrum, a society, occupying a single body. I need to test these limits, to see how I can bring out the side that benefits me. The more I learn, the more I become convinced that, given time, a mere handful of careful manipulations could shape the whole of a *world* into any form you choose. I simply must try that, one of these days."

"You are mad," Myranda stated.

"Am I? Do you realize how simple it was to start this war? Do you even know how it really started?" Epidime asked.

Myranda was silent. A devilish grin came to Epidime's face.

"Oh . . . And I thought there wasn't a single way I could leave you in any more anguish than I had found you in," he said. "Well, it is really a very short story. One hundred and fifty or so years ago, things were going quite well for your little world. In fact, the King of Vulcrest was on the verge of hammering out a mutually beneficial agreement with Tressor. He was not at all well, though.

"As you are quite aware, it is the tradition for the kings of the three northern kingdoms to be buried beneath the ground that they die upon. Thus, when the king suddenly became weak, he was pulled away from the bargaining table and rushed to a carriage, so that should he die, it would happen in the north. A faster carriage was waiting just on the other side of the border, and the king was being led to it when he collapsed. He was found just a few paces on the Tresson side of the border. The government of Vulcrest demanded that soil beneath their king be made a part of Vulcrest. The Tressons refused. And so it began.

"Most of your people do not even remember that simple tale, but there is a bit that no one knew. I was the king's aide. Bagu was the driver of the first carriage, and Teht the driver of the second. Members of the D'karon were the only ones that witnessed his death . . . He died on his own side of the border, but that is not where he was found. Oh, we didn't kill him. His own failing health did that. All we did was move him. And that was all it took. One hundred and fifty years of war only required me to move him a few paces."

Myranda dove at him, stretching the chains to their limit and struggling weakly against them.

"You monster! You *monster!* All of those years. All of those *lives!*" she cried in a frenzy.

Epidime rose, taking his seat with him, and left the enraged girl to her outburst. She strained at her bonds until her strength gave out. With the crystals eating at her, it didn't take long. As she became still, the hopelessness and pointlessness of it all consumed her mind. Nothing mattered. She hadn't the strength to save herself, let alone the others. And even if she could, what was the point? Any world that could plunge itself into a generations old war on such trivial pretext, and allow itself to forget why it fought, scarcely deserved to survive. All she wanted was for death to claim her. For the final darkness to creep over her and take the weight from her shoulders.

Amid the darkness of her mind, a tiny part of her resisted. Some insignificant corner of her soul scratched and dug at her memories, desperate to find something to draw her from the abyss. The events of the valley battle faded briefly into her mind. One of the last things she'd seen was Deacon being hauled through the portal. He was alive, then. Epidime had indicated he still was. At the same time, her own father was at the mercy of Epidime, enduring a torture she herself had only narrowly been able to avoid. The two men that she loved most were both in the clutches of the D'karon, and it was no one's fault but her own. Finally, she understood why the heroes of legend were meant to be solitary. It was to shield others from this hell. To spare those not burdened by divine mandate the wrath of the enemy.

That was why she had to fight. She could not let them pay the price. She had to do something. Something that could cripple the D'karon as they had crippled the Chosen. Saving the world seemed hopeless now, but saving the two people in it who meant the most, or at least avenging them? She had to try.

Slowly, a plan formed. She tested the crystals, seeing how much they could draw from her, and how quickly. Carefully, she practiced isolating just one gem. With purpose behind her actions, the time began to pass more quickly. She choked down what they offered in the way of food. If this was going to work, she would need every ounce of strength she could muster. When one crystal was filled almost completely, she choked off the flow of magic and held it there. It wasn't long before Bagu reappeared. He cautiously surveyed the room.

"I must say, you've managed to confuse the nearmen. And I would be lying if I said I wasn't at least a bit curious about what it is you think you are doing," Bagu remarked.

"I know myself rather well, General. I know how much strength I should have by now, which means I know how much I've given you. It is quite a bit," Myranda said, her words delivered carefully lest she allow her focus to falter.

"Hardly. It is the merest trifle when compared to the amount we've been able to draw from Ether and Ivy. You can be pleased, I suppose, that Lain has been less productive than you," the general mocked.

"Is that so . . . Well, then, I suppose I shall simply need to try harder," Myranda said.

Instantly, she reversed the efforts of her mind. She forced her strength to the surface and into the single gem. The studs in the shackles took on a blinding blue-white glow, some of them bursting. The main gem swiftly took on a similar glow. Cracks of more brilliant light ran across its surface. General Bagu realized what Myranda was attempting and turned to force the gem from its stand, but it was too late. The flood of power was too much for the larger gem, and before he could tear it free, it burst.

The blast was intense, hurling Myranda against the bars of the cage and peppering her with broken shards of crystal. It brought with it a tremendous, sharp clap, like a dozen thunderbolts at once. The flash of light robbed Myranda of her vision and her ears rang and whistled. As her vision slowly began to return, it revealed a surreal sight. The largest of the crystal shards were embedded deep in the walls, creating a fading galaxy of light blue embers all around her. The chain that had been attached to the crystal's pedestal was bent and twisted in the bars nearest to the blast. The bars themselves were bent slightly inward by the collision.

Myranda rose painfully to her feet, brushing away the shards that had found their way to her flesh and limping to the damaged bars to test their strength. With one of the gems destroyed, the end of the chain formerly linked to it was loose, completely freeing one of her arms. One by one, she investigated the bars until she found one that was slightly loosened. She had begun to twist and pull at it when motion caught her eye. A form, as embedded with crystals as the wall, was moving toward her. With an inhuman growl, a hand reached through the bars and grabbed a hold of her, yanking her to the limit of the chains that still held. Myranda could hear the joints of her still restrained arm popping, and the feeling of the half-healed arrow wound opening again made her cry out in pain.

"Congratulations . . ." came Bagu's voice from the darkness, saturated with hatred. "You've earned the third option."

Dozens of nearmen bearing lanterns and torches flooded the room, finally shedding light on the destruction. A large portion of the wall behind the crystal had been obliterated, and of the other three crystals, only one was still intact. Bagu himself was oozing black blood from a dozen wounds torn by pieces of crystal. Half of his face was an unrecognizable mass of ruined flesh. With his free hand, he bashed at the bars. Despite a build that seemed at best average, Bagu's attack was enough to rend the metal bars from ceiling and floor alike. As the nearmen clambered to undo the shackles, he barked orders at them.

"Make the necessary preparations. Tonight there shall be a show," he growled.

With that, he placed a hand on Myranda's head, his will driving the young wizard back into unconsciousness. When she awakened, she was falling through the air, deafening cheers in her ears. She landed painfully on the dusty ground, her twisted joints, skewered arm, and perforated skin all making their presence known once more. After struggling to her feet, Myranda's blurred vision began to clear.

She was in the middle of a large, dirt-covered field. A high stone wall surrounded her. There were doors large enough to pass a carriage through with room to spare at opposite ends of the courtyard. At the top of the wall were downward pointing spikes. Beyond them was row after row of soldiers, weapons in their hands and murder in their eyes. Those nearest to the wall were in full armor, faces hidden behind the face guards. No doubt they were nearmen. Here and there, slung between spikes, was a large example of the storage crystals.

The wizard must have spent some time away from the parasitic gems, as a fair amount of her strength had returned to her. Quickly as she could, to avoid feeding the thirst of the crystals for any longer that was necessary, she healed the more grievous of her wounds. The white cloak she had worn was missing, leaving her only with her thin, hardly adequate tunic. Around one wrist was a shackle, its lock apparently twisted beyond opening by the blast that had earned her this fate. A short length of chain hung from it. An icy wind blew as the setting sun heralded the beginning of a long, cold night. The breeze chilled her, but what chilled her more were the deep furrows and crimson stains that littered the courtyard. There was little question what this place was, and even less question as to why she'd been brought here.

"Myranda Celeste!" came a booming voice from high in the stands surrounding the arena.

Her eyes shifted to the source, though the voice was unmistakable. General Bagu stood upon a balcony isolated from the crowd. Half of his face was a mass of black scars, a smooth black orb where his right eye should be. For a moment, Myranda questioned why he'd not healed himself. Could it be that they were especially vulnerable to their own magic? His thundering voice shattered her thoughts.

"You have been judged guilty of the crime of treason. You have fought against the soldiers of your homeland, and you are responsible for the deaths of two of the generals of the great Northern Alliance," he proclaimed, the crowd screaming for blood. "The penalty is death. However, though we value justice, we value strength still higher. You shall be subjected to trial by battle. If you prove yourself greater than any challenge we can put before you, you shall be allowed to live. Do you have anything to say before the trial begins?"

Myranda's eyes swept over the crowd. The hate they felt for her was palpable. She looked again to Bagu. To one side was Demont, a somewhat impatient look upon his face. Her own father, still clutching the halberd that inflicted Epidime upon him, stood to the other side.

"I have committed no treason. To commit treason, one must injure one's own nation, and I have none. The Northern Alliance is an army, and nothing more. A means to prolong a war. If I must die for resisting that, then so be it," she replied.

"So be it indeed. Let the trial begin!" Bagu decreed.

The doors at one end of the arena were thrown wide and a pair of the beasts Myranda had faced when she first encountered Bagu were released into the arena. Vast, gray approximations of wolves with stiff, stony hides covered in needle-sharp rocky spines, the beasts circled around her. Myranda looked quickly about. There was nothing. Not a weapon. Not a piece of cover. Magic was her only recourse.

She rushed to the wall, as far between the crystals as she could manage. Gathering her mind, she waited as the beasts circled together and charged at her. With a swift, monumental thrust of her mind, she wrenched one of the creatures into the air, one of Deacon's tricks. The heavy creature's momentum carried it into the wall behind her with a sickening crack. There was a rain of the spines that protruded from the creature's back as the beast dropped to the ground to struggle a few last times. After a final twitch, the beast crumbled into a pile of spikes and stones.

Myranda attempted to repeat the attack on the other creature. She managed to get it off of the ground, but the draw of the crystals robbed the spell of the strength it needed, sending the beast tumbling to the ground.

Myranda tried to gather herself for another attack, but the crystals drank everything she had before it could be put to purpose. It was as though the gems were able to attune themselves to her magic, something that they had never done before. There was no time for her to ponder this new discovery, however, as the creature had rolled to a stop and was struggling to get back to its feet. Running was useless, as it would quickly overtake her. With no other options, she ran toward the beast. Just as it got to its feet, Myranda jumped to the creature's neck, slashing one of her legs on one of the few spikes still intact after the tumble. She whipped the chain dangling from her wrist over the creature's neck and pulled it taut.

The wolf bucked, tossing her about like a rag doll, but Myranda held firm. Alas, while it could not throw her from its back, neither did the chain do even the slightest damage. Desperate, and knowing that if she were thrown free it would be the end of her, Myranda raised her hand and summoned a bolt of black magic. The bluish-black ball of crackling energy struck the beast on the head, bringing a sudden and complete end to its rampage. As it slid to a halt, Myranda dismounted.

The lingering aftermath of the attack was quickly drawn into the nearest crystal. Already it had taken on a discernible glow, and the others were not far behind. Myranda shook with anger. It was brilliant, in a terrible, sinister way. They had found a way to turn any outcome to their favor. If she fought, they would have her strength. If she didn't, they would have her life. As the doors began to creak open again, Myranda thought feverishly. There had to be a way out of this.

In the balcony, her tormentors looked on.

"I'm genuinely concerned about the selections you've made," Demont warned.

"I don't know. The spiked wolf has always been a favorite of mine," Epidime remarked.

"They are meant to be beasts of burden. The spines are defensive," Demont countered.

"It is not my intention to kill the girl quickly. We need to wring her out first," Bagu assured him. "When I feel she's given all that she is worth, then we shall end it."

"I don't see why we don't just kill her. Revision IV alone will satisfy our needs in just a few weeks more. We could kill this one, and the rest, and still be assured victory," Demont objected. "But, instead, you would prefer to waste several of my best creations."

Bagu turned to Demont. His scarred face bore a disquietingly collected expression, though the gleam in his eye screamed with rage.

"You've got a thing or two to learn about leadership. Disobedience must be dealt with quickly, harshly, and visibly," he said. "This world will shortly be ours. I intend to show its people what becomes of traitors."

The ground rumbled faintly. A line of churned-up earth traced its way slowly over the arena's floor. Easily a dozen more followed. Myranda knew the sight well. The worms that had protected Demont's fort. She held perfectly still. Last time, they only attacked when something shook the earth, even something as light as a footstep.

As the beasts wove intricate patterns along the ground, the riotous crowd quickly drew their attention. The creatures scattered, colliding with the stone wall--that, it would seem, continued well beneath the arena floor--and surfacing. They were as grotesque as she had remembered them. Horrid overlapping plates of leathery gray hide, with a blossom of snapping jaws at one end and a rapier tail on the other. They writhed briefly against the wall before plunging themselves into the earth as easily as if it were a pool of water.

Myranda held perfectly still, scouring at her mind for some semblance of a plan. They traced quick, ambling paths, crisscrossing the courtyard. The scraps of information were gathered together in her mind. Her spells would work, but only briefly, and at great expense. She would never be able to hold a spell of levitation long enough to clear the wall. Her eyes turned to the wall. It looked ancient, mortar and stone weathered to a smooth finish. Nothing even hinting at a finger hold. There would be no climbing it. What else was there?

As the randomly twisting paths drew ever nearer, her eyes darted urgently, dancing from wall to roaring crowd to churning earth to shattered spikes of fallen stone wolves . . . the spikes. A desperate, foolish, incomplete plan came together in her mind.

She held out a hand and conjured a quick tremor on the far side of the arena. Instantly the tunneling worms carved arrow-straight lines toward it. The ravenous crystals wasted no time drawing away the spell. The beasts reached their target and whipped themselves into a frenzy, churning the earth below the tremor into a rolling boil. The young wizard had taken barely a dozen ginger steps toward the remains of the wolves when the last of the spell was wicked away and the first of the worms turned to her.

With just a few more steps and no chance of another tremor to distract them, Myranda had no choice but to run. Some of the worms burst spindly legs from their sides, others dove below the surface and surged forward, but all rushed toward the girl amid a deafening roar of approval from the crowd. Myranda scooped up a pair of the spikes and threw herself at the wall. The stony tips bit into the mortar of the wall and held tenuously. With terror-fueled strength, Myranda hoisted her feet from the ground. The worms burst from the ground beneath her. They snapped with jaws strong enough to cleave stone and jabbed with sharp tongues. The ground below her was a cauldron of razor edges and needle points.

Myranda took a shaky hand from one spike to change her grip. As she did, the other twisted and drooped threateningly. She pulled herself higher, pushing down on the one well-planted spike and scrambling with her feet. Just above her was the point of impact that had cost the first wolf its life. A few spines had been driven deep into the stone of the wall. She whipped her hand up, yanking along the jangling chain that still hung from it, and closed her fingers around the nearest one. The cries for blood grew louder as she pulled herself further out of the reach of the creatures.

Above her, soldiers left their seats to peer down at the object of their hatred that infuriatingly refused to die. Humans spat at her, screaming incoherent profanities. Nearmen gazed with unthinking eyes hidden behind crude helmets, handcrafted instincts drifting to the surface of their minds.

The hero caught hold of another spike and held the shackled hand low, eying the downward-pointing barbs that lined the top of the wall. With measured precision, she swung the full length of the shackle's chain up. A handful of links tangled themselves in a barb, but the probing hands of the spectators struggled to dislodge it. The cocktail of custom-tailored thoughts that served as a mind for the one nearman finally coaxed it into action. The mindless creation climbed on the barbed wall and drew a sword as those around it cheered in approval.

The weapon came down, chipping away the barb that held Myranda's chain. He then looked down upon his target. The chunk of stone he broke free fell to the ground, driving the worms to new heights of frenzy. Their chaotic writhing shook the very wall. Myranda's grip barely held. The nearman's footing did not. As the helpless creation plummeted to the eager jaws of his fellow monstrosities, flinging his sword from his hands as he did, Myranda swung herself to the next spike. It was not nearly so firmly seated and pulled free from the wall, sending her tumbling to the ground again to land just a few paces away from the swarming worms.

The beasts were busy tearing apart the nearman, but not so busy that they did not take notice of this intriguing new set of vibrations. A pair peeled off from the rest and skittered with spidery speed toward her. Myranda ran, conjuring a short-lived flame before them that the beasts swept through without notice. Her eyes locked on the nearman's sword. It had speared itself into the ground just past the tangle of worms. The girl whirled the chain hanging from her wrist and lashed it at the ground to her left as she skidded to as stop. The worms shifted their path to the site of the impact and Myranda dove. She landed behind them and rolled to her feet, not missing a step. The beasts scratched to a stop and turned to follow, now digging into the earth.

A creak of metal and a flash of light signaled the nearman's end, rendering it nothing more than a pile of twisted armor and pale dust. No longer occupied, the remainder of the worms turned with great interest to the footfalls of the girl as she snatched up the sword on her sweep past.

Myranda flexed her mind. If she wanted this spell to be effective, it would have to be fast, and it would have to be strong. She pulled together most of what remained of her swiftly fading strength and formed it into a tight ball of enchantment. The timing had to be perfect. She reached the opposite wall and turned. All of the creatures were beneath the earth. She let the spell loose.

With the force of a week of blizzard focused into a single moment, a blast of cold splashed against the ground. The already-icy ground frosted over and solidified. It spread quickly, covering a growing blotch of the arena floor with white crystals of ice. The creatures fought to pull themselves from the ground. Some succeeded. Most did not, at best thrusting their heads out of the earth and letting loose unnatural squeals before falling silent and still. As a spell that should have had the force to freeze the whole of the arena three times over crept to a stop under the influence of the crystals, only three worms remained. Myranda tried to ignore the telltale dizziness warning her that she'd reached her limit and grasped the sword tightly.

The crystals stopped the spell, but they could not drink away its effects, as the icy ground remained frozen. Myranda raised the weapon high and brought it down on the first of the creatures, splitting its hide. She raised it again just in time to force it into the gaping maw of a second worm. A heartbeat later and it would have been her arm clamped in the beast's mandibles. As the mindless worm shook madly at the prize trapped in its jaws, the final beast threw itself upon her. Myranda raised her shackled wrist. The monster clamped down on it, buckling the metal and digging a deep gash into her forearm. She cried out and tore the arm free, the ruined shackle still in the worm's mouth.

The sight of blood drove the crowd into a frenzy that made that of the worms a moment ago seem tame in comparison. Myranda managed a sharp pull that slid the slicing edge of her sword along the mouth of the beast that clutched her blade. As it sliced one of the creature's many tongues, a white-hot streak of pain drove into its primitive brain. Its jaws opened. Myranda pulled the weapon back and ended the beast with a thrust. The final creature, curled around the shackle and tearing at the chain, met a similar end.

The blood fell in fat drops as Myranda stalked back toward the center of the arena, the crust of frozen earth crunching beneath her feet. She clutched at the wound. It was serious, but not fatal. It could wait. She continued toward the remains of the stone wolves and the nearman. The armor was ruined. No piece of it could be salvaged. She held in her hand the only weapon the soldier had carried. As the heavy wooden doors creaked open again, Myranda gathered up as many of the remaining spikes as she could find. There were only a few that were whole enough to be considered useful.

Now as armed as she could manage, Myranda turned to the doors. Emerging were three dragoyles. Their sizes varied greatly, each bearing scars from previous battles. Their wings had been clipped. In all likelihood, each had taken dozens of lives in arena battles over the years. They shifted their gaze to her. If Myranda had thought them capable of it, she would have sworn that the abominations looked eager.

Another time, fear would have clutched her mind. More than any other beast of Demont's creations, these creatures had been the face of her fear. They appeared like grim punctuation each time the D'karon flexed their might. Now, the girl looked coldly upon them. She was numb. There was no room for horror in her mind. There was simply no fear left. Memories rose through the increasingly dense fog of her mind. The beasts had a weakness . . . a very pronounced one. A single blow to the back of the throat would end them. It was the trick used to defeat Ether. It was the only hope she had to defeat them now.

The beasts charged her as one. She hurled both spikes she held at once. The projectiles, released with little force and no accuracy from an injured hand, soon redirected themselves and launched at her foes under the influence of her mind. One dragoyle chose that moment to snap its jaws open and attempt a gale of black mist. The spike ensured that it was the last mistake that the creature would make. The second spike drifted off course and drove itself into the ground as the crystals did their work. A shame, because this beast too had chosen the moment for a blast of miasma of its own. With nothing to prevent it, the beast billowed out a thick cloud of the corrosive stuff. A flail of Myranda's mind brought a whiff of wind that pushed the poison aside, just barely enough to miss her. As it sizzled and hissed at the ground, the pair of beasts finally reached her.

Myranda dove aside. One monster thundered past. Something that large moving that fast simply could not turn quickly enough to catch her, but that wasn't enough to stop it from trying. The result was an out of control tumble through the very puddle of venom it had sprayed down just heartbeats before. Alas, the second creature was nearly on target. It caught her with a swipe of its claw that hurled girl and sword through the air to collide painfully with the wall.

She coughed up a glob of blood and turned her blurred vision to the ground to search for her lost weapon as red and white sparks flared behind her eyes. The pounding approach of the creature that struck her rang in her aching head as her fingers closed around the grip of the sword once more. Her ailing eyes brought her a doubled view of the beast when she finally turned back to it. The rising cries of the crowd were a distant hum, like something underwater. Everything around her was moving in long, drawn-out streaks, stretching and twisting as the flow of time slowed to a trickle. She hadn't mind enough to think anymore, her actions instead driven by instinct, luck, and fate. The tip of the blade was raised. The beast's mouth was not open, but the beast did not slow.

When the creature finally reached her, it could not slow itself. She thrust out the sword and released it, rolling to the side with the same motion. The tip just barely breached the creature's thick hide as the beast continued on momentum alone toward the wall. The pommel of the sword struck the wall, and a moment later, the tip burst from the back of the beast's neck, driven through like a nail. The collision with the wall shook the whole of the arena. A moment later, the monster sprang backward. Its uncontrolled death knells sent it in lurching spasms toward its partner. The other abomination, still sizzling from its roll in the miasma and unsteady on its feet, was rocked by the clash.

Myranda's senses crept back to her as she struggled to her feet. The impaled beast twitched once more and was still. The only remaining dragoyle climbed weakly from the ground. Sizzling clumps of acid-soaked earth clung to its skin. A splash or whiff of the black breath had no effect on the dragoyles. The same could not be said for prolonged exposure, it seemed. It took a few halting steps as Myranda limped cautiously away from the wall. Finally, it collapsed.

The hero took stock of herself as she trudged to the center of the arena. Her eyes stubbornly refused to focus. A steady and constant ring was all her ears offered her. From the feel of it, her shoulder and perhaps one of her ribs had been broken. Thoughts flickered in her tattered mind--if she had strength enough for another spell, it would certainly be her last one.

She turned her head slowly, the brilliant glow of the well-fed crystals making it to her mind as bright blue blotches in a blur of gray. A breath dragged a fair amount of blood along with it as it swirled into her lungs and rushed quickly out again as an agonized cough. She was out of strength, out of time--and no doubt out of luck, as well.

Bagu smiled as he watched Myranda stand unsteadily. The time had come. He motioned to a nearby guard. Somewhere far below the stands there was the rumble of a sliding gate.

Out of the corner of her eye, Myranda saw motion near the other door. Until now, her tormentors had been unleashed upon her from the gates below the privileged seats of the generals. She shuffled until she was facing the massive wooden door. It crept open inch by inch. Low, tooth-rattling rumbles came from behind the door. They were sounds that seemed to reverberate off of the very sky and shake the air in her lungs. Sounds that spoke volumes of size, of ferocity.

In a dizzying blur of motion, the doors were thrown wide as something massive burst through them, its patience at an end. Myranda's vision chose that moment to begin to clear. Whatever it was, it was massive. Larger than the three dragoyles combined. Its shape was the same. The image grew gradually less fuzzy. A massive neck craned high into the air. Wings like the sails of a ship unfurled; one was whole, the other hung in shreds. Finally, the last of the haze drifted from her vision. This was not mockery, nor imitation. What towered before her was a dragon of nature's design. Onyx-black scales armored its belly, smooth, with a faint gold sheen. The scales of its back were black, mottled with streaks of the darkest crimson.

Myranda dropped to her knees. There was no use fighting now. Let it end--but let it end quickly. All she could do was hold onto the last glimmer of magic she had. That, at least, the D'karon would not have. The monstrous beast thundered toward her, the very world seeming to quake with every step. She closed her eyes. A few more titanic footsteps came, then a sound like a dozen plows being dragged through the unwilling ground at once. Myranda tensed. A rush of air knocked her backward. She hit the ground.

There was nothing. Complete stillness. Even the roar of the crowd faded to utter silence. Oblivion. Deep in the back of her mind, Myranda questioned why. Why, if her end had come, if she'd been thrust into the void, did the pain of her mortal form persist? Why even in death did she feel the warm trickle of blood down her arm? Then a hot wind rushed over her. A very real wind. She opened her eyes.

The head of the creature, the terrifying face every bit as large as Myranda's whole body, hung over her, staring down. Another breath heaved from its nostrils and washed over her.

As she waited for the horrible mouth to snap open and bring the end she thought had already come, her mind recoiled in anger. Those eyes . . . The torturous life she'd been forced to endure was bad enough, but what demented agent of fate would mock her in her final moment with them? How could the monster that killed her have such beautiful eyes? Delicate slits in deep gold irises. Eyes that seemed so emotional. Eyes that seemed so insistent. Eyes that seemed so familiar. Those eyes . . .

She felt her mouth begin to move, a foolish hope fighting its way to her lips. Myranda tried to pull it back. It was too late.

"Myn?" she whispered.

The eyes were suddenly alight with ecstasy. The mighty creature threw back its massive head and released a roar that was overflowing with the joy of reunion. Both minds were flooded with powerful emotions and endless questions--but, for this moment, joy washed them all aside. Myn dropped her massive head down for Myranda to scratch. The injured girl tried to reach the spot atop her old friend's head but couldn't. The golden eyes turned to her again expectantly, now seeming for the first time to see the state her friend was in. Myn drew in a breath that carried with it the acrid scent of Myranda's blood. The eyes changed. Fury surged up from within. She turned her gaze to the generals. They shot each other looks of anger and accusation.

Finally, Bagu's voice raised.

"All of you! Attack! Kill them both!" he ordered.

The soldiers of the audience instantly leapt to their feet. They flowed like a tide over the walls and into the pit. The dragon's massive maw erupted with flame that licked the ground and pushed back the soldiers. A low sweep with her tail cleared the area behind her. Taking a step forward so that Myranda was directly beneath her, she continued to defend her friend.

Myranda's aching mind pushed her confusion and joy aside. There would be time for that later. For now, they had to escape. Her vision was filled with Myn's black-gold belly scales. Around the edge, lit by the orange light of a burst of flame, she saw the tattered remains of her left wing. A spell hurled by Bagu splashed across Myn's hide and she recoiled in pain.

Myranda didn't know if she had the strength left, but it was her absolute last hope. She swept together the scraps of her spirit and sculpted a healing spell. Slowly, the shreds of leathery flesh began to pull together. The crystals tore hungrily at the spell, but Myranda continued. Darkness began to creep in around her. She struggled to keep her mind about her as the last of the ruined wing became whole.

Myn flapped her restored wings. Gale-force winds swept over the soldiers, knocking them to the ground. Long unused muscles worked like never before. The dragon scooped up her dazed companion and leapt with all of the force her massive legs could muster. She rose skyward and set her eyes on the horizon.

Icy wind rushed past Myranda as she struggled to keep her loose grasp on consciousness. Rooftops, treetops, and open field streaked by her half-lidded eyes and shrank into specks below her. The dark sky and Myn's dark form blended. The only sounds were the whistling of wind, the heaving of breath, and the leathery flap of wings.

It wasn't long before the sound of other leathery wings joined in. Myn peered back. Keen eyes spotted the forms of a veritable fleet of dragoyles among the darkness. She wheeled and soared high into the clouds. The black beasts followed. Soon the world was a haze of gray as they swept through the very clouds. Drawing on instincts developed over generations, Myn maneuvered blindly yet precisely until the vast flock of dragoyles was ahead of her. She could have then dropped below the clouds and made her way to safety. She had other plans.

These men had stolen her away. They had held her, tortured her, changed her. They had hurt her friend. Escape was the last thing on her mind. She drew in close and puffed up her chest. An intense column of flame blasted from her mouth, roasting the riders of half a dozen of their attackers. The others scattered and wheeled. She was twice the size of the largest of them. None lasted long against her. Slashes of claws, whips of her tail, blasts of flame, and devastating snaps of her jaws made short, vicious work of every last pursuer.

The dragon continued onward until the first rays of the sun peeked over the mountains. With the brightening sky, the clever beast knew that it would not be difficult to spot her. She picked out a dense stand of trees and touched down on the ground. As gently as a mother caring for one of her own, Myn placed the shivering form of Myranda on the ground. She sniffed nervously at Myranda. The young wizard tried to pat the creature reassuringly, but she could not stop herself from trembling. The massive creature stood over her ailing friend and lowered herself carefully to the ground, folding her claws over the human's form and gingerly pulling her closer in a sort of embrace. When Myranda was properly nestled in her grasp, Myn let loose a burst of flame.

Myranda could feel the heat rush through Myn's veins, taking the chill instantly from her. Surrounded utterly by her friend, hearing only the distant, deep thump of the massive creature's powerful heart, Myranda, for the first time in ages, felt something she thought she would never feel again. She felt safe. She drifted into a deep, exhausted sleep.

Myn released what could only be described as a sigh of contentment as she felt the tiny form of Myranda slip into slumber. A deep, fundamental happiness filled her as she too drifted into a blissful sleep, finally whole again.

#

Deep in the capital, far to the north, a feeble old man sat in a large, ornate chair. On his head was the crown that had been worn by his forefathers, the Crown of Three Kingdoms. For two generations now, it had been the only crown of the north. It was the very one that had adorned the head of the King of Vulcrest on the fateful day when he lost his life just a few paces too far south and began this endless war. Rescuing it from the Tressons had been the first--and, in many ways, the last--great triumph for his people in this war. Now it sat on his head. To his people, it was the symbol of his power. For the sake of hope, they were allowed to believe it.

Within the castle walls, though, there was no doubt where the true power could be found.

The great doors of the entryway were pulled open by the team of masked soldiers who stood guard. Through the towering doorway passed a small, meticulously-dressed man, a pair of silver staffs adorning his back and glinting with the gleam of gems. The king watched in silence as the man known to him as General Demont marched through the great hall. The sound of his purposeful footsteps echoed off of the vaulted ceiling of a hall designed to be the site of vast celebrations. Save for the occasional honored funeral, it had been unused since the coronation. The general, a stern look in his eye, quickened his pace, walking past the king without so much as a glance. A few steps more brought him to a door.

Demont opened the door, finding the room beyond pitch-black. He closed the door behind him. A dozen candles hissed to life, casting their yellow glow on the form of Bagu, his face a scarred mass of anger. His eyes gazed intently at a massive sand timer. An unnatural, halting stream of grains tumbled toward the bottom. Only a few healthy palmfuls of sand had yet to fall. Whatever the device measured, it was nearing its end.

"Well," he said, fury dripping from the word as it left his mouth.

"The dragoyle riders were defeated. Myranda is out of our grasp," Demont said.

Bagu's fingers locked around the arm of his chair, the wood groaning under his grasp.

"A Chosen one . . . just seconds from death, has escaped. What do you have to say for yourself?" the senior general fumed.

"What do *I* have to say for myself? This is none of my doing!" Demont objected.

"None of your doing? You had in your stables a dragon that belonged to the Chosen One, and you didn't think it was worth mentioning!? You allow me to reunite a divine warrior with a powerful ally and the resulting escape is none of your doing!?" Bagu raged.

"If the intelligence provided by your precious Epidime is to be trusted, then that could not possibly have been the Chosen One's dragon. She traveled with an infant dragon, the size of a dog. The beast my creatures brought back to me was adolescent if anything, nearly full-grown. There can be no confusion on that matter. And as for allowing you to unite them, *I* warned you *not* to use the black dragon. It was not a weapon, it was a target! A brute! A blunt instrument! I plucked that beast from nature and shaped it to my needs to serve as fodder for proving my beasts. It was never under control. It was never *meant* to be controlled. This is on *your* head. You were the one who wanted an example made of her," Demont stated.

Bagu released a long, angry noise somewhere between sigh and hiss.

"Can you track the beast?" he asked.

"Faintly, and not at all if she manages to remove the enhancements," Demont replied.

"She will seek to free the others. Have you recovered the soul gem from the other human?" Bagu asked.

"The largest piece, yes."

"Kill him."

"We've not yet located the smaller piece. Without his aid"

"Kill him!" Bagu demanded.

". . . as you wish," Demont relented.

#

Elsewhere, another figure navigated a large, dimly-lit tunnel. There was an overpowering stench of brimstone, and a thick coat of soot clung to every surface. Ahead, a faint glow signaled the end of the path. Desmeres approached a nearman, his face undisguised and his hands gripping a staff that marked him as one of the rare, spellcasting variety. It was guarding a web of bars that crisscrossed the tunnel with no apparent door.

After flashing a medallion emblazoned with a handful of indecipherable symbols, the creature gave a nod. The staff was raised and the web seemed to come alive, shifting and twisting like a family of serpents until the way was opened. Twice more he was forced to reveal the medallion and await the parting of bars before he finally reached a large, natural cavern. The air was thick with smells that burned the nose and stung the eyes, and combined with the stifling heat it made it difficult to breathe. A channel had been carved into the stone floor of the cavern, from which an ominous red glow radiated. Thin black wisps of evil-smelling fumes hinted at what lie at its bottom. The channel formed a ring around an irregular shaped stone spire that jutted up from the molten rock below.

Attached to the spire was an assassin.

Lain's hands and feet were not secured to the stone. Instead, they seemed to disappear into it, as though the spire had swallowed them and hardened. His head hung limply, his chest painfully drawing in the occasional wheezing breath. The telltale lines of a whip's lash stripped his flesh. Wounds trickled, and blood-soaked bandages cocooned the upper part of his chest and one shoulder. As Desmeres approached the edge of the channel, the head lifted to show faded, cloudy eyes that tried and failed to identify his blurry form. A weak sniff brought nothing but fumes that burned at the lungs.

"It is me, Lain. Desmeres," he said solemnly.

Lain's form shuddered almost imperceptibly at the sound of the name.

"It . . . looks as though they have finally found a cell you can't escape from," he remarked, venturing a peek at the magma shifting along the distant floor of the channel over which Lain hung.

A painful breath left Lain.

"You and I knew it would end this way for one of us. It will please you to know that you did manage to teach them their lesson. I was paid in full for my services," Desmeres said.

"You won't live long enough to spend it," Lain wheezed.

"No one could live long enough to spend that much gold," he replied.

"Why did you come here?"

"We spent seventy years as partners, Lain. I owe you at least a final visit," Desmeres answered.

A raking cough shook Lain.

". . . the others?" Lain asked.

"Captured. All of them," Desmeres stated. "Although . . ."

Lain's eyes shifted to him.

"They don't trust me, Lain. As is to be expected. They only tell me what they think I need to know. Still, it would take a fool to miss the fact that something is going on. Troops are moving, reinforcing forts. It must be the forts where the others are kept. They are all being carefully protected . . ." Desmeres explained, stopping suddenly.

His eyes turned to a half-seen form in the shadows, then to the bandages on Lain's chest.

"Everyone except for you . . . Something has happened and it has got them worried. I've got a feeling that they will soon have a new task for me. Hopefully, it will be a few days more before they contact me. I've nearly finished some . . . items. Things my wife convinced me to make. It would be a shame if they moldered in one of the storehouses rather than finding some use," Desmeres mused.

Lain released another breath and let his head lower once more.

"Well. I'd best try to find what there is to find about this final Chosen. I don't suppose we will meet again. Good luck to you," Desmeres said.

He quickly set off, his back tingling with expectation for a blade.

#

Elsewhere, under a slowly brightening sky, Myranda stirred. Even after a short day and a long night, the black pit of sleep was slow to let the world in. As her mind crept back to her, thoughts clashed. She knew that she was outside, but why was she so warm? She knew that she could scarcely be in any more danger, but why wasn't she afraid? Her eyes opened and beheld the answer. Myn was already awake. She held Myranda carefully against her, all the while keeping a vigilant watch with every available sense. Myranda pushed gently at the grip and the dragon obligingly released it. The shock of cold air that reached her now that she was no longer protected swept the last trace of sleep from her mind.

The dragon stood, its head rising to nearly the treetops. As the young wizard's eyes shifted over the unfamiliar features of an old friend, the dragon suddenly remembered that it had been ages since she had performed her most cherished of duties. Instantly, she vanished into the woods, heedless of Myranda's calls for her to stop. The enthusiasm of the bounding steps was the first thing, save the eyes, that Myranda truly recognized about her friend. Trees swayed like tall grass, accompanied by a creaking and snapping tumult that retreated quickly into the distance. In barely a moment, the earth trembled with Myn's return, a deer clutched in her massive jaws. She dropped it on the ground before Myranda and looked about for a pile of wood to light. Seeing none and growing impatient, she turned to a sizable young tree and, with frightening ease, reduced it to splinters. The act took the merest swat of her massive claws. No sooner had the pile of wood settled than a blast of flame set it alight.

Myranda looked in awe at the results of Myn's traditional morning errands scaled up to her new size. As the glow of the vastly excessive fire cast its dancing light on the trees around her, Myranda's mind began to work. She would need something warm to wear, and quickly. For now, she brought a few spells to mind to take the edge off of the cold that the fire had not. Her stomach reminded her vocally that she was well overdue for a meal, and the fact that a suitable candidate now lay beside her greatly amplified its complaints. That could wait a bit more. The gash that the worms had torn in her arm had been reduced to an abrasion, and her ribs and shoulder were sore but no longer broken. There were any number of things about her body that could have benefited from immediate attention, but none needed it.

In short, she was in terrible shape, but not in danger. This was fortunate, because even if she had been at death's door, there was something else that was far more important to her right now. She took a few steps back and looked at Myn.

The dragon was massive, larger than her mother had been on the fateful day of her birth. Her scales, her claws, even the inside of her mouth were black as night. Here and there, a gleam of gold or a streak of red fought valiantly to be seen, but the black by far overpowered them. There were things about her that were out of scale. Muscles bulged in her forelegs and neck. Her claws were long and cruel. In her great mouth, the teeth ran the gamut from stiletto-sized spikes to stout, triangular, white spearheads. Each was accented with barbs that hinted that they would not so much slice into something as tear into it. The row of scales that ran along her spine seemed to have grown and twisted into a vicious serration. At the tip of her tail was a veritable morningstar of spiked scales.

Every inch of her was a weapon now.

"Myn . . . my dear, sweet little Myn . . . what did they do to you?" Myranda whispered painfully.

The beast lowered its great head, easily as large as Myranda. The young wizard wrapped her arms around the noble beast's neck as best she could and squeezed tight, tears rolling down her cheeks. Myn lowered herself to the ground and angled her head pleadingly. Myranda knew what she wanted. She reached over the dragon's head and rubbed and massaged as best she could without cutting her hands to ribbons. Myn shuddered in ecstasy, her long, powerful tail lashing about and putting deep gashes in any tree unlucky enough to be in its path.

Suddenly, Myranda's fingers found their way to something that should not be there. It was cold and rough. The flesh around it was swollen and tender, so much so that Myn pulled away at even the light touch of the human's fingers. Myranda tried to get a good look, but it was as black as the scales and hard to make out. Still, she tried. It was certainly metal. There seemed to be a row of recessed holes around its rim, with metal studs protruding from them. It reminded Myranda very much of a horseshoe, save for the fact that the shape continued until it met in a point. As the light of the fire and the strengthening sun fell upon its surface, Myranda could just make out some crudely-carved runes. Even to her still-recovering mind, the object resonated with magic.

In the gaping center of the ring-like ornament on the dragon's head, the flesh seemed pitted and burned. There was a residue of something, something that burned at Myranda's fingers. It could have been dragon blood, which stung quite a bit where it touched her sensitive flesh, but Myranda instantly knew that it wasn't. Dragon blood didn't burn like this. This burning didn't stop at her fingers. She could feel it in her soul, tugging and twisting at it. This was the work of the D'karon.

"Myn . . . this . . . thing here. It hurts you, doesn't it?" Myranda asked.

The beast's eyes turned to her with a clear affirmative.

"And *they* put it on your head, didn't they?" Myranda continued.

Again, it was clearly so.

"This is going to hurt, but it has to be done. Hold still, I am going to remove it," Myranda said.

Myn carefully pressed herself against the ground. The dragon's eyes flinched and shut tight as Myranda's fingers probed the edges. The wizard tried to cast a spell to soothe the beast's pain and put her to sleep, but the amulet affixed to her head seemed to turn the spell away. The tingling burn in her fingers grew quickly past the threshold of pain as she found a grip and pulled. The whole of Myn's body shook.

Amid the burning of her fingers, a sharp, stabbing pain in her palm accompanied each tug. She could feel the enchantment reacting to her, trying to tighten its grip as she struggled against it. The metal lifted away slightly, releasing a trickle of blood. It was a mixture of black and red, as though the D'karon's modifications ran through her very veins. The pain in her palm was constant now, and the burning intensified everywhere the blood touched. Myn dug her claws into the icy ground, just barely managing to stop a roar of pain in her throat.

Myranda could feel the spells associated with the piece coiling up her arm, attempting to work its terrible effects on her as well. Before her eyes, streaks of black wound under her skin, along her veins. Her far-from-recovered mind was ill-equipped to force them away. Her clawing at the metal grew more desperate. Myn jerked in pain and the piece slipped from her fingers. Panic began to creep up Myranda's spine, and panic is the enemy of concentration. Desperate thoughts flickered through her mind. She needed a better vantage, and a better grip.

Quickly, the wizard climbed to the dragon's neck and redoubled her efforts. She felt a low, rattling growl of pain from her friend. The metal slipped a bit more. The studs that so resembled nails on a horseshoe revealed themselves to be just that, driven brutally into the agonized dragon's hide, and likely into the bone beneath. Each fraction of an inch that the nails slipped out translated into a shudder of pain and an excruciating hiss. The pain ran up to Myranda's shoulder.

The blood was a steady flow now. The sight of it sickened her. As she tugged at the piece, she could swear she saw flashes of white and violet light pulsing and sparking. She closed her eyes.

Myn fought desperately against her urges. She knew that this creature on her neck was her friend, and that she caused such pain only because she had to. She knew that Myranda was trying to help her. Unfortunately, a wild beast's instincts are strong. They run deep, and they speak with a loud voice. Right now, that voice boomed in her mind. It screamed that she was in danger, that she had to remove the cause of this pain. When one of the nails slipped free from her flesh, the voice finally became too much to ignore.

The dragon burst to her feet. In one smooth, reflex-driven motion, Myn threw her head to the side. If Myranda had been prepared, she might have been able to hold on. As it was, she was fully devoted to freeing her friend of this affliction. Both of her hands were locked about the metallic piece. The motion shook her from the dragon's neck, but did not break her grip. As her body flew through the air, the piece followed, swiftly breaking free and soaring through the air with the dislodged wizard.

The next moment seemed to last an hour. A white-hot bolt of pain shot up Myranda's arm. The same terrible pain drove into Myn's head. A gout of pure black blood poured from Myn's wound, and the air around her began to sizzle and crackle. The black that stained her hide began to draw together and intensify. It looked like vines rooted at her forehead and snaking along her body. They swiftly retreated backward, looping upward into the air in places and dissolving into a thickening black mist about the flailing dragon.

The moment ended with a powerful crack as Myranda's trip through the air ended suddenly due to a collision with a tree. The wind rushed from her lungs, and the world dimmed and blurred. The black, bloodied bit of metal slipped from her fingers and continued in an odd, spinning trajectory into the woods. Myranda dropped to the ground, with the now-familiar pain of a rib being re-broken throbbing in her side.

Her eyes turned to Myn. The massive form was lost in a cloud of black, appearing only as a flash of wing, a hint of snout, or a lash of tail, all thrashing in pain. The frenzy subsided slowly, until finally it was still. The black mist thinned.

Myranda tried to focus her eyes on the red and yellow blur before her. As her reluctant eyes recovered from the encounter with the tree, she slowly saw the results of the short but intense struggle. Myn's coloring was restored. With the notable exception of a black stain where the piece had been, her ruby red and golden yellow scales gleamed in all of their former glory. Her features had returned to the familiar, elegant, natural ones, as well. Her size, however, was another matter. She was no longer the hulking monstrosity that they had turned her into, but neither was she the little creature Myranda had thought she'd failed to save all of that time ago. As the dragon stood, her head rose to easily thrice Myranda's height, and from snout to tail she was ten paces if she was an inch. Truly, she was the spitting image of her mother.

The young wizard's mouth hung open in awe as she looked over her old friend as if for the first time. Perhaps it was because she'd been so changed, but the shock of having her friend back from the dead had not struck Myranda before. Now, tears poured from her eyes as she ran to the beast and wrapped her arms tightly about the base of her neck.

"Oh, Myn. It has been so long. I never thought I would see you again. If only you could speak. I want to know every detail," she cried joyfully.

As her teary eyes opened again, looking over the beast's shoulder, she saw what she believed to be a residual blot of black staining Myn's left wing. No . . . It was too defined for that. It seemed deliberate, intricate. In fact, it looked vaguely like . . .

Myranda wiped her eyes and looked again. The words "it can't be" offered themselves in her mind but were quickly dismissed. A sane person would have spoken them aloud without a second thought. Perhaps a year ago she would have whispered them. Perhaps yesterday she would have considered them. After all that she'd been through, all that she'd seen, those words would never mean the same thing. Today, there was nothing that could not be. What she saw was real. Her beloved dragon had returned from death's door. She had managed decades of growth in a few months. And now, like an insignia on a sail, Myn's wing bore the crisp, black curves of the Mark. The same mark that had been on the sword. The same mark that appeared on Myranda's hand, Ether's head, and the chests of Ivy and Lain. The Mark of the Chosen.

Myranda released Myn's neck and took a few steps back, paralyzed by the torrent of thoughts wrestling for control in her mind. The memories of that terrible day rushed back to her. She'd tried to pull Myn's soul back from the brink. Something had stopped her . . . some power. Then Oriech spoke to her that day; he revealed her role to her. He spoke of the Great Convergence. The pieces slowly assembled themselves.

Myn, the pain subsiding and the world, seeming a bit larger, perhaps, but otherwise as it should be, looked upon Myranda with curiosity. She seemed distant, distracted. The dragon couldn't know what the trouble was, but she tried her best to work it out. Myranda was hungry. She had to be. Yet, for some reason, she did not prepare her meal as she always did. Myn looked about, quickly realizing that Myranda had no means to do so. There was no knife, and neither was there a bag to conceal one. Surely that was the reason. Convinced she'd gotten to the root of the problem, Myn took the job into her own claws. She'd watched the human ready similar beasts to be put over the fire many times before.

The wizard did not notice the somewhat indelicate task being performed before her. She was too deep in her own thoughts. Oriech had pulled her aside to speak of the convergence at that moment for a reason. It had just passed. If Myn was truly the fifth Chosen One, then surely he would have spoken to her before. Surely, he would have shown himself at the moment they had first joined. Unless it was not until she'd been killed that she had been chosen.

The three signs of the Chosen worked their way into her mind. Certainly the dragon was pure of soul, and she already knew that one didn't need to bear the mark on the surface to be Chosen. That only left divinity of birth.

The words of Oriech echoed in her head. They were odd, specific, and deliberate. "Your existence in this world must simply be the work of the direct will of the divine." Could it be that the massive power that had swept Myn from her grasp had been the will of the gods? "The Quickening" affected different people in different ways. Perhaps, in the hands of the gods, Myn had been coaxed into her prime instantly. The explanation was desperate, hopelessly complex, and stretched the rules until they screamed, but it fit.

Far from satisfied, Myranda reluctantly accepted her own explanation and finally took notice of Myn's handiwork. She'd done a remarkably delicate job of separating the beast, though the result was still a bit stomach-turning in its appearance. Myranda plucked up a piece of the meat, prepared it, and consumed it. Myn snapped up the rest. With the hunger dealt with, she looked over the blaze before her, and the pitch-black column rising into the sky. It was a miracle that the whole of the forest had not been consumed in flame by now. Reluctantly, she drew her mind to the task of extinguishing it. The fire gradually died out under her will, leaving a pile of charred wood she could not hope to conceal.

By the time the flames had flickered their last, Myranda could already feel her mind fatigued again, and the chill was creeping into her bones. A spell or two warded off the cold for the time being, and she scanned her surroundings. Nothing seemed familiar. For a moment, she wondered how she could have traveled to this place and not know where it was. Then she remembered the flight. It seemed like a dream. Her eyes turned to the sky. If they could fly . . . then it didn't truly matter where they were, only where they wanted to go. There were two rather severe difficulties, though. First, there could be no hope of entering a town now. Myn simply could not be hidden. Second, unless they flew above the clouds, they could not travel by day. Likewise, nights with a strong moon would present threats of discovery as well.

Discovery. Myranda looked to the column of smoke as it tapered off. Perhaps at night it would not have been noticed staining the sky, but night was gone and day was quickly taking its place. If there was a town anywhere nearby, they had no doubt already seen it. Briefly, Myranda considered conjuring up a rush of wind in hopes of scattering it, but the idea was quickly dismissed. After all, if a sudden and clearly mindful gust of wind perfectly scattered the smoke before someone's eyes, it would bring armed men more surely than the smoke alone. Besides, if she was going to be relying solely on magic to keep her warm, and without the aid of a staff, she would need all of the strength she could spare.

Myranda realized that Myn was looking impatiently at her friend. The young wizard settled to the ground and leaned against a tree near the smoldering remains of the fire. Myn thumped heavily to the ground and gently dropped her head onto Myranda's lap. It was nearly as large as her whole body had been prior to her divine growth spurt. Myranda stroked her head.

"We've got to find them, Myn. Lain, Ivy, Ether, and Deacon are out there, somewhere. If we are lucky, they are still alive. They are going to be under heavy guard, and I have no weapons. I have no staff. I don't even have proper clothing. But I have you. It may just be enough," she whispered.

Closing her eyes, Myranda worked at one of the spells Deacon had taught her, a spell of detection that would not draw the attention of the D'karon. It was different from the one she'd developed on her own. It was less broad, more targeted. Rather than looking upon the whole of the area at once, she focused intently on a small region that shifted and slid along, drawn weakly toward whomsoever one sought, something akin to looking at a map through a keyhole. The greatest challenge of the spell was keeping oneself from succumbing to frustration. Most trying was the fact that Myranda did not search at all, but had to attune herself to her target and allow her mind to be drawn to it.

Slowly, deliberately, Myranda set her mind adrift on the breezes and eddies of the spiritual plane. One by one, she shifted her thoughts to each of her friends. She began with Lain. Her consciousness bobbed lightly on the sea of the mind, patiently awaiting the lightest tug, the weakest current to guide her. None came. Reluctantly, she shifted her aim to Ether, bracing herself, ready for a surge. When she continued to feel nothing but the weak push and pull of the worn, defeated souls of her countrymen, her heart dropped.

Ether's soul was powerful, blindingly so, and she never concealed it. Even when she was weak, it shone like a beacon to the mind. Now there was not a whisper, not a glimmer.

She turned her mind to Ivy. Myranda had found her mind before. It had been after one of her transformations. She had been weak then, and still her mind had smoldered, bright and clear. Now there was nothing but a galaxy of broken spirits drifting though the void.

Myranda fought thoughts from her mind. Could it be? Had they been killed? No. She'd found Myn even after her soul left her body. They were being hidden somehow. Her focus began to waver as fatigue set in. She'd hardly recovered since the ordeal in the arena, and without her staff, she had to work twice as hard at the concentration. The icy-cold wind that swept around her body was beginning to filter through to her mind.

Suddenly there was a flash, like a bolt of lightning. A brilliant gold sparkle in the distance. It shifted to a still-brighter red--then, just as suddenly, vanished. It was sharp, pure, and unmistakable. It was Ivy. Myranda locked onto the indistinct point in the distance where the intense light had pulsed. In the ever-shifting currents of the astral plane, it was maddening, but she could not fail. Everything hinged upon this. She had to succeed.

In her mind, she felt the cold, dark valleys of the north slide slowly beneath her. Another flash came, this time beginning in red and ending in gold. She crept closer. Finally, she came upon something she'd never felt before. There was a sharp, penetrating cold and a deep, fundamental darkness. Not a spark of warmth. Not a flicker of light. Not a whisper of life. She pulled together all of the concentration she could muster to scour for some trace of a soul. She felt something like a heat. She drew her mind closer.

Then it came. An eruption of gold. Myranda could feel the power rush over her like a tidal wave. It permeated her spirit, infusing it and surrounding it. She felt every ounce of strength she had lost pulse, powerful and alive in her very core. Then it shifted to red, and the nourishing warmth turned to a searing heat. She was boiling in an ocean of crimson light that threw her back.

Myranda's eyes shot open. The chill should have taken its toll on her, but all she felt was the heat. Her hand sizzled against the snow as she climbed to her feet. The tree she had leaned upon was black and smoking. After a lengthy search, her mind should be in tatters, but it was sharp as it had ever been. The period of gradually coming to terms with the physical world again was absent, unnecessary. For a fraction of a moment, her mind had touched that of Ivy, sharing some fraction of the power she flowed with during one of the outbursts. It was awesome in the purest meaning of the word. Her eyes turned to the sky. The sun was doing its best to break through the near-constant clouds overhead, and was having brushes with success at some points, turning thin patches of gray clouds a brilliant white. If they flew now, they would surely be seen. If they didn't . . .

Myranda climbed atop Myn's back. There was no choice. They had to move now, while their target was still fresh in her mind. While the strength lent to her, purposely or not, was still coursing through her veins. The mighty creature could feel her excitement. She took a few steps and thrust herself into the air, massive wings unfurling and catching the wind. Myn rose into the sky, circling ever higher.

"That way. West. And hurry!" Myranda proclaimed.

Myn shifted smoothly, her movements fluid and graceful, as though she had been born in the air. Myranda's eyes were wide as the sights that had rushed past her in a blur the night before now found their way into a mind that could truly appreciate them. Forbidding forests and treacherous plains became gray, green, and white patches on an endless painting. Icy rivers became ribbons of silver. Where once there had been half-deserted cities, now there were intricate patterns of streets and buildings, laid out like carvings.

It was a view of wonder, of beauty. No wonder the gods made their home in the sky. From here, all of the fear, all of the sorrow sunk away. There was only freedom. Even the icy chill of the wind seemed far away, so tightly did the spectacle seize her mind.

Myranda tried to imagine herself on the ground, looking up. How small did they seem? A vague form, perhaps mistaken by all but the keenest eyes for a bird? She could only hope. There was a long way to go. Even as hours of travel swept below her in minutes, the place Myranda felt Ivy's spirit struggling was far. She did not know what she would find. She could not plan. All she could do was drink in the peace, breathe deeply of the thin air, and watch as the setting of her life drifted by beneath her in miniature. She saw the thread-thin roads that connected the towns, the same roads she had trudged down since she was a little girl. She saw the

Low Lands. The sheer size of Ravenwood took on a new meaning at this height. It dwarfed cities. Even the mountainside seemed to be little more than the beach on a frosty green sea.

#

Below, the atmosphere in the cities was growing steadily worse. War brings with it a tension. It permeates the mind of every man, woman, and child. In time, though, the tension becomes first tolerable, then comfortable. A constant in a world with so few of them, it can be relied upon. Just as the mind comes to accept it, though, so too does it become sensitive to it. The slightest change is amplified. News of a battle gone badly can almost be felt before it arrives. Messages of lost loved ones seldom come as a surprise. It is intangible, indescribable, but undeniable. Those things that affected the war affected the people, and made themselves known to the people without words. And something indeed was affecting the war.

People paced uneasily in the streets, gazing into the fields at patrols moving too quickly, and too early. Black carriages strayed from their solemn routes. Large groups of very quiet soldiers passed through towns, stopping for neither food nor rest. Black forms in the skies . . . Until recently stories of them were rare and easily dismissed. Now they were frequent and detailed. Creatures like twisted dragons sweeping through the sky in formations. The keen of eye swore they saw men on their backs. And then there were the tales from Fallbrook. The town was ravaged. A swath of the main street bore still visible scars from some manner of substance observers claimed burned without fire. Buildings were left in ruins. The black dragons had been there, the quiet soldiers, the empty cloaks. All under the command of the generals.

And there were others . . . Wizards, malthropes, and an elemental popped up in accounts of the carnage. Tales differed greatly, and no one completely believed them. There was one thing for certain, though. Something was happening. Something important.

#

Perhaps it was the strength that was thrust upon her during her search, perhaps it was the anticipation, but Myranda could still feel the power crackling through her. Hours had passed and the day had long ago given way to night. Myn had flown without rest for these many hours, and she was showing no sign of fatigue.

Myranda gently refreshed a spell against the cold. The air was biting, to be sure, but not nearly so dangerously as it had when the flight had begun. They were quite far south now, and quite far west, farther than Myranda had been in years. Just at the edge of her vision, at the horizon, the western sea could be seen lapping at the land. A cold realization crept to Myranda's mind. She knew where she was headed. Already it was visible in the distance. A high stone wall encircling a half-demolished city. The ruins of Kenvard.

In all of her travels, in all of her wanderings, Myranda was never able to bring herself to come back. Even after fifteen years, the thought burned at her mind. She drew nearer, the jagged, fallen shapes becoming recognizable. The school . . . the temple quarter . . . the market district . . . they all stood as shadows of their former selves. Husks destroyed by siege weapons and eroded by time. The castle, small and sturdy, was the only thing that stood in any meaningful way.

No attempt had ever been made to rebuild. It was too near to the front, the Alliance Army decreed, too dangerous. The thought was madness. The city of Kenvard had stood through a dozen wars. Wars against the old kingdoms of the north. Wars against the lesser provinces of Tressor. Even today, the walls stood proud and strong. No. Myranda wondered how she had ever believed that the Tressons could have taken it so quickly and so completely.

The doors had been opened. Her people had been betrayed.

At Myranda's signal, Myn began to circle slowly down. The forms of the city became more distinct. She'd last seen this place when she'd been no more than six, but the memories stirred bright, vivid, and agonizing. The ghosts of her life stood before her. Once-busy courtyards had decade-old trees pushing their way through the cobblestones. Vines grew over doors and windows. The sight was painful enough--but, slowly, a more searing realization came. There were buildings that were whole, buildings that had not been there before. Paths had been worn here and there by foot traffic. Signs of life . . .

Thin black smoke curled from the chimneys of the new buildings. They were squat stone structures that bore more than a passing resemblance to the forts that she and the others had fought their way into and out of time and time again. A sharp blast on a horn rang out over the countryside and soldiers streamed out into the streets. There were dozens of them, hundreds even. In moments, arrows were hissing through the air toward them, but Myranda brushed them astray with a wave of her hand. She felt a pulse from Ivy, even without searching. It was viciously powerful, a shift from joy to anger. It came from the castle.

Myranda guided Myn in low. The air was heavy with an evil smell, a smell that stung the nose and burned the eyes. She'd smelled it in Demont's fort, but it had not been nearly so strong. Myn swung low, her massive wings inches from the rooftops. Myranda's eyes, tears of anger now streaming from them, beheld the faces of the soldiers. Nearmen, every one of them. Not so much as an attempt had been made to hide the fact.

The streets rushed by below her in a blur, Myn's claws dashing soldiers to pieces below her. Myranda kept the arrows from them and set her eyes on the great castle gates. They were closing.

"Get us through those doors," Myranda urged.

The dragon pumped her wings and they surged through the air. Myranda leaned low and held herself tight to the beast's back, her mind tightly flexed to the task of forcing away the flying arrows. The great wooden doors drew nearer. The opening between them grew smaller. At the last moment, Myn shifted sideways and swept her wings back. The pair of heroes burst through the gap. Digging her claws deep into the stone and ancient carpet of the floor, Myn screeched to a stop in the entry hall. The half-dozen nearmen who had been hauling the massive doors closed now began to push them open.

"Keep the doors shut, Myn!" Myranda ordered, leaping to the ground.

Myn made short work of the nearmen and forced the doors shut against those outside. Myranda held out a hand and focused on the brace, heaving it into place. The alert that had summoned the nearmen outside had left the castle nearly empty. The task now was to keep it that way.

"Good work, Myn. Keep those doors closed! I'll be back as soon as I can!" Myranda cried as she sprinted down the great hall and deeper into the castle.

Walls blackened by fire, great portraits torn to ribbons, and magnificently carved doors whisked past Myranda as she hurried through the castle's halls toward her target. As a little girl, she'd dreamed about seeing this place. Now she was grateful that she hadn't time to linger. The state of ruin around her--and, worse, the corruption that showed itself at every turn--dashed her dreams to pieces. She worked her way through the winding halls. Her echoing footsteps mingled with those of the guards too slow to answer the call in time. Flashes of magic made short work of locked doors.

Finally, she found her way to a massive hall. The throne room.

The vaulted ceilings towered over her head. Moldering tapestries sagged on the walls. On either side of the room, the walls had been modified. Where once were great arched doorways leading to lavish gathering rooms, now there were rough stone walls with heavy wooden doors. The first few were marked with carefully engraved placards, etched with numerals one through five, with the fourth door hanging open to reveal a closet-sized interior--empty. Beside each door, attached to the wall, was a rack. One bore an intricately-carved staff. Another, a massive two-handed sword. The last bore another sword . . . *the* sword. The one that she had found with the remains of the swordsman. The one that had made this quest her own.

Myranda turned back to her task. There, at the far end of the room, perched on a slightly raised platform rightfully occupied by the thrones of a fallen kingdom, stood a sight that boiled Myranda's blood. There was a cage. Inside was Ivy. Fastened about her mouth and neck, and three each on her arms, legs, and tail, were crystal chains. Not the crystal-embedded iron that had held Myranda, but pure, brilliantly glowing crystal. They led through the bars to the walls, where they were affixed first to support pillars and second to head-sized storage crystals. Crystals that even now pulsed with stolen energy. The chains were taut, so much so that they suspended Ivy from the ground. A handful of mystic nearmen, bearing robes and wands rather than armor and swords, tended to the crystals, carefully replacing those that were full with fresh ones.

Ivy's eyes turned to Myranda. Instantly, they were radiant with joy. She struggled and let out muffled screams of excitement. The elation spilled off in scintillating waves of golden light that were drawn ravenously into the chains. The links leapt and danced at the sudden flow of power. The nearmen turned to the intruder, others finally bursting through the door behind her. A wand was raised and a crude spell hurled forth. By some horrible twist, the churning ball of black magic was spared the hunger of the crystals and sailed toward its target. Myranda tried to force it away, but her own will was not offered the same protection. She dove aside, dodging the spell.

A wave of red and a searing heat erupted from Ivy as she shifted suddenly to anger. The force was such that the nearmen nearest to her were thrown aside. As before, the gems soon drank away the power, but it was enough. Myranda sprinted to the nearest of the fallen mystics, the soldiers behind her at her heels. She wrestled the wand from the spellcaster.

No sooner was the item in her hand than its operation became clear to her. The wand itself contained both the spells and the power to cast them. It took the merest thought to set them free. It stood to reason, as the merest thought was typically the best the nearmen could manage. A spray of destructive black magic launched itself from the weapon, bringing the soldiers to a very swift and somewhat messy end. Myranda turned and leveled the weapon at the mystics, but the wand was spent.

Myranda dropped to the ground as a new wave of magic swept toward her. It splashed against the bars of the cage, buckling and peeling back a handful of them, though not severing any of the chains. Myranda took up one of the bars that was broken free and scrambled to her feet. A swing of the makeshift weapon--dripping with a brutality the young wizard hadn't thought herself capable of--destroyed the nearest mystic. The fallen wand made quick work of the rest. The room filled with a brief burst of golden light as Ivy's mood shifted again.

"It is all right, Ivy, I'm here now. I am going to get you out of this," Myranda assured her, as she approached the anchor point of the first chain.

She raised the bar and brought its end down. The link, little more than brittle crystal, shattered after a second and third blow in a tiny burst of raw magic. As the chain fell limp, Myranda moved down to the second. One by one, the restraints fell, each giving Ivy more and more room to struggle. Before long, the jerking chains were yanking themselves free, too weak to restrain the desperate creature. When the last of them shattered, Myranda squeezed through the break in the bars to help her friend. With some difficulty, she pried off the shackle clamped like a muzzle about Ivy's mouth.

"Thank the gods you are here! I knew you would come!" Ivy said, almost too happy to speak. "You have to get this off of me! Quick!"

She tugged madly at an amulet affixed to the neck shackle. It shone with the gold color of her aura, only magnified. As she tore at it, it made a perceptible shift to orange.

"Quick, quick, quick!" she cried with growing desperation. "It makes me happy then mad then happy and if you can't get it off then . . . augh . . . *Get away from me!*"

The ranting creature pushed Myranda forcefully through the gap in the bars and then held tight to them. The gold was washed away in a torrent of red that mixed with screams of Ivy's anger.

"I'll kill them! I'll kill them for doing this to me!" she howled, an anger that was not her own surging though her.

Myranda could feel the raw power washing over her, and the anger prodded at her, trying to force itself into her mind. She shook it away. The poor creature was lost in a torrent of emotion, no doubt spared the full transformation that usually accompanied such rage by the crystals that still tore hungrily at her. Ivy released the bars and took the amulet firmly in her grasp. The thin chain that held it in place snapped like a piece of twine. She threw it to the ground and crushed it to powder beneath her heel. The storm of emotions abated instantly.

Struggling to catch her breath, Ivy crawled through the gap in the cage. Behind her, she dragged easily her own weight in crystal chains, tripping, tugging and pulling at them to get them untangled from the bars. Myranda rushed to her and helped her to her feet. The poor creature looked beyond weary, but the joy and relief gave her strength enough to stand.

"I knew you'd come! Thank you so much for saving me," Ivy said. "Where are the others?"

"Still captured. I haven't found them yet," Myranda explained, guiding Ivy toward the door.

"You came to find me first! I knew you liked me better than Ether. Do . . . do you hear that?" Ivy asked suddenly.

Myranda stopped, prompting Ivy to do the same. With the cacophony of jangling crystalline chains halted, Myranda could hear a rhythmic pounding far ahead of them. The nearmen outside were trying to get in. They had to hurry.

"Quickly. They are beating on the doors. We need to reach--" Myranda began, but Ivy interrupted.

"No, no. Not that. The scratching. It is on the ceiling," Ivy said, turning her keen eyes upward. "There!"

Myranda squinted, a chill gripping her spine as she was just able to make out a bat-like creature nestled in a corner, its unnatural eyes trained on her. It was a tiny beast Lain had called a watcher, a spy for Demont. He knew they were here.

"Quickly!" Myranda urged, running for the door the soldiers had thrown aside.

Ivy tripped and stumbled on the chains dangling from her every limb, trying to keep up. It was no use. The door slammed closed of its own accord. Instantly, Myranda could feel locking spells she could not hope to break fall into place about every door in the room. At the same time, she felt two spells that had been in place drop away. A slow, ominous creak drew the hero's eyes. The doors marked I and II were swinging slowly open. Myranda tried to will them closed again, but the crystals filling the room drank away her spells even more quickly than those in the arena had. With no other options, she rushed to the first door and threw herself against it.

"Go! Find the entryway! I'll--" Myranda ordered.

"No! I'm not leaving without you! We do this together!" Ivy interrupted, throwing herself against the other door.

Myranda's eyes darted around the room as the door shook and rattled against her, pounding blows growing stronger with each passing moment. Ivy's eyes wandered, too, a vague look of recognition drifting across her face as she looked upon the room from outside the cage for the first time. Her gaze locked on the fourth door, open toward her. A shudder went through her.

"This . . . this is where it started. This is where . . . *this* me was born," she said distantly.

"Then these other doors . . . they must be the other revisions. Demont's other attempts at creating a Chosen," Myranda surmised.

A sudden, powerful blow threw Myranda to the ground, whipping the door open. The creature that stepped from inside may as well have stepped right out of Myranda's childhood dreams. He was a man, tall and strong.

His face was the picture of divine nobility; gleaming immaculate armor covered his impossibly perfect form. He was precisely what Myranda had imagined the Chosen would be. At the time, the thought had been enchanting. Now the sight terrified her. Before she could recover, the warrior grasped Ivy by a handful of her chains and threw her with a strength he should not have had. The hero sailed across the room, colliding with the far wall and dropping to the ground in a clattering mound of glassy chains.

The door Ivy had braced opened to reveal a second form in every way identical to the first, though cast in a different role. In place of the shimmering armor, there was a flowing robe, and perched atop his head was a pointed wizard's cap. It was precisely the sort she would have expected all wizards to wear prior to meeting dozens who wore no such thing. The warrior took up the two-handed sword, the wizard took up the staff, and the twin creations turned to their foes.

To an outsider, the sides of good and evil would have seemed obvious. On one side were two statuesque figures, each a picture perfect specimen of heroism, naught but courage and nobility in their eyes. On the other, a tattered woman with desperation and fear plastered on her face and a beast still weighed down by the chains of imprisonment, each at the end of their rope and seeking escape at any price. Never had the unlikeliness of the world's heroes been drawn into so sharp a relief.

Ivy climbed to her feet noisily, brushing shards of broken crystal from where they had bitten into her skin. She sneered in pain, specks of red staining her white fur. The warrior was stalking toward her. The chains wrapped around her legs robbed her of her footing, leaving her struggling to steady herself. All the while, the warrior was drawing closer, his sword raised and a look of triumph already in his eyes.

Myranda rushed to attack the warrior. With her magic all but useless here, she was not entirely sure what she was going to do when she reached him, but she had to do something. Suddenly, she felt a will tighten around her like a vice, crushing her from all sides. Her pained eyes turned to the wizard. His staff was held out, a look of concentration on his face. Myranda struggled, pushing back with her mind, but quickly having any progress wicked away.

How did their spells evade the crystal's thirst when hers did not? Her mind struggled to analyze the spell about her, trying to work out the possibilities. The increasingly familiar sensation of a rib cracking quickly reminded her that now was not a time for academics. A solution came to mind and was immediately put to work.

The crystals tore the power from her spells moments after they were released, but the results of the spells would surely remain. All she had to do was start something the crystals couldn't stop. A short, focused burst of concentration coupled with a muttered arcane phrase conjured a short-lived, intense flash of flame. A moment later, the cloak of the wizard was aflame. The will holding her in place wavered while he attempted to extinguish himself, but it was enough. Myranda broke free from his grip and launched herself toward him. The pair tumbled to the floor with enough force to send the staff sliding across the room.

Ivy was trying to back away from the warrior, but the long chains that still clung to her limbs and tail tripped her relentlessly. They were at once underfoot, wrapped around pillars, twisted around her legs, and entangling her arms. The fear welled up inside of her, bringing with it a sense of panic that further hampered her efforts. One of the chains attached to her wrist had found its way beneath her feet. She struggled with increasing desperation to free her hand. A moment later, she took a step to gain better footing, inadvertently releasing the chain. Her arm snapped back with remarkable speed, trailing behind it the length of crystal chain. It coiled through the air and lashed across the warrior's face like a whip, shattering its endmost link against his cheek.

A few drops of black blood trickled from the resulting wound, and a more stern look came to the warrior's face. The ramifications of the event slowly worked their way into the frightened creature's mind. The blue aura began to fade. A devilish grin replaced it.

Ivy worked her arm in slow circles, drawing more and more of the chain into the air. Each time the warrior stepped near enough, she widened the circle briefly and a lash of jagged crystal pushed him back. Now her other arm did the same. Long tendrils of brilliantly glowing chain drew intricate designs in the air. As she worked more and more of the chain into carefully timed circles, those that remained became less tangled. This was a rhythm. This she could understand. Minute, graceful movements tugged and pulled chains from her legs, tail, and neck into the air. Now she was an indistinct white form in the center of a radiant blur of chains, bending, twisting, spinning, leaping. It could only be described as a dance. The complex pattern of motion that moved the whole of her body finally managed to keep every last link of chain airborne, hissing through the air fully extended and somehow not clashing or tangling.

Myranda scrambled for the staff, ignoring the sharp pain in her abdomen. This was a nearman, and thus the staff was his source of power. She had to keep it from him. He grasped at her, catching her ankle in a punishing grip, but it was too late. Her fingers closed around the weapon. Instantly, the many enchantments of the staff seemed to insinuate themselves into her mind, forcing her to become aware of them. Spells that did not so much need to be cast as selected. Most were harsh and excessive by Myranda's standards, but desperate times have a way of adjusting one's standards.

She unleashed the same vicious, vice-like spell that had been used against her, instantly rendering the wizard immobile and struggling for breath. With virtually no will to resist with, the wizard was at her mercy.

Victory was at hand, but, unfortunately, a sudden and rather terrifying realization made it an afterthought. The gems that had been leeching away all of her strength had been treated to a veritable feast since Myranda's arrival, and many were full nearly to bursting. Deep black scars on Bagu's face and a large jagged hole in the hallway of the arena stood as evidence of the destructive potential of *one* of these gems, and now there were dozens. The light was growing more intense by the moment.

Myranda thrust the struggling wizard with all of the spell's might. In her hands, it was considerable. As she hurried to the most threatening of the gems, his form collided with the bars of the cage and dropped motionlessly, but not lifelessly, to the ground.

A healthy dose of golden light was shining out from the swirl of brilliant blue chains, feeding their radiance. Ivy's flawless motions propelled the azure tendrils with astounding speed and accuracy. She advanced slowly at first, bringing the tips of the chains into striking distance link by link. The warrior raised his sword defensively. The overfilled crystals burst on contact, showering him with faintly glowing shards and scalding him with intense energy. As the chains grew shorter, and she grew more bold, Ivy swept closer still. The strikes became stronger and more frequent. Now the warrior was backing away.

Before long, Ivy's chains had been worn down to a few short lengths, affording her far greater control. The sword-wielding nearman was already on his last legs, the bizarre assault leaving him battered and bloodied, but now the strikes where landing upon undefended flesh without fail. Finally, there was nothing left on her legs and neck but shackles, the crystal bands on her tail having long since slipped away. She wrapped the remaining links that dangled from her wrists around her fingers and advanced on the nearly beaten warrior.

Her ears twitched. The door marked III was creaking open.

Myranda took a large, gently pulsing crystal into her hands. Its ravenous hunger sated, she felt no draw on her strength. She could feel the raw power locked just below its surface. It was a dull warmth--a warmth that she felt not with her body, but with her soul. Tiny fractures were feathering across the surface. Myranda probed the enchantments of the staff. There was a connection, she could feel it. The same power trapped within the crystal fueled the spells. If she could just manage to use the staff to tap into it, she might have a chance.

Carefully, she tugged and pulled at the tools of the D'karon with magic. Reluctantly, a filament of brilliant light wormed out of the crystal and flowed into the staff. Instantly, she felt the enchantments come alive, each seeming to have a will of its own. They all wished to be cast at once. She sifted through them, finally coming upon one that seemed right.

Staff in one hand, gem in the other, she turned to the door barring their way. On the ground lay the defeated warrior, barely moving. Ivy stood over him, the links of chain slowly slipping from her fingers. Her gaze, her mind, her entire being was transfixed by the form before her. A young woman, perhaps Myranda's age, was standing just outside of the third cell. Her eyes were blank and empty, staring at an indistinct point in the distance. From the looks of her, she hadn't seen the outside in years, so pale was her skin. Indeed, she looked frail and weary enough to have been locked away for the whole of her life. The clothes she wore were simple, and seemed almost ancient, worn thin over years.

Ivy approached her.

"What is the matter?" Myranda asked, concern in her voice.

Ivy raised a hand and touched the woman on the cheek. Slowly, mechanically, the woman imitated. A ragged sleeve slid back to reveal, in sharp black against her pale forearm, the Mark of the Chosen. Ivy was fairly trembling. A lone tear rolled down her cheek, her face a potent mix of agony, longing, and confusion. Her mind seemed frozen, locked about a feeling she couldn't describe. Something she felt . . . she *knew* to her very core. Those eyes. They were familiar, but she'd never seen them before. How could it be? What did it mean?

This third foe did not seem to be a threat, but appearances were often deceiving. However, as a quiet crackling emanated from the crystals behind her, Myranda knew that there was a far more pressing concern that had to be dealt with first. She focused her attentions on the door, unleashing the full power of the spell she'd selected. Sure enough, the staff was all too eager to sap the crystal of its stolen strength. As it did, the door began to rattle against is hinges. Myranda could feel the clash of the two spells, the tension as they struggled against one another.

As the two D'karon spells battled, she cast her gaze cautiously about with what little will she had to spare. The woman before Ivy seemed harmless. Beyond harmless. She'd seen a blank expression like that once before, though, on Hollow, the prophet of Entwell. Yet when the spirits gripped him, Hollow was anything but harmless. As she contemplated what precisely it was that Demont had been keeping behind the third cell door, and why Ivy found it so fascinating, the malthrope's expression changed to one of comprehension.

"She doesn't look right because she is . . . she is too . . . old," Ivy gasped in a hushed voice.

Realization cut through her more painfully than any knife could. In its wake, memories long concealed by a dense fog were thrust into clarity. A continuous line of recollection lurched up from the mists, bright and real. The sounds of battle rang in her ears. Scenes of soldiers flashed before her darting eyes. They were the same images she'd recalled when Myranda had asked her to remember, but vivid as life. She saw the eyes of her parents in crystal clarity as they were struck down. She heard the screams of the other children around her. She felt the searing sting of an arcane tool as it was plunged cruelly into her chest.

Her shaking fingers rose and tugged at the neck of the human's shirt. It slid down slightly, revealing a ghastly white scar at the base of her throat. A scar precisely where the artifact had been driven in her memory. Ivy stumbled back as if struck, her eyes riddled with pain. The agony dropped away slowly, leaving Ivy's expression as blank as that of her tormentor. Slower still came its replacement. The change was subtle on the surface. Her lips pressed together slightly. Her eyes drew narrower. Around her, the air seemed to grow warmer and colder at the same time. It had all of the burning bite of the chilliest of winter nights. She drew in a breath and released it as a seething hiss that swirled in front of her as a puff of white mist.

Deep inside, Ivy burned. She burned not with the white-hot flame of anger, a fire that danced blindingly across the surface--this was deeper, smoldering in her very core. This was an emotion she'd never felt so intensely. Her soul and body boiled with it. It was not long before the intense feeling found its way along the channels installed by the D'karon. It came to the surface not as the crimson glow of anger--not a glow at all. Indeed, the light seemed to be drawn from the air around her. Darkness rolled off of her in thin black waves, billowing like mist and thickening as it drifted to the floor.

"Demont," she hissed, blackness beginning to thread its way along her white fur. "It wasn't enough that he killed me. It isn't enough that he tore my soul from my body. He had to lock them both away. Twist them. Shape them. Leave them to wither. I am nothing to him. He tainted everything."

Ivy's words dripped with a hatred the likes of which Myranda never would have thought her capable. She felt the intense emotion at the edge of her mind, eager to get in. It was relentless. Myranda kept it at bay and intensified her efforts on the door. It was not budging, and the crystal was nearly drained. Or, at least, it had been. Now it was drinking greedily of the blanket of black mist that rolled across the floor.

"Ivy, I need you to calm down," Myranda pleaded.

"No . . . no. Now is not the time to be calm. Not when that . . . thing still lives. Not while his little twisted creations still lurk about. He must be punished. He must be ended. And I will use what he gave me to do it," she fumed.

Her voice had a more even, more mature quality. There was no hint of the innocence that saturated her tone normally. Now there was hatred, vengeance, and nothing else. She shifted her gaze to the mock hero, his falsely noble form struggling back to his feet, sword in hand. She stalked toward him. The mist around her feet whisked aside, offering a glimpse of pockmarked, eroded stone where her feet had been. Each step left behind a similar patch that looked as though a century of decay had worn it away.

Myranda looked around. Everywhere the mist touched seemed to age before her eyes. Iron bars rusted. Wood flaked and crumbled. Only two things were spared: the mist parted itself around Myranda, and around the figure that had driven Ivy to this level of madness. The nearmen were not afforded the same mercy. Instead, as Ivy finally reached the battered form of the warrior, the mist seemed to coil up around him. She reached out and grasped him by the neck. A ghostly pallor spread out from her touch, withering flesh to gnarled sinew. Myranda turned away from the horrid sight, only to behold a far worse one.

The wooden racks that held the dangerously full gems finally gave way under the effects of the mist. The crystals tumbled to the ground. Some of them fractured, brilliant light gleaming from within and threatening to burst forth. Most managed to stay whole, drinking in the mist that they were now immersed in. Every last one of them took on a painfully bright glow. Myranda rushed to them, staff in hand. She had to spill off the energy, and quickly, as there was certainly no time to make it far enough away to escape the blast.

She slid to a stop as a form rose up from the mist. The wizard, still clinging to life after Myranda's last attack, struggled to his feet. He hadn't been spared the effects of the concentrated hate that was pouring out of Ivy. His clothes looked as though they had been left at the mercy of a dozen hard winters. His flesh was stark white and drawn. In his hands, though, were a pair of the wands left by Ivy's handlers. With a mechanical look of dignity and nobility still plastered on his ravaged face, the creation began to unleash blast after blast of the black magic. The stores of the wands were depleted quickly, only to be fed by the very crystals Myranda was trying to deal with.

The black energy kicked up a wake of mist as it crackled through the air. Myranda raised the staff and found it more than able to deflect the attacks.

Volley after volley of D'karon magic splashed against the stolen staff--but, if anything, it was merely delaying the inevitable. The crystals would give way before long if something was not done. Myranda cast a glance she could not afford at Ivy, who strode casually along a floor that was now wholly hidden beneath a lightly shifting black mist. She seemed unconcerned with the destructive bursts of magic that lurched in wild deflections across the throne room-turned-battlefield.

The lapse in Myranda's attention let a swath of magic through her defenses. It passed through her. A simultaneous agony of the body and soul burned at her, but she wrestled it from her mind and managed to block the follow-up attack. Now Ivy was beside her.

"See to it that nothing happens to Aneriana," Ivy ordered.

Before Myranda could object, or even agree, Ivy was in front of her. A pair of spells that would have put Myranda on her knees clashed against Ivy. Rather than passing through her, they seemed to curl and scatter. A third seemed to wrap around her, blending with fur that was now more black than white.

Finally, she stopped. Once again the mist swirled up, swallowing the wizard even as he continued his assault. The spells continued to burst from the writhing clouds. A moment later, there was stillness. The mist dropped away. It left behind what looked to be a poorly embalmed cadaver left to the elements for a century. It crumbled to the ground in a dusty pile of gray bones, white skin, and black powder that may once have been blood.

A sound like crackling ice drew Myranda's attention. A sound like scratching claws drew Ivy's. As the girl tried to find something in the staff's arsenal that could buy them some time, she saw a fleeting glimpse of Ivy's eyes. The bright, lively, innocent pink eyes were replaced with a cold, determined violet mockery of them. The eyes locked on the watcher as it scrabbled along the high ceiling to a window. The mere gaze was enough to prompt a choked-off squeal of pain from the creature. A moment later, it fell to the ground, causing a ripple in the settled mist before striking the ground as a dry, shrived husk.

Myranda drew up as much as she could of the power that surged dangerously around her and heaved it at the door. The staff, powerful though it was, simply could not burn enough energy quickly enough to unravel the locking spell, let alone empty the crystals. As a shaft of light burst from a crystal, Myranda turned in a blur of motion and focused the staff's efforts on holding it together. Another crystal got the same treatment, then another. The only thing standing between the castle and its utter demolition was the struggling will of the Chosen.

"Ivy . . . the door. You have to get it open . . . I can't . . . hold this for very long," Myranda pleaded.

"My work is not through here," came a voice as cold and hollow as a crypt.

The black-as-night form of what had once been Ivy stood before the final door. The wood crumbled to dust. The form inside looked up, as though the light that now poured into its chamber brought with it a long-missing spark of life. What she saw was a man, young, but already scarred with the remnants of many battles. He wore armor that was twisted and damaged. His eyes had the same distant, empty stare as the woman who even now stood in the center of the room. Deep inside them, though, was the tiniest flicker of wisdom.

Myranda wove her will with that of the staff, lending as much as she could spare to the weapon's mystic influence. As she did, its secrets began to unfold. She could feel the texture of the spell, see the runes that would coax it from a page, feel the thoughts that had created it. Slowly, she traced it to its roots, the fragment that somehow allowed it to draw its strength from the crystals. The rest of the threads of magic drew back to reveal it.

Quickly, she crafted a spell of her own that incorporated the stolen technique. A shimmering shield flashed into existence, forming a dome over the crystals. She gave her aching spirit a moment's rest. The shield held, but a shudder as a crystal splashed its contents against it assured the young wizard that it wouldn't hold for long. She turned to Ivy, knowing that now was the last chance to escape.

One last time, the black mist rushed in around the work of Demont. It twisted and roiled about the armor-clad form. A hand reached out from among the mist and grasped the hilt of the Sword of the Chosen. Instantly, the mist was swept away. He raised the sword defensively. Ivy grasped the blade, oblivious to the razor-sharp edge, and attempted to wrench it from his grasp. There was a glimmer of dormant magic and a paralyzing sensation that was felt only once before it shot down Ivy's arm. She cried out in pain.

The voice seemed wrong coming out of the dark embodiment of malice. It was Ivy's own, riddled with agony and fear. Myranda looked to the fifth product of Demont's meddling. The image drove itself deep into her memory. She'd seen him before, though never his face. His was the soul that had selected her for this quest. His was the sword that had brought her such trouble. His were the rations that saved her life that night. Somehow, the swordsman that she'd found dead in the field so long ago stood before her now, alive.

A wave of brilliant gold light swept outward from the point where sword had touched flesh. It draped itself along the weapon, and along Ivy's arm. The creature, squealing in pain and a look of desperation in her eyes, released the weapon and rushed backward. The light continued along her arm, leaving white fur where black had been. She dropped to her knees on the now-mist-free floor and clutched at her chest as the Mark burned at her.

As the wave of gold reached the flesh of the swordsman, he grimaced in pain as well. A network of black lines that formed intricate strings of runes shone a brilliant blood-red. Enhancements, alterations, and other manipulations left by Demont reacted with the wave of divine energy. Thoughts and commands implanted by the D'karon generals burned and sizzled in his mind. That which was D'karon and that which was Chosen battled each other. Soon he was little more than a mass of shifting mystical lights in the shape of a man.

Ivy struggled to her feet. The burning was slowly dropping away, and she was once again herself. Her crimes against the Mark had been minor. She'd approached the swordsman, a fellow Chosen, in battle with hatred in her heart and every intention to kill him. Perhaps another day such an act would have drawn a far greater price, but there was precious little left of what the gods had intended in that warrior. Now the man who would have been the leader of the divine warriors was receiving a punishment that his slumber of death had spared him. Much of his mind, body, and soul were now replaced with D'karon. The Mark would not allow that. It burned at him, rendering away the tainted parts at the expense of the rest.

Ivy backed away unsteadily as she watched the swordsman consumed by the same divine fire that had destroyed Trigorah. Myranda rushed to her. The confused creature, recovering from the emotion that had seized control, looked desperately to Myranda for some sort of reassurance, but the wizard had none to give. A threatening glow on the other side of the room drew their attention.

The barrier Myranda had erected around the crystals had been intended to keep their power in, not to keep them from absorbing more. It was an oversight she might not live to regret. The mist may have been dispelled, but in the brilliant spectacle of the Mark's wrath, they had found a far greater meal. Another crystal burst.

It was one more blast than the weakened floor could stand. Ancient and decrepit stones, made more so by Ivy's mist, finally shattered, spilling the whole of the mound of crystals and a fair amount of the throne room onto whatever recesses lie below. Myranda could only spare a moment's glance into the widening hole, but what she saw chilled her: shadowy, vaguely human forms, bathed in the blue light of the fallen gems. She could not be certain, but it seemed that they were incomplete . . . as though they were in the process of being assembled. As the edge of the hole crept closer, she knew that this was a concern for another day. She grabbed Ivy and rushed to the door.

"What are we going to do!?" Ivy begged.

Myranda looked over the heavy wooden portal. The spell sealing it had been weakened, but not nearly as much as the door itself had been. The lowest portion of the door was little more than sparse splinters held together by dusty gray fibers of wood. She gave it a kick and nearly half of the door dropped away in a rush of powder. Ivy did not need to be told what to do next. She scrambled underneath, poking her head back to urge Myranda to do the same. The young wizard lingered for a moment.

The light coruscating over the body of the swordsman was different now. It seemed darker, mixed with something less pure. And it wasn't weakening. The man's face was lost in a pool of light, but somehow she knew that if she could see it, it would be riddled with conflict, as though the D'karon part of him was actively resisting the divine power . . . or, worse, feeding on it.

She looked to the human Ivy had called Aneriana. A flicker of understanding . . . of *purpose* came to her eyes. She turned to the swirling mass of energy. It brandished the weapon, now somehow in control despite the turmoil that consumed it. Myranda slipped under the door as the pair rushed toward each other. The force from the clash, even from the other side of the wall, was enough to stagger the two heroes.

"Is she going to be all right?" Ivy asked, worry in her voice.

"She's bought us a precious few moments; we can't afford to waste a single one!" Myranda said, leading Ivy quickly forward.

She retraced her path through the castle's halls. Every few moments, something between an explosion and an earthquake would shake the very walls, but they did not slow. Finally, they reached the entry hall. Ivy's eyes widened at the sight of Myn. The massive creature was bracing the shreds of what had once been a mighty door. Now it was little more than a collection of splintered holes through which the weapons of countless nearmen clashed and clanged.

"Is . . . is that . . ." Ivy asked, slow to believe that this great creature could possibly be the little one she'd known.

She drew in a deep breath. Her nose wouldn't lie.

"It *is!*" she cried, rushing to the dragon and throwing her arms about the creature's neck. "How could she be alive!? What happened?"

"I'll explain later, just get on!" Myranda cried.

Ivy hastily obeyed, hopping onto Myn's back right behind Myranda. Without a word from Myranda, Myn knew what to do. She backed away and crouched like a coiled spring. The ailing door gave way moments later, and a flood of soldiers were met instantly with a massive beast cannoning out against them. They were easily tossed aside and, after a few wading strides through the throng of attackers, Myn thrust herself into the air.

Myranda again devoted her mind to deflecting the thick volleys of arrows that hissed toward them. So taxing was the task that she was only vaguely aware of the tightening grip Ivy had on her waist.

"Is she . . . are we . . ." Ivy managed to gasp before fear took her words away.

The sight of the shrinking landscape beneath her burned her mind with fear. Only when they were out of bow range did Myranda notice that Ivy's arms were wrapped painfully tight about her. She turned to see a brilliant blue aura and an unmistakable look of still-mounting fear in her eyes.

Myranda forced sleep upon the terrified creature, and not a moment too soon, as the crystals within the castle finally reached their breaking point all at once. The force from the blast was like nothing Myranda had ever felt. Even from so far above, the rushing wind and crackling energy rattled the heroes, knocking the now-limp Ivy from her perch atop Myn. The dragon skillfully plucked up the plummeting form and wrapped Ivy in her tail for safe transport. Once Myranda was sure that Ivy was no longer in danger, she turned back to the spectacle, which raged on still. Brilliant columns of azure fire billowed amid a haze of blinding white light. What had once been the castle of her great land was now a settling cloud of shattered debris. Whole arches soared through the air. Ramparts crashed to earth, demolishing already-ruined buildings.

The sight should have stirred memories of the massacre, surges of guilt that she'd caused this destruction in the place of her birth, or any number of other emotions. Anyone present could have explained why it didn't. In the presence of such power, chaos, there was simply no room for it in one's mind. Watching the landscape shudder. Seeing trees bend aside like grass in a breeze. Feeling the searing heat from hundreds of feet away. Feeling the rumbling roar in one's chest long after it had robbed the ears of their hearing. There was simply no time for thought or remembrance. It was all washed away in a tide of awe.

It was a long moment before Myranda and Myn had the presence of mind to make their escape--but when they did, it was with a speed none who would pursue them could hope to match.

Myranda made a brief attempt to locate her next target, but her head was still swimming after the ordeal. Instead, she used the flight to gather her mind. She directed Myn vaguely north and east. There was no telling where the others were, save the fact that they were in the north. If she kept to the center of the Northern Alliance, she at least would not be far.

With the power that had forced its way into her mind during the search spent, Myranda finally felt the night air in all of its painful chill. She sifted through the enchantments contained within her stolen staff, but it came as no surprise when no spell that could bring her comfort presented itself. It was meant to be wielded by a nearman, and they didn't seem to suffer from any of the effects of cold, or hunger, or fatigue. Myranda dipped into her own quavering spirit and cast a warming spell. Periodically, Myn would huff a flame that sent a surge of heat through her veins. The creature did so in a practiced manner, so that only the merest whisper of light left her mouth.

Now that the cold was dealt with, and hunger was a nagging concern at best, Myranda was left with the unfortunate task of sorting through the images that she'd been forced to thrust aside in the rush of battle. Those new buildings she'd seen in Kenvard. They were D'karon, that was certain. The D'karon had a way of stripping the soul from things, leaving behind only what was needed to perform the task. The thin smoke and vile smell that she'd encountered matched that of Demont's fort perfectly. That had been a place where the horrid beasts she'd encountered were manufactured. So then Kenvard must have served as a source for them. The brief flash of the catacombs beneath the castle forced its way to her mind. Nearmen, half-completed, had stood in countless rows. The abominations had to be made somewhere. Kenvard must have been that place. Her stomach churned at the thought. They had extinguished the whole of a city, killed all of its people, and for what? To craft shallow replicas? To produce lumber to be cast into the flames of war to keep them burning?

There was another reason, though: to get Ivy. Myranda looked back to the sleeping form of her friend. She'd behaved very strangely when the woman had stepped from behind the third door. Ivy had recognized her. Even more strangely, she had claimed that the woman looked "too old." And after the hate had taken her over, she remained concerned with the human's safety, calling her by name, Aneriana.

The name echoed deep into Myranda's memories, taking her back to the days in Kenvard. Aneriana was indeed a name she'd heard often. It was certainly the name of a talented young girl that her mother had taught. It was Ivy's true name, the person she had been before the D'karon had claimed her.

Questions boiled in Myranda's mind. What had happened to Aneriana in the years since her soul was stolen? What had Demont done to her? What had he planned to do? And how was it that even without her soul she'd been able to stand up to the swordsman's raging chaotic form? For that matter, how had she known that she should? And what of the swordsman? What had been happening to him? How had they managed to bring him back?

If anyone had any answers, it was the D'karon. There may as well have been no answers at all. Knowing that only made the flames burn brighter in her mind.

The clouds above began to lighten. Myranda looked over the landscape sprawling beneath them. There was no sufficiently dense stand of trees to hide them for the day, and after the commotion they'd stirred up, it was suicide to remain in the open.

Finally, finding no better solution, Myranda guided Myn to a rundown barn a short distance from the edge of a small lake. After a glance inside to find it mostly empty, Myn cautiously slaked her thirst at the lakeside before slipping inside, keeping a watchful eye on the frosty surface. The dragon settled down and scooped both Ivy and Myranda into her embrace. Wrapped in the warmth of her friend and exhausted from the day's trials, Myranda slipped quickly into a deep sleep. Myn followed suit.

The short day was half over before Ivy, forced into sleep for the duration of the journey, finally awoke. She felt refreshed, and for the moment was mercifully free of her memories of the confrontation in the throne room. After a brief feeling of panic upon finding herself in the clutches of a dragon, she realized she was among friends. A careful, tricky bit of maneuvering extricated her from Myn's grasp and she stretched her sore muscles. She had a quick look over the dusty, disused barn, then turned to Myn. It was the first good look she'd had at the dragon since she'd returned. Myn was enormous now. A real dragon, not the baby she remembered. At the same time, though, everything she remembered remained. The same ruby hues. The same graceful lines. It was still Myn, still familiar, just tenfold the power, and tenfold the majesty.

Slowly, Myn became aware, even in her sleep, that part of her precious cargo was missing. Her golden eyes opened and settled quickly on Ivy. After beaming a broad grin, the playful creature carefully stepped in and wrapped Myn's neck in a tight embrace, planting a kiss on her cheek. After lavishing affection for a few moments more, Ivy stepped back, a finger to her lips and pointing at the slumbering Myranda. Myn gripped the sleeping wizard a bit tighter and watched Ivy with interest as she prowled about the barn once more, rubbing her stomach absentmindedly.

Ivy frowned at an empty burlap sack and poked about in a few crates she found. She was hungry. More than hungry, she was starving. They'd offered little in the way of food while she hung from the chains in the castle, too fearful of loosening even a single one to feed her. Now her grumbling stomach urged her to rummage ever deeper into the recesses of the barn. She turned up a few half-frozen potatoes and a head or two of cabbage that had held up fairly well. She tossed the potatoes to Myn, who snapped them up gratefully. After carefully setting aside half of what she'd found for Myranda, Ivy made quick work of the rest. It was hardly enough to satisfy her. She looked longingly at Myranda's share, but shook the thoughts away. Her eyes shifted to Myn. The dragon would probably be able to hunt something down, but she'd have to wake Myranda, and the two had done enough for her already.

She sniffed at the air. There was something better nearby. Much better . . .

She fairly floated to the door of the barn to get another whiff. The smell was heavenly. Sweet and spicy and warm all at once. A small voice in her head echoed warnings to stay out of sight, but another smell silenced it quickly. She would be fast, she would be sure that she was not seen. She'd watched Lain move. It would be easy.

"You stay here. I'll be right back," Ivy mouthed silently, amid exaggerated gestures.

With that she was off, dashing out the door and across the open field outside toward the lone farmhouse nearby. Myn shifted uneasily, craning her neck in attempts to peek outside. When she failed to do so, she carefully released Myranda and got to her feet, sidling to the doors and gazing out through the gap between. She glanced at the sleeping human, then back at the retreating form, shuffling nervously. It wasn't long before the anxious fidgeting was enough to wake Myranda. She looked about groggily. The expression of anxiety on the dragon's face, coupled with Ivy's conspicuous absence brought her to full wakefulness in a flash.

"Where is she?" Myranda asked sternly.

Myn looked again to the door. Myranda rushed to it, peering out just in time to see Ivy disappear into the farmhouse across the field.

"She knows better than that!" Myranda snapped.

She pulled open the door and stepped outside.

"You stay here. Don't leave unless you absolutely have to," Myranda warned before rushing after Ivy.

It was broad daylight and the field was level. There was no way to avoid being seen by any prying eyes that might turn her way. The crops offered nothing in the way of cover, either, as the field was planted with potatoes on one side and cabbages on the other. The two vegetables were virtually the only ones that would grow in the northern soil, and varieties that would grow any time the ground wasn't frozen solid were the only reason most northerners hadn't starved long ago. In the past, she'd wished there were more wheat fields so that there would be more bread. She'd never thought she would long for the cover that they could provide.

She reached the farmhouse. It was a humble place, somewhat rundown, with two floors. The door was slightly open. For a moment, she considered sifting though her repertoire of spells for something that might help her to remain unseen, but by now the damage was done. The only thing that could help now was speed. She carefully pushed the door wide enough to slip inside. Instantly, there was a gasp.

The whole of the first floor was one large room, centered around a well-stoked fireplace. Cowering behind a cupboard against one wall was a young woman who looked worn well beyond her years. Her eyes were locked on Myranda. Ivy looked up. She'd been hunched over a baking dish on the table, in the process of licking it clean. Her face was covered with its former contents, and bore a look of disappointment.

"Oh, you're awake. I was hoping I could get back without disturbing you," Ivy said, as though she'd done nothing worse than nudge Myranda in her sleep.

"Ivy, we need to leave--now," Myranda scolded.

"I know, but you have to try some of this first. It is called cobbler, and it is the best thing in the world. I finished this one, but she said we can have the other one, too," Ivy said.

"Yes, yes! Take anything you want, just leave!" the woman cried.

Ivy stood and tried to remove a second baking dish from over the fire, touching it gingerly with her fingers before giving up.

"There must be a tool or something for this, right?" Ivy asked, looking about for the offending item.

"Ivy, leave it," Myranda urged again, stepping inside and closing the door. "We have to--"

"Oh, look. She has one of those!" Ivy said, picking up one of the posters the Undermine had been tearing down.

That explained why the woman was just as frightened of Myranda as Ivy. She knew who they were. Myranda looked to the woman, who reacted to the gaze as one might to a raised weapon.

"Please! I swear to you, I will not tell a soul. Just don't hurt me! I am the only one here! No one ever has to know," she hurriedly assured.

"We do not mean you any harm. We just--" Myranda attempted to explain, only to be interrupted again.

"You aren't the only one here," Ivy said, sniffing the air. "There's someone upstairs."

The woman's eyes shot open.

"No! Please! Leave my father be! He is very ill! He's no threat to you! And without me he will die!" she begged, dropping to her knees.

"Ill? What is wrong with him?" Myranda asked.

"Please, please," the woman sobbed. "We've done nothing to you."

"No, you can tell her. She heals people," Ivy explained offhandedly, looking over the poster critically.

"I may be able to help him," Myranda offered.

"You . . ." she began, her eyes flashing with hope before distrust rushed back in. "You just leave him be."

"Very well," Myranda said. "Quickly, Ivy."

"But the cobbler!" she objected.

"Leave it," Myranda said sternly.

Ivy slouched and reluctantly followed as Myranda opened the door and moved quickly outside. They had gotten only a few steps into the icy field when the door was pulled open.

"Wait," the woman cried.

The heroes turned.

"Can you . . . can you really help him?" she asked in a shaky voice.

"I can try," Myranda said.

The woman opened the door. Myranda and Ivy entered.

"I knew you'd come to your senses," Ivy said, picking up the poster again and taking a seat at the table.

Myranda was led up the stairs to the second floor. The steps were practically worn through by worried footsteps. At the top, she found a number of doors. Behind one was a bedroom. A thin old man lay in a bed that clearly had not been empty in weeks. He was at death's door. His skin was gaunt, a sickly gray. Beads of sweat rolled down his face and dampened the sheets. The smell of illness permeated the air. At their approach, his face turned weakly to them, clouded gray eyes staring past them.

"It started a month ago," the woman said, nervously. "He was--"

"Working by the lake," Myranda surmised.

"How did you know?" she asked.

Myranda pulled aside the blanket slightly and lifted his arm. It was wiry, but even shriveled by sickness as it was, it seemed like it could pull a stump from the ground. She turned his hand. Nothing. She picked up the other. Nothing. Finally, she uncovered his feet. Sure enough, across the ball of his foot was a hair-thin black scar. The woman's tears began anew at the sight of it.

"It isn't . . ." she gasped.

Myranda nodded. Residents of the north knew it well. There was a plant called the cutleaf. It had broad leaves with hard, thin, upturned edges. It grew only near water, and was very rare, but it hadn't always been. For years, people who worked the land had been trying to kill them off. The edges carried a powerful toxin. Even a few drops of it just under the skin was more than enough to ensure a withering death. The vision faded, strength was sapped away. The appetite vanished, and finally a burning fever set in. It was a terrible, slow, and certain way to die. As a child, she'd heard the lecture a thousand times. Watch for them just beneath the ice, and if you aren't sure, stay away. In the winter, the leaves would freeze, the ridges standing straight with a cruelly sharp edge. The larger plants could easily slice through the sole of a boot. It was likely what had happened to the poor soul before her.

The woman was beside herself with despair. Myranda placed a hand on her shoulder.

"What is your name?" she asked.

"Sandra," the woman managed between sobs.

"Sandra, I am going to try to help him, but it will take some time, and a great deal of concentration. If you will leave me to my work, I give you my word that if he can be saved, he will be," Myranda said earnestly.

"I won't leave him," she answered with resolve.

"Very well," Myranda replied.

In the rare and brief discussions she'd had with the healers of Entwell, cutleaf poisoning had come up more than once. To many, it was considered one of the most difficult maladies to cure. The poison nestled itself deep in the body of the victim, soaking into every tissue. As she searched with her mind for the toxin, it appeared in her mind's eye as a thin haze across his entire body. It clung to him, entwined with the very fibers of his being.

Myranda knelt and put her mind to the task. Immediately, she saw why it was so great a challenge. Separating the poison from his flesh was infinitely more complex than any of the tests she'd had to endure in Entwell. If there was a spell to do it, she did not know it. That meant she would have to do so consciously. There could not have been more than a drop of the vile stuff in his entire body, and it slipped easily from her will and settled back each time her concentration wavered even slightly. She had to move all of it, and all at once, without doing any further damage. It had to move against the flow of blood here, with the flow of blood there, never mixing. Progress was slow and painstaking.

After a few minutes, the elderly man had stirred once or twice. Myranda managed to allow for it, but the sight had brought hope to Sandra, who grasped at Myranda's shoulders encouragingly. It broke her concentration and cost her a great deal of ground. When it happened a third time, Myranda's frustrated sigh convinced Sandra she would serve her father better elsewhere. She slowly descended the stairs.

Ivy was rummaging through a cabinet. Seeing her host, she stopped and smiled sheepishly.

"I'm sorry. I was, um, looking for something. I don't mean to overstep my bounds. How is it going up there?" she asked.

"I am not sure. But she is trying," Sandra said, giving Ivy a wide berth as she made her way to the table.

"She'll do it. She can do anything. We are the Chosen, you know," Ivy said with pride.

Sandra's eyes rested unsteadily on the poster. The woman upstairs had earned a slice of her trust, but this creature was another matter. She was a beast, a malthrope. Even if the Alliance Army had not marked her as an enemy of the state, she would have been terrified. They were murderers, thieves, and worse. She looked up to find that the monster was standing right beside her, looking over the poster again.

"It is an awful picture, isn't it? Look at me. So lifeless. So bland," Ivy said with a frown.

Sandra slid her chair away a bit and locked her eyes on Ivy.

"It does the job," Sandra said.

"That it most certainly does not!" Ivy objected, her raised voice startling the woman, who pressed back into her chair. "Art is supposed to tell a story. It is supposed to be a piece of the soul that created it. Art is supposed to be alive, vibrant. It is supposed to speak directly to the spirit. To say things words alone could never say. Art is the essence of being. This just *looks* like something. This is just a picture. It is a shame."

Her words had carried a passion of which Sandra hadn't thought a beast of her ilk was capable. She ventured a peek into the crude, animal eyes and found them bright and friendly. It didn't mean anything. She'd managed to survive this long, she must know all sorts of tricks to lower people's defenses. The childishness was an act. She would *not* be fooled by this beast. As the eyes stared questioningly into hers, Sandra felt a nervousness at the deepening silence growing in the pit of her stomach.

"What was it that you were looking for?" she asked, eager for something to push the silence back.

"Well, um . . ." Ivy began, looking down at the floor as she spoke. "I realize you just offered us whatever we wanted because you were afraid of us but . . . I need something to eat. Rather a lot, actually."

She was standing self-consciously, her hands clutched behind her back. She was ashamed that she'd scared this woman so. It was something of a reversal for her, and knowing how terrible fear could be filled her face with hot shame and embarrassment.

"The cobbler wasn't enough for you?" Sandra replied, somewhat accusingly.

"Oh, it was wonderful! But even if you are willing to part with the other one, it is for my friend. She hasn't had one yet. This food isn't even for me, though," Ivy explained. "It is for Myn."

"Myn? I . . . I thought the woman's name was Myranda," she said, casting her eyes again at the poster and scanning it for the name.

"Eh? Oh, no," Ivy replied, smiling and shaking her head. "No, Myn is still outside. She's the dragon in your barn."

Sandra drew in a sharp breath and held it. She could not have truly said that. No one could say such a thing in so casual a manner.

"D-dragon?" she ventured.

"Mm-hm!" Ivy said with a bright nod. "She must be hungrier than I am, because she flew here. So, well, there's only one thing around here that she'd eat, and it happens to be one of her favorites."

The color dropped from Sandra's face. Everyone knew what dragons ate. It was the subject of nearly as many tales as the malthropes. Tall towers. Deep caves. Always with a dragon. Always awaiting an offering to satisfy their hunger. She swallowed hard.

"P-please . . ." she began.

"It isn't so much to ask, I don't think," Ivy offered, fearful of being turned down. "Myranda is helping your father. It is the least you can do in return."

"I . . ." she began.

"Look, it won't take a moment. We can head out there together," the creature offered, perking up at a thought that might tip the bargain in her favor. "*You* can feed her!"

Sandra tried to swallow again, but her mouth had gone dry. She was backing away slowly.

"There's got to be some other way . . ." she croaked hoarsely.

"But Myn always is so much easier to get along with if you give her a treat. I'm sure she'll like you after she gets a taste," Ivy added desperately.

"I'm quite sure she will, too," Sandra whispered.

"It's settled then. Where do you keep your potatoes?" Ivy said with relief.

"But . . . potatoes?" she asked, so disoriented that she nearly lost her balance.

Ivy rushed in to steady her.

"Easy there. Yes, potatoes. What did you think I meant? Cabbage?" she asked.

"But dragons don't eat potatoes," Sandra objected, for the moment forgetting what the alternative was.

"Not as a rule, I suppose, but Myn loves them. Can't get enough, really. Come on, you must have bags and bags of them around here. She will be beside herself!" Ivy chirped, positively--and literally--aglow with the thought of Myn's reaction.

Sandra's eyes widened and she backed away from the faint but undeniable golden light. Sorcery as well? What *was* this creature who spoke such madness?

Ivy recognized the fear in her eyes and quickly surmised what was causing it. The renewed shame quickly wiped the joy away, and with it the glow.

"I can explain. It wasn't anything dangerous! Oh . . . I'm making a mess of this," Ivy began, tears welling in her eyes.

She gritted her teeth and forced the tears away, absentmindedly rubbing at her wrists.

"Look. I . . . do you have something that can get these off?" Ivy asked, defeated. "Their edges are very sharp, and they burn a little. I think if I could get rid of them, I might be able to think a little better. Maybe then I could stop botching things so badly."

Sandra's eyes drifted to the crystalline shackles. The wrists beneath them were badly cut, white fur stained with blood. There was a similar shackle on each ankle, and another on her neck, each similarly injured. Ivy was rubbing a particularly reddened bit of her wrist with her thumb and wincing. Against all of her instincts, Sandra felt a twinge of pity.

"Why are you wearing them?" she asked.

"Ask the army. They put them there," Ivy replied glumly.

"Then I think they ought to stay," Sandra replied, aghast at how fiendish she felt for saying it.

Ivy slumped against the wall and slid to the floor, huffing a dejected sigh and nodding. She rubbed at the tender skin under the shackles some more. While she was distracted, it didn't bother her so much, but the sadness and stillness made the wounds itch horribly.

As she did, Sandra watched her. It was a pathetic sight. Slowly, she felt her revulsion weaken, turning steadily to pity. She tried to remain resolute in her hate, but she couldn't help it. She felt sad to see the creature this way. Even a monster didn't deserve this.

"Don't pick at it. I may have something," Sandra relented, standing and heading for a cabinet. After a bit of digging, she produced a small hammer.

Ivy's eyes perked up as she was offered the tool. She grasped it, and after hesitating for a moment, Sandra let go.

"Thank you so much. Yes, this should work. It is really very nice of you," Ivy gushed, crossing her legs to press the ankle cuffs against the floor.

She raised the hammer slightly, but stopped.

"You don't suppose the noise will bother Myranda, do you? I wouldn't want that," she said.

"It is an old house with thick floors. Just be quick about it," Sandra replied, a nagging doubt in her mind begging her to take back the weapon she'd just provided to this monster.

Ivy raised the tool and dropped it with a good deal more force than was warranted. The crystal shattered into dozens of shards, and the hammer continued down onto her ankle. She clenched her teeth and fist until the pain subsided, then ventured a glimpse at her ankle. It was rather bloodier than it had been before, but not much worse. She shifted, and broke the second shackle with a bit more care. Another blow took away one wrist cuff. By the time she broke the other wrist free, she'd managed to break it into two neat pieces. Finally, there was the collar. Try as she might, she could not maneuver herself into a position to break it easily. After a few attempts that resulted in little more than bruises, she looked to Sandra.

The young woman had been watching through the corner of squinted, half-turned-away eyes. A part of her was terrified of what Ivy might do to her. Another part was terrified of what Ivy might do to herself. She was caught somewhere between feeling as though she'd given a weapon to a maniac and feeling as though she'd given it to a child.

"I can't quite manage the neck. Um . . . could you?" Ivy asked, holding out the hammer hopefully.

Sandra took it slowly. No sooner had she done so than Ivy placed her head down across the edge of the table, pressing down so that the collar stood upward slightly. The young woman looked nervously at the beast that, for the life of her, looked to be offering herself up for execution. She hefted the hammer in her hands. The voices of suspicion rose well above the voices of compassion. They screamed for her to take this opportunity, no doubt the best she would ever have, to end this creature now. One sharp blow would be enough to knock the beast cold. After that, it would be easy enough to end it.

She looked down at the creature, eyes shut tight and hands braced about the leg of the table. Not a hint of fear, not a dash of suspicion, just bracing for the blow she trusted would take this last remnant of her bonds away. Sandra looked at the neck beneath the cracked collar. It was raw, the white fur stained a dozen shades of red. It must hurt terribly. She looked over the creature. There were no weapons, no armor. The clothing was ratty and worn. If this was a fiend, surely it would be armed. If it was a trickster, surely it would be better dressed. Sandra took a deep breath and raised the hammer.

Myranda appeared at the top of the stairs in time to see it fall. The rough metal head clanked off of the crystal band, feathering it with fresh fractures and knocking a flake or two free. Ivy opened her eyes and tested the damage with her fingers.

"I think that'll do it," she said, gripping it and pulling it apart with ease.

"Sandra . . ." Myranda called from the top of the stairs.

The young woman's eyes shot to the voice from above. Myranda had looked weary before. Now she looked dead on her feet. Sandra was by her side in a heartbeat, skipping most of the stairs on the way up. She pushed past and burst into her father's room. The difference was like night and day. The color had come back to his face. She placed the back of her hand on his head and found the deathly burn of the fever virtually gone. His eyes were hazy, but active. They focused on her briefly before closing.

"Is he . . ." Sandra squeezed past the knot in her throat.

"He is going to sleep for some time. His strength is going to return slowly. It may be a few weeks before he is himself again, but he is going to be fine," the wizard explained.

All of the grief, pain, worry, and sorrow burst from Sandra in a torrent of joyful laughter and tears. She threw her arms about Myranda, nearly knocking them both to the ground. Years seemed to uncoil themselves from about her. Life returned to her teary eyes. She stood back and tried to find the words to thank Myranda, but nothing would make its way to her mouth but more sobbing laughter. Ivy appeared at the top of the steps. Sandra turned to her and rushed forward, embracing her. She didn't see a monster anymore. This saint that saved her father's life would not allow a monster to be by her side. There were only friends here. There were only heroes.

"How can I ever thank you!?" Sandra said when the emotion finally began to subside.

"No thanks necessary. I am just glad I could help," Myranda answered.

"No, no. I won't hear it. Look at you. You need clothes. You need food. You need rest. Here, my bed is just in the other room. Go, sleep," Sandra said, leading the wobbly healer through a door.

"I really couldn't. We've too much to do. I wouldn't dream of putting you in that kind of danger," Myranda replied, trying her best not to look longingly at the bed.

"There is no one for half a day in any direction. Sleep. I owe you that at least," she urged.

It took a bit more insistence, but Myranda finally relented, dropping into sleep almost the instant her head met the rare luxury of a pillow.

"Now what can I do for you? Anything! And not because I am afraid," Sandra said, her eyes looking upon Ivy as if for the first time.

"Really? Well, if you are going to make food for Myranda, I could use a bit more for myself. And there are the potatoes for Myn," Ivy hazarded.

"Oh . . . oh, yes, yes. The dragon. We shall see to it she has all she can eat. That is the one item I can offer an abundance of," Sandra said.

A moment later Ivy was following a bundled-up Sandra down into the cellar. A dusty bag bulging with potatoes was hefted onto Ivy's shoulder and the pair made off toward the barn. After pausing only briefly at the door, Sandra pushed it aside. Had Ivy been thinking, she would have asked to enter first. The sight of an unfamiliar human stirred the anxiously waiting dragon quickly to her feet in a blur of motion that would have startled the steadiest of minds.

Myn looked at Sandra with the deep stare that a predator reserves for its prey, dark thoughts of what this stranger may have done to the others fueling a primal fire--a fire that would have burst forth had Ivy not teetered into view with a bag that had the dry, starchy smell of that rarest of treats. The anger dropped away, but not the suspicion. The enormous eyes locked themselves on Sandra, who would swear that the gaze was cutting straight through her. Ivy fumbled the bag open and thrust some of the contents into the shaking hands of her host.

A look of hunger that did little to ease Sandra's paralyzed nerves came across Myn's face. She edged closer to the human who stood transfixed by the gaze. When she was near enough, the forked tongue slipped from her mouth and deftly plucked the treats from her trembling grip. After savoring the all-too-brief flavor, she looked expectantly at her host, who hurriedly held the bag open. The bag was empty in moments, a look of satisfaction rolling over the surprisingly expressive face of the beast. The massive head lowered down to the ground and slid forward until it was directly in front of Sandra.

"She wants you to scratch her head," Ivy whispered.

After a few moments of convincing her unwilling limbs, she managed to do so. She was rewarded with a rumbling from deep within the dragon. In another creature, it might have been a purr. The bone-rattling sound rose to a crescendo as she found her way to a very precise place above Myn's eyes. When Sandra was through, Myn lifted her head, gave one more glance, and retreated to the center of the barn to settle down comfortably again. When her heart stopped pounding, Sandra turned to Ivy.

"There must be a story behind all of this," she said breathlessly.

#

Later, Myranda pulled herself reluctantly from the bed. At the edge of the shrouded window was the dying light of the day. They would have to be on their way again. She fumbled about in the dark and unfamiliar room until she found the door, opening it to be greeted by the warm, inviting smell of food simmering below. As she made her way down the stairs, she found Ivy and Sandra chatting at the table like old friends. Set out on the table was by no means a feast, but as the first meal she'd seen in ages that wasn't hastily cooked over a meager flame or served by guards, it was perfect.

"You really didn't have to--" Myranda began.

"Oh, hush. I've heard the whole story. I'm not sure I believe all of it . . ." Sandra began.

"Hey!" Ivy objected.

". . . but I certainly don't believe everything the Alliance has said either," she continued. "I don't know if you are the Chosen or a group of traitors, but you have done something for me that even the Alliance Army couldn't. For that, at least, I owe you the benefit of the doubt. And a hot meal."

A hot meal it was, and a good one. It featured things like fresh bread, wine, mugs, and plates. Things Myranda had forgotten were supposed to be a part of mealtime. She ate heartily, savoring the flavors as much as she could. It might be the last real meal she would have for some time. As she ate, she and Sandra spoke.

"You . . . you work with the Red Shadow," she said.

"I do," Myranda admitted.

"Then you *are* criminals," Sandra said gravely.

"We do what we have to do. If that makes us criminals, so be it," Myranda said.

"But he is a killer. Knowing what little I do about you, I cannot imagine you would willingly help him," Sandra said.

"I cannot speak for what he has done in the past, but he is dedicated to the task at hand," Myranda explained.

Sandra stared at her, considering the answer. Myranda took a final bite of the cobbler that had attracted Ivy to begin with. To taste such a divine concoction at a time like this made her feel like a prisoner eating her last meal.

"Where will you go now?" she asked.

"I've two . . . three more friends that I need to reunite with," Myranda said, Deacon flitting across her mind. "I will find them."

"I . . . I cannot believe that I am saying this . . . but I wish you the best. I hope that you find your way to a solution that will spare our soil any more blood, and I hope that you find it soon. The north needs people like you. You have compassion. You are a healer. And the country is suffering," Sandra said.

"I shall do my best," Myranda said, standing up from the meal.

Sandra stood.

"Before you go, at least take a cloak," Sandra insisted.

She walked over to the hook upon which it hung. A cloud of dust billowed into the air as she shook it clean.

"You've done so much already, I couldn't--" Myranda replied.

"It belongs to my younger brother. He left for the front a few months ago. If giving it to you means he comes home to find it missing, I don't think I will mind the scolding," she said earnestly.

Myranda took the garment from her and the two shared a hug. Sandra turned to Ivy.

"Goodbye, Ivy. I am sorry for how I treated you," she said, opening her arms.

Ivy pounced upon her, offering up a more enthusiastic hug than Sandra had been expecting.

"It's okay. You didn't know any better. Sorry for scaring you," the playful creature said.

"It is all right," Sandra assured her.

With that, the two heroes set out, Sandra by their side. When they reached the doors, their host stopped them.

"Myranda," Sandra said. "If they come to me, I will tell them you were here. I won't keep this a secret."

"Do what you think is right. That is all we are doing," Myranda replied.

Sandra pulled the doors open. Myn stood, her eyes filling with excitement and relief as her two friends appeared. Myranda offered a friendly scratch on the head. Myn offered a raspy tongue on the cheek in return. The dragon looked to Sandra with a vague look of recognition followed by a gaze that instantly made it clear to the farmer that she should be holding another bag of potatoes. Ivy scrambled onto Myn's back.

"Are you sure you want to ride there? We will be flying again," Myranda warned.

"I'll close my eyes. I don't want to be asleep if something happens," Ivy replied, wrapping her arms tightly about the dragon's neck.

Myranda climbed atop Myn, taking her place just behind Ivy. Sandra stepped aside and held the doors open. A few powerful strides and one mighty leap later and the heroes were soaring into the crisp night air. In moments, the massive form was nothing more than the quiet flap of leathery wings. A moment later, even that was gone.

Sandra walked slowly back to her home. For the first time in months, the veil of sadness was gone. For the first time in years, she felt something else. Hope.

#

High above the frozen ground, Ivy was clutching Myn tightly enough to make even a dragon take notice. She was trembling, her breath coming in swift, terrified hisses and leaving in quiet whimpers. A blue aura struggled every few moments to flicker to life, but Ivy managed to push the fear deeper inside.

"Ivy, you need to calm down. Breathe slowly," Myranda urged.

"I can't. I can't. How much longer? Say we're landing soon!" Ivy squealed in terror.

"We will be flying all night. I'm not certain where we are headed yet," Myranda replied.

Ivy responded with a louder whimper and a flash of blue.

"Ivy. You are in no danger. Myn would never let you fall," Myranda said.

The word "fall" shook Ivy, and she clenched her eyes even tighter. This would not do. It was true what she'd said earlier. If something happened, it was important she be awake--but to have her in abject terror would do no good at all.

"Ivy, do you trust me?" Myranda asked.

Ivy nodded stiffly.

"And do you trust Myn?"

She nodded again.

"Then open your eyes," Myranda requested.

"But . . ." Ivy objected.

"Ivy . . . it will be all right," she said softly.

Ivy braced herself and fought her eyes open, momentarily letting the fear through to the surface. She was greeted first with nothing. Just a cold, black abyss all around her. The flare of blue began to fade. Slowly, she gazed upward. The clouds were close. So close she felt as though she could touch them. The moon was nothing but a pale glow behind them. She looked down. Her head felt like it was spinning. It was the ground she was looking at, but she'd never imagined it would look like this. The fear fell far into the back of her mind, pushed aside by the very same sense of wonder and beauty that had struck Myranda on her first flight. She leaned aside to get a better look, then shifted quickly to see what the other side offered.

"It's . . . beautiful," she whispered.

Her wide eyes darted all over the spectacle, eager to take in as much as she could. The fear was still there, but it was tempered by exhilaration and discovery into something different. Something new. She turned her eyes to the clouds.

"Can . . . can we go higher?" Ivy asked.

"Well, Myn?" Myranda asked with a smile.

The dragon angled herself toward the sky and started to climb. The clouds drew nearer, then suddenly the world vanished as they drifted inside. There was nothing but gray in all directions, and the tingle of suspended particles of ice danced across their skin. A few moments later, Myn emerged from the top, trailing a few streamers of mist behind her. She may as well have traveled to another world. Below them, the clouds stretched out as far as the eye could see, like a stormy gray sea with cresting waves frozen in place. Above was the sky. Not the dismal blanket with rare patches of starlight that Myranda knew as the sky, but the true sky. A field of stars, crystal-clear and sparkling.

Myranda had never looked upon a cloudless night sky, but she'd dreamed of it. Even her imagination paled in comparison to the jewel-studded eternity before her. And the moon. She'd thought she'd seen it before, but she'd been wrong. What she had seen could not be the same glorious, mottled, ivory disc that hung overhead. It was like polished marble, and it gleamed with a brilliance that seemed to rival the sun.

Ivy's mouth hung open in awe, the dazzling sight sparkling in her eyes. Myranda was not blind to the beauty, but to Ivy it was so much more. Her keen eyes traced marvelous patterns on the moon's surface. Her mind, attuned to the finest nuances of art in all of its forms, was buzzing with inspiration. It was almost too much for her to bear.

"I never could have dreamed of anything so wonderful . . ." Ivy managed in a hushed voice.

Myranda reluctantly closed her eyes. She had a job to do. Now that Ivy was calm, it was time to choose a direction. Soaring through the icy sky on the back of a dragon would not have been her first choice as a place to meditate, but it would do. Myn was gliding smoothly and easily, and but for the rushing wind, she could not have asked for more tranquil surroundings. A night of proper rest and a decent meal had served her well. A staff in hand, even the D'karon one, was a help as well. She sifted over its enchantments one last time, hopeful of something that might help her find the others, and wary of something that might help the D'karon find her. Finding nothing she could identify as useful or dangerous, she set her mind to the task as she had before.

The cold air and howling wind slowly drifted away as her concentration deepened. The galaxy of stars above vanished and a duplicate seemed to appear below as the tiny burning embers of the souls of her people revealed themselves to her. Briefly, she sought the others as she had before, but it soon proved itself fruitless. She reached into her memory, scouring her discovery of Ivy for clues. In her mind's eye, the world was awash with a mild, warm glow. It was faint, but it was everywhere. Myranda had never been taught precisely what it was. Perhaps it was the spirit of the very world. Perhaps it was the energy of nature. Whatever it was, it was everywhere . . . Everywhere but where Ivy had been.

She turned her gaze to the staff she held. It was dark, darker than its surroundings. So it was with everything that they touched. She changed her search, seeking not light but darkness, not fountains of life but barren voids. If the D'karon were hiding the Chosen, then she would find the residue of their treachery.

It didn't take long. A horrible darkness and soul-searing chill seized her mind. She focused on it. It was far, but that word had come to mean very little now that Myn had returned. Associating true distance to its strange counterpart in the astral plane was far from simple, but it was a task she'd been forced to become adept at. Slowly, the indistinct destination resolved itself to a point on the map. They had their target.

"That way, Myn. More to the east," she guided.

Ivy turned.

"Who did you find?" she asked.

"I don't know," Myranda replied.

"I hope it is Lain . . . or Deacon. Anyone but Ether," Ivy said, sneering at the offending name. "It is a good thing she wasn't around to meet Sandra. It would have been a disaster. I never would have heard the end of it, either."

"You did take a big chance," Myranda reminded her. "You should have stayed hidden."

"I know it. But sometimes I see a house, or a city, and . . . I don't know . . . I feel . . . wistful, I think is the word," Ivy said.

Myranda thought back to the throne room.

"That human, back in the castle. Was she . . ." Myranda began.

"She was," Ivy replied.

"Then should I call you . . ." the wizard attempted.

"No," Ivy shook her head slowly. "That isn't me. Not anymore. I might have been Aneriana once. That was a long time ago. She couldn't have done some of the things I did. She wouldn't have done some of the things I did. I'm Ivy now. For better or worse. I couldn't go back . . . even if I could."

She furrowed her brow at the last cryptic line.

"Do you remember any of it now?" Myranda asked.

"Some of it. Some of it is very clear now. The last part. The rest is still a blur, except here and there," she said sadly. As her fists clenched, she seemed suddenly frantic. "Uh, let's talk about something else. Quick! When I think about that I think about *him* and when I think about him I start to feel that way again. The hate. I didn't like that. It wasn't the same as the others. Anger and fear are bad, but at least they throw me aside. I don't even remember it. When I felt the hate, I was still there. I remember it. I just couldn't stop it . . . It was *me.* I don't think it would have let go if I hadn't touched that sword."

Ivy paused to consider it, shuddering at the thought.

"You know, I don't think you told me about Myn yet. How did she get so big? And what happened to you? Did they get you, too?" Ivy asked.

Myranda explained her own trials since they parted, and explained to the best of her ability what had happened to Myn. It should have been a quick tale, but Ivy pressed her for details relentlessly, eager for every last nuance. If Myranda hadn't known any better, she would have sworn that she was imitating Deacon. After quite some time, when every last avenue of the ordeal had been explored, Ivy turned to Myn's wing, eagerly seeking a glimpse of the mark she'd failed to notice before.

"Is the mark big? I don't know how I could have missed it. I guess . . ." Ivy began, stopping suddenly.

When she spoke again, it was with a steady, serious voice.

"Myranda. We're close to where we are heading, aren't we?" she asked, with little doubt in her voice.

"Yes. How did you know?" Myranda asked.

"You'll hear it before you see it, I think," Ivy said ominously.

Myranda listened closely. She heard the wind. Aside from that was the beat of Myn's wings. The dragon seemed to tense beneath her. Something had her on edge. She listened closer. The leathery flapping was different. It sounded as though . . . there was more than one pair of wings at work. Before long, there was no doubt: something else was in the air with them.

"Where is it?" Myranda urged. Her knuckles were white around the stolen staff.

"There," Ivy said, a finger indicating a vague form blotting out a patch of stars ahead. "And there . . . and there."

The wizard trained her eyes on the darkness, searching her memory briefly for something that might cut a bit deeper though the pitch. It didn't make sense. The moon was nearly full. It was more than enough light. She should see the threat as plain as day.

"Do you think if I was to get afraid enough to change it would help at all?" Ivy asked, flickers of blue making their way through despite her best efforts.

"Anger would be better," Myranda said, her eyes finally making out the full silhouettes of three dragoyles, each as big as the beast that had threatened them in the valley of the dead.

"Yeah, it p-probably would, but f-fear is all I've got to offer," Ivy struggled to say.

"Stay calm, Ivy. We've got Myn. We can get through this," Myranda assured her, scouring her mind for anything that might be effective against the behemoths.

"C-can't calm down. It's one thing to trust Myn to catch me if I fall, but what if *she* falls!? What if she gets hurt!?" Ivy raved.

"Just hold tight and don't think about it. I won't let them touch us," Myranda said.

Briefly, the wizard considered casting sleep upon her again. No. The task at hand was difficult enough without having to keep a helpless body from slipping off.

"I can't stop thinking about it! I can't do anything! You shouldn't have rescued me! You should have left me for last! I'm no good to you up here! All I am is another thing for you to worry about! The best thing I could do is . . . THAT'S IT!" Ivy said, a burst of yellow mixing with blue for a moment as she turned to Myranda. "Let me fall!"

"No! We will get through this together, I can't let--" Myranda attempted to object.

"Myranda, listen! If I fall, I'll be afraid. I'll turn into whatever it is that I turn into when I am afraid. There'll be a lot of light and a lot of sound and then I'll wake up safe and sound, far away. That's how it always happens! It won't get rid of them, but it'll give you one less thing to worry about," Ivy explained.

"It is too risky. We don't know what will--" Myranda cried.

"Myranda, there's no time to argue. You have to trust me," Ivy said.

The hulking forms were close. They would be upon the heroes in moments. Myranda could not bring herself to agree. It didn't matter. She didn't have the chance. Ivy hopped to her feet on Myn's back and ran a few steps along it, leaping in a graceful dive over the dragon's head.

"Don't catch me, Myn!" she piped in a crazed cry of mounting terror as she blurred past the beast's vision.

Myn dove to follow.

"No, Myn! She knows what she's doing," Myranda said uncertainly.

With all of the will she could muster, she turned her eyes from the brilliant point of blue light disappearing through the clouds and faced the dragoyles. She could only see one well. It would be her first target. She waved the staff in a circle, stirring the wind with it. In moments, she had a howling gale. It circled around them, growing in force and dragging up trails of mist. First they were thin streamers, then fat ribbons, and finally vast sheets of cloud. They whirled and mixed into a growing maelstrom.

The dark creature fought against the wind, frost building to ice on its black hide. It wasn't enough. Myranda could hear the massive thing ripping though the wind. Now it was Myn's turn. She gave a powerful pump of her wings and lurched upward suddenly, placing her claws in the perfect position to strike. And strike she did. Stout, powerful talons came down with crushing force on the creature's head. As the dragoyle's momentum carried it past, Myn raked her foreclaws along its back, lashing with her hind claws at its wings.

The roar of pain that burst from the thing's mouth was deafening. It faltered, disappearing into the clouds. Myranda recovered from the sudden shift and searched desperately for the second creature while still maintaining the intensity of their shield of wind. Before she could find it, the creature made its presence known. The massive dragoyle, easily triple Myn's size, collided from the side. The rocking blow all but threw Myranda free. As she clung for her life, the monster clutched Myn with massive claws. The brave dragon struggled, spouting flame that scattered uselessly in the wind.

Far below, Ivy plummeted earthward. The wind screamed in her ears as she tore through the clouds. She screamed at the top of her lungs. Fear burned her mind and fluttered in her chest, but it did not bite to her core. Blue sparks of intense aura danced in front of her eyes, but stopped just shy of consuming her. Deep inside, she knew that she would be safe. The fear would protect her. The intricate designs of the ground spiraled and grew slowly, filling her vision, stirring something in her mind. It began as surprise and built quickly to confusion. Where was the transformation? She brushed the concern mounting in her aside. There was no need to worry. The fear would save her. There was no need to worry . . .

The realization struck her like a lightning bolt. If there was no need to worry, then she wouldn't be frightened enough to change! She would be killed! The epiphany thrust the reality of the situation into the foreground once more, and a renewed terror carried her to the very brink of transition. Unfortunately, the familiar feeling of slipping away from the world brought with it the relief that she would indeed be safe, quickly banishing the fear. The fading aura made the rapidly approaching ground clear to her, surging the fear again, and again came the relief, extinguishing it. Her mind raced in ever tighter loops as the cycle of panic and calm grew faster.

"I WAS WRONG! CATCH ME!" she cried.

The tangled form of Myn, Myranda, and the dragoyle dropped into the clouds. The dragon managed to clamp her jaws onto the beast's wing. Vicious teeth tore leathery hide and creaked against hollow bone. Puffing up her chest, Myn belched a column of flame onto the limb still caught in her maw. The dragoyle howled in pain and released them. After a few moments to steady herself in the air, Myn made ready to circle back and face the creature again, climbing to the surface of the ocean of clouds.

"No! Stay in the mist!" Myranda ordered.

Myn obeyed. Myranda scrambled across the dragon's back to her proper position and held the staff high. The freezing cold of night grew deeper. The mist became grainier. A lurching blackness approached from below as the first beast, still suffering from the long furrows scoured into its back by Myn, finally made its way back into the fight. Myranda made it the focus of the cold. Tiny crystals became fat flakes around it. A crust of ice stiffened the beast's joints.

Myranda pushed her mind harder. The crust became a layer, then a blanket. Soon it was not only the water around the dragoyle, but the creature's very blood that was freezing. It squeezed a pathetic, strangled screech out. The cry was cut off as even the monster's throat hardened into stillness. Just as the paralyzed form started to drop from view, Myranda hurled a ball of flame. The intense heat splashed against the frozen creature and, pushed from one extreme to the other too quickly, it came apart at the seams. What dropped out of the clouds was a barely recognizable scattering of frozen anatomy.

Without a word from Myranda, Myn knew what was next. Find the others, and avoid being found.

Ivy screamed through the air like a brilliant blue comet. She swept every terrifying thought she could muster from her memory and piled them one on top of the other. Nothing could upset the stalemate. She flailed at the air, as though if she tried hard enough she could dig her fingers into it and hold tight. As she did, she inadvertently turned about. Her maddened eyes came to rest on a sight that managed to be even more frightening than the ground.

It was one of the dragoyles. It was not a tiny, blurry speck among the clouds as it should be, either. What she beheld was a creature just a few seconds behind her, serrated beak trailing a billowing cloud of miasma behind it. It wasn't flapping its wings, instead tucking them back and straightening its body into a streamlined dart. It was falling. And it was falling faster than she was. Ivy's mind clamped onto the image. It would do.

A blaze of blue surged like an azure sun as Ivy's fear took over. The cry of fear echoed over the hilltops and through the trees. A sudden and intense will forced her earthward far faster than the dragoyle could manage, but still it worked its wings to catch up. The ground turned swiftly from patches of silver, gray, and white to icy water, frozen trees, and barren fields. When she reached the ground, she struck with enough force to sway the trees of the forest that was unfortunate enough to be her target. No sooner had the branches swayed to their maximum than a blue blur flashed out from between the trees and into the field. A moment later, the enormous monster, far too large to overcome its own momentum, shook the forest again. It was a grotesque sound, a crunch louder than thunder mixed with the splintering of trees and a short, agonized squeal.

Then there was only silence as the forest attempted to recover.

High above, Myn pulled herself up through the clouds and locked her eyes on the remaining dragoyle. Its partially roasted wing was doing a barely adequate job of keeping it airborne. Its maw hung open and vast swaths of black breath were erupting forth. Myn circled to the side. The ponderous beast attempted to wheel to follow, but it couldn't match the agility of the smaller creature. Myn clamped down on the beast's afflicted wing, planted her feet against the monster's body, and pulled with all of her might. The pair began to plummet through the clouds again. Myranda kept the thick motes of black mist from them as the bones and flesh yielded to Myn's jerking pulls. Finally, the whole wing came free. What was left of the creature spiraled and writhed as it fell.

Myn turned her sharp vision earthward, locking onto the bright blue streak below that blazed across the field and over the lake's icy surface toward a small, rocky island at its center. Perhaps her fear-crazed mind believed it offered the best cover. Perhaps some small part of her knew what she would find there. Regardless of the reason, the island was the very place they sought. Someone the D'karon did not wish to be found was being held within.

A sturdy wooden door in a stone wall splintered as she roared through it. The dragon dove toward her, but the better part of the distance between the clouds and ground still lay before her. Ivy blazed through the narrow courtyard, around what looked to be an outcropping of stone with a doorway carved into it. When she reached a point behind it that was reasonably hidden from sight, she disappeared inside, the fading blue glow betraying her position. A moment later, a scattering of nearmen climbed from the hole in the stone and inspected the shattered remains of the door.

Myn was drawing nearer, but as she did, she began to slow, even though there was a long way to go. Her eyes were locked on the shifting layer of ice that had yet to settle after Ivy's trip across it. As they approached the surface of the lake, Myranda felt the same tenseness that had marked the approach of the dragoyles, only more so. Her heart raced. What could lie beneath the waves? They'd never faced a creature of the water before. There was no way to prepare for it.

Now the water was just below them. They were just approaching the shore of the island when a pair of ice drifts collided, sending a spray of icy water high enough to sprinkle Myn's scales. Something inside her mind gave way. She pumped her wings madly, as though at any moment the water would reach up and grab her. There'd been no motion but the ice. Nothing had touched her but the water, but still she was mad with fear. Of course . . .

It stood to reason. Myn had always been afraid of the water, ever since the flooding of the cave when they were heading to Entwell. Her last serious encounter with it had literally cost her her life. Even the stoutest of minds would falter at the sight of it after that. Myranda tried to steady her friend.

"Myn, just get me to the island, you can leave me and come back for me after!" Myranda called out.

The terrified creature fought every instinct in a mind trained for eons to embrace them. She forced herself to approach the ground at the water's edge. The instant Myranda tumbled to the frozen stone, she shot skyward. The wizard surveyed the threat before her. As with her rescue of Ivy, the nearmen before her were magic users. They held black wands at the ready--but at the sight of her, they did not attack. Instead, they scurried back into the carved hole in the stone, securing it shut with a wave of a wand and an uttered word. The door was also stone, and fit so securely into the opening that if she'd not seen it move into place, she scarcely would have imagined there was a hole at all.

Myranda stepped back. Upon closer inspection, the structure, if it could be so called, was a low dome of stone that sloped until it was flush with the ground. In fact, it actually connected to the ground. Had they simply carved a chamber into a solid stone island? Or had the whole of the little isle been created by them? She rushed around the edge of it, seeking another door. The closest she found was a shallow recess on the far side, the very one Ivy had nestled herself in for protection. The creature was still there, the blaze of fear replaced by the deep, unnatural sleep that always followed. The wizard shook her, hoping to wake her. It was an act of pure optimism. After such an outburst, Ivy was seldom awake in anything less than half a day. Sure enough, no amount of jostling produced anything beyond an uncomfortable shift.

Whatever had to be done, Myranda would be doing it alone.

So be it. Myranda made her way back to the door and thrust the point of the staff into what little there was of a seam and put her mind to work. Slowly, a tremor was summoned. The pebbles at her feet began to dance around her. Something was wrong. Try as she might, she could not will anything stronger than a light rhythm from the earth. There was an enchantment working against her. A powerful one. She abandoned the spell and switched to flame, but no sooner did it splash against the door than it flickered away. She didn't need to test wind and water to know they would be similarly ineffective.

"So they've protected it against elemental magic. That means Ether is inside," she reasoned out loud.

For a moment, she brought to mind some of the more destructive spells that fell outside of the elemental realm, but a thought occurred to her. The staff she held was of D'karon design. A quick perusal of the enchantments clinging to it revealed one that had much the same feel as that which held the door shut. A second seemed its logical opposite. She fed the appropriate spell a dose of her will and it eagerly leapt to work. A smile came to her face. The door was slowly grinding aside. In taking the staff, she may well have stolen the very keys to their defense.

"This is quite the useful tool," Myranda quipped.

The smile dropped away as the sounds from within finally made their way through the widening gap. There was a commotion inside. Splashing water, twisted unnatural voices, clinking, scratching, clawing. Myranda placed a foot inside the opening when it was wide enough. Almost instantly, she was pushed back. Out from the inky depths of the place came a cacophonous rustle and flutter as dozens of black forms burst from the darkness. For a moment, she thought she was being attacked by bats. She was wrong on both counts.

It was not a colony of bats tearing past her, but a veritable army of cloaks, and they were not attacking. The disembodied garments seemed utterly unconcerned with the human, save for the fact that she was in their way. She tried to oppose them but was thrown aside, sprawling to the ground as the sky filled with the creatures and the ground crawled with them. Myranda's eyes darted from one beast to the next. Deep within the folds of their cloth forms was a crystal, phantom claws locked about it in a protective grip. They drifted through the sky and across the surface of the water like ants carrying eggs from a flooding colony. By the time the flow from the opening trailed off, there were easily hundreds of them, all drifting north.

"Myn!" Myranda called out. "Stop as many of them as you can, and keep Ivy safe! I will be back as soon as I can!"

With that, she disappeared inside.

The dragon went to work. Sweeping as low along the water as her mind would allow, she sprayed the creatures with flame. They scattered, but each blast of fire took a handful of them with it. Myn managed a few more runs before the flow was too scattered to manage any more than one at a time. In truth, she'd roasted only a small fraction of the torrent of creatures, but destroying any more would take her too far from Ivy. She circled back and took up a patrol in a tight circle over the tiny island, her sharp gaze locked on the sleeping creature.

Inside the dome, Myranda was greeted with the only light ever to be found in the depths of D'karon structures, the blue-white light of captured magic. This time, however, the light came in a way Myranda scarcely could have imagined. An intricate pattern of crystalline rods had been gathered together into a sequence of interlocking shapes, like an array of enormous snowflakes fixed point to point. The grid formed a shell in the center of the largely hollow interior that now seemed to have been bored into the island. Half of it was submerged in water, refracting and reflecting the light into dazzling blobs of light across the ceiling, and a trio of wooden struts stood from water-obscured floor to ceiling.

At every point where one crystal rod met another, a gem was affixed--or, at least, had been. Even now, a smattering of cloaks and nearmen were harvesting them and sweeping toward the door, showing little regard for the human who stood in their way. Myranda stepped aside and let them pass. Myn would stop them if she could, and there was a far more pressing matter at hand.

In the very center of the vast crystal shell was a smaller one attached to stone at the bottom of the deep hollow center of the island. Inside of it, shifting wildly, was a swirl of water that clearly had a will controlling it. It was twisting and writhing, trying to snake out through the space between the bars and recoiling back inside when it touched one. A moment later the bundle of water darkened and shifted to stone, dropping a short distance to the rocky floor. Beside it, standing completely beneath the rippling surface of the indoor pool, was a pair of creatures Myranda had never seen before.

Each looked to be a man in a suit of armor, but even through the shifting wavelets, she could see that there was no flesh beneath the metal plates. They hung loosely in place, an empty shell in the vague shape of a man, and a formidable man at that. Red runes traced arcane patterns across every surface. The only semblance of a being within the armor was a ball of flickering amber light behind each chest plate. They each held in their gauntlets a tall spear.

In a fluid motion that stretched the unseen limbs further than any natural being could, one of the demon armors thrust the weapon into the newly-formed stone. A gem flickering in the blade drew in a dose of power and the rock shuddered and shifted back to water to start the struggles anew.

The final crystal was hurried out the door and finally notice was taken of the intruder. Only two nearmen remained, sloshing around the shallow water at the edge of the flooded room. As Myranda raised her staff to face them, she was quickly reminded that the gem structure was ravenous enough to limit her to the D'karon spells, but that was of little concern. She'd become quite comfortable with their use.

A bolt of black ripped through the air at her, but it was easily deflected. She clamped the crushing spell so frequently used upon her around her attacker and hurled him at the stone wall. The other nearman aimed a shot at the curved roof, his destructive spell punching a jagged hole through it. A second blast destroyed one of the wooden struts.

Impossibly, the whole of the island shuddered and tilted, sagging against the remaining struts. The door Myranda had entered through dipped below the waterline and began to gush water. Myranda scrambled through the icy water to the high ground at the opposite end of the flooding room. She regained her footing just in time to deflect another blast from the sole surviving nearman. The blast reversed neatly on itself and destroyed its caster. Myranda turned to a sharp hissing sound overhead. It came from the hole above her. Air was escaping. The island, which she now knew was certainly anything but a proper one, was sinking!

Outside, the sight of the sudden movement of the island cast a fresh spike of fear into Myn's mind. She couldn't believe her eyes. The waves were working their way up the shore. The water terrified the creature, but the thought of losing her friends terrified her more. She dove low, snatching up Ivy before the water could reach her. Working her wings for all they were worth, she skimmed across the water's surface to the shore, depositing Ivy there and charging back. The water would not claim Myranda.

The wizard splashed out to the crystal shell and climbed atop it, blasting at it with whatever the staff seemed capable of. Fractures curled their way around the bars, but they seemed to shrug off the worst of the damage. Below, one of the demon armors was scaling the sloped floor beneath the water. When it reached the shell, the various plates and straps of the armor spread and scattered, finding gaps large enough to slip through, reassembling around the amber glow on the other side.

Myranda worked at the shell. One bar broke, then another. Suddenly a grip, literally like iron, closed around her ankle and tore her from atop the crystal structure. She was tossed effortlessly aside.

Water that was cold as ice drained the feeling from her limbs as she struggled to reach some manner of foothold. Alas, the last of the floor was slipping ever deeper into the water, leaving little more than the peak of the crystal cage above the surface. The steely grip closed around her ankle again and she was yanked beneath the waves with barely a gasp of breath. Nearly blinded by the freezing water, Myranda managed to dodge the thrusting spear of the armor, but only just. She forced aside the agony tearing at her mind and summoned another blast. The gauntlet clutching her leg flew to pieces, allowing her to fight her way to what little air remained and take a much needed breath.

Myn crashed down on the sinking hunk of stone, clawing madly at the tiny hole she found. She felt the waves close around her legs and every ancient instinct and ingrained fear demanded she take to the air again. She denied them, finally breaking though. There was the wet snap of wood and the entire island seemed to drop out from under her, sinking into the depths. The terrified dragon flailed about in the water before managing to catch enough of the wind in her wings to hoist herself skyward. The former island drifted out of sight, the remnants of the sheet of ice that had been the lake's surface closing over it.

The last of the air slipped out of the widening hole. It was large enough to escape through, but Myranda turned her back to it. She still had a job to do. The icy water stung at her eyes as she gazed down at the still-intact shells of crystal. The remaining hand of the demon armor had caught hold of the edge of her cloak and she was being pulled into the darkening depths. A sizable chunk of the ruined roof drifted down beside her. Again, she called upon the vice spell, clutching it and guiding its fall. It broke easily through the first shell, but the armor creature that had stayed behind managed to deflect it from the smaller shell, the shell that held what remained of Ether. A moment later, the still-intact demon armor hurled its spear. The weapon hissed through the water like a harpoon and grazed Myranda's side.

Exertion of mind and body were squandering Myranda's last breath of air, and pressure squeezed painfully in around her. The inner shell still held strong. She ignored the pain and cold and held out her staff, groping with its spells for something to smash Ether's cage. The whole of the structure around her lurched as it struck the floor of the lake, sinking slightly into the icy mud. The shock was enough to dislodge a piece of the damaged roof. Myranda tried to swim aside, but the injured armor creature clamped her wrist in its remaining glove and twisted it viciously. The fingers opened of their own accord and her stolen staff floated instantly out of reach, rocketing to the surface. The stone pushed her to the tilted ground and pinned her there. It was all Myranda could do to keep from losing her last few moments of air in a scream of agony.

All that she knew of water magic flashed through her mind, but what remained of the enchantments protecting this place, and the crystal shell feeding off of it, prevented even the simplest spell from taking hold. Levitation and a dozen other spells fell flat in a frenzied panic of casting. Her lungs burned for air. Her chest heaved for it. The demon armors stood about her as her vision began to darken.

Then came the sound.

It was strange and far away, like thunder filtering though the fathoms of water. Myranda and her attackers turned their eyes to the surface as one. Thrusting toward them with waving motions that rippled along her whole body was Myn. Madness flashed in her eyes. She came down upon the ruins of the structure like an avalanche, snapping her jaws around one suit of armor in a maelstrom of bubbles and twisted metal and smashing the other apart with a wildly flailing claw. The beast quickly levered aside the stone that pinned her friend and snatched her up. Myranda gestured wildly at the shell of crystal. Myn cast a fleeting glance and whipped at it with her tail, reducing it to powder. She then planted her feet on the stone floor and thrust herself toward the surface.

The pair erupted from the surface, shattering a chunk of ice and soaring into the air. The dragon unfurled her wings and darted to the shore as Myranda gasped a burning cold breath of the icy air and collapsed into a fit of coughing. Myn belched out column after column of flame until the water that clung to her boiled and sizzled. She shook and rolled in crazed fear, as though the drops that nestled among her scales were at this moment trying to kill her. By the time she was through, Myranda had finished coughing and now lay in a trembling heap on the ground. Without the crystals near, her spells would work. Warmth and health were but a few whispered words away, but that could wait. She struggled soggily to her feet and looked to the lake.

The whole of the surface was surging with waves and churning ice. In the center, a small, clear mound of water had heaved itself up. It resembled a human form in the very loosest of terms, but stood perfectly still, in stark contrast to the stormy surface. Slits of light where the eyes should be flared. Slowly, the water around it settled to stillness. A circle of water centered around the form dropped flat and calm, and the circle began to grow. More and more of the lake was struck by the sudden stillness. With each wave that sunk to nothing, the humanity of the form became more distinct. Finally, the whole of the lake was a dead calm, smooth as glass-- and, in the center, Ether.

She sunk beneath the surface, providing it with its first ripples. An instant later, her form emerged from the shore nearest to the other heroes. Now near enough to see, the expression on her watery face was far from the serene, complacent mask of superiority she normally wore. It was a mosaic of fear, fatigue, desperation, and--perhaps most out-of-place of them all--gratitude.

"Thank you . . ." the shapeshifter managed. Two more unlikely words had never been spoken.

Ether dropped to her knees on the dusty pebbles of the shore. The rough gray texture crept up her legs, and in a few moments she was entirely composed of stone, motionless. Myranda made her way to the form and looked into its eyes, little more than orbs of smoother white stone set against the rest--but in them, she saw the flicker of power that she was hoping for. Ether was out of danger. All she needed was time to rest and a good strong fire. Indeed, that was all that each of them needed.

Having baked the last of the dampness away and finally calming down again, Myn seemed to suddenly realize she'd been remiss in her duties. She bounded off toward the nearest forest, no doubt on the trail of a fresh meal. Myranda took the opportunity to look after herself. She willed the wound on her side closed and wicked away the water that was chilling her to the bone. With a few more words and a flex of her mind, her trembling subsided. For a moment, she smirked at how simple it was, almost an afterthought. It was not long ago that falling in the water without someone to start a fire would have been a death sentence. Now it was, at worst, an inconvenience, rectified in moments, even without a staff.

She looked to the lake. Bobbing on the surface, tossed lightly by the small ripples being driven by the wind, was her stolen staff. She held out her hand and willed it to her. It obliged with little effort. In the calm after the battle, she regarded it as if for the first time. A curious little thing, it was. Certainly not something she would have imagined the D'karon putting to work. That, of course, was the point. It was a tool of deception, meant for the hand of a deceiver. There was no gem, nothing to mark it as a weapon. It seemed harmless, rather thin and ancient-looking. Gnarled and knobby in just the way a wizard's staff ought to be, the sort of staff that a kindly old wizard would lean on as he ambled through a village. It was comforting. It put one at ease. It was a lie.

A closer look revealed mystic runes etched over every surface that would hold a mark. The merest touch opened a dark tome of spells. Spells that required no training, no *soul* to cast them. Just a whisper of words, the tiniest thought. They were spells designed to destroy. Spells designed to control. Even holding the thing made Myranda feel soiled.

At the same time, though, it held many keys to trials she and the others had failed to overcome before. Spells to undo their locks. Spells to drop their shields. Somewhere among the enchantments, she felt something very close to what she'd felt whenever one of the generals vanished into the swirling voids--the very spell that allowed them to move so quickly at times, to escape so readily. She touched at the spell experimentally, but quickly withdrew. It was different from the rest. It needed a target of some sort, something specific. A simple point in space would not do. It seemed to crave an indication of which of many doors she wanted to open. The destinations were fixed, leaving her only to choose. Where those doors led, however, she did not know, and the potential danger of choosing the wrong one made choosing any one of them ill-advised.

The pounding steps of Myn returning pulled Myranda from her thoughts. It had surely only been a few minutes, but Myn dropped a young stag in front of her with the sort of pink-toothed contentment that betrayed a recently filled stomach. Without a word of request, the dragon bounded off again to gather wood, while Myranda faced the task of preparing the night's meal without a knife. Even with magic, it was an ungainly task. Still, she managed.

Before long, Myn was back to dump her prize on the ground. She was new to the task of fetching wood, and it showed. She'd brought an entire tree, dirt still clumped on its roots.

"Good, Myn, good," Myranda praised, offering the customary scratch. "Next time, though, try to find wood that is a bit less green. Something that snaps without much effort."

Such fresh wood should have been difficult to light, but in the presence of a wizard and a dragon, fire is seldom a long time in coming. Soon, a roaring fire was crackling. Ether's statue of a body was heaved onto the flames, Ivy was situated comfortably, and the food was prepared. The stone form of their friend reddened and eventually shifted to flame, tearing at the energy of the flame far more hungrily than Myranda gnawed at the meat. A few minutes allowed the shapeshifter to regain her composure and, unfortunately, her usual disposition. Her eyes came to rest on the dragon and, despite being composed of flame, took on a cold glare.

"The lizard has returned from the dead, I see," Ether said, as though there was nothing particularly impressive about the feat.

Myranda nodded, swallowing her current mouthful before adding, "She's got something to show you, as well."

Myn unfolded her wing enough for the Mark to reveal itself. For a moment, Ether was silent. When she spoke, her words shook with intensity.

"She counts herself among the Chosen. Well then--fate's mockery of me is complete. My exalted place at the zenith of cosmic import must be shared with a common beast," she fumed.

Myn's eyes narrowed.

"Myn saved your life *and* mine a few minutes ago. That fire, this food, and every day you and I live from now on are thanks to her," Myranda reminded.

"She is not without her usefulness. However, at least the *other* mindless beast is small enough to escape notice," Ether remarked, turning her gaze to the sleeping Ivy. "And the dragon will make us a target regardless of who sees us. There is not a human in this world who would trust such a monster."

Myn climbed angrily to her feet.

"Easy, Myn," Myranda said with little result, before turning back to Ether. "The whole of the north sees us as enemies already, and at least with Myn we will be able to move more quickly."

"Yes, well, considering how slowly you all recover, it hardly seems useful to be rushing to the next battle. At least for you," Ether countered, stepping from the flames and easily turning back to her human form as if to hammer home the point that days of torture could be erased in minutes.

Myn's scornful stare took on a predatory depth once more.

"I'm a healer. So long as I am able, I can see to it that we are all in fighting shape after little more than a night's rest," Myranda offered. She felt strangely as though she were arguing to be allowed to remain a part of the team, despite the fact that it was Ether who had just been rescued. Likely this was simply the shapeshifter's way of saving face after undeniably owing her freedom to another.

"Mmm. So long as you are able. Of course, that is far from a foregone conclusion at the end of a battle. Indeed, one could scarcely deny that you are the weakest link in our little ill-formed band of--" Ether began.

"MYN, DON'T!" Myranda shouted.

The shapeshifter turned to find the dragon reluctantly frozen in place, her massive jaws gaping just above Ether's head. From the mixed look of hunger and fury, there was little doubt what her intentions had been.

"I assure you, beast. Had you swallowed me, I would have created my own exit," Ether warned, turning back as though nothing had happened. "Regardless of the qualifications, it would appear that you three have managed to escape where even I have failed, evidence that the insight of the gods is not to be doubted. Tell me, then, how it came to pass, and why it is that Lain is not among us."

Myranda began the tale again.

#

Far away, huddled around a similar fire, a small band of different heroes plotted the events of the coming day. A bottle was passed around that held a different kind of fire. It passed first to Caya, a fresh scar striping the back of her hand. Then it passed to Tus, leather armor against leathery skin. Next it was passed to the shaky hand of a newcomer, a runner who carried information. It then passed away to the shadows, from hand to hand of the best of what little the north had left to staff the Undermine: Men, women, and virtual children.

"So, what do we know?" Caya asked.

"There's a-a lot of action. A lot of m-motion. The flow of troops to the front has stopped. They're . . . coming back. Coming north," he said nervously, as though such news would get him a hand across the face--or worse.

"Right . . . you know what that is called, boys? Desperation!" Caya cried.

A chorus of cheers erupted.

"The generals are losing control!" she spurred on.

A second roar rang out.

"Our time is coming, my soldiers," she added in serious tones. "The times have been hard. Victories have been scarce, but now the Alliance

Army is gasping its last breath. Mark my words, this war has seen its last winter!" she cried.

All in attendance raised their voices in triumphant approval. More bottles were produced and passed about, clinking together and lifted high. The hoots and hollers of the tired, battered, rejoicing soldiers filtered through the dense trees of Ravenwood. They'd been chased from these woods before, but in a forest so large and so thick, there was always another place to hide. Even now, their shouts became lost among the trees within barely a hundred places, and the light of their fire in half that.

Caya smiled as she looked upon her troops, their spirits riding high on her words. She'd never been the best on the battlefield, but give her a man's ear and he'd fight the gods themselves by the time she was through. As she basked in the warm glow of the fire and the admiration of her followers, something wiped her smile away. Despite the boisterousness about her and the deadening effect of the forest, ears sharpened by well-justified paranoia had latched onto something.

"Quiet!" she ordered.

Silence descended instantly. Somewhere in the darkness around them, there was the snap of a twig. The stand of trees echoed with dozens of swords pulling free in unison. She held out a hand. A bow was placed in it. She readied an arrow.

"Tus . . . find our visitor and bring him to me, would you?" she requested.

The monster of a man stalked into the forest. Tus was aware of stealth, but he'd never felt compelled to employ it. His thumping footsteps sent little cascades of snow drifting down from the trees as he passed, and despite the slow appearance of his gait, the length of the enormous man's stride carried him at what some would consider a run. He'd only just vanished among the trees when there came the sound of a man's voice, choked off in mid-sentence, followed by the plodding footsteps of his return.

When Tus came back into view, he was dragging an average-sized man by the throat. The man struggled uselessly at the ham-sized hand wrapped almost completely around his neck, while Tus looked, if anything, disappointed that he'd not put up a better fight. When he reached Caya, he hoisted the man to his feet, released his neck, and spun him around to face the commander.

"How did you find us!?" Caya demanded. "Did you follow the messenger!?"

The scrawny runner, his face perpetually with the look of a scolded dog, froze at the words, sweat rolling down his face. Tus shifted his stone-faced gaze in the poor man's direction, managing to deliver an unmistakable threat of punishment without changing his expression at all.

"No, I assure you the fellow is blameless," said the intruder roughly, as he rubbed his manhandled throat a bit.

"Wait a moment. I know you. You're that fellow Myranda was traveling with. Devon," she realized.

The mention of the hero's name sent a stir through the crowd. Myranda was the reason half of them had joined. It was the one name all of them knew for certain.

"Deacon, actually," he corrected.

"Right, right. Deacon. Have you come alone?" she asked.

"Unfortunately, I have," Deacon replied.

The crowd lost interest instantly and audibly.

"Right--well then," Caya said, motioning to Tus, who clamped his hand on Deacon's shoulder. "That warrants an explanation, I'd say. You see, Myranda we trust, and people who travel with her we trust as well. People who travel without her . . . well, that is another matter. You can start with how you found us."

Deacon winced at the grip on his shoulder.

"I am a wizard, and I've had quite a bit of practice at locating people in the past few months. For a wizard, practice is typically all we need," Deacon said.

"I've got more than a few wizards as enemies, my boy, and most have met me more times than you. Why is it that you found me and they didn't?" Caya asked.

"Maybe they aren't looking," Deacon offered. A paralyzing pain in his shoulder informed him that it was not the correct answer.

"Aspersions on my infamy aside, perhaps you'd like to tell me about Myranda. I first received word that she and an assortment of oddities were captured and moved to undisclosed locations, then that she entranced a demon dragon during an arena battle and escaped. Might you be able to verify?" Caya asked firmly.

"I was one of the oddities captured that day. I can't say for sure about the *demon* dragon, but she *has* been able to escape, and I think she's been busy freeing the rest of them as well," Deacon explained.

"I presume that you were one of the rescued, and yet you travel alone. Have you fallen out of her favor?" Caya probed.

"I freed myself. I imagine she has been tracking down the others because she can't find me. I've been concealing myself to make sure Demont doesn't follow me, but she's been flexing some considerable mystic might, so I've caught glimpses of her. As for me, even if she could detect me, the others are far more important than I," he said.

"Demont, you say. *General* Demont? That's a powerful enemy you've made for yourself," she replied, suddenly far more interested. "Let's hear it, then. Why come to me? And how did you manage to get away?"

Tus released his grip, allowing blood to flow back into Deacon's arm.

"My escape was somewhat complicated," he said, adjusting his ring uneasily. "Suffice to say that fully disarming me has a paradoxical effect."

"I really don't think that suffices at all," Caya said with a furrowed brow.

"I'll go into greater detail later. As for coming to you, I need to reach Myranda and the others, and I am not certain I can do so alone. She is moving very quickly."

"Demon dragons move quickly," Tus remarked, eager to believe the stories about a hypnotized beast.

"Err, indeed," Deacon conceded.

"Needed a bit of muscle to see your way safely, did you?" Caya asked.

"Well, if combat was my only concern, I might have managed on my own. My difficulties lie virtually everywhere else. I hail from a place very different from this. It has left me ill-suited to survival tasks," Deacon explained.

"Can't handle the wilds?" Tus asked.

"Not particularly well, no. The cities are no better for me, either," the wizard admitted.

"Listen. I'm willing to lend you a few of my troops, myself included, if it will bring us to Myranda, but how do you expect to catch up with her?" she asked.

"We can't. But we can get ahead of her. I know where she's going to go next. If they have been hiding the others as they had been hiding me, then there is only one such place that she hasn't visited. After that . . . well, there is only one target that makes sense. Northern Capital," Deacon said.

Caya considered his words.

"What do you say, my brave warriors? Do we help the wizard? Do we go to the capital? Do we take this war to the very doorstep of those who prolong it?" she asked.

The earth shook with the force of the reply.

"There you have it, wizard. You have the Undermine. For now, you can fix up the men and women that need it, and warm yourself by the fire," Caya said, snatching up a bottle and placing it in his hand as she grasped him tightly across the shoulders with the other arm. "And put a little fire in your belly, as well! And when the sun rises, we begin the march!"

#

The cold night drew toward its end, the faint glow that the people of the north knew as a sunrise beginning to hint at the edge of the mountains to the east. Myranda slept sitting up, enfolded in Myn's front legs. Ivy was left undisturbed on the shore of the lake to sleep off her outburst.

Out of dead sleep came a sharp gasp of air as the malthrope's eyes shot open and her claws dug into the ground. Her mind had done her the disservice of picking up precisely where it had left off, and it took a few moments for her to realize that she was no longer plunging through the sky toward the ground.

When her heart stopped racing and she'd caught her breath, she climbed dizzily to her feet. Her eyes scanned her surroundings. There was the lake. She'd seen it from the air, so they hadn't gone too far . . . though it did look different. Myn and Myranda were sleeping beside her. But there wasn't anyone else. Had they failed to rescue anyone? She shook more of the sleep from her head and looked again. There was food for her and a fire. She squinted her eyes at an indistinct form in the flames, the sight bringing a frown to her face.

"It was *you* we rescued," she said sulkily.

Ether stepped from the flames once more and resumed her human form.

"Who would you have preferred?" the shapeshifter asked.

"Pff. *Anybody,*" she said, crossing her arms and looking away.

"The antipathy is mutual, I assure you," Ether replied, scooping up the raw remainder of the meal that had been set aside for Ivy. "However, the resurrection of that beast has dispelled any doubt--or hope, for that matter--regarding the Great Convergence. She is the fifth, and we had indeed been united. As such, we are, by dint of poor consideration on the part of fate, partners until the D'karon are defeated."

Ether held out the food. Ivy eyed it suspiciously. Hunger got the better of her and she took it.

"So does this mean you aren't going to be mean anymore?" Ivy asked, mouth full.

"I will behave as I have. I will merely no longer anticipate your death with eagerness," Ether said.

"How nice of you," Ivy said flatly.

"It is the circumstances that have changed, not I," she replied.

"The circumstances *didn't* change. Myranda *told* you that the . . ." Ivy began, struggling to remember the appropriate word. ". . . *Convergence* happened way back when Myn died. If you'd have listened to her, you could have been not hoping I die for all of that time."

"Indeed. Her insight into the course of destiny has been somewhat more accurate than I would have expected," Ether admitted.

"Yeah, because she *trusts* people. She *believes* in people," Ivy jabbed.

"A practice that continues to confound me with its success. I, for instance, would have never allowed your little experiment in constructive cowardice," Ether mused.

Ivy furrowed her brow and ran the words through her mind again. If it had been spoken by anyone else, she would have asked what was meant by "experiment in constructive cowardice," but she would not give Ether the satisfaction.

"When I fell from the sky, you mean!" she spouted triumphantly after a moment.

"Indeed," she replied.

"Oh, yeah, I guess that worked. I'm glad she let me do it, but . . . I don't think I'll do it again," Ivy said with a shudder.

They were silent for a few moments. Ivy looked about once more, her eyes locking on the lake, considering it as she finished her meal. She remembered seeing it when she broke through the clouds. The terrifying proposition of falling to her death in its frozen waters had managed to cement the image in her mind. As she looked at it now from ground level, she could not shake the feeling that something was missing.

"Didn't there used to be an island, a little one, right in the middle of this lake?" she finally asked.

"Something resembling one. Myranda's rescue destroyed it," Ether explained.

"Really? I . . . I think that means that every place we've been held in, we've wrecked!" Ivy said, a smattering of pride in her voice.

"If Myranda is to be believed, the arena was still standing when she left it," the shapeshifter corrected.

"That's true . . . close, though. Maybe we can get another shot at that one later," Ivy chirped cheerfully, as she shifted energetically. "I'm excited. I want to go now! Deacon's next, or Lain! How long have they been asleep?"

"Long enough," Ether decided. She told herself it was because she wanted to waste no more time. The fact that it was not until Lain's name was mentioned that she felt the urge to move forward was irrelevant.

The shapeshifter marched up to the sleeping dragon.

"Awake, beast," she stated, in a voice powerful enough for it to seem like a command.

Myn's eyes hoisted open sleepily, focusing on Ether and narrowing into angry slits. Myranda stirred and managed to pull herself from the dragon's grip.

"She has a name, Ether," Myranda reprimanded.

The wizard crawled out from under the dragon's craned neck and found her staff. The sky was brightening.

"We can't travel during the day, we will be seen," Myranda said, stifling a yawn.

"Now that you are not limited to the ground, there is always cover to be had," Ether said, gesturing toward the clouds.

"Well, Myn. Are you up to it?" Myranda asked.

The great beast sprang to her feet and unfurled her wings. No sooner had Myranda and Ivy climbed onto her back than she was in the air. A moment later and the windy form of Ether was beside them. Myn wheeled and pumped her wings, spiraling higher and higher in a less than subtle attempt to out-fly her airy rival. As she did, Ivy held tight and closed her eyes tighter.

"I thought you liked to look at the ground," Myranda remarked.

"I do. I like the way it looks from up close and I like the way it looks from far away. It's in between I don't like," she explained shakily.

The trembling creature didn't open her eyes until she felt the familiar damp chill of the clouds. When they emerged above them, she thanked the gods that she had. The sky was a tapestry, beginning in the deepest of star speckled blues and progressing to violet and purple, to red, orange, rose, yellow, and blue. The feathery tops of the clouds were fiery yellow and radiant gold. And the sun . . . it had never been so bright and glorious. The biting chill of the rushing wind was tempered by the warm rays that fell upon them unfiltered by the dismal blanket of clouds.

Only Ether seemed immune to the wonder before them. She looked upon her fellow travelers with mild irritation, finally breaking them from their trance.

"Why, might I ask, have you chosen to head in this direction?" said the shapeshifter.

"I hadn't made an attempt to locate Lain or Deacon yet. I shall do so immediately," Myranda said, realizing her oversight.

"No need. He lies in that direction," the windy form said with a gesture.

"How do you . . ." Myranda began, stopping when she realized the answer.

She could sense him already, without even putting her mind to it.

"They aren't hiding him anymore," Myranda said, her voice edged with concern.

"That's bad?" Ivy remarked in confusion.

"It means that they want us to find him. It means he is the bait in a trap," Myranda said solemnly.

"Oh . . ." Ivy replied. "Well, what do we do then? Find Deacon? Try to get more help?"

"The other human is meaningless and there is no one who could hope to offer aid. Lain must be freed," Ether decreed, bursting off toward her target.

With a word from Myranda, Myn was after the speeding form. It required a good deal more effort than before, but the dragon managed to keep pace with the determined shapeshifter. The golden sun rose slowly into the sky, but the beauty of it all was lost to them now. Tense minds were focused about the task at hand. Myranda ran a thousand possibilities through her mind, trying to work out what sort of dangers she might expect. Ivy breathed deeply and steadily, trusting that the others would know what to do when the time came. Myn's mind was a razor, the whole of her being focused on summoning all of the speed she could. She knew that Lain lie ahead and nothing in the world would keep her from him.

Ether's mind was a torrent of conflicting thoughts and emotions. Lain's soul smoldered ahead of her, weaker than it had ever been, and yet she'd never felt anything so intensely. She needed to free him. The purpose, the one guiding constant in the eternity of her existence, should have been the first thing on her mind. It was the last. In its place, she felt a symphony of emotions, most for the first time, and all focused on him. Fear of what may have been done to him. Hatred for those who had done it. Vengeance, desperation, desire . . . A chorus of discord, but all in agreement on one single thing: Lain must be freed.

#

In the capital, the king lowered his withered form onto the throne, the crown heavy on his head. He looked to the portraits that lined the hall, paintings of his predecessors. Each head wore the same crown. For some, it had been a symbol of their leadership of the kingdom. That had been long ago.

The land was ruled by no king now. There had been no ceremony, no coronation, but, nevertheless, the power had passed to the generals long before his own time. He turned to the heavy door to his right. Raised voices echoed from behind it. Names he'd heard spoken more and more frequently, and with more and more fury, were again ringing out. One name rang out above the rest. Myranda.

The door burst open, the general called Demont rushing out. His superior, Bagu, called after him.

"I don't care about anything else. Keep the Chosen from the capital! I shall punish you for your idiocy later, just make sure that they find Lain, and that they do not leave, understood!? Pull back your men from the front. Bring every available nearman to the capital immediately! We are too close to victory. There can be no more mistakes! I don't care about missing papers. I don't care about stolen crystals. Nothing matters but the gateway!

Once it is open, all else will be an afterthought! Now go, you imbecile! Do as I say!" the general cried.

A smile came to the face of the king.

"Is something wrong, General? Feel as though things have slipped from your grasp? As though you've lost control? Perhaps you should seek my council. It is something I've had much experience coming to terms with," the king said.

"Silence, old man," Bagu hissed.

"I held my tongue while you controlled my kingdom thus far, because at least the land was protected, but I can keep silent no longer. I have heard you order Demont to pull back his men. What of mine?" the king challenged.

"They will fight and die as their fathers did. They will learn what this war would have been if not for the aid of the D'karon," Bagu fumed. "It was not so long ago that this was what you'd sought."

"I'd sought for our men to lay down their weapons, not lay down their lives. If you will not aid in the battle, then the battle must be ended. If you will not support my kingdom, then what use are you? Get me a messenger! No, get me a carriage! I shall deliver the proclamation of surrender myself!" the king demanded, leaping to his feet.

"I cannot allow that. The war is a necessary distraction," replied the general.

"The war was your only purpose! I will not leave my kingdom in your hands! I will not forsake my people!" the King raged.

Bagu's fists tightened.

"Your Majesty, I've something to show you. Something that might make things clear to you," Bagu smoldered.

He disappeared into his office, emerging a moment later with a sand timer.

"Do you see this, my king?" he asked, holding the delicate glass apparatus to his face.

There was barely a sprinkle of sand left in the top bulb, and it slipped through, grain by grain.

"This is your world, Your Majesty. Those are the final moments of your people drifting away. When the last grain of sand falls, a gateway will open, and through it will flow *my* people. This world will be ours. Were I you, oh mighty king, I would busy myself with the task of proving why we shouldn't crush your people in their entirety. North, South, Tresson, Alliance. You will *all* fall before us, and there is *nothing* that can be done," Bagu explained with grim steadiness. "You can kill me. You can kill the other generals. It won't matter. The end is here."

Bagu placed the glass on the ground before the throne and stalked back into his sanctum. The king collapsed into the throne, his eyes fixed on the silvery sand that remained. He'd known throughout his life that he had no real power, that his whole purpose was to give his people some comfort and hope. In his years on the throne, he'd heard many whispers, collected much information on these men that had ruled in place of the crown. He knew they were not human. He knew the men they commanded were little more than shells.

Somehow, he had managed to convince himself that it was as it must be. That the way things were now was the best he could hope for, and that they would not change so long as he allowed the generals to continue. He had assumed that control of the Northern Alliance was all that they sought. Never had he imagined that through his inaction, he had doomed his kingdom and all others. For a few moments, his anger and resistance persisted, but the weight of hopelessness could only be heaved aside for so long. He hadn't the strength to resist, nor did his people. The D'karon had seen to that expertly. All that was left was to wait for the end, and pray it was a swift one.

#

The cold, gray noon shined dimly down upon a small, ragged group marching north. In the sky was the unmistakable look of a blizzard. Deacon looked nervously at his new allies. The night before, there had seemed to be quite a few more soldiers. Indeed, there had been, but with the rising sun, most had scattered in all directions, carrying messages to be passed on to the others, and in search of others bearing messages. What remained were perhaps a dozen of the sturdier troops, an assemblage of men slightly past their prime, boys who had yet to reach their prime, a pair of women, and Deacon himself.

"We usually traveled at night, when I was with the others. To avoid being seen," Deacon explained anxiously, as he watched riders on a road at the far end of the field pause to watch them pass.

"Too many of our own runners looking for us. If we hide, they won't find us," Tus stated.

"Tus is right. What we need most right now is information. The Undermine is not the most sizable force, and it is spread *very* thin. We can't afford to waste the time of our messengers by staying out of sight if we want to be able to coordinate. Besides, you said yourself, the generals aren't paying attention to us. 'Bout time to change that, I'd say," Caya said with a grin. "Let 'em know who they *ought* to be afraid of."

The comment met with a roar of approval that startled Deacon. He looked to the sky. He couldn't see anything, but he could feel it. Ether. She'd never made an attempt to hide herself before, and she certainly hadn't started. Even the most novice wizard would feel her presence from days away in any direction, and those they faced were no novices. The others were more subdued, requiring a skilled mind and a bit of luck to spot. He could not be sure, but they seemed to be traveling just slightly behind the shapeshifter. It wouldn't be long until they'd reached the mountain in the distance, the place from which Lain's soul suddenly began to shine like a beacon just hours ago.

"Have you ever fought any of the generals? They are formidable," Deacon reminded.

"As are we. We've got soldiers and a wizard. That makes us a match for anything that they can throw at us," Caya said.

"Except more soldiers and more wizards," Deacon corrected.

"What happened to your courage, man? Don't tell me you are afraid to die for this cause!" Caya said, slapping him on the back.

"I don't mind dying for a cause. I just don't want to die beforehand," he said.

Deacon tried to calm himself. He was unaccustomed to fear. It had never occurred to him to be afraid of something before. Things were not to be feared, they were to be understood. He was to learn from them. Now anxiety burned in his chest. He was not fearful for himself, or even for Myranda. He was fearful for the world. In the time since his escape, he'd felt a rhythm in the air. A barely detectable frequency at first--but, as time passed, it grew. Now it buzzed in his head, like the whole of the world was resonating with it. It was a power he couldn't identify, and it was massive.

The first flakes of the blizzard began to fall and the group shifted its path to a nearby town. A figure standing at the city gates disappeared inside and reappeared a moment later, on horseback. He galloped toward them, slowing only when, at a word from Caya, bows were drawn and angled at him. He sat silently and sized up the group before him as Caya returned his calculating stare. He was dressed oddly, in that the ubiquitous gray cloak that served as the national garment was conspicuously replaced with a long rider's coat, accompanied by a scarf wrapped about his face. His horse was not a farm animal, but a beast of rare breeding. Everything about him screamed wealth and privilege, save for the fact that he was in the middle of a field in a quickly mounting blizzard. His steed was weighed down with a number of cloth-wrapped bundles.

"Undermine!" the rider said, raising a hand in a peculiar sign, evidently to signal his allegiance.

"Are you now?" Caya said with irritable familiarity. "I don't remember accepting you."

"I know that voice," Deacon said, raising his crystal. "That is Desmeres. He is a traitor."

"Impossible, Desmeres can't be a traitor. A traitor has to have some sort of loyalties to betray--or, at least, some principles. I've dealt with him before, he has nothing of the sort," Caya said, motioning for the bows to be lowered.

"No, you don't understand, he is the one who helped the D'karon capture us," Deacon said frantically.

"D'karon?" Tus questioned.

"Err, the worst of the Alliance Army," clarified Deacon.

Caya took on a stern look and motioned for the weapons to be readied again.

"That association is over, I am afraid," Desmeres remarked casually, hopping to the ground. "And I will have you know that I am a man of very strong loyalties. It just so happens those loyalties are to myself. As for principles, I am about to betray them all."

"Oh?" Caya said.

Desmeres released one of the bundles and--slowly, so as to avoid triggering a salvo of arrows from the soldiers--undid its bindings and unrolled it. There, seeming to gleam with their own light, were blades of every shape and size. Short swords, long swords, hatchets, axes, daggers, knives, and shapes too unique to name. Each was a masterpiece, emblazoned with careful mystic engravings meaningless to all but Deacon and Desmeres.

"Take them," he said in a pained tone.

"These are your own creations. As I understand it, there are only two beings in the world you've deemed worthy to hold them," Caya said, looking over the weapons with hunger in her eyes.

"Yes, and the Alliance has seen fit to destroy one such being. I offer them to you to see to it that the other worthy party is not similarly destroyed. And to taste a bit of this vengeance that seems so popular these days," Desmeres replied. "So take. One each and there should be enough for all of you. The balance will be off; I designed them for the Red Shadow."

Caya snapped up the weapon nearest in size and shape to her own.

"I don't know what you mean. They seem perfect to me," she said with glee, experimentally slicing the weapon through the air and beaming a wide smile at the satisfying ring it produced.

"Compared to the relics you've had to use, I'm sure they seem that way," he replied.

The others clambered for the weapons greedily. As they did, Desmeres pulled Deacon aside.

"You might buy *them* with weapons, but *I* am slower to--" Deacon began.

"Yes, yes. Healthy suspicion. Commendable. I don't have time for it, though," Desmeres said, thrusting a deceptively heavy bundle under Deacon's arm. "Don't open it until you find them all. *All of the Chosen,* understood? And here. I know you'd have little use for anything I might have had time to make, but I managed to liberate these. I think you might be able to get some use out of them. You may read them at your leisure."

A thick leather messenger bag was pushed into his hands. Desmeres turned back to find the mat of weapons picked clean. He gathered it back up and mounted his steed once more.

"Wait!" Caya called. "How is it that you found us? And how is it that you knew that Deacon would be with us?"

"Our networks of informants have a good deal of overlap," he explained, turning his horse to the open field. "Oh, and do not get comfortable with those weapons. I'll be getting them back when you are through."

"Over my dead body." Tus grinned, holding the bulkiest weapon, a battle ax. It looked like a toy in his hands.

"If it comes to that," he replied, casting a final glance at his weapons, as a mother might when her children leave the nest.

With that, he was off. Deacon pulled open his satchel and slid the large bundle inside, eagerly pulling open the messenger bag once both hands were free. He'd only managed to pull the first page out when Caya put her hand on it.

"What was that?" she asked.

"What? The page?" Deacon asked in confusion.

"Where did you just put that big bundle Desmeres gave you?" she asked. "It couldn't have fit into that little bag."

"It is a localized distortion of dimensional . . . it is bigger inside than out," he explained.

Caya nodded. "I see. Well, I'd say we find someplace out of the wind until this storm blows over. Once--"

"No. No, there is no time for that!" Deacon objected.

"Look here, wizard. Dedication is one thing, but we've got to reach them in one . . ." Caya began.

Deacon pulled his crystal free and released it. The gem floated up slightly and took on a bright glow. The wind around them slowed to a slight breeze, the snow sprinkling gently down. All around the group, the wind whipped and raged, but among them it was gentle as a lamb.

"Right . . . well, then we continue," Caya said, leaning over to Tus to add, "We should have gotten a wizard a long time ago."

#

Above the clouds, the others flew until the sun neared the opposite horizon. Then, suddenly, Ether dove through the clouds, her windy body boring a tunnel through the icy mist. Myn dove after her. The clouds were thicker and denser than they had been that morning, and they had taken on an ominous darkness. Fat crystals of ice pelted them mercilessly as they made their way through, soon emerging into a swirling tempest of falling snow. There was no hint of the blizzard from above, but now it raged all around them. The wind whipped Myn side to side and threatened to tear her riders from her back.

Ether was lost among the swirling flakes, but Myranda managed to guide Myn. What little light made it through the clouds served only to turn the world around them into a blur of gray and white. When the ground came, it seemed to leap out at them from nowhere. Myn landed as softly as she could, dislodging an unprepared Ivy in the process. Myranda climbed down and helped her to her feet.

"Where are we?" she screamed over the howling wind.

"The Eastern Mountains, about midway between Entwell and where I found you, but deeper among them," Myranda explained.

"What's that smell?" Ivy asked, covering her nose.

Myranda ventured a sniff of the freezing air. Even among the snow and bitter cold, she could detect something. It was a hot, acrid smell that clutched at the nose.

"Brimstone," she replied.

"This way! Quickly," came Ether's voice through the gales.

They set off toward the sound and soon found her in her stone form, making her way steadily along the mountainside.

"He is inside. We need to find a way in," Ether stated.

"A way inside a mountain? I didn't know there were places to *be* inside a mountain. I thought there was just more mountain," Ivy said in confusion.

"This mountain is different. It is that rare sort that is alive inside. Molten and vital, like the land when it was young. A fire mountain," Ether said, purposefully stalking along a steep bit of slope, crouched low and running her fingers along the rocky ground.

Slowly she paced, until she seemed to find what she was looking for. Clasping her hands together, she hammered at the mountainside. Blow after blow rained down, seemingly with no result. Finally, she shifted to air and launched skyward. Moments later, her stone form came crashing down with earthshaking force. Cracks began to radiate outward from her crater, and the rumbling sound of stone giving way managed to momentarily surpass the din of the storm around them. With an earsplitting crash, a whole section of the mountainside slumped inward, crumbling to boulder-sized stones and exhaling a scalding hot breath of sulfurous fumes. The dust and snow settled around it to reveal a jagged, pitch-black tunnel leading into the heart of the mountain.

"How did you--" Ivy began.

"Never mind that--this way, quickly!" she ordered, leaping inside.

Myranda looked hesitantly into the gaping hole in the mountain. It was large. Large enough for Myn to slip through with room to spare. With great care, she navigated the broken ground down into the tunnel, Ivy on her heels. It was like walking into a furnace. The air was heavy with choking fumes. When the others had cleared the entrance, Myn slipped in. Whereas for Myranda and Ivy the heat pressed down on them like leaden weights, Myn seemed instantly revitalized by it. Her eyes closed as she let the intensity of it replace the biting cold she'd left behind. The satisfaction was more than apparent on her face.

"Well, at least *she's* happy," Ivy said.

After a few moments to adjust to the massive swing in temperature, the heroes rushed to catch up with Ether. Myranda lit the way with her own magic, as the staff she held contained no enchantments for illumination. In contrast, it had quite a few for extinguishing light.

The walls of the tunnel were rough and wavy, and colored a lustrous black. As they moved on, it twisted and folded upon itself, taking a meandering path toward the recesses of the mountain. The heat grew steadily as they moved deeper. With it grew the understanding of Ether's words. The mountain did seem alive. Deep in the walls were faint rumbles and groans. Periodically, there came shudders, the walls trembling as though something were moving just beyond their surface. The air swept past them in ever-warmer breezes.

Then there was the glow. It came in tiny shafts from cracks in the walls; a deep, primordial red.

#

In a field, surrounded by the Undermine as they rested, Deacon was in a panic. They were far, too far to be reached in anything less than a few days, and they had stopped. They had found Lain--or, at least, found where he was hidden. If their past encounters were any indication, they would be moving on soon after. There wasn't enough time to catch up with them. This was troubling, but it was not the source of his panic. Indeed, he had expected, even anticipated it. What concerned him was the presence he felt elsewhere.

The pages offered to him by Desmeres were a very detailed summary of some of the more fundamental principles of D'karon magic, as well as personal notes made by Epidime himself. With their help he'd been able to attune himself far more closely with the unique energies their magics created. It made them clear to his mind's eye like never before. What he discovered was a focus of activity near the capital--a massive force gathered about a gleaming ember of magic. The ember was a dormant but powerful spell, waiting to be awakened, and it had a counterpart very near to where Lain was located. The scenario was revealing itself to him, and it spelled ambush.

The contents of the messenger bag had clearly been selected with great care. Desmeres was no fool. He knew that too much information would take too much time to pore through. No, he'd plucked choice bits of data, specific dispatches, individual pages. Desmeres had a plan for these pages, and it was a brilliant one. There were no instructions, no indication of what Desmeres had in mind, but the pieces he'd provided opened a single avenue of possibility. It was a narrow one, and called for considerable risk, but it was nonetheless a possible route to salvation.

"You should get some sleep. That mind of yours must need a fair amount of rest to work those wonders," Caya suggested.

"No time. Besides, I don't know if I could keep the storm from burying us if I am asleep," he muttered.

"Oh, yes. The storm. I'd forgotten," Caya said, glancing at the impossible way that the wind and snow seemed to purposely avoid them.

Deacon looked to her. "How quickly can your troops ready themselves when the time comes?"

"My soldiers can be ready at moment's notice. Pray tell, what time is coming?" she asked.

"The time for battle. If I am right, it will come soon, and suddenly," he said, continuing to mumble to himself aloud. "I can't create it . . . they have to create it . . . can't close it . . . but once it is open . . ."

#

After a few narrow bends proved a tight squeeze for Myn, the path began to level. It merged with a handful of similar tubes, eventually leading to a still-wider passage that had some signs of use. The rough floor had been walked smooth, and scattered among the walls were glowing gems. At choke points in the path, there seemed to be thin metal bars clinging like vines to the curved walls. Nowhere was there the slightest hint of resistance, not a single guard.

The heat was beginning to wear on Ivy and Myranda. The latter was wringing wet with sweat, her boots hissing gently with each step. Ivy's mouth was slightly open and every few moments she had to consciously prevent herself from panting. It was difficult to say how long they had been trudging though the dark interior of the mountain, as each moment seemed to crawl by. The stone-on-stone clack of Ether's footsteps guided them onward tirelessly.

Then, suddenly, Myn stopped. She drew a deep breath of air through her nose and flicked her tongue. A moment later, she was running as quickly as the confined passageway would allow, Ether's pace quickening to a run as well. The others forced their tortured bodies forward. When they reached Myn again, she was scrabbling to get through a bottleneck in the tunnel that was far too small for her. Her claws dug long grooves in the stone and her heaving thrusts fairly shook the walls, but still she could not pass.

"Easy, Myn. Calm down and let us through. If Lain is in there, we will find him," Myranda said.

With eyes wide and maddened with desperation, the dragon let them pass and watched pleadingly as they entered a cavernous chamber on the other side of the opening. Ivy and Myranda pushed into the intense heat of the room. The fumes here were a thick haze that burned the eyes. Glowing crystals speckled the tall, domed ceiling, but what little light there was came not from them but from the deep crimson glow in the floor. A ring-shaped trough engraved into the floor released an ominous red light, illuminating the stone spire at its center. There, his hands and feet fused into the very stone, was Lain himself.

The signs of torture were too numerous to count. There was not an inch of exposed flesh that did not bear some manner of scar, gash, or burn. The skin hung from withered, emaciated arms and legs. He was breathing, but only just, with the breaths drifting painfully in amid a quiet, painful wheeze. Ether had already leapt to the spire and was easily cleaving the stone with her rocky claws. In moments, his feet were free. His weakened form was draped over her shoulder as the last of the stone was carefully chipped from around his hands. She leapt from the spire and lowered him to the ground. Instantly, Ivy and Myranda ran to his side.

"Do your work quickly. We need to leave this place," Ether said, eying the crystals shining above them with suspicion. One with a bluer tint prompted a more prolonged stare.

"Is he all right? Is he going to be all right?" Ivy asked desperately, amid a flare of blue.

"Just be calm. I will do my best," Myranda said, looking with concern at the tremendous task ahead of her.

Lain was more dead than alive. The fact that he had been freed was only now registering in his savaged mind. Eyes veiled in a gray haze attempted to focus on the blurry form bending over him, but to no avail. His ears, however, were still healthy, and he recognized the voices. Thoughts were moving slowly and vaguely through his usually razor-sharp mind. He could feel magic at work on him. Wounds were closing. Fog was lifting. As a hint of clarity returned to him, a single, burning thought brushed the others aside. He tried to shift his eyes to the exit, a ragged breath fighting its way into his tattered lungs.

"Go . . ." he croaked.

"We've come to save you, Lain, we won't leave without you," Myranda replied.

Lain struggled and gulped down another breath of the acrid air.

"R . . . Run!" he ordered, fingers closing about Myranda's cloak.

As if in reaction to his cry, there came a metallic sliding from the opening and a renewed clawing from Myn. The bars that had lined the walls were slithering into place, nearly strangling Myn until she managed to pull her head free. Before Myranda could raise her staff to offer the slightest counterspell, one of the long metal tendrils lashed out, knocking the weapon from her hand and wrapping around her, and drawing her back against the wall. A second and third bar pursued the others. One caught Ivy about the leg. The other twined about Ether, but a moment later, it was writhing uselessly about in the air she had become.

The shapeshifter burst toward the blue gleam above just in time to see it dislodge itself and launch through her, revealing itself to be the accursed halberd they'd faced so many times before. The crystal tore at her as it passed through, but Ether shrugged off the pain and chased after it. It was too late. The weapon had thrust itself into Lain's hand. Instantly, a terrible and all too familiar look of cold intellect came to his face.

Ether tried to attack, but Epidime willed Lain's lightning reflexes to the task and deflected every attempt. Ether's airy form was ill-equipped to defend against the assault. Before long, she had to pull back and regroup. The usurped Lain surveyed his surroundings. The living metal bar wrapped tightly about Myranda was on the verge of crushing her. What little concentration she could manage was entirely dedicated to holding off its grip. Ivy was fighting both the tendrils that gripped her body and the fear that gripped her mind valiantly, but with a metal bar coiled about each limb, she was beginning to tire. Myn stood just out of the range of the flailing metal bars and watched helplessly from the tunnel.

"I must say, I was beginning to grow weary of waiting. I've always prided myself on my patience, but once I'd weakened this assassin's surprisingly firm mind, I had very little worth doing while I awaited your arrival," he remarked. "Not that this little encounter is what I would call worthwhile. It is a victory, to be sure, but you will be pleased to know I consider it to be a hollow one. You were defeated not by the D'karon, but by the rules of the game. Worthy opponents such as yourselves deserve better. That said, I am not so foolish as to allow you to survive."

With that, he swung his halberd to speed and leveled it at Myranda's throat. There was a deafening clang and a spray of sparks. Ether had swept in and assumed her stone form, her arm held defensively.

"Well," Epidime said. "You've gotten a bit faster at that. I rather *thought* that you might be the greatest challenge."

The possessed form of Lain stepped quickly back and twirled the weapon in a sequence of wide loops, building speed as it went. Soon, the tip was fairly hissing through the air. Ether stalked toward him. With carefully calculated timing, Epidime directed an attack at the shapeshifter. A clang of steel echoed off of the walls as a blow powerful enough to chip away at Ether's stony form met its mark. She recovered quickly and continued to move toward him.

As the weapon clashed again and again, Ivy watched, her mind ablaze as she fought the metal grip
. She felt fear, anger, desperation, hatred. None of them would do. Anger would bring pain, and possibly death. Hatred . . . no, never again. Fear took the place of the other emotions, but this too was no good to her, and she did her best to bury it down. There was only one thing that could help her now. She knew what she needed to do, but she didn't know how. It had happened once before, if only she could remember . . .

Expert timing and inhuman speed landed countless attacks on Ether without so much as a single blow being returned. Her rocky form was striped with cracks and lacerations, and the repeated strikes with the crystal had reduced her strength to nearly nothing. The shapeshifter needed relief, needed to escape, but she knew that any other form would be instantly struck down--or, worse, would squander the last of her energy and leave her a helpless, drifting mind once more.

Epidime sensed this, raising the intensity of his attacks. When victory seemed certain, he began to highlight his attacks with mocking taunts.

"Remarkable creatures, these malthropes. I've seldom encountered such boundless stamina. And after days of starvation and torture, as well. Truly a wonder, and truly a shame that very shortly they shall be extinct," Epidime said with a grin.

He rained blows upon Ether, the battered creature no longer strong enough to mount a defense. As he raised his weapon to deliver what would surely be a final blow, a blaze of white light filled the chamber. The sudden outburst proved distracting enough for Ether to fall clear of the strike, collapsing weakly to the ground. Epidime turned to the source of the blaze, shading his eyes against its intensity.

There, amid the groan of straining steel and the creaking of stone, was Ivy, immersed in a pure white aura. Her eyes, now piercingly white, fixed on Epidime. There was no anger, no fear, just iron determination in her expression. Only once before had she managed such a transformation. Driven only by duty, she'd achieved it in her escape from the fort that had nearly claimed Myranda's life. With the strength brought by her new form, she levered her feet free and now stood with them planted on the wall, pushing with all of her might against the failing grip of the metal tendrils that coiled about her arms. Her clothes rustled in the arcane wind that seemed to surge from her in all directions. Steadily, the writhing steel tentacles began to lose their grips.

Epidime turned his focus to this new threat, directing his will to the failing restraints as he charged at her. The iron grips tightened, causing Ivy to falter and crouch lower to the wall. The charging halberd-bearer was mere steps away when the stone that anchored the tendrils finally gave way. Ivy uncoiled and cannoned into the form barreling toward her. The pair became a tumbling tangle of flailing limbs and brilliant light. Drawing upon instincts and training deep within Lain's mind, Epidime shifted and angled his body with each roll. Finally, planting his feet on Ivy's midsection, he launched her off of him and rolled to his feet in a single, fluid motion. Before his eyes, Ivy pivoted in midair, landing in a dead run.

The dark wizard scarcely had the time to admire the poetry in motion he'd witnessed before he was forced to ready his weapon. What followed was a true sight to behold. Two minds, each rivaled only by the other in acuteness of the senses and sharpness of the reflexes, engaged in the most unusual of battles.

Epidime knew not what to think. Ivy was attacking, but she wasn't. In motions both graceful and awkward, she was bobbing, weaving, lunging, and diving. Now she reached toward the retreating halberd, now she backed away. She seemed to have no interest whatsoever in striking Epidime himself. It was not until she finally succeeded that Epidime understood her goal.

Ivy's fingers closed around the shaft of the halberd, grasping the weapon just below Epidime's own grip. Steadying herself, Ivy attempted to tear it away from him, but it would not move. Epidime contorted Lain's face into an out-of-place, sinister grin once again. There was a flare of light within his crystal and the whole of the halberd seemed to darken. It had been black before, but now it seemed to devour the light around it until it was little more than a shaft of pure, ebony midnight. The surface was cold, an agonizing, sizzling cold that burned and bit at Ivy's hands, but her grip would not relent. She stared into his eyes, through them, into his soul. Epidime stared back at her, his madness in Lain's eyes.

"Remove the evil weapon and it will release your friend, eh? A clever realization. I wouldn't have thought one of your surging transformations capable of such an epiphany. Intriguing. Blue is fear, red is anger, but what is white? Is it hate? Is it love? Is it an emotion at all? Or have you somehow learned to control what we've done to you? Only one way to find out, I suppose," he mused as the pair struggled against one another.

The crystal flared again. Instantly, the burning in Ivy's hands was joined by a pressure on her mind, an unwanted influence trying to work its way in. In its natural state, Ivy's mind would have been simple to enter, but there was nothing natural about the state her mind was in now. It was consumed by a singular, pure, all-encompassing purpose. A will hard as diamond poured energy from her. Epidime fought the current, pouring more and more of his will to the task.

"You may be able to resist me now . . . but you cannot keep this up for long, can you?" Epidime managed to taunt.

Suddenly, Ivy lurched forward. Lain's body and Epidime's mind had been fully committed to keeping Ivy from pulling away the weapon. Now she was pushing. Before he could compensate, Epidime found himself running backward to keep from falling. He withdrew from her mind to probe for Lain's instincts once more. Just as the perfect counter maneuver surfaced, time ran out. The pair met the wall with crushing force. Lain collided with the narrow section of wall beside the entryway. A heartbeat later, Ivy collided with him. The wind rushed from his lungs, but he did not release the weapon. Suddenly, Ivy buckled to the ground as, through her clothes, the burning of her Mark became visible.

"Lain is still a Chosen. Every action against him is a knife in your own back!" Epidime gloated.

The blazing white aura about Ivy had faded somewhat, but still she held firm. As the Mark finished meting out its punishment, she climbed to her feet and resumed her tug of war on the halberd. Epidime staggered a bit before he managed to mount an effective resistance again.

The general opened his mouth to issue another taunt, but something interrupted him. Something tightened about his waist with crushing strength. He looked down to see a bundle of muscle and gleaming red scales pulled taught around him. A glance over his shoulder revealed that he'd let his attentions stray too far from the task of controlling the metal vines. Myn had managed to bend and rend enough of them to snake her tail through, and now it was locked about him with every ounce of strength the dragon could muster. She didn't understand what was happening, but she didn't need to. The only thing that mattered was getting her friend away from this place, and she meant to do it.

The dragon pulled in one direction, the malthrope in the other. Lain's body dangled off of the ground, bones creaking and tendons straining. Epidime split his mind between the tasks of augmenting Lain's failing muscles enough to maintain his grip and summoning a spell that would end the meddlesome dragon. His joints popped and twisted, sending a shudder of pain through Ivy and Myn alike as their actions took their toll on a fellow Chosen. The hesitation was enough of an opening for him to launch the spell, a ball of crackling black energy, at the dragon.

He watched with morbid interest as it streaked through the air. A shimmering wall manifested in the path of the destructive spell, dispersing it. At the same time, Epidime could feel his fingers being levered open by an unseen force. He turned his head and spat a string of otherworldly syllables, words never before uttered in this world but nonetheless understood for the profanities they were.

Myranda was standing, free, with her staff in hand.

With Epidime's mind otherwise occupied, Myranda had managed to escape from her restraints. Now she focused all that she had into loosening Epidime's grip. For a few long moments, the only sounds were the crackle of bones and the stifled agony of Myn, Ivy, and Myranda as they incurred the wrath of their marks. Finally, Lain's fingers opened. Ivy was thrown back, the weapon hurling from her fingers. As Lain's body fell, motionless, from Myn's grip, the halberd took a wild, clattering path across the ground, screeching to a stop. A moment later, the crystal flared and it launched itself toward them. The heroes braced themselves. There was an ear-shattering clash as the weapon struck something.

There, twisting and shaking to get free, was the halberd. Locked about it were the crumbling fingers of Ether. Powerful arcs of black magic were surging from the weapon, splashing against her stony form and pushing back the others. The shapeshifter staggered to her feet and took a few unsteady steps before a thick bolt of power shattered one of her legs. She dropped to the ground. The failing glow that was her eyes shifted about the floor. Finally, she gripped the halberd with her other hand and with one final heave, lurched into the channel carved into the floor.

There was the crackle and scrape of stone on stone as she plummeted down the narrow crevice, but Ether's grip held. A moment later, the bundle of stone and weapon was driven deep into a thick, molten flow. The halberd shuddered as its metal took on a brilliant glow. The air buzzed about it one last time before it was swallowed by the liquid stone. The still-faintly flickering form of Ivy strode to the edge of the channel and peered into the glowing depths. Assured that her task was complete, the transformation released her and she collapsed to the ground, eyes still faintly open.

"Wha-what?" She panicked, struggling against restraints that weren't there.

Myranda rushed to her and pulled her away from the edge. Ivy slowly realized that something had happened.

"I . . . Did I do something?" she asked, climbing shakily to her feet.

"You did so much," Myranda said, helping her. "But come, we need to help Lain and get him out of here."

The mention of Lain's name shook the cobwebs from Ivy's mind. She hurried to his side, but skidded to a stop.

"What is happening?" she cried.

There was the sickening pop of joints pulling back into place on their own amid sudden jerking motions. He was rising to his feet unnaturally, seemingly hanging from unseen threads that pulled him upright with little concern for things like gravity or balance. The writhing of the metal tendrils near the door began anew, forcing Myn further into the narrow tunnel. Lain's head lifted and his eyes opened. An awful, impossible smile came to his face.

"No . . . It isn't possible!" Myranda said in horror.

In a blur of motion, Lain's fingers were about her neck, closing with strength they shouldn't have. He lifted her from the ground.

"You are to be commended. I took up the halberd centuries ago. No one until now has been able to destroy it," he said.

Myranda tried to put her mind to a spell, but he sent her crashing to the ground with a vicious throw. With the wizard dazed, he raised his hands to finish the job. Ivy dove onto his back.

"You can't be Epidime!" she cried.

A pulse of magic threw her from his back. He turned and stalked toward her, the greater threat. The same darkness that had encompassed his weapon now seemed to be pooling about his hands, trailing from them as he walked. He grasped at the air and Ivy suddenly felt a crushing force about her. She was hoisted into the air and held before him. Slowly, he paced toward the channel of lava with her.

"A weakness is a useful thing, Ivy," he said calmly, as though to a student. "Once those who would destroy you discover it, it is all that they target. It makes people predictable. They rely upon it, expend all of their energy on it. I don't have a weakness, so I provided myself with one."

With his other hand, he willed Myranda into the air.

"It is just as well you destroyed it. In the years since I selected the halberd, I've been through the minds of hundreds of warriors skilled in thousands of other weapons. In truth, I was beginning to feel constrained. In the future, I shall have to select something more benign. A medallion-- or a ring, perhaps."

Myranda's eyes slowly began to focus. She raised her hand, only to have it pinned down again. The blow had dizzied her, but already her senses were returning. She focused her mind on Lain. Not the body, but the soul within. Epidime was on the surface now, a greasy black slick in her mind's eye, staining Lain's form with his influence. Far behind it was the tiniest flicker of the soul she knew. She reached out to it.

"No, no, no. That will not do," Epidime scolded.

With a flick of his fingers, Myranda was hurled to the center of the room, bouncing painfully against the spire that had held Lain. She fell, barely catching the scalding hot edge of the channel. Instantly, there came a crash strong enough to shake the walls--then another.

Epidime turned to find Myn throwing herself against the entryway. Cracks were creeping along the walls. What remained of the metal vines were little more than twisted, useless lengths of metal. With one final heave, she shattered a piece of the wall away, charging into the chamber. The dragon pounded past Epidime and skidded to a stop at the edge of the channel, scooping Myranda to safety. She then turned to Epidime, a look of betrayal in her eyes.

"Ah, Myn. You bring an interesting mix of emotions to Lain's head. Surprise, relief," Epidime said, eying the gashes the creature had suffered in her attempts to enter. "Concern. I wouldn't have thought the old assassin capable."

Myn was growling, though the word had not been conceived with a dragon in mind. It was a sound like distant, rolling thunder. It was a sound that shook the earth. Epidime dropped Ivy unceremoniously from his grip.

"Well, Myn, what will it be?" Epidime said.

Myn took a few significant steps toward him, placing the stricken heroes behind her.

"You know, I have the greatest respect for dragons. They have minds capable of great wisdom. Far greater than most mortals, given the time to develop it. Unfortunately, the assortment of instincts that keeps you alive in the wild is, alas, ill-suited to understanding abstract concepts. You thus cannot be blamed for your failure to grasp why your beloved Lain has begun to act so strangely. Nor can you be expected to realize that standing between a wizard and his target is a worthless and foolish gesture," Epidime explained slowly.

Myranda and Ivy cried out simultaneously. Myn turned to see waves of black energy burning around them like dark flames. She turned back to find Epidime volleying a pair of attacks at her. As the crackling energy splashed across her scales, blistering them in a way that no fire could and wracking her with pain, the part of her that would not allow her to hurt Lain was finally pushed aside by a far more fundamental instinct. In a blur of movement, Myn pounced on Lain's body, pinning him to the ground beneath a massive foreclaw. Her talons curled over his shoulders, cleaving the stone on either side of his head. Instantly, she felt the burn of divine punishment surge outward from the Mark on her wing.

"Cruel, isn't it?" Epidime wheezed. "The Mark punishes you for disloyalty to the cause, and in doing so has made you helpless. As I said, it is the rules of the game that have beaten you."

A flex of his mind lifted Myn into the air and launched her at the spire in the center of the room. She shattered through it and slid to a stop on the opposite side, writhing in pain. Lain's body rose from the ground and alighted on his feet.

"Now I am afraid it is time to . . ." Epidime began.

There was a new rumbling now, one that made the growl of the dragon seem like a kitten's purr. The whole mountain was shaking. Without the spire in its center, the circular channel was nothing more than a pit, and from within it came a glow like the fires of hell. It grew brighter, and the rumble louder, until the very ceiling seemed ready to collapse. There emerged from the pit a massive form, glowing like the inside of a kiln and throwing off a heat to match. It was Ether. A few minutes immersed in the molten lifeblood of the mountain had brought her a strength she'd not known for thousands of years.

The shapeshifter climbed out of the hole, stooping to fit in the chamber. The floor beneath her feet melted and boiled. Her eyes, brilliant golden pools set in a radiant crimson face, turned to Epidime, who stepped toward her.

"Resilient little things, aren't you? This is all very impressive. What will you do now? Kill me? I do hope so. It would destroy you, and after this demonstration, I must say I am not sure how else to achieve it," he taunted, stepping so close that the heat that poured off of her was beginning to make Lain's fur scorch and smoke.

Ether moved cautiously away from him, but he pressed closer. The black fire continued to plunge the others into mind searing agony, and soon began to roil across the body of the slowly recovering dragon. The shapeshifter had never been so powerful, and yet had never been so helpless. There was nothing she could do to stop his magic from doing its work without hurting or killing Lain. Epidime stepped closer still. The bandages on Lain's chest began to smolder, blacken, and fall away. Beneath, there was the glint of gold.

Lain's face wore a look of arrogant satisfaction as he brought up another cascade of black fire to torment Ether's massive form. Deep in his mind, Epidime knew that the easiest, most certain way of destroying Ether was to coax her into destroying a fellow Chosen, but doing so would take time and the others could not be allowed to escape, so he turned his attentions to them. The spells were doing their work, dark flames sapping what little strength they had left, but these were durable creatures, resilient and resourceful. The magic had always been quite enough in the past, but not this time. No matter. If magic alone was not enough, there were simpler ways.

He approached Ivy and picked up a stone that had been dislodged from the ceiling. He raised it. He brought it down.

One of his legs faltered, sending him stumbling back and shattering the stone on the ground. Epidime grunted in anger. Something was wrong. He could feel the spells holding the others at bay tapering off. He poured more of his will into them until they met with his satisfaction and attempted to approach his prey once more, but his leg would not obey. Just as a dim realization came to his mind, his left hand shot to his chest, claws closing about the gleaming golden badge hidden beneath the bandages there. He gripped the fingers with his right hand and attempted to pry them free, but slowly the golden disc began to pull away. Beneath it, a brilliant gold light began to flare.

"Think about this, Lain. This will only destroy you. You are doing my work for me," Epidime urged, the beginnings of pain in his voice as the spirit of Lain fought to regain control.

Still, the fingers did their work.

Epidime sighed in frustration and extended his right hand to the glowing pit in the center of the chamber, twisting the fingers into an arcane gesture.

"It is my own fault, of course. I overextended myself. I shall have to resort to a somewhat less elegant contingency plan," he struggled to say.

There was a flash of mystic light in his eyes. Instantly, the bowels of the mountain began to stir, rattling the whole of the chamber and producing an ominous rumble from its central pit. Finally, the golden seal was torn from his chest and he cried out in a howl of pain that seemed to echo with two voices at once. He wavered and finally dropped to the ground. At the same moment, the dark flames that tore at his allies wafted away.

Myranda struggled to her feet and rushed to Lain just as the divine light of his Mark faded to nothing.

Lain was alive, but whatever vitality Epidime had brought to the tortured form had left with him. He was weak, drawing slow and painful breaths in a sort of half consciousness. Myranda tried to pull her weakened mind to the task of offering some sort of aid, but she hadn't the strength for the simplest of healing spells. Epidime's attacks had cut deeper than any physical attack could.

"Is he all right? Is he . . . is he Lain again?" Ivy asked, as she limped to Myranda's side and handed her the staff.

The ailing Myn joined them a moment later, nosing the half-dead form of Lain. Her eyes were a swirl of sorrow, concern, and guilt.

"He's Lain," Myranda assured, sensing nothing of the influence that had tainted him before, "but he is hurt badly. He needs help, or I don't know how much longer he will last."

"Get him out of this place. Epidime has started something that I am not certain I can stop!" Ether declared, looking down into the growing glow within the pit in the chamber's center.

"Myn, you can move far more surely than we can in this place. Can you get us to the outside?" Myranda asked.

Myn responded by crouching low. Lain was loaded onto her back and the others joined him.

"I will hold it as long as I can," Ether said. "But go--quickly! It will not be for long!"

With that, she dove back into the pit.

Myn launched herself out into the tunnel. Her sensitive nose followed the scent of fresh air. Her injuries were many, but she forced the pain aside. She had a job to do now, and she would succeed. She navigated the darkened corridors with catlike grace. The crooked, roundabout path that had brought them here was abandoned for what seemed to be a far more direct and more traveled one. Before long, the air began to carry the chill of the still-raging storm outside. There was the sound of crushing collapse behind them, followed by a rush of hot air. Then came a long, low rumble. The roar grew steadily, growing sharper and more distinct. Soon it was joined by a hot wind and amber glow from behind. Not a moment too soon, the group reached the frigid exit to the tunnel.

The dark cave emptied into a tall, narrow valley. Snow crunched beneath Myn's feet, the icy wind instantly chilling her riders to the bone. The dragon leapt into the air and spread her wings, but the frenzied efforts to reach Lain had taken a considerable toll on them. After a few painful and abortive attempts to remain aloft, Myn resigned to running. Myranda huddled close to the dragon's back, holding Lain down. She trembled uncontrollably, her sweat-soaked clothes already crackling in the mountain air. The cold managed to cut through the dizziness that clouded her mind, making her acutely aware of a very powerful and terribly familiar power in the air.

"Faster, Myn! Faster!" she urged.

Myn thundered through the swirling snow of the blizzard, her mind resolutely focused on the most direct path down the mountain, but already the threat Myranda feared was beginning to form.

It started as a ripple in mid-air, a distortion amid the white wall of raging snow. The ripple darkened and spread--slowly at first, then surging. In moments, the whole of the valley was blocked by a massive, churning, black void. Finally, the void cleared from the center outward. It revealed a torchlit courtyard, calm in spite of the blizzard in the valley. It was lined with row after row of nearmen and demon armors, and the hulking figures of five massive dragoyles.

Myn skidded to a stop and began to back away from the army that faced them. The nearmen were marching through by the dozen, and one of the massive beasts strode out among them, followed by a second.

The faithful dragon turned to the steep walls of the valley and began to scale one, the others clinging desperately to her back, but the massive dragoyle roared into the air and swiped at the comparatively tiny form, missing narrowly. Myn half slid, half climbed back to the valley floor, barely avoiding the shattered rubble knocked away by the attack. The ranks of troops were closing around them as Myn looked frantically for some means of escape. As she gushed gouts of flame at the soldiers nearest to her, and lashed her tail at others, one nearman climbed atop a nearby outcropping. He shuddered for a moment, then addressed them with an unmistakable tone of confidence.

"It always reduces to brute force, doesn't it?" declared Epidime in his new host, his voice ringing out with unnatural clarity amid the clash of sword on scale and the roar of fiery breath. "This time is different, though. There will be no offers of mercy. There will be no chances to surrender. This time you die."

He drew his sword, but quickly regarded it with disdain. Slowly, his gaze turned to the hulking dragoyle. It opened its serrated maw and heaved a breath of miasma that whipped away uselessly in the winds of the blizzard. The smile broadened on his face. Suddenly, the intellect left the face of the nearman. A moment later, the largest of the dragoyles froze momentarily. The empty hollows of its eyes took on a distinctive orange glow and looked upon the heroes with intelligence and resolve.

Myn plowed through the tide of foes that flooded the valley, but there was no place to go. Epidime charged after them, trouncing his own soldiers with little regard. Dozens more flooded in with every moment. Ivy flared weakly with the blue aura of fear as she held tenaciously to the dragon's back, but the transformation inside the mountain had left her with little more than the strength to remain conscious--and barely that. It was all that Myranda could do to keep Lain from being hurled from Myn's back into the bloodthirsty throng. There was naught but madness. Then came the sounds.

The first was a crack like thunder, but from deep inside the mountain. A fault erupted boiling hot fumes as it ran down the mountainside to the mouth of the cave. The second sound was a hissing whine, almost beyond the range of hearing. It seemed to emanate from everywhere at once. Then, more distinctly, from the portal. The mountainside quaked again, and deep orange molten stone erupted from the fault. It did not rush forward. It seemed to mound upward, rolling up itself and pushing the slope aside. Finally, it settled into a towering figure. The arctic winds turned the surface onyx-black in moments.

It was Ether, her eyes radiating orange heat, towering even over the massive dragoyles. One of the still-mindless beasts charged her. She pulled back, white-hot molten stone showing through cracks when she moved, and sent the creature hurtling into the valley wall with a massive backhand.

As the piercing tone grew louder, all eyes turned to the portal. The edges had turned from black to a feathery white. Another dragoyle was stepping through. Just as its forelegs touched the snowy earth, the edge of the portal surged inward. The window into the courtyard shrunk toward the center of the massive mystic gateway; in its place, there came a new view, a view of a hilly countryside. Finally, the edge of the portal passed through the dragoyle. The half that had made it into the valley fell away from the portal and writhed briefly. There was no sign of the rest. As the neatly-bisected monstrosity came to a rest, a dozen wild-eyed warriors rushed into the valley from the portal's new target. The nearmen and armor beasts unlucky enough to meet them first were torn to pieces. Gleaming blades split the shields of their foes like clay as the frenzied troops carved a swath through the nearmen.

Epidime launched himself at the new foes, but Ether brought down a crushing blow that knocked him to the ground. The other beast recovered and attacked her.

As the titanic clash continued, Myranda looked through the chaos of snow and battle. On the other side of the portal, a look of complete concentration on his face, was Deacon.

"Myn! Through the portal!" she cried.

The dragon took off like a bolt. She bounded through the valley of clashing swords and battle cries, leaping from one clearing to another and knocking aside D'karon soldiers like a ship cutting through the waves. As she drew nearer, the rundown but maddened soldiers who had come to their rescue began to pull back. The nearmen pulled together and put up a final defense, their swords cutting notches into Myn's thick scales with every step. Behind, the thundering footsteps of a dragoyle were drawing near.

With a final leap, the group of heroes plunged through the portal, crashing to the icy ground on the other side and grinding to a halt.

Myn turned to the portal. The ragged soldiers were making their way back through. The ground on the other side of the portal was shaking as the massive dragoyle pounded ever closer. Only a pair of soldiers were left on the other side. Myranda tried to steady her shaky nerves enough to recognize them. One was a massive man swinging an ax with one hand and a sword with the other. It could only be Tus. The second, then, could only be Caya. Tus reduced a swath of soldiers to powder and twisted metal, shouldering his way through to the other side of the portal. The dragoyle was so near, the hissing breath could be heard even over the crashing of claws and howling wind. Caya leapt through the portal a half-step ahead of the beast. Its head passed through the portal, scattering the assembled soldiers, but a stony black hand clutched it about the neck and brought it to a halt. The monster drew in a breath of icy air. Next would be a cloud of black death.

Suddenly, the portal snapped shut about the beast's neck and its wrangler's wrist. The two massive forms dropped to the earth, and rocked to stillness. After a moment, there arose a thunderous cry of victory. Warriors young and old slapped each other on the back and reveled in the thrill of the moment. Only one man was silent. His head was heavy from the exertion, but the concern he felt could not be set aside. He approached Myn. She'd settled to her haunches, her head resting on the ground as she heaved great clouds of exhausted breath. Her eyes regarded the approaching form with weary suspicion before she closed them and rolled her head lightly toward him. Deacon offered a vigorous scratch. Myranda half climbed, half fell from the dragon's back.

"How ... how did you find us?" she managed.

"Myranda, I could find you anywhere," he said, throwing his arms about her shivering body.

She hugged him back, tears rolling down her face. For a moment, the two stood, holding each other tight. Emotions flooded over them. There was so much to say. So much to hear. An eternity in that warm embrace would not have been enough, but each knew that there was more to be done. Reluctantly, they parted. Ivy had made her way to the ground and was tugging at Lain. Together, the three managed to lower their barely-conscious friend to the ground.

It did not take the eye of a healer to know that Lain was near the end. His breath was leaving his body in thin wisps. Clouded eyes wavered slowly and refused to focus. Every joint was swollen or crooked. Every muscle was shriveled or torn. Every inch of skin was blistered, bleeding, or scarred. Myranda's numb fingers closed tighter about her staff. She tried to form the first incantations of a healing spell, but she couldn't shape the words. Her will was in tatters. Her soul was wrung dry. She simply didn't have anything left.

Deacon placed his hand on hers.

A cool steadiness smoothed the wrinkles of her mind. Neither she nor Deacon had much left to give, but together they amounted to something more. Slowly and deliberately, the spells were formed. Lain passed into a deep, healing sleep. Wounds were closed. Bones and joints clicked back into place. Swelling drifted away. It took great effort, and greater care, but the two minds working as one finally put Lain's broken form in order. He was by no means healed, but he would make it through the night.

Ivy had been watching anxiously, but slowly the fear melted away. She knew nothing of healing, but she knew a proper slumber when she saw it. With her friend safe, she turned to the soldiers behind her. While the wizards had been doing their work, the celebration had settled down. Now there was nothing but a powerful silence as every last warrior looked upon the spectacle before them.

Myranda they had expected, and they had known of the others as well. No one had actually believed it. It had never occurred to Deacon that a dragon and a pair of malthropes might come as a shock to them, that perhaps they'd distrusted the Alliance Army's poster. He'd come to accept them; there was no reason why anyone else might not. Now there was the whistle of windblown snow and the cold stare of a battalion of warriors, some nervously gripping their weapons and worrying that they might have let the wrong group through.

"Hello!" Ivy said brightly, eager to break the silence.

The response was the long slow slide of steel from its sheath and the crackle of hot stone cooling on the icy ground.

"Um. I'm Ivy . . ." she offered. "What are your names?"

"Ivy? The prodigy?" asked a soldier doubtfully, recognizing the name.

"Yes, yes! That's me! You've heard of me?" she said excitedly.

A crackle coming from the severed head and stone hand that marked the former site of the portal drew the attentions of the soldiers. There was the hiss of steam escaping. It seemed odd to all in attendance that such a thing would not have occurred sooner, and odder still that it seemed to grow stronger with each passing moment. The steam condensed quickly into a swirling cloud. The cloud grew denser and tighter, finally taking on a very definite form.

"Oh, good! Ether made it, too!" Ivy said, even glad to see her old adversary.

Sure enough, a few more moments of hissing revealed the human form of Ether standing beside the cracked obsidian husk that had once been her hand.

Caya turned to Deacon and Myranda.

"I would say that drinks are in order," she proclaimed.

Packs were emptied, producing a tent for every few men and enough rations for perhaps one in three. As short as the other supplies seemed to be, there was plenty of drink to go around, as a fiery wine and an assortment of other spirits served to settle nerves, warm blood, and dull pains. The soldiers first clustered tightly about Myranda and Deacon, eager to share tales of battle and triumph. They soon found themselves in a wide, cautious circle around the heroes. Myn, it turned out, had had quite enough excitement for one day and was slow to trust so large a group of strangers. As such, she took a seat beside them and cast a threatening look at any who ventured too close.

With a bit of effort, Deacon managed to raise the spell necessary to shelter them from the worst of the storm once more.

Ivy looked about uneasily from her seat beside her friends. The eyes of the soldiers seemed to be scrutinizing her and the dragon in particular. Ether took up a position among the flames, which caused a bit of a stir, but once the exclamation and surprise had dulled, the eyes turned back to their steady circuit between Ivy and Myn. She felt something was expected of her. Suddenly a thought struck her.

"Deacon! Do you have my violin?" she asked.

"I believe so," he said, poking around in his bag until he was able to produce it.

Ivy snatched it and the bow away from him and quickly struck up a tune. After the initial shock of yet another unexpected truth, the music began to take effect. The feeling came back to Ivy's fingers as they danced nimbly over the strings, the joy of playing filling her soul, and bathing those around her in a warm, golden aura. The happiness was infectious, no doubt aided by strong wine on empty stomachs, and before long, grizzled soldiers were clapping along, and the youngest among them were dancing. As the joy spread, the pain and strain of the day melted away. Injuries and aches that had lingered for years, pains that had simply become a fact of life, wafted away along with fatigue and sorrow.

For a time, Caya and Tus watched with satisfaction as their soldiers rejoiced--but before long, their curiosities got the better of them.

"Not entranced," Tus said flatly as he and Myn exchanged hard stares.

"No, just a friend," Myranda said, using the strength brought by Ivy's influence to speed its effects on Myn as Deacon did the same for Lain. "Why would you think she was entranced?"

"The trouble with getting information quickly is its tendency to become a bit mangled during the trip," Caya explained. "We had all assumed such was the case with the images the Alliance had distributed. Who would have thought the Red Shadow was really a malthrope as they said? It stands to reason, certainly, but one wouldn't imagine a monster like that being clever enough to avoiding capture for so long."

Ivy hit a sour note and stopped, glaring at Caya.

"The tales about malthropes have had more than their share of mangling as well, I can assure you," Myranda said.

"Er, yes, so it would seem. No harm meant," Caya said.

With a satisfied nod, Ivy commenced her playing

"I don't think they fed him at all. Lain is going to need food when he awakes," Deacon said to no one in particular.

The words hit Myn like an order and she sprinted into the whipping snow on greatly restored legs to fetch a meal.

"Try to bring back enough for all of us!" Myranda called after her speeding friend.

"Just a friend . . ." Tus said doubtfully.

Myranda looked over Lain, finally satisfied that all that could be done had been done. Her mind released from its most pressing concern, she decided the time had come to indulge her curiosities.

"Deacon, what happened to you? Where did they take you? How did you escape?" Myranda asked.

"Yes, I'd say you can spare a few moments to share the details now," Caya encouraged.

"It was nothing, really. More their oversight than my action. They'd taken me to a small outpost. Demont wanted to retrieve both halves of Ivy's crystal, but finding something in my bag is difficult, so he wanted me alive until it could be found, just in case killing me would keep it from them forever. When he left, I realized that they had taken all of my equipment, but they hadn't taken my ring. I tried to get it off, but one of the nearmen caught me. Apparently, he was under orders to confiscate any sort of mystic paraphernalia, because he actually removed the ring *for* me once he discovered it.

"The shackles were ideal for restraining hands. It would appear that they were woefully inadequate for restraining first a cluster of tentacles, then a three-fingered talon, then a variety of other disturbing forms it managed to take before I located the ring and put it back on the first form that had a roughly finger-sized protrusion," Deacon explained.

"Eh, what's that? Tentacles?" Caya said, confused.

"It is really quite fascinating. You see, I had a bit of an accident involving chaos magic, and now it would appear that the natural state of my hand is to exist at some sort of variable probabilistic displacement from the norm that causes it to leap from one staggeringly unlikely configuration to another unless manually maintained at a more typical status," Deacon said enthusiastically.

"That was supposed to be an explanation, was it?" Caya said.

"Because of a miscast spell, his hand changes shapes unless he wears the ring," Myranda offered.

"Ah." Caya nodded.

"I thought I'd just said that . . . well, at any rate, I realized that you were moving far too quickly to catch up to, and that things were getting out of hand. Caya turned out to be fairly nearby, so I sought her help," Deacon finished.

"And the portal?" Myranda asked.

"Oh, yes. Desmeres tracked us down and provided us with some weapons and a good deal of literature about the D'karon's methods. They provided details enough to allow me to manipulate the entrances of their portals, once they were opened. The exit cannot be moved, it seems. Something about the target requiring an actively maintained focus," he added, pausing for a moment of thought. "Curious that there was no backlash when the portal closed. The notes indicated that there would be. Perhaps repositioning the entrance spilled off the surplus energy, or perhaps it happened on the other side due to--"

"Right, that's enough of that," Caya said, cutting off what she had already learned was sure to be a labyrinth of terms and concepts no sane person would understand.

"Oh, uh . . . I stole their portal. I made it lead here," he clarified.

"Right, stick to explanations like that," Caya said.

Distantly, there came the thunder of returning footsteps. Myn burst into the region of relative calm afforded by Deacon's spell. She was plastered with snow, her jaws stretched to their limit around what was likely the better part of a herd of deer. She dropped them near the fire and proceeded to pelt all around her with caked snow shaken from her head and neck. The complaints of soldiers wiping snow from mouths and eyes were quickly silenced by Myn's angry glare. Some of the more courageous soldiers attempted to help themselves to the kill, but Myn resisted, snapping at grasping hands.

"Myn! Be nice!" Ivy said, ducking beneath the protective creature to snag her share.

At Myranda's insistence, Myn finally relented, but not before snatching up a hearty portion to place beside Lain. She then plopped to the ground and moodily watched the rest divided up among the soldiers as a larger fire was built. Myranda took a seat beside Myn, the dragon placing its head in her lap and unfurling a wing to lay over Lain.

"Thank you very much, Myn. That was very kind of you," Myranda praised, as she stroked the faithful beast's head.

Caya looked on in astonishment. She turned. Here, her men cooked a meal provided by a dragon. There, the flame complained and stepped away, becoming a woman. All around them, a vicious blizzard raged, while seemingly ignoring them. At the edge of this calm was a monstrous dragoyle head in the grip of a massive stone hand.

"Things are moving in curious directions," she said, slowly processing the experiences of the day. "Half of me feels as though we are in over our heads. The other half is trying to figure out how to bring that monster's head home as a trophy. This is bigger than a war, isn't it? This . . . this is the prophecy, the work of fate. What else could bring such creatures together? You have my full support, of course. The call has gone out. My men will be rallying near the capital. They will help you in any way they can.

"That leaves us with two wizards, a dragon, two malthropes, a shapeshifter, and a few dozen soldiers to assault the most heavily fortified city in the world against the generals, an endless supply of their men, and likely the people of the city itself. The scales are tipped--but the real question is, in what favor?"

When the food was finished cooking, the Chosen and soldiers alike feasted. The raging snow diminished slowly, finally to the point that Deacon's protection was no longer called for. As the warriors grew more comfortable with the Chosen and more deeply inebriated, questions were asked and stories were told, Deacon scribbling madly to record them all. Only Ether and Myn avoided the curiosity of the newcomers, each taking a place beside Lain and weathering the questions and stares in silence.

The sun was beginning to appear again by the time the group sought to retire. The Undermine divided themselves among the available tents until only one remained.

"Take it with my blessings," Caya said, holding the flap open.

"I couldn't. By rights it is yours and . . ." Myranda began.

"We can argue about this, but I assure you, it is a waste of time. You'll find me rather obstinate on the subject," Caya said with a grin. "Besides, Tus here tried to give *his* tent up to for Lain, but the dragon wouldn't allow it. Surely you wouldn't want *both* of us to be denied."

"Myn, I really think you should let them move Lain inside," Myranda said.

Myn looked to Myranda, slowly and deliberately lowering one of her paws gently over Lain, digging the tips of her claws into the icy ground in front of him. With that one simple motion, it was made quite clear that she had spent far too much time away from him and seen far too much happen to him to allow Lain to be separated from her so soon.

"I'll stay out here with them, Myranda. You know as well as I do she'll keep us good and warm. Besides, after ending up in a cage again, then baking in that awful mountain, I think I'd like to spend a bit more time in the fresh air," Ivy said.

"Yes, Myranda. I think you deserve a night of comfort. I'll stay out here with the rest," Deacon said.

Myranda relented, slipping inside. Deacon took a seat beside the tent's entrance. Almost immediately, Caya motioned for him to stand and pulled him aside. Tus joined them.

"I've listened to the stories you've told, and I've watched the way you act. This goes deeper than just lending a hand for you, doesn't it?" Caya whispered.

"What could go deeper than . . ." Deacon began, confused.

"No, no, no . . . You're going to make me be blunt about it, are you? Fine, then. You love the girl, don't you?" Caya interjected with a sigh.

"I do. With all of my heart, and more every moment. How did you know?" he asked.

"It isn't subtle. Ahem . . ." Caya whispered. After a conspiratorial glance, she added. "Have you ever slept in a tent that big, Deacon? It can get awfully cold without two people in there."

Tus gave him a slap on the back that knocked the air from his lungs.

"Keep your woman warm," he stated.

"And for heaven's sake, man, have a drink. You look pale as a corpse and tighter than a bow string," Caya said, pressing into his hands yet another bottle of the seemingly inexhaustible supply of powerful wine.

He put the bottle to his lips. Immediately, she tipped it up so that nearly half of its contents went down his throat or all over his face. After catching his breath, he stepped into the tent.

"Honestly! And to think I wondered why there weren't more wizards," Caya snickered to Tus, before raising her voice. "You there, er . . . Ivy is it? Do you suppose you've got another song in you? I'd say the occasion demands it."

In fact, Ivy had already nestled herself against Myn, eager to get some real sleep, but almost reflexively she put the violin to her chin. The hilly clearing began to lilt with a soft, deep, soulful song. A song that crept into the background, weaving with the thoughts of those that heard it. It became a part of the surroundings, as in place and proper as the rising sun. Most of the camp drifted quickly into a well-deserved slumber to it. To some, it served another purpose, but equally well.

#

Deep in the heart of the capital, Bagu sat, his eyes focused intently on the man before him. It was Greydon Celeste, Myranda's father. He'd been bound and set aside when the bait for their latest trap was put in place. Now the senior general watched the barely conscious form with seething attention. A shudder went through the frail body, its eyes opening wide, and for a moment he fought his bonds. When a sharpness and anger replaced the fear in his eyes, Bagu broke the silence.

"Tell me you did not fail *again!*" he bellowed.

"*I* failed? What happened to the portal? What happened to the rest of the troops?" Epidime countered.

"It shouldn't have *come* to that, Epidime. They were forced into your hands and you let them slip through! They should have defeated themselves!" Bagu raged. "You had every advantage!"

"Every advantage!? It was five against one! You pit me alone against four full-strength Chosen *and* charge me with keeping a fifth in check and call it an advantage!" Epidime replied. "And then you somehow manage to turn *our* ambush into *theirs!* In the veritable eternity that I've been aiding you in these endeavors I have *never* heard of a portal being stolen! *Never!* When they reach the capital--"

"They will *not* reach the capital," Bagu interrupted, "because you and that other idiot are going to take every soldier, every creature, human, D'karon, or otherwise, and you are going to find them! You are going to *end* them before they can get here! The moment is hours away! They will *not be allowed to reach this place before then!*"

"You've lost what little there is left of your mind, Bagu! If we leave the capital and take the best men with us, then what will be left to resist them if they reach the capital before we find them!?" Epidime reasoned, his voice dropping to a steady, smooth tone. "Yes, there has been a failure. Mine or yours, it is unacceptable, but we must not let it coax us into a mistake we cannot recover from. We bolster our defenses here. We stop them where our defense is strongest."

Bagu tensely wrung his fingers and considered the words.

"Yes. We harden our defenses here. The strongest will remain within our walls. Gather some of the dregs, the weakest of the dragoyles and the like, and send them out. At best, we defeat them; at worst, we soften them and learn their position," he said, fury dripping from the words.

The bonds securing Epidime dropped away of their own accord. He stood and exited Bagu's sanctum with measured slowness, a grin coming to his face as he felt the general's anger smolder behind him. Bagu was always much more entertaining when he was angry. No one else he'd worked with had ever reached the level of fury Bagu seemed to constantly hover around. As a connoisseur of the mind, it was something he enjoyed witnessing. He chuckled lightly, savoring the surge in anger it brought, before disappearing to issue the orders he'd been given.

#

The sun had not yet set when the small encampment of heroes showed its first signs of motion. The ragtag members of the Undermine were awakening, expecting the customary consequences of too little sleep and too much drink. One by one, they realized first that their heads were not throbbing nearly as much as they ought to be, and second that the artifacts of the impossible events of the previous day were still present.

The sudden realization that Lain, Myn, and Ivy were not, in fact, just a dream prompted enough startled cries to rouse the rest of the camp to wakefulness. The last to emerge were Myranda and Deacon, each looking a bit more disheveled and a great deal more invigorated than the handful of hours of sleep would warrant. As the wizards blinked at the light and wiped sleep from their eyes, Myn leapt to her feet and padded over to them. After sniffing Deacon up and down and giving him a brief, accusatory look, she gave Myranda an imploring glance and led her quickly to Lain. As Myranda knelt over the still-slumbering assassin, Myn curled her tail behind Myranda to give Deacon a sharp lash on the arm.

"Ouch!" Deacon exclaimed. "Now that you've grown, I'd appreciate it if you were a bit gentler."

"Why is he still asleep?" Ether demanded, a quite out of place look of concern on her face.

"We placed him in a *very* deep healing sleep. It isn't the sort of thing you wake yourself up from," Deacon explained.

"That has never stopped him before," said Myranda.

Lain appeared to have recovered from the torture at the hands of Epidime. His physical wounds were healed, save for a burnt and swollen patch of skin around his Mark and the lingering effects of starvation. His mind and soul were another matter. Epidime had left them in tatters, savaged and weakened. Myranda set herself to the task of coaxing it to the surface. As she did, the members of the Undermine attempted to gather around, but Myn quickly made it clear that doing so would not be tolerated.

Deacon admired the work Myranda was doing. White magic, where it was concerned with the mind, was a very tricky area. Every mind was different, necessitating a level of improvisation that was difficult to teach. Myranda, it seemed, had a natural knack for such things. Watching her carefully untie the knots left by the D'karon's actions was like watching a sculptor at work. He would have been hard-pressed to achieve in a day what she had done in just these few minutes. It was best she be left to the task.

He stepped between Myn and Ether. The dragon's anxiety was apparent, and though Ether had managed to regain her composure, she too was clearly upset. Deacon placed a hand on Ether's shoulder.

"Remove your hand from me or I will remove it from you," she stated in an even voice.

Deacon hurriedly did so. He turned to Myn and gave her a reassuring pat. She turned to him briefly, coiling her tail for another lash. Deacon cringed, but Myn relaxed her tail and settled to the ground, resting her head on the ground beside him.

"Lain will be all right, Myn. Myranda will have him on his feet in no time," he said, scratching the creature.

Ivy wandered over and climbed on Myn's back, absentmindedly scratching the dragon as well. She leaned close to Deacon, an uneasy look on her face.

"Look at how the others are looking at us," she said.

The Undermine did indeed appear to be surveying the heroes with a combination of fascination, disbelief, and distrust. Only Caya and Tus behaved otherwise, with the former seeming to be feeling little more than impatience as she awaited the completion of Myranda's treatments and the latter chiefly directing a blank faced stare at Myn.

"No one is talking to me anymore. They were talking to me last night," Ivy whispered.

"Last night they were drunk. First on victory, then on wine. It has a way of silencing some of the more insistent voices in the mind. I dare say those voices are speaking now," Deacon said.

Ivy gave him a puzzled look.

Deacon sighed.

"The average person can only tolerate things that are different in small doses. You and the other Chosen are something of an overdose," Deacon clarified.

"Oh," Ivy said. "I was afraid of that. Is everyone like that?"

"Mostly," Deacon replied apologetically.

"That's going to have to change," Ivy decided, "because I don't see us becoming any less different, and we're about to save the world. It'd be pretty silly if folks had a hard time accepting the people that saved the world."

"Agreed," Deacon said.

Suddenly, Lain's eyes opened and his hand shot to his chest. Myn leapt to her feet so quickly, Ivy had to grab on to avoid being thrown. His eyes had a desperate, crazed look about them. They swept over the faces of the Chosen around him. Myn nosed the jealously protected share of the previous night's hunt to him. With a disquietingly feral snarl, he tore into the long overdue meal, scarcely taking time to breathe. As the burning in his stomach subsided, a measure of his sanity returned. A hastily provided canteen was emptied into his mouth. Only when its last drops were swallowed did he finally seem to calm, surveying his surroundings as if for the first time. As he did, Myn crept forward and lay before him, placing her head on his lap.

"How?" he asked, as his stroking brought about a purr almost as formidable as her growl. It was the first he'd truly seen of the dragon since he and the others had believed her killed.

"She was touched by the divine. They brought her back to us, and made her what she is now. She's Chosen, Lain," Myranda said.

"Another soul on the pyre," Lain said solemnly.

He climbed to his feet, Myn reluctantly pulling aside. The eyes of the Undermine fell upon him, and the air was alive with tension. Lain was rigid and silent, as though the gaze of each and every soldier was boring into him.

The soldiers felt a cocktail of feelings. Some admiration, most disgust, but all felt a measure of comfort. This creature they knew was deceitful and murderous. In short, he was precisely as they knew a malthrope should be. Amid things like an obedient dragon and a lighthearted, musical malthrope, finding a being that did not challenge their preconceptions was akin to meeting an old friend.

Caya approached him, standing for a time with their eyes locked, measuring one another. Caya broke the silence.

"I can't say that I ever thought the Undermine would be working with you. We can't afford your fee," she jabbed.

There was a general stir of chuckles from her men. Lain remained silent.

"I want to make this clear, Shadow. We are not like you. You would *never* have been allowed to join us if not for Myranda. We are freedom fighters. We are rebels. We are not murderers," Caya added, again to the raving of her troops.

"Caya, stop it. We have to work together in this," Myranda said. For a moment she dwelled on the fact that, somehow, she'd managed to forget Lain's past. She was not sure whether she should feel pride or shame for having done so.

"Indeed. We've saved your life, Shadow. When this is all over, and we've gone our separate ways, I want you to remember that if ever one of our names comes up from one of your employers," Caya warned before turning to the men and women who followed her. "Come on, Undermine. The day has come. I want this entire campsite on your backs, now!"

To the great relief of some, each soldier set to work. Myranda began to help them, but Caya pulled her hand from the task.

"These men and women are real soldiers, Myranda. They have a routine. You couldn't offer a hand without slowing them down," she said.

And so the Chosen found themselves left alone, their privacy strengthened when Myn planted herself resolutely between them and the Undermine. The dragon focused a dagger-sharp gaze on Caya, radiating displeasure at the tone she'd adopted. Ivy took the opportunity to prance up to Lain and give him a hug.

"I am *so* glad you are safe, Lain," she gushed, kissing him on the cheek. "We had to fight you! I thought for sure someone was going to die, but we all made it! Myn and Ether were so worried, but once Myranda started to heal you, I knew you'd be fine."

Ether's fists tightened at the mention of her concern. She slowly turned to avoid Lain's gaze.

"You should have *seen* Ether," Ivy continued, realizing the shapeshifter's discomfort. "She was practically on the verge of tears. And when we were fighting! At the end, she was *huge!* And . . . wait . . . *she wrecked the mountainside!* That's another one of the forts we destroyed! We are good at that!"

"Where are we?" Lain demanded.

Deacon scrambled to retrieve the map.

"Now that Myn can fly, precisely where we are isn't much of a concern. She can have us to anyplace in the north in hours," Myranda said.

"We need to get to one of Desmeres's storehouses, and quickly. He told me he had finished something, but Epidime was in my mind. We need to reach it before--" Lain began.

"I . . . I think he's given it to me," Deacon realized, hoisting the massive bundle from his bag. "I think there is something for all of you in here. He'd been very clear that I should only open it when all of you were present."

He carefully unrolled the leather mat. What unfurled before them was an array of glistening blades, elegantly carved wood, sparkling crystal, and rolled pages. Beneath them was a carefully folded and tied pile of exotic-looking cloth and mail. Every item Desmeres had provided the Undermine with had been a masterpiece, but the pieces before them now were something else entirely. They had the hallmarks of his design, and a precision and craftsmanship bordering on perfection, but there was more. They seemed alive, pulsing with energy. A small bundle of pages sat atop everything, sealed with wax and scrawled with the words *Open first and read aloud.*

Deacon broke the seal.

"'Chosen,'" he read. "'By now I am certain that I've made an enemy of all of you. It is to be expected. If the messenger has followed orders, these pages are being read in the presence of the united team. If not, listen carefully and act quickly. I believe Lain has been subverted in some way. Do not allow him to take up the enclosed sword unless you know him to be himself. Likewise, if you must face him, do not make use of the other weapons. If memory serves, the death of one Chosen at the hand of another will end them both, and one of these weapons clashing with anything but one of its peers is sure to end in death.'"

"Wow. Desmeres is smart," Ivy said.

"'Assuming things have gone well, this package contains what I consider to be my finest work. If you must kill me, Lain, kill me with this sword. I would be honored to be killed in such a way.'" Deacon continued as Lain picked it up, "'I made one like it for Trigorah many years ago as a gift. My brief time in the confidence of the D'karon has exposed me to techniques that have enabled me to improve it immensely, and in a fraction of the time I'd have thought possible. The gems in the blade will draw strength *only* from the D'karon and their creations. Once stored, the stolen energy can be used to fuel any of the five effects I've engraved upon the handle. I imagine that by now Deacon should be able to explain them.

"'I've enclosed a weapon for Ivy. It took a bit of research because of a few quirks about her, but I settled upon modified katars. They are a pair of double-edged, straight blade, horizontal-hilted punching daggers. For the sake of brevity, and for other reasons that will soon be apparent, I've called them Soulclaws. To my knowledge, these weapons are utterly unique, and necessarily so--but, regardless, I think they may suit her well. I only wish I could see them in action. The effects of a few of the unique enchantments I've placed on them should be truly interesting.

"'Finally, there is the staff. Myranda has certainly proven herself worthy of it, and I am in eternal debt to her for giving me a reason to craft such a device. It is mounted with three of the D'karon gems, treated to react in a more flexible manner. Providing the gems with a charge is not perfectly straightforward, but I've every confidence that Myranda will master the process in no time. It has a pair of mounts for focus gems, though lamentably I was only able to create a single crystal I would consider worthy of a place on this staff. I think you will find it a vast improvement to anything you've used before, regardless of its failure to reach its full potential.

"'I realize that there are five of you, but a shortage of time and information has denied me the opportunity of equipping the rest. Ether, the shapeshifter, I am in particular saddened that I've been unable to address. Designing a weapon useful to her limitless abilities may well be the ultimate challenge. If I've interpreted the events correctly, and the information that I've intercepted can be trusted, the dragon has been raised from the dead, which I sincerely doubt can be explained by anything other than a touch of the divine, and thus Chosen status. Interesting as designing for a dragon's physiology may have been, there simply was not time to do such a thing properly. I've provided ancillary weaponry as well as protective garments.

"'Finally, there are a few notes that Deacon will no doubt find quite enlightening. I wish you all of the luck in the world, my friends. Desmeres.'"

"Ooh," Ivy said, eyes wide, as she picked up her weapons.

Each consisted of a blade half the length of her arm and a bit wider than her fist, mounted on grips. The grips braced against her arm and placed the base of the blade across Ivy's knuckles. As a result, the blades continued the lines of her arm until they tapered into a point. As with all of Desmeres's weapons, the blades had a flawless mirror finish and were carefully etched with arcane symbols and designs. In addition, each blade had a small, clear crystal mounted in it. Ivy gave the weapons a few experimental sweeps through the air.

"Wo-o-ow," she said with a wide grin. "I love them. They feel like I'm not even carrying anything. And they are so-o-o pretty. Look at the jewel! It changes color!"

The gem had indeed taken on a distinctive yellow hue, one that grew more intense as her excitement grew. Accompanying the change was a change in the blade itself. The razor-sharp edge was taking on a decidedly frilled, intricate shape, like the shell of an exotic sea creature. Ivy watched it change with a look of awe and fascination.

"I have to show everyone," she said insistently, bounding off toward the busy Undermine soldiers.

"'Unique enchantments' indeed!" Deacon said, turning to look over the remaining bundles of pages.

They were written in an unfamiliar hand. Several unfamiliar hands, in fact. Every few paragraphs seemed to have been written in an entirely different handwriting, yet the tone and voice of the notes remained constant. As he read, he discovered it to be notes taken by Epidime regarding the mental and spiritual aspect of Ivy's creation. In contrast to the somewhat mechanical and sterile writings of Demont, Epidime's words were lively. At times, they even seemed enthusiastic. Deacon poured over the words, stopping only when Lain thrust the engraved handle of his sword in front of his face.

"Yes. Yes, of course," he said, taking the weapon and beginning to analyze it while gushing about the notes to Myranda. "So much so quickly. All of this information. It is torturous to have to sprint through it . . . Yes, there are five spells here . . . Those notes--is Ivy busy? She probably shouldn't hear this. Those notes were about her, most of them . . . This very clever, this design here . . . Desmeres had to create a new type of weapon for her, because she's been given all of the same training as the nearmen--if you could even call it training . . . What does this mark mean again? Ah, yes . . . Apparently the nearmen have a sort of instinctive training for most types of weapons installed into their minds. You put a weapon in their hands and it activates it . . . This grouping here is clever . . ."

"Focus on one thing at a time, Deacon," Myranda insisted, her head spinning as he alternated between topics.

"Right. Ah, the sword first. There are five spells. This first is fire. It heats the blade to glowing. The second is time dilation--or speed, I think. Activate it and the time around you will slow to a crawl. This one should render you invisible. Remarkable. This increases your strength. This heals you. The string of D'karon runes defines the spell, and this ring with the single rune must cast the spell. It is the activation rune, the spell won't be cast without it. Simply twisting it to align with the appropriate line of runes should be enough," he said, turning to Myranda. "Now, this nearman training. Ivy must have forced most of it aside, but the weapons training is different, almost a reflex.

"If Ivy brandishes a weapon covered by D'karon training in battle, she will be able to use it as well as they do--at the price of using it with their intention, as well. In short, if she uses the skills they gave her, her actions will be as mindless as those of the nearmen. The training covers virtually everything. The only gaps are blunt weapons and some of the more complicated rope and chain-based weapons. Desmeres had to make something she could use, but the nearmen couldn't. Brilliant. There are more pages here. Not about Ivy. They look older. Much older, and they are written entirely in D'karon . . . odd. In the other writings, it seems D'karon is a proper noun, but here it seems broken up. It means first . . . first . . . oh, blast it, where are my notes . . ."

Myranda reached down to pick up her staff. A hand grasped her wrist. She looked up to see Ether giving her a stunned look.

"Have you no sense? These weapons were left by Desmeres. He betrayed us. He is a known agent of the D'karon. There is no telling what he could have done to the weapons. To touch them is madness. Actually using them is suicide!" Ether cried.

"Desmeres would do many things, but he would never taint his weapons," Lain said.

"He would endanger the very future of the world, but he would not do so with his creations? How can you be so sure?" Ether objected.

"You can't always trust a man to do what you ask. You can't always trust him to do what he should do, or even what he wants to do. The one thing you *can* trust him to do is be himself," Myranda explained. "Desmeres defines himself with his weapons."

The shapeshifter relented. The mortals and lesser beings had always been a mystery to her. She'd managed to convince herself it was because their minds were too simple to be understood--that they had no structure, no reason. Anything beyond securing food, finding shelter, and continuing their bloodlines boiled down to randomness, from her point of view. Her time among them had served to make two things clear to her: she would never understand them, but they just might understand each other. Their potent mixture of muddled thinking and fractured viewpoints did, at times, result in something quite akin to insight. Of all mortals, Myranda seemed keenest in this regard. If she believed something to be so, it deserved the benefit of the doubt, at least.

Myranda picked up her present from Desmeres. The D'karon staff had been adequate until now. At least, it had seemed to be. With the work of art Desmeres had created in her grasp, she realized just how inadequate it had truly been. She could feel her mind sharpening. Her eyes traced the long, intricate strings of runes carved into an ancient-looking silver wood. The lines seemed to shift and coil under her gaze. Though she could feel no discernible draw, the moment her fingers touched the surface of the staff, the gems embedded in its length began to pulse to life. Before long, they had taken on a definite glow. When the glow reached its peak, the effects of the staff seemed to compound. The miraculous weapon literally became weightless, drifting from her grip and standing obediently at attention. Somehow, the focusing effect persisted even without contact.

"Astounding . . ." Deacon said in awe. "The . . . the staff has an *area* of effect, and yet . . . I can't feel it. I can feel that it is there, that there is a force at work, but I can't feel its effects. Somehow, he's managed to create a staff that lends its strength only to its owner. I've never seen such a thing achieved without the binding of a soul to it . . . you don't suppose . . ."

"I doubt Desmeres would do such a thing. He would probably consider it cheating," Myranda said.

Myranda experimented with the levitating staff. It drifted along beside her when she walked, and with the merest thought, leapt to her hand or swished to any location she required.

Lain, Myn staying close beside him, had outfitted himself with some of the light armor. The thin chain mail, covered by close-fitting black cloth that had the dull texture of velvet, made him seem, save for his head, a featureless silhouette against the white snow. The hilts of a dozen or more throwing daggers protruded in groups of three from any portion of this outfit large enough to accommodate them. He finished by throwing a white cloak about his shoulders. Anyone who doubted that he was truly an assassin needed only look upon him now.

He drew the new sword. It slipped from its sheath with a barely audible hiss. The weapon bore a marked resemblance to Trigorah's, though with a gentle curve along its blade. Lain took a few cuts, the thin, elegant blade whispering through the air silently and flawlessly. Satisfied, Lain slipped it back into its sheath.

Myranda found a hooded robe that seemed tailored to her. Somehow, merely putting it on seemed to add to the already formidable effect of the new staff. As she moved, she noticed a slight shifting of what felt like cold sand, but turned out to be small swatches of the same exquisitely fine mail that Lain wore placed strategically about the garment.

"Ooh, what's that?" Ivy asked, snatching up the last of the items on the mat.

The equipment was indeed meant for her, and she slipped discreetly out of view behind Myn to try it on. She emerged transformed. They were quite like Lain's equipment, though entirely white. The back of the cloak had a slit up half of its length and the body suit was more form-fitting, no doubt to permit a more full use of her preternatural agility. As they were the first clothes she'd ever worn that were made specifically for her, wearing them made her instantly seem older, more serious, and more formidable. Gone were the saggy, shredded cloak and charred gloves and boots. Where before had stood a childish, seemingly harmless, silly little creature now stood an individual to be dealt with. She hung her new weapons on the straps she found on either side of the leggings.

"Do you like it? I feel a little strange," Ivy said, trying to look herself over from every angle.

"You look like a warrior," Myranda said.

"Oh. Well, I like it, anyway. Not quite as comfortable, but lots easier to move in," she said, attempting a few graceful turns, leaps, and pirouettes.

Myn sniffed at the new outfits and their unfamiliar scents. Myranda looked over her friends, and herself. Each dressed in new white, they seemed to be wearing a semblance of uniform. Of the Chosen, only Myn was unchanged, Ether having quietly altered her clothing to match theirs. Myranda thought hard. The greatest battle of their lives lay ahead. Surely there was something to help Myn. It didn't take long to realize that there was.

"Deacon. The charm from Myn's neck, do you still have it?" Myranda asked.

"I ought to," he said.

He removed a sequence of items from his bag. A bundle of papers, a bottle affixed to a long length of thin chain, and finally the charm. The piece had once adorned the helmet of the now-deceased Trigorah. It carried a powerful enchantment that protected its wearer against nearly all magics.

Myn had worn it when she was small, having snapped it free of the late general's helmet with her own teeth.

"What is that vial?" Myranda asked, as she removed the dragon head figure from its tattered thread.

"I don't know," he said, picking it up and gingerly removing the stopper. The scent was potent and familiar.

It *seemed* to be something he'd encountered during his brief discussions with the alchemists in Entwell, but it couldn't be. There had never been more than a few drops of it, and this vial seemed to hold perhaps a quarter-cup. He stoppered it again and began to put it away.

"Do you need the chain? I think we may be able to use it," Myranda said.

Deacon nodded and attempted to unhook the chain, only to find it fused to the vial. He conjured a simple spell to break it, but somehow it was not enough. Only after summoning an intense heat, one hot enough to make the chain glow, did he manage to unravel a single link and free the chain. Whatever this vial was, it was *very* valuable, and *never* intended to leave the chain. He gave the sturdy chain to her, only to have her hand it back, with the addition of the charm, to have its ends connected. He managed it, and carefully stowed the vial.

"Come here, Myn," Myranda said.

The dragon turned and inspected the trinket, seeming to recognize it. She offered her head. The loop of chain allowed it to hang against her chest comfortably. Once adorned, she stood again, radiating pride. The addition of the long-absent ornament gave her a regal bearing, and she stood tall, with the air of one who has just been knighted. Ivy turned and beamed a broad smile.

"Look at you! Now that just leaves . . . oh. You're dressed like us now!" Ivy said, realizing Ether's change for the first time. "This is incredible! You actually changed to be more like us! You are acting like we are a team, instead of just a bunch of people you tolerate."

"Only you could read so deeply into a simple act," Ether sneered.

"Uh-huh. You look nice, anyway," Ivy said, the excitement rising in her voice. "We all do. What are we waiting for!? Let's go!"

"What do you say, Deacon? Are we ready to go?" Myranda asked. Deacon did not answer. "Deacon?"

The young wizard was looking over the bundle of pages that accompanied the vial with puzzlement. It was strange . . . the language was his own shorthand, but he didn't remember writing it. It was describing, with a very grim tone, the inevitability of the coming of something he called "The Age of Ignorance." There were numerous mentions of the perpetual war, but they were all in the past tense. Near the bottom of the page, the text stopped abruptly and a single message, written in plain Northern and covering the entire bottom edge of the page, took its place. It read, "Stop reading. The knowledge will come in its own time."

"Deacon!" Myranda called, finally drawing his attention. "Is something wrong?"

"Er, ah, no. I do not believe so. I . . . I suppose I've gotten a bit ahead of myself. What was it you wanted?" he asked.

Before she could answer, Lain, Ivy, Ether, and Myn all turned as one to the northern horizon. There was a blotch of black forms against the red sunset.

"There are a lot of them. Looks like . . . maybe ten dragoyles. I think they have riders," Ivy said, Myn nodding in agreement. "I don't think . . . no. They aren't heading toward us."

"They are going to start where the battle was and search out from there, no doubt," Deacon said. "We should have little trouble avoiding them."

"No . . ." Myranda began, an idea forming in her head. "No, I think we can use them. I never let you look at the D'karon staff, did I?"

"No, I suppose not," he said, catching it when she tossed it to him.

Instantly, a look of awed realization came to his face as the spells of the staff revealed themselves to him. Ideas poured through his mind. It didn't take long before a plan began to form. Myranda could tell by the look in his eyes that they were of one mind on the subject.

"Can it be done?" Myranda asked.

"Almost certainly. It will take a bit of effort. I dare say the most difficult part will be convincing the Undermine soldiers," Deacon said quickly.

"Leave that to Caya," Myranda said. "Ether. Would you be able to attract the attentions of that search party?"

"Instantly," Ether replied.

Without another word, Ether flashed into the air. Myranda quickly pulled aside Caya and explained the plan. A grin came to her face.

"Attention, Undermine!" she began. "This war has seen its last sunset!"

#

Northern Capital was uncharacteristically silent. Despite the fact that it was the northernmost city in the empire, its streets were seldom quiet. So far north, the air carried a deathly chill year round, but fate, geography, and climate had conspired to produce a small patch of land spared of the brunt of the arctic freeze. The people of the north, never ones to let a windfall escape them, perfectly ringed the anomalous region in stout walls and founded the castle town of Verril.

Those were the days before the war, before the empire, when words still had the benefit of history and soul. Now it was simply Northern Capital, a sterile description that fell well short of capturing the bustle and clatter of what had become the largest and most wealthy city in the empire. As simultaneously the furthest place from the front and nearest place to the king, the capital was home to the richest and best-born the north had to offer. There was no shortage of young men and women of age for military service here, their positions affording them the privilege of a civilian life. Now they passed their days overseeing the constant trade in goods and information that filled the streets with people and the air with commerce. That was--until today.

A pair of generals stood in a watch post as the massive wood and iron doors were drawn closed for the first time in decades. Ancient hinges protested, and teams of horses strained against the mounded snow that was pushed steadily ahead of the closing gates. The people had been ushered indoors, the sounds of trade now replaced with the march of boots as nearmen filled the streets. Dragoyles and nearman archers lined the roofs. There clicked among the cobblestones of the streets the footsteps of scattered other beasts, creations of Demont. Rocky wolves, gleaming metallic hawks and centipedes, and all manner of other beasts lurked in shadows once lit by torchlight.

The doors creaked shut like a coffin lid. The horses and their drivers were quickly and wordlessly sent to the stables, and the ground outside the walls boiled with the movement of Demont's blind worms. The residents of the city locked their doors. The D'karon owned the city now.

"Explain again why we've closed the doors?" Epidime asked, still in the body of Myranda's father.

"You yourself said that they had troops now," Bagu said.

"What do we care if they have troops? Unless I am mistaken, it is the Chosen *themselves* that we fear," Epidime quipped.

"We fear *nothing!*" Bagu snapped. "Demont is attending the portal. It will be open in minutes. Once it is, this world is *ours.* The Chosen have already failed. There is nothing that they can do."

"Then why have we closed the doors?" Epidime repeated.

Bagu released a slow, hissing breath and tightened his grip about the handle of the sword that now hung at his belt.

"Where is the force we sent to search out the Chosen?" he asked with rigidly enforced steadiness.

"You would have to ask Demont. I never could get much of a feel for his toys. All I can say for certain is that they are alive. Most of them, at least," Epidime said.

Bagu looked beyond the walls. There was no moon, dark clouds leaving the sky a shroud of black hanging over the field of white. A few flakes of ice kicked up by the wind blew into his face, stinging the black scars left by his last encounter with the Chosen. Eyes adapted for the darkness picked out the thrusting forms of Dragoyles approaching.

"They have come, and empty-handed. Come, to the castle. I have a few words for the king before we attend the portal's opening," Bagu said.

The pair descended and strode up the long central street of the capital leading to the castle.

"My, but the dragoyles seem attentive tonight," Epidime mused.

Indeed, even after the generals had made their way inside, the dragoyles stood alert, the eyeless hollows of their heads universally focused on the handful of their brethren that were returning. As the group of wayward beasts drew nearer, a ripple of motion seemed to sweep through the creatures. They stiffened and stood. Slowly, as if through great effort, they each turned to the closest nearman. At the very instant the returning squad touched down within the city walls, there was a flurry of motion. A hundred jaws snapped at once, bringing a hundred nearmen to a swift end.

Instantly, the city was plunged into chaos. Silence was replaced with maddened, inhuman cries. The freshly landed dragoyles shed their riders--not nearmen, but Undermine. One oversized dragoyle leapt to a roof, two other forms climbing from its back. The rocky black hide wafted away to crimson and gold. As Myn took to the sky, Myranda clutched the D'karon staff tight. Her mind was split in a hundred different directions, pouring all that she had into the enchantment of the staff that made her the master of the beasts.

The Undermine were carving thick swaths through the nearmen that crowded the streets. Dragoyles lurched awkwardly through the air under Myranda's untrained guidance, crashing into the throngs of dark warriors choking the courtyards. The weapons of Desmeres made short work of the enemies lucky enough to escape the blunt attacks of the dragoyles, but for every nearman that fell, ten more seemed to rush in to replace him. The streets were a sea of crude armor and flailing weapons, moving like a tide toward the heroes.

Inside the castle, the armageddon outside did not fall upon deaf ears. Both generals rushed to the barred slits that served as windows. Somehow, a solemn silence that waited to bring a swift end to any who threatened the capital had turned into a storming battle in an instant.

"What has happened!? What is this!?" Bagu demanded.

"It looks as though the dragoyles are revolting," Epidime replied. "And our guests have arrived."

Bagu scanned the rooftops until his eyes came to rest on a hated form.

"Go. Mind the gateway," he ordered.

"I think perhaps you may need . . ." Epidime attempted.

"GO!" Bagu bellowed, twisting his fingers into an eldritch gesture and coaxing a portal into being.

"As you wish, General," Epidime said before slipping through.

The portal clashed shut behind him, filling the room with a splash of dark energy.

#

As Deacon poured his mind into maintaining a shield against the torrent of arrows that rained upon Myranda from all sides, Myn roared through the air. The wind hissed past her wings as she cut and dove just ahead of the flurry of arrows. Her talons slashed at archers, tearing through them without sacrificing an ounce of speed. As more bolts launched into the air, she dropped even lower, here and there planting a foot on a roof for an extra surge of speed. Ancient instincts of the hunt and battle set her mind aflame as she dipped among valleys of buildings to scoop a pair of stone wolves into the air and hurl them into a dense crowd of soldiers. Fire billowed in her maw, but the last trace of her mind that was under her control held it back. She was protecting this city. Fire would destroy it.

A blur of black and white burst from the streets to the rooftops. Lain was sprinting. What few soldiers could get in his way offered little resistance to his sword, and as unholy bodies flashed to dust, the crystals of his weapon drank deeply of whatever arcane energy fueled them. His eyes were set on the castle. Like Myn, it was instinct that drove him now--but a different kind of instinct, an instinct learned rather than innate. His blade swept of its own accord, guided by training so deeply ingrained that it existed beneath the level of thought. He was on the hunt. His prey was within the castle. He'd not seen him, heard him, or even smelled him yet, but he knew just the same. Some sense unique to the assassin burned the image of his target into his mind. It was Bagu he would find.

In the streets below, there was a barely noticeable ripple moving through the densely packed streets, nearly matching Lain's speed. Ivy was insinuating her way through the horde of soldiers virtually untouched, fluidly sidestepping, shouldering, and squeezing past before most realized she was present. At a swift glance, it almost appeared that she was trying to hurry through a crowded street of uninterested bystanders. That illusion was dashed when she came upon a shoulder-to-shoulder wall of soldiers with swords raised. She made a quick, panicked swipe with her as-yet-untested weapons. The keen edge passed through weapon, armor, and nearman alike.

Had she taken the time to notice, Ivy would have seen the gems in her weapons take on a dim glow. She also would have seen the blades become a measure stouter, roughly in proportion to her confidence. Instead, she launched herself through the opening and continued her sprint after Lain.

There was a thundering sound in an adjacent street as one particularly dedicated dragoyle trounced into a courtyard. Demont's creations were in full force there, tainted versions of nature's most vicious creatures. For a moment, the beast paused to survey the abominations. Those D'karon soldiers with minds keen enough to determine that the dragoyles were no longer allies set about hacking and slicing at the creature.

When a blade finally cracked the rocky hide, it was not black blood that rushed forth, but a hiss of air. The hulking form wafted into a screaming gale that scoured across the ground of the courtyard. First the smallest creatures, then the largest, were caught up in the tornado. When every last creature was bouncing, struggling, and scrabbling against the icy cobbles and aged edifices, the wind erupted skyward. As the dark creations rained down on their brethren and shattered against the architecture, the wind coalesced into the form of Ether, satisfaction in her eyes. She looked across the rooftops from high above. Some of the dragoyles were heading toward her.

"Something is wrong," Myranda said shakily. "I . . . I can feel them slipping away from me."

Myranda was pouring all that she had into fueling the spell that controlled the dragoyles. The stolen staff was beginning to smolder and warp.

"The generals are taking them back?" Deacon asked, his own efforts beginning to take their toll, though not without benefit. The roof beyond the shield was piled high with deflected arrows.

"No . . . they . . . they are cutting them free. The spell that controls them is being undone. No one is controlling them!" Myranda cried, as the last of the creatures were released from their enchantment.

The change was immediate--and horrific. The beasts were never meant to be uncontrolled. Their minds were not crafted for it. The fragments of consciousness and crudely-formed instincts and reflexes that were etched in their minds were firing randomly. Suddenly gouts of miasma were sprayed at the slightest movement, friend or foe. Those creatures in flight flailed madly until they collided with a building or each other. As soon as one of the creatures made contact with anything, mad convulsions consumed it until the unfortunate creature or structure was no more.

"We've got to stop them, and warn the others!" Myranda cried, turning to her faithful dragon skimming the rooftops. "Myn!"

The mighty creature, half a city away and surrounded by chaos, pulled a tight turn and charged toward Myranda at the sound of her name.

"Myranda, wait. Leave the city to the Undermine and me--you've got to stop the generals. They are desperate now," Deacon said.

"But--" Myranda began.

Deacon took her hand and placed his casting gem in it.

"Take this with you," he said.

"How will you--" Myranda attempted again.

"Don't worry about me. Just go," he said, guiding her hand to click the gem into the vacant socket on her staff as Myn arrived. "And survive."

With nothing left to say, Myranda nodded, throwing her arms about him and sharing a kiss before climbing atop the dragon and taking to the sky. It may have been Deacon's crystal, or it may have been the knowledge that the whole of this ordeal had been leading to this moment, but Myranda's mind had never been so focused. She secured the D'karon staff to her back and willed her new staff to her side. Arrows from the few archers that remained were not merely deflected, but snatched up and hurled at the largest threats.

Myn blazed forward, now high above the city. Tiny, hawk-like beasts of Demont's design flitted around her, mere insects in comparison, but insects with a powerful and deadly sting. An intense swath of flame turned them to plummeting cinders. The castle loomed before them, an imposing and seemingly impenetrable fortress. It had withstood uprisings, invasions, and generations of the harshest winters. Now it faced the Chosen.

Deacon allowed himself a few moments to watch her, as the warmth of her embrace slowly faded in the winter cold. Finally, he turned. There was work to be done. Without his crystal, he was at an immediate disadvantage, but it didn't matter. He'd been trained properly. Drills in unaided spellcasting had been a part of his weekly regimen. Now it was time to put those skills to good use. He pulled the gray blade from the bag and it whirred to life. A leap and a surge of levitation brought him swiftly and safely to the streets below. The dragoyles had punched vast holes in the tide of nearmen. Caya and her men had pushed far forward, but now the gaps were filling, and the battlefront was retreating. Deacon carved his way to the nearest cluster of Undermine. The ragtag soldiers, on the strength of surprise, confusion, and Desmeres's weapons, had made their way to the center of the city, a vast courtyard. Deep in a sea of slashing swords was Caya, barking orders with frenzied energy.

"Caya! The dragoyles are out of control! Stay away from them!" Deacon cried out, as his blade sparked and buzzed against a thickening throng of armor and weapons.

"That won't do!" Caya managed between clashes. "If they are not with us, they have *got* to be neutralized!"

"There are too many, and they are attacking anything that catches their attention!" Deacon said, finally forcing his way to her.

"Shift their attention elsewhere, then!" Caya ordered, Deacon now just another of her soldiers.

"I will try!" Deacon cried.

"Don't try! DO IT! NOW!" she bellowed.

Deacon's eyes darted about the landscape. An idea presented itself. Without a word, he shredded a path to the ancient, ornate doorway at the north end of the town square. After a heave against the heavy doors that served only to knock a crust of ice from them and injure his shoulder, he whispered a few words and wrapped his flagging mind about the beam that was bracing the door from the other side. It reluctantly slid aside and he forced his way in. It was the church, a building second in age only to the castle itself. A building containing a tower that was a match for all but the castle's tallest. A tower that contained a bell . . .

In the distance, a white form scaled the wall around the castle as effortlessly as a ladder and launched itself over the moat, clearing it by inches. A crusted-over stone plummeted into the icy pit, sloshing aside the half-frozen water. It contained no beasts, but it needed none. Salt kept the water liquid and far colder than nature intended, making it deadlier than any beast.

Lain did not attempt the doorway, nor did he scale the walls in search of windows for entry. This was a castle built not to show wealth, but to stand against any army. Windows were scarce, and those that could be found were little more than barred slits that would barely allow a finger to slip through. Outer doors were heavy, well secured, well guarded, and led only to other doors. A scattering of nearmen, heftier specimens no doubt created expressly to defend these walls, attempted to pursue the intruder, but no sooner did he turn a corner than he was lost to them.

Lain knew precisely what was needed to enter this place. He'd had targets within the castle before. Silently, he stalked to a tiny, barred opening at the base of one of the castle walls. It was ancient, corroded-- and, to the trained eye, carefully bent. The castle guards never guarded it, because it did not lead into the castle. The assassin surveyed his surroundings one last time before wedging himself through, dropping lightly into an inky black and burning cold cell.

It was the dungeon. This particular cell no longer had an occupant--not because the north hadn't enough prisoners to fill it. It was because an uncovered window to the frigid night and bed with no blanket was as effective, if not as efficient, as any executioner. After a moment of his skilled efforts, the cell door swung open and the assassin sprinted down the labyrinthine hallways.

The gems mounted in Ivy's weapons were burning like radiant sapphires. As she drew nearer to the castle, she'd been forced to put them to use more than a few times, and each time with a dash more precision. A mind honed to rhythm and grace had carefully entered the weight and shape of the blades into its many equations and made the proper adjustments. Leaping turns, diving rolls, handsprings, and slides all returned to their former flawless state and now carried a deadly bite. Any fear at all was lost in the exhilaration. The nearmen were now little more than sluggish and rather fragile obstacles to her, no longer a cause for concern. Alas, her artful navigation of the narrow alleys and crowded streets had not gone unnoticed. With a force that shattered the cobblestones of the street, one of the dragoyles struck the ground before her.

Having emotions with consequences as significant as hers had eventually taught Ivy a single-mindedness that would have been the envy of any wizard. To avoid being overcome by fear or anger, she devoted her whole mind to the task at hand, in this case following Lain and reaching the castle. Thus, the rampaging and out of control change that had seized the dragoyles had managed to escape her notice. In her mind, these beasts were still under Myranda's control, a misconception strengthened when the monster's first act of business was to trample the nearmen between them. The unsuspecting hero attempted to simply slip past the hulking beast. A heartbeat later, it was only through the combination of sensitive hearing and razor-sharp reflexes that Ivy avoided having her head ripped from her shoulders by a powerful swiping claw.

"Easy, now, Myranda, it's me!" Ivy said as she backed away from the beast.

A second monster dropped down behind her.

"What . . . what is this?" Ivy stammered.

Fear had managed to catch up with her and was making its presence felt both in her blue aura and her weapons. The blades began to reconfigure themselves to suit the emotion, curiously curling and twisting until they resembled the long, curved blades of a scythe. Both dragoyles snapped their maws open mechanically and hissed a stream of black acid. Ivy crouched and sprang into a long, graceful backflip. She peaked just over one beast's head and carefully shifted in air, crossing her blades and lowering them. At the same moment she landed, she crouched, planting her feet on the back of the creature's neck and hooking her blades around it. Before the momentum of the flip was spent she stood again, carrying herself into a second flip and neatly shearing the monster's head free.

The malthrope landed and watched as the dragoyle dropped lifelessly to the ground. Ivy's mind treated itself to a brief surge of amazement and joy before it allowed the image of the remaining dragoyle, mid-charge, to be processed. The beast hadn't managed a second step toward her before the fear finally took hold. She turned and bolted toward the wall of a rather tall building, now little more than a fear-crazed streak of light. The newly-curved blades made the purpose of their shape clear as they bit into the wall, permitting a streak along the ground to become a streak ascending a wall. She reached the top of the wall and continued upward, the momentum of the climb carrying her into the air above the city like a beacon. A beacon that gave a single target to the crazed minds of the remaining dragoyles.

There was a very strong, very precise wind tearing through the streets below. It dashed silvery centipede-like creatures against walls, hurled insect-mawed panthers into the air, and even churned up the earth outside the gates to tear apart spider-legged worms. Ether had decided that Demont's lesser creations must be destroyed. The nearmen and dragoyles were atrocities, but they at least did justice to their stolen forms. They had a perverse sort of purity.

The lesser beasts burned at Ether's mind. They were combinations, unions of one creature and another, or of a creature and an element. The hybrids were small, evasive, and they sullied nature. The humans and other Chosen might have overlooked them, but Ether would not. Indeed, she had not. As she gathered herself into a vaguely human shape and swept the city one last time, she felt only the dragoyles and the nearmen left to be dealt with. However, within the castle, she felt something more. Something that had turned her away once before. Something that needed to be dealt with. She whisked toward the castle.

Myn touched down in the castle courtyard. The inhuman guards who opposed them were reduced to ashes by a carefully-aimed blast of flame. Myranda climbed to the ground and thrust her will at the door. A ripple of magic visibly distorted the air, but it splashed uselessly against the door. Myranda focused her mind and released another volley. This time, the air crackled, but still the door stood. There was a magic far more powerful than hers set against her.

"Myn, can you get us inside?" Myranda asked.

The dragon turned to the door. She retreated until the gates of the castle wall were at her back, then slowly lowered her head. Iron-hard muscles under gleaming red scales propelled the massive creature to frightening speed. When she struck the door, it was like a crack of thunder. Wood splintered and creaked. Rust-encrusted metal twisted and warped. The very frame that held the doors in place buckled--but they held. Myn shook her head and retreated again. A second time, the ground shook and the walls shuddered, knocking free months-old ice and snow. A third and final charge hit like a battering ram. The ragged remains of the door exploded into debris as Myn blasted through.

A red carpet slid and bunched under Myn's claws as she tried madly to stop herself. Myranda rushed in after her. This was the castle's entry hall. Once again, Myranda found herself in a place that, as a girl, she could only have dreamed of seeing. Unlike her mad dash through Castle Kenvard, this place actually met and surpassed the dreams of her youth. Intricate tapestries lined the walls. War banners hung proudly. Suits of ornate armor worn by kings and noblemen stood at attention between massive, towering columns that disappeared into the darkened vault above them. The air was warm, and the smell of burning candles still hung in the air. This place was empty now, but it was alive. Perhaps just minutes ago there had been servants and guards here.

Myranda turned. Ropes had been thrown over the edge of the wall. Boots scratched against the wooden gates of the castle's outer wall. The hordes outside were fighting their way past their own defenses to get in. Her eyes turned again to the wonders around her.

This was the true history of her people. The very history that had been stripped from them. Marble was engraved in ancient languages. Above the hallway leading into the castle proper was a map of the world that still bore the old borders, the old names. The world before the war. Here and nowhere else, the identity of the north seemed to have survived--and it was about to become a battlefield. Already it was scattered with the splintered remains of the door.

"Myn, you won't fit through the hallway, you have to stay here . . . but I have another job for you. You see this? All of this? This must *not* be destroyed! Myn, keep those soldiers from entering this place. I'll be back as soon as I can," Myranda stated.

Myn shot out the shattered door and planted herself just outside, a predatory gaze focused on the wall. She heard the echoing footsteps of her friend retreating down the hallway behind her and longed to follow, but Myranda had spoken. Her talons flexed in anticipation, splitting the stone of the courtyard, and her mighty tail swept and coiled. The scent of the enemy soldiers was in her nose. It was a scent she would never forget. The D'karon creatures came in many shapes, but there was a quality of the scent that never changed. It was out of place, not a part of nature, and it was etched permanently in her mind. Dragons have a long memory, and the scent of those who had killed her was not one she was going to forget. She intended to return the favor.

Deacon finally forced his way to a staircase. When he'd wrestled the doors of the church open, he somehow had expected to find it empty. What he found instead was a huddled crowd of aristocrats and dignitaries. These men and women hadn't known a moment of true hardship in their lives. The war was, to them, a distant thing. Something others dealt with and hardly worth noticing. Now it was on top of them.

Deacon's arrival found them pressed against the opposite wall, not a single one of them willing to risk holding the door shut against the onslaught. When it was clear he meant them no harm, the pleading came. In the space of a few minutes, he was pulled in every direction, had half of the kingdom offered to him, and turned down many a daughter and dowager's hand in marriage in exchange for safe passage from this war zone. It continued as the more desperate of them followed him up the steps.

"Please," begged a round, red-faced man dressed head to toe in silk. "I own a great deal of land. Help me to escape and you may name your price. Be reasonable!"

"I mean to help all of you--now stay back! This could get dangerous," Deacon said, pulling free of the man's insistent grip and rushing up the stairs.

The heavy footfalls followed him for a half a dozen steps before wheezing to a stop and slowly thumping away again. Deacon spiraled up the steps, urgency and duty driving his failing limbs. Soon he was high enough that the battle was just a distant clamor below him.

At what had to be the top of the precarious flight of stairs was a locked door. It did not remain locked for long, the merest whisper from his skilled mind springing the delicate mechanism open. He rushed inside. There were ropes nearly as thick as his arm leading into the darkness overhead. He cast a spell at the bell itself, but the massive piece of brass barely budged. Reluctantly, he grasped the heavy rope and heaved. His feet lifted from the ground, and slowly the rope drifted down.

The voices below rose in terror once again and the sound of pounding footsteps echoed up the tower. In the back of his mind, he realized that he'd not managed to heave the brace back into place. The bell thumped faintly. He leapt and heaved the pull again. A second weak ring echoed down the tower, but as it echoed back up, it was joined by a familiar voice.

"Stop!" Caya cried, as she finally made it to the landing. "No need for that. The monst . . . the prodigy is doing an excellent job."

"Ivy? How?" Deacon asked, slowly releasing the pull.

"She's leading them on a circuit around the city, zigzagging through the streets. I've never seen anyone move so fast," Caya explained.

"She's changed . . . what color is her aura!?" he asked urgently.

"Blue. Does it really matter?" the veteran asked in puzzlement.

"Blue is fear. It doesn't last long. Please, you've got to help me ring this bell!" Deacon begged, leaping to the task again.

"I don't understand," she replied.

"Ivy can only stay that way for so long. When she tires, she'll be helpless. They will tear her apart!" he cried.

Caya dropped her sword and grabbed a hold of the rope. Ivy was still a monster. She and Lain were malthropes. From time immemorial, they were enemies, the plague of humanity. She'd never seen one before, but the tales of her parents and her parents' parents were vivid. Malthropes had blood on their hands that Caya could not ignore. As a race, they were the lowest of the low.

It didn't matter. Ivy was a monster, but she'd saved the lives of Caya's troops. Both Ivy and Lain were putting their lives on the line for a cause she'd devoted her life to. As a race, they were irredeemable. As individuals, they were godsends. They were owed a debt that could not go unpaid.

After a third pull, the bell rang out, clear, and *loud.* The sound was bone-rattling, knocking dust from rafters and rolling over the city. Citizens cowering indoors raised their heads. Undermine soldiers tightened their resolve. The dragoyles turned their hollow eyes to a single point. In their unguided minds, the flaring blue form that had held their attention was instantly replaced and utterly forgotten. Leathery wings nearly tore themselves from their sockets in a frenzied rush to direct the beasts at this new target.

Inside the tower, Caya and Deacon retreated to a lower landing, where a door led to a rooftop. Deacon threw it open and stumbled outside, Caya behind him. He scanned the city madly. There, at the far end of the town's main street, too many massive black forms to count were making their way toward them with maddened, mechanical thrusts of wings. Behind them, unnoticed, a brilliant point of blue faded away. Deacon breathed a sigh of relief.

"Thank you!" Deacon shouted between tooth-shaking clangs of the massive bell.

"It was my duty! I only wonder why you'd needed me! Surely your magic could have done the job," Caya cried.

"What?" he called out.

"I said, why couldn't you have used your magic!?" Caya repeated.

"Haven't the strength. Keeping us disguised and hidden during flight here, the shield, and now with no crystal? I can barely think!" he admitted.

"You haven't . . . you . . . YOU MEAN TO TELL ME THAT WE'VE JUST DRAWN THE ATTENTION OF EVERY LAST ONE OF THOSE MONSTERS AND YOU HAVEN'T A SPELL TO CAST AGAINST THEM!" Caya raved, pulling her sword.

Deacon nodded, fumbling through his bag.

"I can understand wanting to end your life on a high note, but I would have appreciated a bit of warning! I'd have preferred an audience for my death!" Caya fumed, as she gripped the sword tightly. "Ah, well. At least we'll take a building full of cowards with us! Shame it being a church!"

Deacon did not answer. Partially because taking his hands away from his ears to rummage through the bag had cost him what was left of his hearing, and partly because he was busy running some calculations. He pulled the small, clear vial from the bag and pulled it open, smelling it. It certainly smelled like the substance he knew as moon nectar. He recalled the portion of his education devoted to it. Collected from the leaves of special herbs only on the nights of blue moons and eclipses, moon nectar was nothing short of condensed, distilled magic.

He hadn't taken it from Entwell. Even in Entwell, there simply wasn't this much to be had. There was no telling where it came from--it would have taken ages, perhaps thousands of years to collect this much. Had he been more certain that it was what he believed it to be, he'd have sent the bottle with Myranda. Now, well, if it turned out to be poison, whatever death it might bring to him could only be an improvement over the one heading toward him on rough leather wings. One drop, he worked out, would provide him with all of the strength he'd squandered and then some. His body might *just* be able to contain the strength in two. Slowly, he put the edge of the vial to his lips.

"Trying to gird your loins? No sense being genteel about it," Caya said, quite literally to deaf ears.

In a smooth, practiced--and, at any other time, predictable--way, she placed a finger at the vial's base and tipped it up, pouring the entire contents down Deacon's throat. The wizard silently swallowed. Even facing the death sentence it represented, he would not allow himself to waste a drop. A moment later, the sensation began. It was a fire, though the word falls far short, that burned in the center of his mind and the pit of the soul and built. He shuddered as he tried to spread the effects, feeling as though if he allowed it to remain concentrated, it would burn a hole through all of reality. The liquid was the spark, and his spirit the tinderbox.

"Strong stuff?" Caya asked, eyes wide as Deacon turned slowly to her, his eyes already taking on a brilliant white gleam.

"Get your men and bring them indoors," he calmly instructed, his unstrained voice louder than the bell and gaining dimensions with each word, as though it echoed not only through space, but time as well. "I do not know what is going to happen, but it is going to be spectacular."

With that, Deacon paced toward the edge of the roof and, without hesitation, off of it.

Caya had opened her mouth to warn him, but something about the crackling, glowing footprints he'd left a few inches above the roof behind him made her realize it would be a waste of breath. Reluctantly pulling her eyes from the spectacle, she rushed down the stairs.

Deacon hung past the edge of the roof for a moment, then he was atop the tower. He hadn't appeared to move at all, as though he'd remained still and all of existence had shifted to accommodate him. Once in place, he turned his mind lightly to a spell.

The mystic act reached Myranda as a distant, brilliant flash of light. The flare was impossibly bright, somehow gleaming through the stone walls of the castle. It lasted for less than an instant, so brief that she dismissed it, but she could not dismiss its effects. Myranda's trip down into the heart of the castle brought her against spell after enchantment after curse, as though the castle itself was composed of the blasted things. They bored at her soul, pushed against her from all sides. But now they were gone, every one of them, swept away by Deacon's will. The door ahead of her swung open.

A thousand questions and a hundred concerns fought for a place in her mind, but Myranda ignored them. She could not afford to waste this opportunity wondering if it was a trap. Already the spells were slipping back into place and the door was closing. She dove for it, gathering the might of her body and mind to keep it open. It was enough to halt it, but only just, and not nearly wide enough to slip through. Slowly, the enchantment against her strengthened and she began to lose ground.

Behind her, there was a whipping of wind. Outside it might have been dismissed, but her mad dash had taken her deep into the castle. There was only one explanation for such a sound here. Myranda cast a look over her shoulder and saw the swirling form of Ether rushing toward her.

The shapeshifter had spent the last few minutes attempting to enter the castle. As a creature of pure magic, Ether found herself far more affected by the recently dismissed enchantments, and the look on her face made it clear that she was in no mood to allow them to bar her way any longer.

In a single smooth motion, Ether transitioned to stone, gently brushed Myranda aside, and clashed against the door before her momentum had begun to dissipate. The collision neatly knocked the heavy wooden construction from its hinges, sending it sliding a short distance into a particularly ornate hall.

Myranda pulled herself from the floor and clutched the growing lump where her head had met the wall. A gentle brushing aside from a stone form moving at blinding speed was, indeed, anything but gentle. She'd barely brought the thought of healing the injury to mind when her new staff obligingly dipped into the filled-to-bursting reserve crystals and did so for her.

Ether stalked into the tall, elegant chamber beyond the door, but clearly something was wrong. She walked as one through a storm. The magic that merely slowed Myranda hit her like a hurricane gale. Finally, she reluctantly took on her human form. As the focused mana turned to mundane flesh and bone, the arcane pressure parted around her rather than pounding against her. The expression on her face was one of determination and concentration. The human form was useful for many things, but battle was not one of them. If her elemental forms were vulnerable in the presence of this magic, she would need an alternative. She mentally searched through the handful of forms she'd managed to memorize from the samples Deacon had stolen. Surely one of them would be adequate for an indoor clash . . .

Myranda hurried in after her. One of the generals was near, she could feel it. What little light there had been in the hallway gave way to utter darkness in the massive new room. The light from her staff glinted off of hints of gold and silver in the blackness. The hall had a luxury to it that was felt, even though it wasn't seen. Slowly, carefully, as though she might not be ready for what it would reveal, she coaxed more light from her staff. It fell upon portraits in gilded frames, ornamental and ceremonial swords, shields and daggers . . . and a throne.

Myranda dropped to one knee and lowered her gaze, managing. "Y-your Majesty."

Somehow, Myranda hadn't thought she would find him here, that she would have found instead one of the generals in the throne, gloating, with the crown of the empire upon his head. Instead, she found a man. Though frail and old, he seemed to be authority and wisdom itself. Even with her eyes averted, she could feel him looking at her.

"Rise, child. I deserve no such reverence. Not anymore." He spoke in a voice to match his position, rising slowly and stepping down from the throne as he did.

"But you are the king. The emperor. You rule this land," Myranda said.

He placed a hand on her shoulder.

"A ruler has power and wisdom. Power I never truly had. Wisdom . . . wisdom I had only believed I had. I realized too late that even that was not so," he said. "Now stand. You are Myranda, I believe. Myranda Celeste. My generals would have me believe you mean only harm for my kingdom."

Myranda stood.

"The generals. Sire, you must understand, the generals are--" Myranda began.

"I know. I know more, perhaps, than you. You've made a valiant effort, but you are too late," he explained.

"That is not your decision to make, human. Now reveal the generals. Bagu is near," Ether growled.

"Ether, please this man deserves respect!" Myranda scolded.

"Yes, Ether. Where are your manners?" came a voice, seemingly from everywhere at once.

The words echoed around the room, masking the slow, deliberate opening of a door. From within emerged Bagu. His scarred face bore an arrogant expression, an expression of extreme satisfaction. In his hands was an hourglass. Myranda raised her staff, Ether took a step back, settling on one of the more aggressive forms she could remember. With a burst of wind, she assumed the form of a tiger. Massive teeth bared, plate-sized paws sprouting finger-long claws, the shapeshifter pounced.

"Enough!" Bagu shouted, raising a hand.

A pulse of energy knocked the heroes back.

He grinned, continuing. "This is a momentous occasion. It is for your benefit that I allow you to live to see it. You see, you are about to witness the death of your world."

As Myranda struggled to her feet, the last grain of sand slid with painful slowness into the bottom bulb. It struck the pile. Instantly, there was a rumble like continuous thunder. The ground began to shudder under their feet. The roar grew steadily until antiques rattled from their shelves and smashed upon the ground. Dust and mortar sprinkled from the walls and ceiling. Bagu laughed. It was a dark, demented laugh, dripping with evil.

The sound stabbed at Myranda's mind. The young wizard steadied herself on the shaking ground. No. It would not end like this. Not here. She charged. Bagu raised his hand again. A wall of magic shimmered into being, crackling with energy and strong enough to stop a stampede. Myranda did not slow. As she came to the wall, she slashed at it with the D'karon staff. The impenetrable barrier rippled and spread apart like the oily surface of a swamp, Bagu's spell countered by one of the same design. She hurtled through the gap. The wizards clashed.

Outside, those soldiers who had not managed to reach shelter before Deacon struck were left with an image that would linger in their nightmares for the rest of their lives. The whole of the first attack occurred in an instant, but that instant seemed to last an eternity.

A sphere of light burst out from around Deacon. Those creatures nearest to it were simply undone. First, their body divided into separate pieces--heads, limbs, wings, and segments of tail and neck hanging in midair. Then they too disassembled, hide, flesh, blood, and bone pulling apart--not in a gory way, but as though they were simply components that were being dismantled. Then, somehow, even these things seemed to divide further into whatever constituent parts made them up. It continued, further and further, finer and finer, until nothing remained at all, the whole sequence analyzed by Deacon with a cool, scientific eye.

Those luckless beasts who found themselves just outside of the sphere suffered the same fate, albeit to varying degrees of completeness. They remained in such a state when time finally came flooding back, some clattering to the ground, others dissipating like a cloud, still others spattering as a liquid, and the rest in some horrid combination of every stage. None lasted for long. All told, perhaps ten beasts remained fully intact once the moment had passed, those fortunate enough to have been slower than their brethren.

Deacon's mind was fragmented, with each part working feverishly on its own task. One aspect stored the wealth of information gleaned from the dissection of the dragoyles. Another skillfully navigated him to the ground. A third carefully tallied the remaining threats and tasks at hand. The largest part was taking special notice of the effects an overdose of moon nectar seemed to be having.

The mystic energy he'd consumed was greater by many orders of magnitude than he was able to contain or control. Were it a more traditional type of energy, the effects of would have been brief, immediate, and messy. Instead, the power he could not contain was escaping. It was not like his own strength, nestled inside and waiting to be harnessed. This power was pouring out of him, slipping through his mind and soul like water through a sieve. Whether he gave it form or not, it slipped away, crackling and baking the air as it did.

As each facet of his mind finished its task, it merged with the rest, until finally there was but one Deacon within his mind once more. He was busy debating on what to do next. This power would be gone soon. The bulk of it was gone already. Briefly, he considered joining the heroes and striking down what foes he could, but he knew it would not last, and there was no telling what state he would be in when it ran out.

The outside world, having recovered from his onslaught, made its presence known, quickly putting any other prospective tasks to rest. The ground was shaking, a mysterious blue light was painting the clouds to the north, and he was surrounded by nearmen.

Their numbers, despite the long battle against superior foes, were still in the hundreds. The creations had been imbued with a carefully measured amount of intelligence. They were smart enough to identify him as the chief target, but not so clever as to determine their odds of victory. Fear and common sense existed in precisely edited forms so as to ensure that orders were followed no matter the cost and no matter the risk. They raised their weapons and rushed at him.

Deacon's mind was still floundering in energy enough for an army of wizards, but it was rushing out rapidly. Already he knew that any attempts at the reality-defying manipulations he'd managed moments ago would fall short. What was called for now was conventional magic . . . in massive quantities. He attempted a quick assessment of the surplus of energy but failed miserably, the constantly shifting effects of the overdose having evolved into a sensation akin to looking into the sun while simultaneously another sun was looking out from the inside. This was a situation that called for successive approximation.

He drew his gray blade and spun it up to speed and beyond, until the weapon was little more than a shimmering disk producing a terrifying whine. He hoisted a sword from the ground with his mind and set it spinning. It quickly became clear that this was taking too long, and the circle of nearmen charging toward him was growing nearer. Like birds rising from a field, every stray sword left by a defeated soldier lifted from the ground. There were dozens. One by one, in rapid succession, the swords matched the speed of his blade.

Deacon nodded. This would do.

Across the city, the thump and clang of blunt blades encountering poorly-made armor filtered and reverberated through streets and alleys until it reached the motionless body of Ivy as a chorus of dull percussions. She was sprawled on the ground, barely breathing in the aftermath of her outburst of fear. Desmeres's blades were scorched but intact in her still-clenched fists. At some point, they had resumed their original shape, but the near-blinding glow of the embedded crystals persisted. As Ivy drew in a slow, shallow breath, there was a sudden, sharp pulse. The breath came out as a scream. The stored energy forcibly and painfully returned to its source, tearing Ivy from her repose and restoring her to a wakeful, albeit dazed, state.

"What was that? Oh . . . Oh, no. Where am I! There were dragoyles! Are they gone? Hello! How long has it been? Did we win?" Ivy stammered, as her eyes darted around the street.

Slowly, she became aware of her surroundings. The ground was littered with broken armor, flecks of black blood, and gray dust. Debris was clattering about the cobblestones as the ground maintained a constant, low rumble. The nearest sound came from the north. She turned to find, a short distance away, a gate. A smattering of nearmen were hacking at it with swords and axes, and a few were in the process of scaling it using ropes hanging from the top. Beyond that was a castle. Far in the distance behind it, there was a pool of white-blue light on the clouds.

With her investigations thus far offering up more questions than answers, Ivy looked herself over. She was certain she'd changed, and fairly certain it had been fear. That usually cost her a few days and left her with scorched clothes. Her outfit was none the worse for wear, and she was not nearly hungry enough for days to have passed. There was something strange going on, and she had a feeling Desmeres's equipment was to blame, but that didn't matter right now.

"We were heading for the castle, so that's where I'm going," she decided.

She ran to the castle gate, her head slowly clearing. By the time she reached it, she felt tired, but no more so than after a long day of walking. She wasn't at her best, but she was hardly at her worst.

There was something very noisy happening on the other side of the gate, something that clearly was far more interesting to the nearmen than she was. Jumping from ground to shoulder to rope, she managed to make it halfway up the wall before a single foe noticed her.

"Off! Get off!" she cried as one of the soldiers grabbed at her foot.

A firm yank managed to dislodge the foe above her on the same line, and moment later she was atop the gate. A moment after that, she was dangling from the edge, a column of flames lancing over her head.

"Myn!" she scolded, peeking up. "It's me! What are you . . . wow. You've been busy."

At the base of the other side of the gate was a mound of ruined armor and ruined soldiers as tall as Ivy. Myn reared up and leaned against the gate, bringing her to eye-level with Ivy atop it. The malthrope stepped gingerly onto Myn's head and navigated down her back to the ground. Myn finished the remaining nearmen with a sweep of flame down the outside of the gate. The immediate threat gone, Myn looked with confusion at the streets that were mysteriously free of nearmen. She gazed vaguely in the direction of the city's center, where periodically what looked like long metal insects flitted above the skyline, Deacon's spinning swords. The dragon looked in confusion to Ivy.

"Don't ask me, I just woke up! Where is everyone? In there?" Ivy asked, indicating the splintered doorway.

Myn nodded.

"All right. I guess you stay here. I'll try to find them," Ivy said, venturing inside.

The castle shook from a blast somewhere deep inside.

"I don't think it will be hard," Ivy called, as she disappeared down the hallway.

Myn watched Ivy go until she could no longer see her, then padded uneasily about the courtyard. She pawed at the smoldering pile of armor briefly, then plopped down to the ground, huffing in irritation.

The air in the throne room was alive with magic. The king sat on the throne, looking upon the battle with the distant, helpless interest of a man watching the icy water lap up the sides of his sinking ship.

Myranda held the D'karon staff in one hand and Desmeres's staff in the other. Powerful spells arced across the room. It was quickly becoming clear that Myranda was still no match for Bagu, but between the robe

Desmeres provided and quick work with the D'karon staff, the young wizard found that she could shrug off most anything the general could summon mystically. The same, alas, could be said for Bagu. Fire hot enough to melt stone faded to nothing as it neared him. Black magics had no effect at all. The only progress at all was made by Ether.

The shapeshifter was on her third form, abandoning the form of a tiger for that of a wolf, and the wolf for that of a bear. Myranda's uninterrupted assault had created a handful of openings, and Ether had filled every one with tooth and claw. Thick black blood leaked from slashes across Bagu's back, but the wounds were quickly closing. Worse, the animal forms, though immune to whatever persisting spells had been tearing at her elemental forms, were defenseless against the perversions of magic that Bagu unleashed upon her directly. A sizzling patch of fur served as a reminder.

In a single move, the tide turned against the Chosen. Bagu's fist closed about the D'karon staff and wrenched it from Myranda's grasp. No sooner did the staff leave her grip than the full force of a dozen lingering spells dropped upon Myranda at once. Black energy wracked her body with pain enough to snuff out the spell she'd been readying. With a thrusting kick, he knocked Myranda to the ground and hissed a mouthful of arcane words that nearly incinerated Ether's hulking form. She shifted to stone and gathered herself, searching for a form that might do some good.

"Stupid creatures," Bagu spat. "The battle is lost! There is nothing you can do! You have failed at your purpose!"

The dark wizard punctuated each sentence with a new and worse twist of magic. It was all Myranda could do to hold them off. Bagu's hand finally reached for the hilt of his sword, left untouched at his belt. He'd not had the opportunity to brandish it, but with the momentum on his side he revealed its obsidian blade. Myranda's faltering spell of protection buckled and quavered. Without words, Bagu raised the weapon.

A blur of white flashed through the room and clashed with the sword. Ivy stood unsteadily, blades crossed against Bagu's weapon.

"You won't kill my friend," Ivy hissed, red flaring in her eyes.

"It is long past time this failed experiment was brought to an end," Bagu replied, coils as dark as shadow working their way up Ivy's legs as he bore down on his blade.

The general's mystic strength seemed bottomless. Ivy clenched her teeth in agony as Bagu's spell burned at her soul. He seemed determined to overpower her, to show her that he was stronger. Slowly, Ivy began to lose ground. The blade sagged nearer to her face. Then, without warning, the pressure was gone. A hole had opened on Bagu's breast plate, seemingly on its own. There was silence. Not a gasp of pain, not a grunt of effort.

Gradually, a polished silver blade, now smeared with black blood, wavered into view within the wound. The general staggered aside. Behind him, no longer hidden by his sword's spell, was Lain.

What followed next was chaos. Scalding, black as death energy began to erupt out of the wound. Like water from a ruptured dam, the power came. In the center of the storm was Lain, sword firmly held in hand, and Bagu. The general lurched, clutching desperately at the blade and bellowing words that twisted reality. He cast out his hand and a trio of curls of darkness drew together, swirling and opening. From the hole in the air came a shaft of piercing blue light--the very same hue as that which painted the skies to the north. He heaved himself free of Lain's blade and stumbled though the portal. It snapped shut, the unspent energy lashing outward and tearing at the heroes, crumbling the stone and warping the ceremonial shields on the walls.

Then there was quiet. A distant rumble, the ping of cooling stone, and the clatter of debris settling were the only sounds. Here and there, the masonry of the walls was striped with a swath of glowing red heat like veins in marble. It was the only light. Slowly, it was joined by Myranda's magic. The light that had so recently fallen upon splendor and history now fell upon ruin. Ancient portraits lay dashed upon the floor. Tapestries smoldered. The heroes slowly gathered themselves.

"Is everyone all right?" Ivy said, as she helped Myranda to her feet.

Ether was slowly returning to her human form. As massive as the battle had been, she was not much worse for wear. The animal forms that were so often forsaken in favor of her elemental ones had been virtually effortless to assume, and as most of the attacks had merely damaged her physically, the injuries were whisked away with the form. Lain had once scolded her for squandering her abilities. Now it seemed that he may have been correct--she could have been more efficient.

The special equipment provided by Desmeres had taken the brunt of the damage directed at the others with barely a mark to show for it. Lain slid the ring of his sword to the position Deacon had indicated would heal him. Within a few moments, at the cost of the remainder of the sword's stolen power, Lain's injuries were nearly gone. Myranda put her mind to repairing the damage she'd taken, then turned her attentions to Ivy. Of all of the heroes, she'd fared the best, barely requiring more than a moment of the healer's ministrations. The king was another matter.

"Your Majesty!" Myranda cried, rushing to the throne.

The burst created by the closing of the portal had struck him unimpeded; the elderly monarch was slumped across the arm of the throne. Myranda ran to him. It was the work of a few moments to revive him, but to restore him was another matter entirely. The D'karon magic had a cruel, almost poisonous quality to it. It wrapped about one's soul and remained long after the injuries were closed.

"Enough. Leave me," the king said.

"You are my king and I will not allow you to die," Myranda said.

"See to the city. They deserve what little time you can give them," the king said, pushing Myranda away.

"The city is fine. I don't think we knocked down a single building," Ivy said, a hint of disappointment in her voice. "The streets are pretty much clear. I think the Undermine are mopping up the rest. And Deacon, I suppose. I don't know, I missed most of it."

"Still, it doesn't matter. It is over now. Perhaps my ancestors truly thought they were saving the kingdom. I was still a boy when I learned the truth, that *they* had all of the power. This kingdom ceased to be ours the very moment one of those things wore the colors of the north. I knew I couldn't take it back, I could only delay the awful realization from hitting my people. I never would have thought that it was the *world* I was failing," the king rambled.

"Be still, Your Majesty. You are out of danger, but you will need to rest," Myranda said.

"Your Majesty . . . *Your Majesty!* I am no king. I am barely a *man.* My name, my kingdom, my bloodline is tainted forever," he raged, throwing his crown to the ground.

"We are wasting time. We need to find and end the generals while Bagu is still wounded," Ether insisted.

"The generals don't matter. The sand has run out. The gateway is open now. They have succeeded, you have failed," the king muttered.

"Gateway?" Myranda asked.

"Their world to ours . . . indeed, their world to theirs," the king said vaguely.

"A gateway is open? Where?" Myranda gasped.

"I think I know! There was light on the clouds to the north. That has to be it, right?" Ivy said, her voice radiating the simple joy of being helpful.

"Let us go! That gateway must be closed," Myranda said. "But the king!"

"Go! There are some yet within these walls who would defend me," the king replied.

Lain was already padding swiftly down the hallway. The others quickly followed. With a final look to her king, Myranda joined them.

"Myranda! You have to hear what happened! These things that Desmeres made, I think they woke me up! And . . ." Ivy began.

"Ivy, we've still got a job to do. You can tell me later. If there *is* a later . . ." Myranda said solemnly.

"There'd better be. I have a *lot* to say," Ivy stated.

Myn leapt alertly to her feet when the heroes arrived. Myranda, Ivy, and Lain climbed to her back. After a few words, Myn began to charge along the courtyard, building speed and spreading her wings. The load was half again heavier than she was used to, and she was lifting off with a day of flight and a night of battle between her and her last real rest. The wings caught the air and pumped experimentally as she made a few successively longer hops. Then, with a final leap, she launched herself into the air.

After a few powerful flaps of her wings, it was as though she carried no weight at all. She wheeled and set off toward the piercing point of light on the horizon to the north.

#

Deacon's rampage was coming to an end. He'd adopted a spectrum of different manipulations with the swords as his power had waned. Rotating blades that cut through armor gave way to sweeping swarms of swords that he directed as a conductor might direct his musicians. As his strength dropped further, so too did a number of the swords. Those that remained orbited him in a complex pattern, separating and obeying his whim when the time came to attack. Blades assembled to mimic his fingers clutching and tearing at massive dragoyles. Others swept into place to block blows and keep soldiers at bay. When his mind weakened further, he thinned the cluster of swords to ten carefully arranged about him, floating and striking as though in the hands of invisible warriors defending him.

Now what swords remained sagged and drifted sluggishly. He carefully made another mental note on the effects of the overdose of nectar. It would seem that the flood of energy escaping him had the same effect as a siphon on a barrel of water. It continued to draw energy much at the same rate even after it had reached quantities he should have been able to maintain. In short, he was far worse off now than before taking the tonic.

Surrounding him was a single, badly injured dragoyle and perhaps fifty nearmen, the very last vestiges of D'karon influence in the city. Though it meant he had sawed, slashed, and bludgeoned his way through the vast majority of soldiers, this remaining fraction may as well have been an entire army. He simply didn't have the strength to face them.

As the final sword slipped back to the ground and Deacon staggered over the heaps of shredded armor, he quietly thanked his good judgment for not offering aid to the others. No doubt Myranda would not have let him die without a fight, and what energy she wasted on saving him might well have cost them the battle, and thus the world. Here, at least, he could be killed without consequence. He smiled weakly as the fate he'd been expecting all along stalked inevitably closer.

They were nearly upon him when a chorus of war cries from the opposite end of the courtyard startled him out of his reverie--and, more importantly, distracted the nearmen.

Deacon faintly remembered, an eternity ago when he'd taken the dose of moon nectar, that he'd warned the Undermine to seek shelter. At the time, they had been a dozen or so men and women. Unless one of the lesser effects of the potion was to confuse one's hearing, that number had grown greatly. He turned to the church to find, alongside the well-armed and poorly armored soldiers, were poorly-armed and unarmored aristocrats, screaming for blood. His addled mind tried to work out how the terrified gathering of social elite had been stirred into a maddened mob of berserkers. Caya claimed not to be a wizard, so it was not magic that had set their spirits aflame. Regardless, Caya seemed to have a power of persuasion that any wizard would kill for, and she wielded it through words alone.

On the strength of numbers and frenzied enthusiasm, the D'karon quickly fell to Caya's force. The most skilled of the soldiers spread out, each leading a small band of civilians. Names were shouted, doors were opened, streets were filled. Quickly, the city came to life again, this time populated by those to whom it belonged. The air filled with voices passing the tale from ear to ear. Curses of anger, cries of disbelief, and gasps of fear mixed with a universal feeling of relief. Whatever had happened, whoever was to blame, at least now it was all over.

Caya and Tus approached the weary sorcerer, the latter delivering a slap on the back that nearly threw him to the ground.

"Why didn't you do that in the first place? For heaven's sake, my boy, you practically could have taken the city on your own!" Caya cried.

Deacon did not answer. He was too busy keeping his eyes focused on the retreating form of the Myn, carrying the other Chosen north. It wasn't over. Not yet.

#

There were few who had ever seen this part of the world. Well outside the curious pocket of livable temperatures that made the capital possible, this mountain range that stretched to the very top of the world was nothing short of suicide to traverse on foot. The mountains had no individual names. No adventurer or explorer had yet to challenge a single summit. A half-circle of mountains that stood noticeably above the rest were known collectively as the Ancients. The rest were known simply as the Dagger Gale Mountains, and with good reason.

The wind seemed to cut like a knife, as though the air itself was freezing into jagged, pointed sheets. Myn heaved a heavy, streaming breath of flame every few minutes and basked in the all-too-brief warmth it brought. Despite the near fatal cold, though, each hero had a far more pressing concern, and it lay just ahead.

Nestled in the shallow bowl of a valley half ringed by the Ancients was a trio of triangular columns. The obelisks were gray, wide as a small building at the base and towering taller than the tallest tree. They tapered gradually along their lengths, then suddenly near the top, such that the massive towers were topped with small pyramids. Each tower stood many hundreds of paces from the other, evenly spaced as the points of a sprawling triangle, so large it took up most of the northern half of the valley. A small city could have comfortably fit between the towers.

Myn circled closer. The towering columns were perfectly smooth, seeming almost polished. Neither a line of mortar nor a single brick marred the surface, as though each tower had been carved from a single massive stone. The only interruption to the glassy sheen was on the inward-facing side, where massive runes were embossed into the surface. They covered the entire inner face, and led to a point of intense blue light that floated in mid-air just in front of the final rune. Each tower had such a point, and from each point emerged a single shaft of tangible mystic energy, bright as a bolt of lightning. The shaft buzzed and crackled, lancing down through the icy air to a point midway between the two towers opposite it. It came to a stop at a point above the ground precisely half the height of the tower. The point where the shafts crossed was brighter than the brightest sun on the clearest day. Directly below it, paper-thin and defined by the points where the shafts ended, was a triangle of pure black.

The whole of the structure had a terrible, geometric precision. The thought that something so enormous could be so exact was chilling.

"What is it?" Ivy asked in awe.

"It can only be the portal . . ." Myranda answered.

Ether, without a word, hurled her windy form to the ground. Myn followed, wheeling gradually toward the only other thing whole of the valley. It was a lone figure, a man, casting a long, black, twisted shadow. Ether took on her stone form, but held firm a few paces away from him. When Myn touched down and the heroes spilled from her back, it was clear why she hesitated. He was standing just within the area traced by the towers, and the power that poured out of the border felt as though crossing the line that separated them would tear flesh from bone.

"Astounding, isn't it!?" shouted the man over the diabolical mix of sounds the portal produced.

His back was to the Chosen as he admired the monstrous configuration. He continued:

"The end result of centuries of constant work. Two *hundred* fifty-five years, eight months, eleven days, fifteen hours. In your time, at least. Every moment of it filled with conjuring, sapping, chanting, and focusing. First ourselves, then a few of your own wizards, and finally a veritable army of Demont's nearmen made especially for the purpose. Even so, we'd estimated over three hundred years to get the gateway in place. That is, of course, until we captured you," he said.

The figure turned. It was Myranda's father, but his face made it clear that such was the case only on the surface. Epidime looked out from within.

"Ivy and Ether were the most help, but you all made a contribution. Those crystals. You filled *hundreds* of them. Each one took months off of the process. In just a few days, we made great bounds toward completion. If only you'd been a few minutes sooner, you might have seen it all come together. It is a sight to behold. The towers aren't built, you know. They are summoned. They are utterly impenetrable, every aspect of them carefully shaped in the mind. One moment a shifting mass of focused magic, the next three perfect towers coaxed instantly into existence. They draw the power to hold the portal open from your very world. A marvel. Every detail a marvel.

"You made it interesting, I can tell you. I had actually begun to believe we wouldn't get the gateway open. Now we have, and only three worlds in all of our experience have ever closed one. None of those worlds exist any longer."

"Where are the others!?" demanded Ether. "The time has come. You shall meet your fate, and your creation will die with you!"

"Bagu went through. He took Demont with him. They are gathering the army," Epidime said.

"Your army is destroyed," Myranda called out.

"No. *Your* army is destroyed. Those were Demont's toys. Made in your world, of your resources. The D'karon was a force of four. Three, now that Teht is dead. Ah . . . but, then, you never did understand that part, did you? I suppose now is as good a time as any. You thought the name for our race, for our *kind,* was D'karon. You were wrong. D'karon is a military term. It means 'first wave.' You thought you'd been facing an invasion. The invasion hadn't even begun," he explained, with a grin that cut to the soul.

The vast field of black above him began to ripple. Whirls of clouds wafted and twisted, revealing whispers and glimpses of things unspeakable. Epidime's grin grew to a smile.

"Until now," he added.

On cue, the whole of the triangular void erupted. Black clouds rushed out with the force of an avalanche, tearing the heroes from the ground and whipping them through the air. The howling of the fetid wind was joined by a rumble and quake. The ground shook as though a landslide were bringing the very mountains down upon them. The wind slowed, not as though it was cut off, but as though the pressure behind it was slowly being equalized.

By the time the heroes found themselves on the ground once more, they were scattered to the far reaches of the valley. The blackness was still. It hung like a fog in the air, filtering the light from the obelisks into a pale haze. The stench was a choking combination of arcane odors. In the shifting, smoky fog, dark forms moved indistinctly at the threshold of vision.

A cold wind began to pour into the valley. Ether's windy form rose up, the swirling mass trailing behind her, lifting the black veil that hung over the valley. It revealed a sight worse than any one of them could have imagined. The ground was alive with creatures, wretched beasts that had no place in this world. No two seemed the same, each a mass of spidery legs and lashing tendrils, snapping mandibles and gyrating wings, chitinous shells and glistening claws. The horrid creatures ranged from the size of a large dog to as massive as an elephant, with the exception of three.

The first was barely a creature at all. In shape, it vaguely resembled a root that one might find in an apothecary jar. A leathery indigo hide stretched over a body tapered at either end and massively thick in the middle, studded over its entire surface with spiky barbs. The barbs along the bottom sprouted deep violet stalks, shiny with something the consistency of syrup that dripped from the barbs, and tipped with swollen, spherical orange ends. The stalks hoisted its body, easily the size of a house, from the ground like legs.

Behind it was a creature almost twice as tall. Its body seemed to be composed entirely of three thick appendages joined to a central bulge. The limbs were tubes thick as Lain was tall and ended in a ring of flat, pointed teeth that spread like toes as it walked. Its skin was hidden beneath a coat of white fur. On the misshapen bulge where the limbs came together, hundreds of small black eyes, scattered across top and bottom, blinked randomly.

The last was a beast so tall it was not until it had come out from beneath the black void that it was able to unfold itself to its full height. The thing was standing on seven narrow legs, thick as a tree trunk where it left the boulder-sized body, and tapering to a point along its segmented length. It resembled a daddy long legs, the body sagging between the upward-arcing limbs. While only seven touched the ground, the twisted thing had more legs than could be counted. Most were tiny, twitching things that spiked the body like an urchin. Randomly scattered among them were larger ones, a trio of which surrounded a clacking, squid-like beak, the only part of its body not sprouting limbs.

Standing among the hell's menagerie were the three remaining generals. Epidime's infuriating look of satisfied superiority stood in stark contrast to the deep, penetrating look of madness that twisted the remnants of Bagu's face. His obsidian sword was joined by a second in his other hand, and his gaze was locked firmly on Lain. Demont was atop the reared-up neck of a beast that looked to be a horse-sized combination of a serpent and a centipede. He had a distracted look on his face, as though he had more important things on his mind than battle. With a single gesture from this third general, the demon horde washed over the icy ground like a tide.

The Chosen hurled themselves into the fray. Lain's sword was in constant motion, lightning-quick slashes opening gaping wounds on the larger beasts and dividing the smaller ones into pieces. Streaks of silver flashed toward the airborne creatures that strayed to near to him, sending the beasts crashing to the ground with daggers buried deep in each. The gems of his blade quickly took on a brilliant glow. Most of the creatures were left behind, hopelessly slower than their target. Speed, however, could only overcome so much, and before long Lain found himself facing a wall of creatures too large to avoid and too well-armored to strike down. Lashing talons and snapping jaws closed in around him. The assassin tightened his grip on his weapon and angled the blade against their attacks.

Myn took to the air. The towering, spider-like creature was moving across the valley with staggering speed, and she knew that it could quite easily be a threat to any of her friends. Slashing and searing those winged beasts foolish enough to face her, Myn climbed high into the air. When the chaos was far below her, she turned, tucked her wings, and dove, flames streaming from her gaping maw and fury burning in her eyes.

The ponderous, many-legged creature lumbered blindly, only seeming to become aware of the dragon's approach a moment before she collided. Tooth and claw clamped about the thick base of one of its legs with the full force of momentum behind them. The shell-like surface creaked, cracked, and split, gushing dark green blood. The beak released an earsplitting wail and the legs long enough to reach Myn began to slash and scrape madly at the dragon's scales. Myn ignored them, working industriously at removing the leg.

Ether's form flickered to flame, anger burning in her mind like never before. To the others, these beasts were merely a threat. To Ether they were a personal slight, a slap in the face of all that she embodied. She was nature given form, but these beasts . . . they were creations of another nature entirely. She dipped low, charring a path through the smaller beasts, injuring as many as she could as she made her way to the indigo skinned beast, a very definite sequence of events forming in her mind. She swept below the creature, her blazing touch sizzling against the tendrils that held it aloft. As each one was scalded and blistered, it retreated into its barb.

By the time she'd passed completely beneath the monster, too few tendrils remained. It teetered and finally collapsed to the side, its massive bulk rolling over a cluster of its fellow invaders, crushing them utterly. New, glistening tentacles were already sprouting out from beneath it to raise the beast again when Ether landed atop it. No sooner had she done so than she leapt back into the air, searing pain stabbing at her everywhere she'd touched the beast. Her flames flared brighter as she dove for another attack. Again, she was repelled. The creature's hide glowed lightly where she'd touched it. The glow then spread and faded. It couldn't be . . . this beast *fed* off of her energy.

Myranda thrust her staff into the earth and cast a tremor forward. The ice and stone rolled forward like a cresting wave, hurling beasts aside. She sprinted through the wake behind it. The scrabbling of beasts trying to right themselves after being whipped aside and the screech of beasts trampling them to get to her stabbed at Myranda's ears. None of it mattered. Her eyes were focused on a form wading unmolested through the sea of demons, grin on his face.

Epidime stood stone-still as the wave of earth approached. A flex of Myranda's mind split the rippling earth around him, throwing aside the beasts that stood guard around him. A moment later Myranda stepped into the clearing. A wave of one hand coaxed a ring of stone spires from the ground, walling off the creatures. A whispered phrase supplemented it with a glimmering shield that curved up over them. The pair stood in a personal arena, for the moment sealed away from the rest of the conflict.

"Just the two of us, once again. So this is it. This is all it takes to break you. I spent hours trying to find my way to that last corner of your mind. Weeks trying to weaken you enough to loosen your grip on it, and all of this time I needed but to find your father. One glimpse of him and you abandon everything you believe in," Epidime remarked.

"Release him!" Myranda hissed, her staff raised and swirling with a spell ready to be cast.

Epidime waved a hand dismissively and the churning magic slipped away.

"For the sake of privacy, I will allow the shield and the stone, for now. This is far too delicious a torment to share with the others," Epidime said, his sinister tone turning Myranda's stomach. "You've more power now than you've ever had before, and what can you do with it?"

He thrust his hand forward. A wave of energy smashed Myranda against the wall.

"Nothing," he said.

Ivy tried to gather herself. She was afraid. Maddeningly so. The light of it burned in her mind, but she simply didn't have the strength to slip over the edge. Perhaps it was something to be grateful for. Perhaps another time she would have been. It wasn't the towering behemoths that concerned her. It wasn't the rush of unidentifiable forms before her. Monsters and beasts were things she had faced so often in her short time with the others that they were almost comforting. What filled her with fear was the sight of Demont, though even the threat of the horrible things he had done to her and the horrible things he might to do her friends was not what frightened her most.

What frightened her most was what thinking of those things stirred up in her. Behind the fear, and growing stronger with every moment, was the hate. A hate that might be strong enough to do what the fear was failing to. A hate that might make her into what she'd been before. A hate that might not let go. The frightened creature backed slowly away as Demont drew nearer. She raised her weapons.

"Get away from me!" Ivy cried.

"You are my experiment, and there is still much I can learn from you," Demont said. "Now come."

"I won't! I'm not your experiment. I'm one of the *Chosen,* I'm one of the ones who . . ." Ivy began, her voice trailing off and a familiar, empty look drifting into her eyes.

Demont's fingers were wrapped tightly about the largest half of Ivy's crystal. All of her thoughts stopped cold, save for the deepest, least controlled of her feelings. Demont pointed firmly toward the portal. Ivy slowly began to march forward. There was no hesitation. There couldn't be. There was only obedience. Her face twitched slightly.

Lain's blade was hard at work. The monsters were sturdy, but nothing that they had to defend themselves with could withstand the bite of his sword for more than a few swipes. Despite this, the sheer number of beasts attacking had kept him at a standstill. Worse, the number continued to grow as the flow of creatures dropping through the portal continued. Of course, Desmeres's blade had more tricks up its sleeve. The gleaming crystals, having filled to bursting on the dark power that dwelled within his foes, were turned to the spell Deacon had identified as strength.

At first, nothing seemed to change. He felt as he always had. The weapon felt no lighter. Only when he put blade to foe did the effects of the spell become obvious. His sword passed through the thick shelled horror before him without hesitation, and without resistance. A second and third swipe left the three largest threats in pieces. A quick leap, one that carried him far farther than he'd intended, landed him well behind the crush of enemies. His eyes turned to Bagu. The general seemed to be waiting for him.

Twin black-bladed swords were raised defensively. Lain leapt again, now familiar with the extent of his strength. The agile assassin soared through the air, pivoting himself and angling his sword. When the time was right, he brought the weapon down, the lightning-fast motion adding its momentum to his own. Bagu's swords were crossed before him. The three blades met. The air in the shallow valley rang with a screeching far louder than any of the beasts that filled it. A moment later, Lain was on the ground. A moment after that the tips of Bagu's swords fell as well, sliced through.

The general lurched back. The weapons he held, weapons that had been able to withstand anything that had been turned against them on a dozen worlds, had barely managed to deflect the assassin's blow enough to spare him its cut. Indeed, the front of his breast plate, already damaged by Lain once, now bore a new long gash. Bagu's flesh had been spared by a hair's breadth.

He looked to the malthrope only to see another slash aimed at him. A reflexive bit of magic sent Lain sliding back. In the few heartbeats that the distance had afforded him, Bagu uttered a dark incantation and his weapons were restored. Then he uttered another one. When Lain's weapon met Bagu's again, both blades held.

"You've been given magic, assassin. You think that it will give you what you need to defeat me. I shall teach you how wrong you are," Bagu hissed.

Lain fell back, shredded a few of the lesser beasts to restore his weapon's strength, and clicked a new spell into completion. Once again, it was the world that seemed to be affected, not he. The writhing mass of demons, the massive monsters, and the general before him all slowed to near stillness. When he moved, Lain almost felt as though he was in water. The air felt thick, pressing against him. He charged in, thrusting his sword forward, but an instant before it made contact, the general's weapon shot down, knocking it away.

"There is nothing you can do that I cannot," Bagu said, matching the spell's effects.

The general traced an arcane symbol in the air and hissed a few more arcane words. The already dense air took on a tingling, living quality. Lain could feel it begin to burn and tear at him--not via some tangible wave of magic that could be deflected by his weapon, but directly. It was weak now, but each moment it grew stronger. Worse, he knew instantly that the slow onset of the spell's effects were due to the effects of the spell he'd activated in the sword. The faint and fading glow of the weapon's gems assured him that if he did not cut this attack off at its source soon, he would be fully in its grasp with nothing to defend him. He rushed at Bagu, determined to end the foe before his spell could take full effect.

There was a creaking snap, like the felling of a half-rotten tree, and one of the legs of the spider-like creature dropped to the ground. Instantly, Myn turned her attention to the veritable thicket of lesser limbs that had been making steady progress at scraping their way through her hide. A blast of flame and a few mad rakes with her claws cost the creature's back nearly its full complement of waving feelers, the narrow things snapping like twigs.

Suddenly, a rapier-sharp talon carved a shallow gash down Myn's back. The dragon turned to find the monster had coiled one of its primary legs beneath itself and up the other side in hopes of skewering the fire-breather. Myn simply clamped her jaws on the groping point, dug her claws into the half-roasted back, and unfurled her wings. The vast sails began to beat at the air, tugging the already unstable creature further and further off balance. The beast struggled to free its trapped leg and stumbled to right itself. All it managed to do was bring those beasts nearest to its feet to swift and sudden ends. Finally, the monster toppled over, falling in a slow, flailing arc. Myn leapt free at the last moment and hung in the air as the fragile creature collapsed like a bundle of dry reeds and finally became still as the swarm of smaller creatures flowed over it.

Ether had assumed her stone form and was industriously tearing at one of the long seams along the side of the creature she fought. The beast's hide had withstood flame and cost the shapeshifter much of her strength, but the tendrils were vulnerable. That meant that it was the skin and the skin alone that could stand against her attacks. All that she had to do was find an opening, a point of entry.

Impossibly, the beast seemed to have no eyes, save the bulbs at the end of the tentacles, and no mouth. Those things that served as a beast's traditional points of weakness were wholly missing. That left her with the task of creating her own, and as stone fingers made slow progress to that end, the entire surface of the creature began to flutter and ripple. Finally, the seam split.

Ether shifted to fire and took to the air. The other seams were splitting as well, and one end of the beast was curling back. Like the blooming of some horrid flower, the beast opened. A bundle of tendrils lashed about inside what could now only be a mouth. Ether rushed inside.

In an instant, the monster snapped shut again. For a few long moments, there was nothing--then came the sound. The beast seemed to have no means of making such a sound, but still it came, a subdued, hissing, sizzling noise. The sound was accompanied by a glow that began at the seams, brilliant orange. The barbs on its surface soon took on the same radiant glow. Finally, the glow became more general, spreading across the beast's skin until the whole of the creature shone a smoldering red color, like a paper lantern. The glow faded as patches of the beast's flesh darkened to black.

A blazing orange form, for the moment surpassing even the portal in brightness, burst from inside and watched with grim satisfaction as the blackened husk cracked and crumbled away. The glowing form then shifted to stone and plummeted into the throng below her with the force of a battering ram.

#

"You should have left me to one of your allies--Ether or Lain. Someone who would have done what needed to be done. Instead you take me for yourself," Epidime mocked, assaulting Myranda with mystic attacks that, to his mild surprise, she was managing to fend off. "What can you do? The Chosen have not marked *this* body. Nothing can chase me from it while it still serves my purposes. Considering that my purpose is to torture you, I assure you, I do not intend to relinquish control until there is nothing left of your father."

"No!" Myranda cried, lashing out.

She held out her hand and wrenched Epidime aloft with her mind.

"I will do . . . what I *must* do," Myranda struggled through tears.

"Are you trying to convince me or yourself? Regardless, you are fooling no one," he jabbed. "You won't kill your own father. He is the last link you have to your life, your history. Besides, you know it would do you no good."

Myranda scoured her mind for anything she might be able to use to take her father out of the fight. Something had to exist that would render the body unusable for Epidime but would leave it whole. She lobbed sleep, paralysis, and a dozen other spells at Epidime, but she felt them fizzle and die. He seemed to raise defenses against them, one by one, that made the blasted spells useless. Her maddened mind finally came upon something that slipped through. It was clear from Epidime's expression that he was ill-prepared to deal with it.

"Well, now . . . aren't we the clever one," Epidime struggled to say.

The effects were subtle at first. Epidime's struggles slowed. He became heavier. As Myranda lowered him to the ground, the spell finally took full effect. His complexion grayed. His body turned to stone. After a few moments of stillness, a twisted shadow separated from the petrified form. First it launched itself at Myranda. There came the intense and familiar sensation of the general attempting to force his way into her mind. It only lasted for a moment. Then the shadow whisked away, effortlessly shattering the shield Myranda raised.

The wizard rushed after it, willing the protective stones aside to allow her to escape, then forcing them back in place, in hopes of protecting the stone figure of her father left behind.

Ivy had been carefully navigated toward the portal, and was very nearly there. Demont was treating her carefully, as though he was afraid of damaging her. As such, the creatures surrounding her were ordered to give her a wide berth. One creature was venturing near, and was not responding to his unspoken commands.

"Back!" he ordered.

The beast, a small mass of legs and snapping jaws, broke into a run. Demont swiftly retrieved a dagger-like tool from his belt and raised it. The creature collided with the general. Its jaws first closed around the gleaming crystal extractor, crushing it to powder. It then turned and snapped at the crystal in Demont's other hand, but Ivy's blade caught it in the back.

Both Ivy and the rogue beast released a cry of agony. The beast writhed and struggled, finally exploding into a burst of wind. Ether launched Ivy back and turned to Demont, but he thrust the crystal that controlled Ivy into Ether's swirling form. The ravenous stone tore at her more intensely than any of the crystals she'd encountered before. She began to shift to stone and stumbled back, taking the stone with her.

The half-shifted form lurched away, collapsing to the ground and clawing at the now fully-stone abdomen that had closed around the offending crystal. When she finally managed to reach it, she pulled the ravenous thing free. The strength to move quickly wicked away with her fingers still closed around the broken gem.

Demont got to his feet and stalked over to the paralyzed form. He pulled the gem from her grip and retreated quickly.

"Destroy it!" he ordered the surrounding beasts.

Instantly, the stone form was buried beneath a wave of creatures.

"To the portal," he ordered Ivy.

She turned, but lingered.

"To the *portal,*" he commanded, brandishing the gem.

Something was wrong. He looked to the familiar crystal. It seemed less lustrous than it should be, less transparent. Before his eyes, it faded to a dull stone color. The same exact color and texture Ether's body had been. An instant later, it rushed into a gust of air, accompanied by an identical burst from beneath the mound of attacking beasts. The wind reformed into Ether, madness in her eyes and the true crystal in her hands. She hurled the offending gem with the force of a hurricane, sending the faintly gleaming fragment nearly to the southern horizon.

Demont's eyes jumped to Ivy. The creature was herself again, eyes locked on him and darkness sweeping in around her. Before he could manage a command, spoken or mental, the malthrope holstered one of her blades and wrapped her fingers around his throat, hosting him high.

"Call off your beasts or I slash your throat now," Ivy hissed, the blackness of hate spreading over her, forging her still-brandished blade to a needle point.

"If you don't kill me, the others will for betraying them by calling off the beasts," Demont croaked.

Ivy pressed her blade to his throat, a trickle of black blood dripping down.

"I promise you, it will be cruel. It will be torture, and it will still be better than you deserve," she growled.

"They will be crueler," Demont gasped.

"So be it," Ivy said, a hideous satisfaction in her voice.

She drew the blade slowly, opening the slice ever so slightly. As she did, she saw herself in the reflection on her stained blade. She saw the darkness in her eyes. The madness. She withdrew her blade.

"No . . . no. You aren't worth it. You aren't *worthy* of my hatred. I will not allow you to draw that out of me. I won't become what you wanted me to be," she proclaimed.

She turned to the portal, just steps away, and threw him through its border. He struggled to his feet. Above his head was the black triangle, the gateway between the worlds.

"Go! Return to your darkness. Before I change my mind," she warned.

"Your world is lost. I am quite through with it. I was wrong about you, experiment. You are nothing but a failure," Demont replied.

With that he seemed to vanish, his form replaced with a dense black smoke that coiled its way through the portal.

Ivy turned back to the fray. Just ahead of her was Ether. She was struggling to pull her windy form together into solidity. With a final burst of effort, she managed to assume human form. The beasts she'd thrown aside were quickly closing in around her, even without their master to command them. Ivy rushed to her side, madly swinging her blades until any too foolish to back away were in pieces on the ground.

"You . . . you saved me, didn't you," Ivy said, almost in disbelief, while staring down a threatening monster.

"I did . . . what was required of me . . . as a Chosen," Ether replied.

"Uh-huh," Ivy said knowingly.

The ring of beasts witnessing the clash between Lain and Bagu were wisely keeping their distance. To outside viewers, the pair was little more than a blur of motion and energy. One began to slow, crackling waves of energy rippling over him. Finally, Lain's energy was spent and he fell to one knee, pure agony twisting his features. His foe slowed and stood over the stricken hero.

"This moment has been coming since the day you were born," Bagu taunted, the crackling energy intensifying with each word. "The prophecy spoke of a malthrope who would be Chosen. On that day, your kind were marked for death. I am glad I was able to finish the task personally. Ivy will suffer. I will see to it myself."

Lain's sword fell from his fingers and clutched at his arm. Bagu raised his weapon. There was a blur of black. There was a flash of silver. The crackling slowly died away. Lain was on his feet again, the dagger in his fist hilt-deep in the general. The assassin heaved the stricken general to the ground and wrenched the black blade from his stunned grasp.

With a mighty thrust, he drove the weapon through Bagu's chest and into the frozen earth beneath him.

"Fool! Weakling!" Bagu wheezed. "Have you learned nothing!?"

Already the spell was falling back into place.

"I cannot be defeated!" proclaimed Bagu, as he wrapped his fingers around the blade and heaved it from the earth and out of his chest.

There was another flash of silver. The assassin knelt and clutched the general's head, dragging it up. The body remained where it was. Without a word, he hurled the head to the portal. There was a rush of blackness as a horrid black mist rushed from both body and head, each coiling up through the portal as Demont had.

Lain turned. There was more work to do. The massive white-furred creature, until now merely lumbering slowly southward, had turned and was now pounding toward Myranda. Myn rushed to her aid, scorching black lines across the beast, but it refused to turn from its task. Creatures continued to flow out of the portal, now marching in a continuous stampede over the hills to the south. Already, a black tide could be seen creeping up the slopes of the mountains in the distance. They were heading toward the capital . . . toward the rest of the world.

The earth rumbled with the constant flow of abominations of all shapes and sizes, and thumped with the thundering blows of the white creature's single-minded attacks upon Myranda. The monolith-sized limbs drove themselves into the earth, spade-like teeth sinking in and tearing up vast stretches of earth. It crushed and trampled dozens of its fellow beasts with each attack. Myranda ran, lacking the mind to spare to offer up a spell. The quaking earth split before her and each crushing stomp threatened to hit its mark. Myn burned at its eyes, slashed at its skin, and tore at its fur, but nothing seemed to do enough damage to distract it, let alone defeat it.

Finally the dragon swept down and plucked up her friend, wheeling high into the air.

The young wizard fought to catch her breath. Below, the beast ceased its rampage, the few eyes that had remained unburned watching her intently. Myranda felt the telltale sensation of a spell slipping together around her and managed to dispel it. Surely no beast could have even begun to cast a spell. She turned her eyes to the long shadow cast by the beast as it thumped along to stay below her. It was even more hideous and twisted than the beast itself.

Epidime had taken its body as his own. Sensing that he had her attention, the possessed creature took a single, purposeful step toward the arching stone ring that had been their last battleground. With that single motion, even without words, Epidime had issued a threat Myranda could not ignore. The monster was heading for her father.

"Stop him!" Myranda cried, guiding Myn into a dive.

Her cry made its way to the ears of Ivy. The malthrope had been keeping a watchful eye on the still-recovering Ether, warding off any would be attackers, but with the disappearance of Demont, the beasts had steadily lost interest. Now they marched mindlessly south, dividing around the heroes as they might a tree or other meaningless obstacle. Myranda's voice drew her attention. She looked back and forth between Myranda and Ether, desperate indecision on her face.

"Are you . . . going to be all right if I help Myranda? You still look weak," Ivy asked Ether.

"Go; I don't need your help. I could *never* need your help," Ether replied, mustering up enough strength to show the proper degree of indignation.

Everything beyond the word "go" went unheard, Ivy sprinting madly toward the rest of her friends. The flow of beasts was dense now, far too dense to try to slip between or hack through. With no other option, Ivy climbed atop it, leaping from shell to back to carapace as nimbly as one might across stepping stones in a pond. A final leap brought her into the wide clearing around the beast, a churned-up, craggy battleground littered with the broken remains of the demons that hadn't been wise enough or fast enough to escape.

Lain, still limping from Bagu's attacks, slashed his way into the clearing a moment later.

"Ivy! In the ring of stone! Help my father!" Myranda cried, as Myn swept low and threw all of her momentum against the ponderous beast.

The blow was enough to stagger the monster, tipping it up on a single limb. Ivy scrambled up the side of the tooth-like protrusions and tumbled inside. For a moment, she stared curiously at the statue she'd been sent to help. The ground shook as the monster came crashing down. Instantly, she crouched and hoisted the form to her shoulders, and eyed the wall of stone around her. This was strangely familiar. She lowered her shoulder, the heavy form heaving forward. Behind her, the massive beast smashed at the earth.

Ivy looked back to see one hideous leg flail up and strike the earth. The ground trembled from the force. The stone spires, already weakened from previous tremors, cracked and split. Ivy knew that she wouldn't have a better chance than now. With all of the strength she could muster, she charged at the point in the stone most riddled and worn.

There was an explosion of dust and gravel as the spire gave way, and not a second too soon. The monster was on its feet. Ivy ran, smoldering fear and heartfelt duty forming a potent mix that urged her forward. She could hear the slash of a sword behind her and the thunder of the feet all around her. The fear that had festered in the back of her mind began to drift to the surface again. Until now, she'd been rushing past, over, or through the flood of beasts. Now they were beside her, in front of her, behind her. They were matching her speed, giving the frightened creature her first prolonged looks at the misshapen beasts. Something deep inside of her reminded her that the same mind that produced this horde had produced her as she was now. She shook the thoughts away.

Lain slashed at the towering beast anywhere that his sword would meet flesh, but he could make no progress. It was immune to pain, and any wounds that posed the massive creature any threat at all were closed immediately by Epidime's magic. Worse, the creatures flowing from the portal were steadily larger than those that came before them. A second and third beast, identical to the one occupied by the dark general, had dropped out of it and now stood ominously ready to replace his current host.

Seeing no end in sight, Lain retreated, disappearing among the lumbering beasts.

Myn circled over the valley, Myranda staring down from her back. The wizard watched helplessly as the monsters rushed like ants across the landscape, spreading until they were nothing more than a vague movement on the dimly lit landscape. Something had to be done. The portal had to be closed. With barely a word, Myn spotted Ether, and dropped quickly to the ground beside her. Lain emerged a moment later. All eyes were trained carefully on Epidime, the beast under his control wading through the rush of like-sized demons.

"Fire, quickly," Ether demanded, sparking quickly and weakly to the suitable form.

Myn complied, more out of the desire to roast the infuriating creature than to help her.

"That is sufficient," the elemental instructed after few moments of flame, though the dragon belched a few more blasts at her for good measure.

"How do we close the gateway?" Lain asked.

"I . . . I don't know. The D'karon . . . or whatever they are . . . their spells are all very similar. I wish Deacon was here. He knows them better than I," Myranda struggled to say, watching the massive beast draw nearer.

"We don't have time for him. Every second releases more of those wretched things into this world. They do not belong here. Look at them. They don't care about us. Their task is to devour this world. To claim it for their masters," Ether hissed.

"The . . . the spells. They don't have counterspells. They are cast to be permanent. The only way to stop them is to cut off their power," Myranda said distantly.

She was distracted. Somewhere deep in her mind, she could hear a voice from her memories. His words were echoing through her thoughts, dredging up images she'd just seen and attaching to them. The meeting of the three shafts of light, the dark triangle that served as the doorway, they were cryptic warnings she had received, long ago. It was all falling into place, but what came next? Suddenly, she knew.

"Get to the edge of the valley. Get far away. Find Ivy and stay with her. I have an idea, but I don't know what is going to happen. Let's go, Myn," Myranda barked with authority. Her tone was clear, confident, and decisive.

The dragon leapt into the air, the other heroes launching themselves southward. Myn spiraled upward and out of reach of Epidime not a moment too soon, the massive beast finally reaching the Chosen as they parted. Myranda held tight, purpose in her eyes, and coaxed Myn high into the air. When at last they were higher even than the titanic obelisks, the pair headed toward them. The mystic, unnatural sound of the energy hissing through the air filled their ears. They drew nearer.

Now the energy itself was reaching them. It had a heat to it that went beyond fire. It was a heat that burned the body, mind, and soul all at once. Myranda urged the dragon forward. Below them was the white-hot, blindingly bright point where the three shafts of light met. Myranda leaned forward and placed a hand on Myn's neck.

"I'm sorry," she whispered.

She jumped.

The wind whipped by her and mixed with the screech of the life force of the world being leeched away. The heat grew, consuming her entirely. Myn dove after her, but the rush of raw power that wrapped around Myranda pushed the dragon back. She fell further, tears streaming from her eyes and memories sizzling in her mind. At the southern edge of the valley, the eyes of the others watched the tiny form fall, almost invisible against the brilliance. The searing pain seized Myranda, then dropped away--and, for a brief instant, she had clarity. Her thoughts turned to her father, to Deacon, to all of the people she cared about, and who cared about her. Her body passed into the point of energy and, for her, the world vanished.

Pain is a thing of the body. It could not be applied to the sensation that permeated Myranda now. The agony felt was greater than any single body or spirit could contain. What she felt stretched further than the boundaries of her body. She felt the torment of all beings at once. She felt the torture of the world itself. Her individuality wavered, the whole of her self was blending and mixing with existence itself. For a moment and an eternity she was not Myranda, she was all. The eye of creation looked upon her expectantly. The gods themselves watched her and waited.

There was more to be done.

Her will fluttered and fought, clinging to the spark of divinity within her that was holding firm against the onslaught. Gradually, her mind and body drew back into being. The all-encompassing agony focused into a pinpoint of physicality once more. Her eyes drifted down. The portal remained beneath her. She had hoped that, just for an instant, she would have been able to choke off the flow of energy, but she simply could not contain that much power. All that she was could not interrupt the flow of power for even an instant.

Very well--if she could not contain it, she would use it. She gathered together the energy that filled her to bursting and, without the focus necessary to give it form, cast it out all at once.

From the edge of the valley, where Ivy had finally been joined by her friends, the rest of the Chosen watched a shining ring of brilliance erupt out from the meeting of the lights.

The halo of light was filament-thin, but trailed light behind it as it spread. The sheer power of it threw its heat to the far ends of the mountainside. Where it met the obelisks, striking each at once, there was a flash that robbed all who watched of their vision. The segments of the ring that did not splash against the towers continued, passing through open air-- then, unimpeded, through the mountains themselves.

With a sound like the end of the world, the band of light sliced a surgical line along the slopes, sweeping the peaks away like dust. It then continued off into the night sky, illuminating the landscape beneath it as it moved. The dust of the devastation rolled into the valley like a fog, briefly concealing the traveling horde of creatures. The dense cloud of debris settled quickly. When the air was clear, the mighty Ancients, the massive mountains that formed the rim of the valley, stood flat topped and equal. The towers still stood.

Myranda's mind was boiling. In the crucible that surrounded her, memories surged to the surface and burned away again and again. She felt the sum total of her experience cycle through her mind over and over, in ever-smaller circles. Not just her experiences, but others. Thoughts she'd never had rushed through her mind, feelings she never would have imagined flitted in and out of her soul. Every one of them dealt with the towers.

The power flowing through her, consuming her, carried something with it. It carried the residue of its purpose. The knowledge of how to produce the towers drilled itself into her mind. Alongside it came the firm, irrevocable realization that there had never been any intention to cast them away. All that could ever be done was to summon more.

Her thoughts wrapped around this. That was the answer. Her eyes turned to the final mark on each tower. It was the activation rune Deacon had spoken of. Without it, there would be no spell. She drew together the power that was destroying her, forced it into the shape that resounded ever louder in her mind, and directed it at the runes, projecting it toward all three towers. The magic struck, weaving itself into a shape--then, suddenly, attaining substance. When the spell had run its course, the embossed form of the rune was filled, erased. The spell was incomplete.

There was a flicker and a shudder. The streaming light pinched off and trailed away. Darkness replaced the pale blue glow that had lit the valley. Now the only light came from the edge of the black gateway and a point of failing glow that dropped toward it.

A pair of wings approached the dying light as Myn, no longer facing a torrent of energy to hold her back, darted toward the glowing form. Snatching it out of the air, she carried the blue ember of energy toward the others. When the noble beast reached them, it lowered the form reverently to the ground before them. It was Myranda.

There was an intense aura about her that grew weaker with each moment. She was not moving. She was not breathing. Her eyes were unblinking, featureless pools of light. In her hand was the weapon crafted by Desmeres. Each of the three D'karon crystals along its length had shattered and her fingers had sunk deep into its surface, as though the staff had been soft as clay for a time.

Her body was whole, but broken. Bones were fractured. Blood trickled from her mouth. The Chosen looked upon her solemnly. Lain crouched beside her, putting his ear to her chest. He felt her head, her abdomen. His eyes conveyed a grim message. Every part of her was in ruins. For a moment, no hero spoke, their heads hung low. When the distant crackle of the portal and the thinning rumble of the flow of monsters was joined by a voice, it was Ivy.

"No," she stated. "No . . . they . . . they can't do this . . . They can't kill her . . ."

"I knew it would be one of us . . . I never thought it would be her. Fate made--" Ether began, for the first time a gentleness to her tone.

"*Shut up!*" Ivy hissed, a flare of red accompanying the cry. "If they are going to kill Myranda . . . then . . . there is only one thing to do, isn't there? If death is all that they understand then *death* is what they shall get!"

Each word surged the red aura brighter. Anger was succeeding where hate and fear had fallen short. The gems set in each blade adopted her hue of fury, thin red lines tracing their way along the wide blades in crooked, cruel patterns.

"Ivy, this can do no good. We have no way to heal her. Whatever can be done has been done," Lain said.

"No! You are *wrong!*" she said with a smile of madness. The blades split into three jagged blades. "I can make sure they never do anything like this again. I can make sure that NO ONE SURVIVES!"

With her final words, the anger finally took hold. The blaze of red consumed her and she charged into the black mass. Beasts large and small were reduced to ribbons by the vicious, serrated shape her blades had taken. As the rampaging form carved a path through the thinning herd, Lain stood and placed a hand on Myn's neck. The beast lowered her head, tears rolling from its great eyes as the still form of Myranda cooled.

In the darkness, someplace between this world and the next, the defeated wizard's vision fell upon a new view. They were familiar, almost comforting surroundings for Myranda. Shifting, distorted shapes replaced land and sky. Bright, pure lights marked the souls of the living. The astral plane faded weakly in and out around her as the last lingering grip on her shattered body gradually slipped away.

She watched with relief as the portal, in this place a colossal, churning mass of pure energy and light, began to slowly draw together and close. The power that had surged through her was wicking away. Oblivion awaited her--and, though she was sorry to leave the others behind, she was ready for it. The ordeal had left her ruined. Spent. She was tired, and a final sleep lay invitingly ahead of her.

As she waited for whatever was to come next, she became aware of a presence. It was a blackness, without features, but in a shape the stung her mind. A shape she'd seen twist the shadows of far too many.

"Epidime," she said.

"You do fine work. Your world is now the fourth to close the door, and the first to do it so quickly. It is truly a shame to lose your world," he said, borrowing her own voice, as he had in his earliest torments.

"You had no claim on this world. It was ours and it will remain ours," Myranda replied.

"Yes . . . for the next few minutes, at least," Epidime remarked.

"What do you mean?" Myranda asked, concern in her voice.

"I realize that memories of life tend to slip quickly from your kind, but surely you recall all of the other portals, and what happened when they were closed," Epidime scolded.

Myranda searched her thoughts. She didn't have to search for long. The images of walls of raw energy flashing forth in her mind.

"No . . ." she said in horror.

"Yes. I had mentioned that the worlds that closed their portals no longer existed. Obviously, I've never seen it, but the shock wave from a portal this size must be a true thing of wonder," the black form mocked.

With that, Epidime vanished. The tattered remnants of Myranda pulled themselves together. Death could wait. Slowly, she clawed her way back to her body. Myranda's physical form began to struggle.

Myn's head shot up. The human made horrid, strangled sounds as she tried to draw breath into lungs that could no longer hold it. The broken gems of her staff took on a glow as her shattered mind gathered into a shaky focus. In fits and starts, the spells of healing began to flow, breaking through the agony and feeding on the residue of power that lingered from the onslaught. When air finally made its way into her half-restored lungs, she cried out, the words coming straight from her memory.

"Victory is a prelude . . . the . . . white wall . . ." she wheezed.

"I may have underestimated the human form," Ether marveled.

Myranda struggled unsteadily to continue as her wounds faded away. "The shock wave! The burst of energy that comes when the portals are closed!"

Ether's eyes turned to the portal. The creatures had entirely stopped pouring out of it, and the still raging form of Ivy had nearly cleared the valley, leaving behind little more than twisted remains. The shapeshifter's eyes looked past what physical eyes could see. Her mystically attuned mind judged the power of the failing portal, and sifted through what she'd seen of the other portals. With an intuitive knowledge of magic that Deacon could only dream of, she worked out in moments the potential threat. The result was immediate, and unprecedented. A look of total horror came to her face.

"We have to leave this place. Quickly. QUICKLY!" Ether cried. There was fear in her voice. A creature who had shown nothing short of cold, steady, unshakable confidence now was trembling.

"There has to be a way to stop it. It . . ." Myranda said, leaning on Myn's head to get to her feet as her recovery began to slow.

"No! You don't understand! We can't stop it! Nothing can! It will be the end of us, all of us! The end of everything!" Ether cried. "Power like this . . . It will sweep the world clean. So much raw, unshaped magic. What it leaves behind . . ." she cried. "There is no telling . . . just a terrible randomness. Chaos incarnate!"

From within the valley there was a choked-off cry of fury, as Ivy's strength finally failed her. Half dead creatures that had been lucky enough to escape the bite of her blades were slowly hobbling toward her motionless form. Without a word Myranda climbed atop Myn and wiped away her wounds with more of her borrowed energy. With that, Myn took eagerly to the sky once more. As they turned to the task of rescuing their friend, Ether turned her attentions to Lain.

"Lain, we must go. We MUST!" Ether repeated.

Lain's voice was steady. "We will face it, and if it can be stopped, it will be stopped."

"How can you say that? I . . . I know you see yourself as a mortal, and for mortals death is a certainty. When a human dies it only loses a few years. You and I, we are losing eternity. You've got to come with me! The blast will weaken with distance. If we can get far enough away . . . I . . . I might be able to protect us," Ether pleaded.

In the distance, Myn swept down to the prone form of Ivy, plucking her up. Myranda managed to pull the unconscious creature to the dragon's back. Desmeres's weapons chose that moment to jolt her to wakefulness. Ivy roused from sleep with a cry of pain. As her eyes focused on the rushing darkness below her, it was followed by a scream of fear.

"Easy Ivy, it is all right. How did you wake so . . ." Myranda asked, she was interrupted by a squeal of confusion.

"But you! You! YOU did it AGAIN! I thought you were dead!" Ivy yelled, shoving Myranda in mock anger. "Stop doing that!"

With that, the freshly awakened creature threw her arms around Myranda. For a moment Myranda marveled and admired Ivy's ability to so quickly accept the impossible events that seemed to occur so frequently in her life.

"Ivy, something very dangerous is about to happen, I am not sure . . ." Myranda began again, only to again be interrupted.

"Where is she going?" Ivy asked.

Ether had taken on her windy form and was making her way south with a speed only fear could bring.

"Myn, get Lain and my father and follow her!" Myranda cried.

The dragon dove, snatching up the stone form as Lain leapt to a place on her back. The load was great, and Ether was well ahead, but Myn didn't care. The blasted thing had been a thorn in her side since they'd met. Ether never ceased to look down on the others, to behave as though she were better than them all. For Myranda's sake, the dragon had let it pass, but now it was different. Now was her chance to prove something to the shapeshifter. She wouldn't get away.

Myn flew like never before, the icy breeze rushing over the heroes with gale force. Her mighty wings sliced through the air faster and faster, then cut back and let the wind rush over them. She skimmed in the mountain currents of air, taking every ounce of speed from them that she could. Slowly, steadily, the indistinct swirl of wind ahead drew closer. Below, the army of otherworldly creatures, beasts that had made it clear of the valley before Ivy's rampage, was marching. Before long, even the leading edge of the mob of demons was behind them, and Ether just ahead. Myranda called out to her.

"Ether! What are you doing!?" Myranda cried.

"I must not be destroyed, Myranda. I *will* not be destroyed!" Ether cried.

"You just have to face this danger. We have to face it together!" Myranda urged, Myn managing to bring the two heroes side by side finally.

"It is easy for you, human. Anything can take your life. You face death every moment of every day! For me, death was an impossibility until now! I had no use for courage because there was nothing for me to fear! How can I face this now!?" came Ether's reply.

"You can face it because you must! You can face it because this is your moment. The moment you were created for! Every second for you, since the dawn of time, has been counting down to this day! You can either rise to the occasion, damn the consequences, and do what you were meant to do, or you can run away and at best survive to live in an empty, ruined world for an eternity that can never redeem you!" Myranda said.

Ether was silent, slowing her flight. She considered the words. Deep inside of her, she felt something she'd always believed had driven her, but until now she'd never truly known. Duty. She looked upon the land with new eyes. When she spoke, the fear was gone, but the tone that replaced it was not the superior preen of old. It resonated with--for the first time-- sincerity and respect.

"Very well, human. Lead the way. I am not certain we have a chance, but if I must die, let me die by my brethren. Let me die doing what is right," she said.

The Chosen backtracked to the level top of a low mountain to make their stand, a wide expanse only a few mountains removed from the valley. Ivy slipped from Myn's back and wavered slightly. The repeated outbursts without real rest between had wrung her spirit dry. She had the strength of body to stand, but barely the strength of will. Lain was weary, but no ounce of it showed on his face. Myranda, now devoid of the surge of power that had briefly used her as a conduit, was fighting to undo the ravaging effect it had had on her mind. Myn was breathing great, heaving breaths of the stingingly cold air, taxed to the limit by the chase. Ether merely stood, human once more, her eyes looking expectantly to the north. Had it not been so far and so dark, she might have seen one last form drop from the nearly closed portal.

"What can we expect?" Myranda asked.

"Chaos. Madness. Hundreds of years of energy released at once without will or form. Raw, untamed mystic carnage," Ether replied.

"How do we stop it?" Myranda pressed further.

"It cannot be stopped. It will continue until its reserves run dry," came the answer, Ether's voice a resigned, steady tone.

"If it is pure mystic energy, can we harness it?" the wizard suggested.

"I would imagine so. Insomuch as you can drink the ocean," she answered.

Myranda put her staff to the ground and traced out a large circle. Within it, she inscribed a triangle. Finally, she stood her staff in its center. It was a practice described in careful detail by Deacon as one that aided a link between wizards when they were to work as one. Ideally, she would have traced out a five-pointed figure, but Myranda's recent experience with the vast expenditure of borrowed power made it clear to her that it was an undertaking unsuitable for the untrained mind. Were Myn or Lain to be included, they might well be able to draw in the power, but there was no way that they would be able to release it again.

No, this was a task for herself, the shapeshifter, and . . .

"That last spot isn't for me, is it?" Ivy asked nervously as her friends took up positions at the other points.

"We need you," Myranda said.

"But I don't know magic," Ivy offered meekly.

"All you need to do is waste it. You are uniquely suited to that," Ether said, a hint of her old self in her tone.

Reluctantly, she took up her position at the corner of the triangle pointing toward the portal. The three joined hands and waited. They did not have to wait long. The tiny, faint fleck of blue light that was the portal winked out in the distance. It was silently replaced by a blindingly white filament of light that began at the ground and continued into the sky, piercing the clouds and showing through them. The line spread slowly, as though reality itself was being spread aside like a curtain to reveal the plane beyond. The sound came next. It was a tone at the edge of hearing, high-pitched and haunting, like a distant choir echoing through the dimensions.

The shaft of light bathed the whole of the mountain range in its unearthly glow. It painted the clouds chalk-white and brighter than day. In Northern Capital, all eyes turned to it. Residents stopped their rejoicing and rebuilding. In a dozen forests across the north, woodland creatures stood frozen in terror of the sight. At the battlefront, soldiers standing at uneasy attention, awaiting long overdue orders and longer overdue reinforcements turned their backs to their counterparts across the border and watched as the hair-thin line of light pushed back the clouds.

In Entwell, Num Garastra, wizards, and warriors watched the light over the edge of the mountain and waited. They alone knew what it was. It was the last of Hollow's prophesies.

"What is that? What is behind me?" Ivy asked nervously, turning to look over her shoulder.

"No, Ivy. Not yet," Myranda instructed. "Just close your eyes and open your mind. Ether and I will do the work for now."

The shapeshifter and the wizard began to sink deeply into focus. What little energy was left inside of them began to spread and flow between them. Slowly, the line between their minds began to blur. The thoughts, feelings, and strengths of each hero joined with those of the others. The timid mind of Ivy rose beside the complex thoughts of Ether and the dutiful focus of Myranda. Like a boat caught in a current, without truly understanding how, Ivy felt herself aiding in the construction of a spell.

Outside of the ring, the drawn circle and triangle now beginning to glow, Myn and Lain became aware of something else. In the light cast by the beam, the mountainside spreading below them seemed to be alive. A low rumble was growing steadily louder. The twisted forms of the army of demons that had flooded from the portal had reached them. Myn looked upon the horde almost with relief. Now, at least, her role was clear. She stalked a few long paces down the slight slope of the mountain, dug her claws into the rocky soil, unfurled her wings, and waited. Lain drew his sword and followed suit.

By the time the first of the dark creatures clashed with the warriors, the shaft of light had grown into a wall. The surface, from a distance featureless, now seemed to ripple with prominences and tendrils. It slid in eerie near-silence, only the distant wail accompanying the smooth, undaunted motion of the cataclysm. It devoured whole mountainsides, the occasional filament of light twisting out and tracing a random line along the ground, offering a terrible insight into what the wall was leaving behind it.

Earth and stone shone brilliantly and then . . . changed. Much of it vanished. More troubling were the other effects. Here, a cluster of stones shifted to a flock of winged creatures that scattered. There, a patch of field miraculously sprouted a lush garden of magnificent flowers and trees. Monolithic stones rolled to the ground as liquid. All manner of random, inconceivable effects flashed into being at the touch of a tendril from the wall, only to be swallowed as the band of light pressed forward.

One by one, thin threads of light drew away from the surface of the wall, twisting and winding through the air and finally coiling about Myranda's staff. The power began to build and pool within the three focused minds. It came slowly at first, but as the wall drew nearer, threads of energy became thicker and more numerous.

Myranda's mind pulled and twisted at a spell she'd used a dozen times before, a shield against magic. It had served its purpose in the past, but now it was not enough. It was possible nothing would be enough, but she could not afford to think that now. She modified it, catering it to precisely the sort of energy that made up the wall, and cast it forward. The surface of the wall rippled slightly and bowed inward. It slowed, but did not stop. As Myranda gave form to a tiny fragment of the well of stolen power, Ivy and Ether fought to contain and spill off the rest.

The energy poured in as a torrent, then as a flood. It was wicking away from the wall, now only a mountain away, in a tendril of energy, nearly filling the mystic circle. Myranda's efforts were as great as any spell she'd cast before this battle had begun, and even so she was making a barely noticeable draw on the ocean of energy that was every moment threatening to drown them.

Ether gathered up her share of the surplus power and hurled it skyward. She was a being composed of magic, and had been host to energies that could have reduced a city to rubble, but even she could not release the power quickly enough. A shaft of energy surrounded her and stretched high into the sky, twisting and curling into complex shapes. Her flesh and bone body began to hiss and sizzle. It was clear she needed a new form, but none that she'd taken before would do. Even her flame form was too efficient; it could not waste the power that needed disposal, nor could it serve as a suitable conduit. There was, however one that just might. A form she never would have dared assume otherwise. Mystic strength leaked from it like water from a sieve. Taking the form would tax her to her limit while achieving nothing. In the circumstances, it was perfect.

To the others the change came merely as a distant sensation of a warm, soft hand shifting to a cold, hard one in their grips, but that was far, far away, in the physical world. The far more important and far more impressive change came in the world within their minds. It was as though floodgates had been thrown aside and the sea of energy had an escape. The pressure scorching their minds and roasting their souls lessened, and the remaining energy sloshed and shifted, distributing itself among the others a slice more thinly.

Outside of the mystic circle, madness reigned. Myn was grappling with beasts as large as she, tearing and incinerating them, while lashing her tail against hordes of smaller creatures. Lain's sword slashed and severed beasts several at a time. The crooked tunnel of energy coiling toward the others was a constant threat, sweeping and twisting across the mountaintop like a snake. Swift kicks and well-placed throws sent unlucky creatures into the writhing form, their swift, spectacular ends making it terrifyingly clear what would happen should Lain or Myn be too slow to avoid it. Then there was the wall.

It was at the base of the mountain now, and moving steadily up, as though the end of the universe was creeping toward them. It was bulging outward, to either side of the battleground, as portions unhindered by Myranda's ambitious spell began to pull ahead. It cast a glow brighter than day. There were no shadows, as though the abundance of light rushed in to fill any crevice, or perhaps passed through solid forms uninhibited. Despite how near it was, the distant wail remained distant, as though it was not made by the wall, but by some far-off creature, fearing what the wall might bring. The thunder of hooves, claws, and tentacles should have drowned it out, but the haunting sound cut through the tumult easily, ringing at once clear and indistinct in their minds.

As Lain hurled a hawk-like creature into the beam that erupted from where Ether had once stood, his eyes caught something a few hundred paces down the mountain. It was not one of the creatures. It was something worse, something that could not have been more out of place in the valley. It was a patch of darkness. Even the inky menagerie they fought was painted by the white light to appear gray at best. Below was a shape that managed to resist the light.

An instinct deep in Lain's mind told him that this thing, whatever it was, was the real threat. The rush of creatures, even the wall of energy, were meaningless. Carving himself an opening, Lain launched himself toward it.

I can't stand it. It is agony! What do I do! The energy! Ivy screamed in her mind as she struggled.

The flow of stolen energy had been growing exponentially, and Ivy was approaching her limit. Until now, she'd done her part, passively letting the energy that the others could not handle seep into her soul, but now she was full to bursting. She'd learned nothing of focus, nothing of discipline, nothing of cordoning off energy within her soul and reserving a piece of her mind for thinking. The energy permeated her. Every cell of her body and every nuance of her soul dripped with it. The others had been watching within their linked minds, concern building but tasks of their own to see to.

A solution had been prepared from the beginning, held back until now due to the very real threat that it might cause--but the time had come.

"Ivy," said Myranda and Ether at once, each bracing herself. "Open your eyes."

The malthrope did so. A single image entered her mind. Ether was a barely visible, perfectly transparent crystalline form within a shaft of light. Myranda was almost hidden behind strips and strands of mystic energy that orbited her as she formed her spells. Directly in front of her was an undulating, untamed tower of twisting energy. Shapes never meant to be seen whorled across the surface. The corners of her eyes contributed half seen struggles between Myn and more of the very beasts she'd fought in the valley. At the very limits of her vision, there was nothing at all . . . only a complete, unbroken wall of white. She turned her head, taking in the wonder and horror of the wall.

The poor creature's mind never had a chance.

When the fear took control of her, the others had to direct a part of their minds toward a spell to augment their strength enough to keep the struggling creature from slipping from their grasp. The brilliant blue aura around her rivaled the wall for brightness. The mystic load tipped in her direction as her soul dumped its reserves and feasted on theirs in an all-consuming attempt to escape the chaos by any means necessary. Her voice rose into a scream of terror that rang loud and clear in even the distant capital.

#

Thousands of residents in the Northern Capital shuddered at the sound of the sudden shriek as they stared in silent terror at the wall approaching. Deacon's face alone wore an expression besides that of abject horror. It was plastered with a look of wonder and fascination.

"What is it?" Caya managed when she found her voice.

"It is . . . the end," Deacon replied.

#

Lain charged toward the wall. The air around him tugged and pulled. It was alive, almost with a mind. It was something a wizard was trained to feel, but one needed no training now. The distortions were real. Reality was turning and stretching, warping in the mystic heat of the furnace of energy a stone's throw away. He ignored it, along with every instinct in his mind--save one. His eyes were in agony as they locked on the black form against the whiteness of the wall. It was moving swiftly, just ahead of the rippling chaos. Whatever it was, it had no details, like a vaguely human void cut out of the universe. It was unrecognizable, yet it was unmistakable.

It was Bagu.

Gone was whatever human form he'd had constructed when he first came to this world. What was left was the black as midnight essence that had festered within it, his true form. What might have been arms extended forward, twisting what might have been fingers into arcane positions. A voice that came from nowhere was uttering syllables no mouth could form. If the blight on the landscape had eyes, they were focused intently on the circle of heroes just visible as a nexus of energy past the next rise. He was on the cusp of completing a spell that would shatter the circle--and the Chosen within it.

A blade swept through his immaterial form, the carefully selected and etched runes of its surface reacting with the unnatural energies. There was nothing to cut, yet the sword made its mark. Bagu cried out and collapsed to the ground. Lain stood over him, placing the tip of his sword in the center of what should have been the demon's back. The air around him swirled and churned. Around the pair, a glimmering shield rose up just in time to absorb a bolt of energy bursting from the wall just steps away.

"Stop!" pleaded a voice that mixed with Bagu's own tones with a fractured, echoing chorus of others. "If you destroy me, you destroy yourself!"

The wall reached the dome of magic and flowed over it like the ocean flowing over a pebble. The energy of the shield buckled but held, albeit tenuously.

"You would destroy my world," Lain replied.

"Wait! Your world is lost already! The wall cannot be stopped," the form struggled to say as the protective shield pressed closer. "Join me! I can take you to one of our worlds. You could rule a kingdom. A whole plane of existence! I can give you anything you desire! Death is nothing for us! I can restore your race!"

Lain hesitated. Among the still-echoing voices, some turned again to the eldritch words of the spell he'd interrupted. Lain drove his weapon home. At once, all of the voices united in a single cry of pain. The shield vanished. The wall swept in.

Myranda, Ivy, and Ether suddenly felt the wave of energy crest, as though a vast portion of it had been sloughed away. A final mad surge of power seemed to roll over itself, the wall nearly spent. They redoubled their efforts. Ivy's fear raged. Ether drew in and poured out untold amounts of mana. Myranda's mind was focused entirely on the spell pressing against the wall. The thunder of beasts trying to escape the approaching cataclysm rose to a roar. Myn forced them back until the area between the heroes and the wall was completely covered with them.

The bulging edges of the wall threatened to surround them. The light was fading, the fringes of the wall dropping like a curtain. There was the wail of wind rushing to replace where the energy had been. The three fought to hold their focus. Each was ready to break, but still they held. Just a few moments more. The last of the wall slipped forward, a whisper away from Myn. Just a heartbeat more . . .

Darkness.

An eternity might have passed in that darkness. The three linked minds were snuffed out like candles when the energy gave out. The rumble and wail was replaced by a deafening silence. The blinding light was replaced by a dense blackness. One chaotic extreme had shifted instantly to another. The tightly coiled souls relaxed. The horribly taxed bodies collapsed. The only sound was a long, heart-wrenching wail of sorrow that could only have been Myn. It was a mournful sound of pure sadness, but it only just reached their minds. They hadn't the strength or will to care. They had nothing. If this was death, it came as a friend.

Myn took to the air. In a frenzied burst of anger, the dragon utterly destroyed every beast that might even venture close to her friends. Now her eyes were fixed on the weak glow of street lanterns in Northern Capital. She flew with a heavy heart and a set mind. There was only one creature in the world left who she trusted. He could do many things she didn't understand. Like Myranda, he knew magic. Like herself, he cared about Myranda. If anyone could do something, it was he. And he *would* do it.

The fact that Deacon was standing in front of a large group of people, helping Caya to calm them and assure them that the worst was over made little difference to the dragon when she arrived at the capital. She darted out of the air, snatched him up, and headed back to the battleground.

"Myn! It is wonderful to see you! I am so glad you've survived . . . though you may have hurt my credibility with the townspeople," he said.

He struggled for a moment to try to get to the dragon's back, but it quickly became clear that she had no intentions of carrying him anywhere but clutched tightly in her claws.

#

The faint glow of dawn colored the eastern edge of the sky by the time Myn reached the battleground. Deacon's eyes widened at the sight. There was a vast, roughly heart-shaped chasm. No bottom was visible, just an infinite well of blackness. Its edges were straight, as though they had been carved with great care--and yet this failed to be the most astonishing sight. That honor was bestowed to what waited within the chasm. It was a galaxy of small islands. Some stood rigid and still. Others drifted like icebergs in the sea. They ranged from barely the size of a carriage to hundreds of paces across. Nothing held them aloft. Even more bizarre was their variety.

Many were simply the same icy gray rock that made up the landscape, cleaved free and floating of its own accord. The rest represented a spectrum of impossibility. There were magnificent forests populated with trees that should not have had a chance to grow in such icy weather. There were clumps of earth that looked to have been shifted entirely to silver and gold. One island spouted a river with no possible source, dumping it as a long waterfall into a large lake that rippled blissfully, unaware that it had no banks. On some of the larger islands, dense thickets of foliage rustled with the motions of animals that no world had ever seen before.

Jutting out toward the center of the sea of impossibility was a narrow, tapering crop of untouched land. At its very end, motionless about a mystic circle, were three of the other Chosen.

Myn landed and dropped Deacon. The wizard got to his feet, still dizzy, and approached them. Myranda, Ivy, and Ether were motionless, but weakly alive. Standing in the center of the circle was the staff Desmeres had crafted. Where once it had been immaculate, straight, and true, it was now gnarled and blistered like an ancient tree root. His own crystal and the one that Desmeres had provided, remarkably, seemed to have survived whatever gauntlet the tool had been put through. Plucking it from the earth proved difficult, as its tip seemed to have been fused into the center of the circle, which had a vaguely glassy look to it now. Finally, he pulled it free and breathed a sigh of relief as clarity and focus worked their way back into his mind.

A few words and a few thoughts brought Myranda to consciousness again.

Her eyes fought to focus, finally coming to rest on Deacon. A moment later, Myn pushed him aside and stared into Myranda's eyes. Before the girl could speak, a tongue like a rasp dragged across her face. Myn then placed her head gently on Myranda's chest. The freshly awakened wizard scratched at her dragon.

"Are you--" Deacon began.

"See to the others," Myranda interrupted.

Deacon nodded and turned to Ivy. A similar application of magic brought her around as well. She managed to sit up, looked around, and then looked to Deacon.

"Did we do it?" Ivy asked blearily.

"Of course," Deacon answered.

"Oh, good . . . I'm going back to sleep," she mumbled, leaning back to the ground.

"You've certainly earned it," Deacon admitted.

Finally, he turned to Ether. This might be a challenge. The shapeshifter was completely rigid, her expertly crafted beauty now locked in a form composed entirely of the very same type of crystal affixed to the end of the staff. He pondered how best to undo such a change. He knew any number of spells designed to restore the proper form of a being, but for a creature such as Ether, every form was equally proper. He ruminated on the possibilities. Finally, he reached down, touched her on the shoulder, and passed a bit of his own strength to her. The form stirred and slowly began to shift to flesh again. Deacon smiled proudly.

"Where is Lain?" Myranda asked, Myn helping her to her feet.

The answer came as a mournful gaze. Myn padded to the edge of the outcrop and stared down what had once been the mountainside. A short distance away, floating above the yawning chasm, was a patch of rock. Driven into the stone was a sword, Lain's sword. Beside it, scored into the stone, was a pair of footprints. A blackened shadow stained a silhouette around the sword's base. Aside from a few shreds of cloth and a few drops of blood, it was all that remained of the assassin and his final target.

"It can't be . . ." Ether whispered.

"It *isn't,* right?" Ivy said, rubbing the sleep from her eyes and staring at the evidence incredulously. "This is . . . this is like the other times. When Myranda died . . . right? He's . . . he's coming back, right!?"

"No . . . no, he . . ." Ether stuttered, another new emotion spilling over her. Sorrow.

"Fate has made its choice. Lain's life for our world," Myranda said sadly, consoling Myn with a hand on the neck. "He began his life hated. In life, he came to earn the hate, becoming what the world believed him to be. In death, he's earned redemption. In death, he is truly a hero."

The remaining Chosen took their place atop Myn and the dragon slowly plodded along, picking up the stone form of Myranda's father from its place behind the mystic circle before taking to the air.

Ether remained for a time, eyes resting painfully on the sword. She stood perfectly still. In all of her existence, she had always had complete control over her form, body and soul. So long as she had the strength, if she wanted to do something, she would do it. If she did not, she simply didn't. A pain deeper than any she had felt before sliced through her, and she could not put it aside. Thoughts of the things said and unsaid seized her mind. Unwanted and yet at the same time cherished memories asserted themselves. When she was finally able to pull her eyes from the scene, a tear trickled down her cheek. She did not wipe it away.

#

The days that followed were tense. A generations-old war is not ended in a single stroke. Even before the orders reached the front, though, combat had reached a temporary halt. Without the will of their masters to drive them, the nearmen would no longer fight. The weakest of them collapsed with a flash of light and a puff of dust. Others crumbled limply to the ground. Those blessed with some semblance of a will of their own dropped their weapons and fled. By rights, the Tresson force should have swept over the broken remains of the Alliance Army, now composed of what few human soldiers remained at the front. Ironically, the very thing that had threatened to destroy the Alliance--and, indeed, all of the world, is what held the Tressons at bay for a time.

The southern force was not without its wizards. They were a small, but well-trained--and, above all, *wise*--part of the military. The sheer intensity of the unexplained power that had erupted from somewhere deep within the heart of their enemy's land had convinced them that, for now, perhaps caution was in order. Clearly they were in possession of a vast power, one that should be carefully assessed before they continued hostilities. By the time the first troops were readying themselves to take advantage of the virtually unprotected battlefront, flags were being raised requesting parley.

For the first time since the very earliest days of the war, diplomats met. Discussions began, but progress was slow. The truth of the five generals and their treachery was slow to spread, and even slower to be accepted. Much of the blame for the continued hostilities and lack of negotiation fell on the shoulders of the northern king.

In time, concessions from each side were made. The first was that King Erdrick III be removed from the throne. It was a fate he stoically accepted. Leaders of Tressor were adamant that his line never again be allowed to rule, and that his successor not be chosen from the military. For those who witnessed firsthand the liberation of Northern Capital, an event that would be known for generations as the Battle of Verril, the list of suitable replacements was a short one. The crown was offered to two individuals. One of them accepted.

#

It was the day of the coronation. The actual crowning had been a small, solemn ceremony, witnessed by a small group of royal officials and clergy members. Now was the grand banquet, the celebration of the crowning and the traditional introduction of the ruler to the public. Assembled in the still-scarred Northern Capital were representatives of the oldest and wealthiest families of the Alliance and, for the first time in over a century, a small delegation from the Kingdom of Tressor. They found themselves carefully sorted among the tables of the Castle Verril's enormous banquet hall. The elite of the kingdom sat nearest to a broad dais at the head of the hall. The chief among them occupied a coveted seat at the table itself. Each had been carefully introduced, and now all eagerly anticipated the arrival of the guests of honor.

For the honor of doing the introductions, the highest ranking officer of the military had been sought out. So much of the power of the Alliance Army had been held directly by the generals, their defeat had left the chain of command in shambles. Only a handful of individuals had been given any positions of power, and most had either been nearmen, or had abandoned their position for fear of sharing the blame that had been heaped upon the generals. Finally, a young elf by the name of Croyden Lumineblade had come forward. He had been a minor field commander, but had steadily ascended the ranks, and was currently the only remaining member of the Alliance Army willing to admit to a rank higher than lieutenant. There were rumors that his estranged mother had, in fact, been one of the five generals, but the lack of detailed military files and his own silence on the issue left it unproven.

He now stood before the dais, parchment in hand. On it was a very precisely written list of titles and instructions.

"Silence, please," he requested. "as I announce this evening's guests of honor."

Conversations hushed to an excited whisper.

"Announcing Heroine of the Battle of Verril, Guardian of the Realm-- the great elemental, Ether," he spoke.

There was a smattering of polite applause. Ether was known, by name alone, to be one of the others involved in the battle, but she'd not been seen since. Indeed, if not for the application of the title of Guardian of the Realm, an honor greater than knighthood and just beneath royalty, Ether might have received no reaction from the crowd at all. The shapeshifter walked toward the dais and coolly surveyed those in attendance. After judging them, she altered her gown, transforming it into a masterpiece carefully envisioned to outshine the best the nobles and aristocrats had to offer. This sent a wave of impressed whispers and a second round of more genuine applause through the crowd. She took a seat near the end of the dais.

"Announcing Heroine of the Battle of Verril, Guardian of the Realm, Royal Poet, Composer, and Painter--Ivy," Croyden announced.

The crowd hushed to near silence as Ivy appeared, interrupted by the occasional nervous clap. Every attempt had been made to allow her to fit in. Her gown was made especially for her, and was every bit the match for any in the room, save Ether's. She walked with grace and regal bearing. Nonetheless, the distrust of her kind was a deeply rooted one. At best, her heroics were seen as a testament to the others for having coaxed such greatness from her. Despite this, Ivy walked to the dais with a wide smile on her face. If there was one thing she had learned in the months gone by, it was that society might still hate her, but individuals were easy to win over. As far as she was concerned, it was only a matter of time and patience before she was as well-liked as any other. She needed only make the effort. There was a dash of mischief to her grin though, as she took a seat.

"I cannot help but notice that your title is longer than mine," Ether said as Ivy sat beside her.

"That's because I'm more talented than you," Ivy said.

"You most certainly are n--" Ether began.

"Shh. This is going to be good," she said, her grin widening as she watched Croyden swallow hard.

The herald read over the next line again, and eyed the doors at the end of the main hall.

"Announcing," he said, "Heroine of the Battle of Verril, Guardian of the Realm--Myn."

A gasp arose first from those people who recognized the name. A moment later, a few stifled screams rose from those who didn't.

Myn stepped lightly along the floor of the banquet hall, attempting to keep a watchful eye on all around her at once. Those nearest to the walkway shuffled and skidded their chairs in attempts to put some distance between themselves and the massive beast. Baubles of gold adorned Myn's head and neck, in much the way a woman might wear earrings and necklaces, and her scales had been polished to a high gloss. She looked resplendent.

Ivy applauded enthusiastically and raised her voice in encouragement. A smattering of the crowd weakly followed suit. Myn took her place at the end of the dais and sat on her haunches. Ivy threw her arms around the dragon's neck and gave her a kiss on the cheek. The audience turned first to the four remaining seats, then expectantly to the door.

"Announcing Hero and Heroine of the battle of Verril," Croyden said, raising his voice as a standing ovation began. "Full Master and Full Mistress of the Mystic Arts--Deacon, Duke of Kenvard, and Myranda Celeste, Duchess of Kenvard."

The pair appeared and made their way down the walkway hand in hand. The roar was deafening. Deacon was the other great hero of the day in the eyes of the people of the capital, and the long disused title of Duke had been bestowed as recognition. In the months since, he and Myranda had been a part of the peace talks, and helped to wipe away as much of the remaining scourge of the D'karon as they could. They were now equally beloved as warriors, healers, and diplomats. They took their place among the others.

The doors opened once more, and an honor guard of soldiers arranged themselves on either side of the walkway. Myranda recognized most of them. Chief among them was Tus, dressed in the unmistakable uniform of the Commander of the Royal Guard. The rest of the guard was made up of fellow members of the Undermine.

"Announcing Her Royal and Imperial Majesty, Queen and Empress of the Northern Alliance--Queen Caya the First!" cried Croyden.

The mention of the final hero of the Battle of Verril roused all in attendance to cheers. Half of the people in the hall had been present on that fateful day, and each told a different version of the tale. Only two aspects of the account remained constant. The first was that it was a glorious and sweeping victory. The second was that two great warriors, Deacon and Caya, were the greatest heroes of that day.

While the defeat of the generals in the mountains to the north was known only to the heroes, stories of their deeds within the capital grew more spectacular with each telling. The dragoyles grew in size and number, and the nearmen gained all manner of gruesome descriptions. Indeed, the nearmen of the recollections were massive, hideous beasts that clearly could never be confused with the soldiers who had patrolled the city each and every day for the decades prior to the battle. Deacon's legendary acts were performed in full view of the people of the capital, going so far as to earn him the honor of being the first to be offered the throne. He declined, but as the only other hero the people had seen leading the charge in their defense, the former leader of the Undermine as equally revered and more than willing to accept the crown.

Caya was radiant. She looked every bit the queen, dripping with jewelry, the freshly polished crown perched upon a bun of immaculately prepared hair, and a dress made of the rarest and most expensive of fabrics. One could easily envision her portrait hanging among the others that lined the walls--and, indeed, it very shortly would be.

Her behavior, however, was another matter. Even now, rather than the stately and stoic approach to her seat of honor that the servants had prepared her for, Caya was eagerly shaking the hands of the dignitaries and aristocrats. Croyden had been carefully briefed on the proper protocol for the occasion, and tasked with seeing to it that Caya behave appropriately. He quickly approached her as she was nearing her seat. Her eyes were scanning the crowd, lingering with particular interest on the faces of those who seemed disgusted by the creatures who had been given seats of honor. She turned to Croyden when he arrived.

"Ah, Croyden, is it? Excellent work announcing us. I was thinking I might address my public," she said. "Perhaps you would like to call them to attention?"

"Your Majesty, it is not traditional for the monarch to speak on the day of his or her coronation. Tradition states that if speeches are to be given, they are to be delivered by high-ranking members of your court on your behalf," he stated politely but firmly.

"Is that so?" she asked.

He nodded. Caya turned to the rest of the banquet hall.

"The good Captain Lumineblade has informed me that tradition requires I not speak to you great people on this, the first day of my reign. I would say we are long overdue for a break in tradition," she declared.

The response was an immediate and enthusiastic roar of approval from the honor guard and many of the other guests, and a somewhat more reluctant round of applause from the nobles of the audience. It was rapidly becoming clear to them that things were going to change a bit more than they would have liked.

"Take a seat," Caya said to Croyden, indicating the position next to her own, which had been abandoned by its previous occupant in favor of one a bit further from Myn. "You can come to expect this sort of thing."

With that, she turned back to the expectant crowd.

"Let me begin by making my first proclamation as queen. I hereby pardon the members of the notorious and subversive group known as the Undermine for all crimes and acts of treason committed on behalf of the group," she began.

Once again, the honor guard let up a cheer, while the nobles and the handful of military in attendance voiced their disapproval.

"With that out of the way, let me announce, once and for all, that until you good people saw fit to place the crown upon my head, I was the *leader* of the Undermine," she said with a grin.

Now even the cheers of the honor guard could not be heard over the growls of disapproval.

"And yet I am now your queen," she declared. "Will anyone deny that it was I and my friends that liberated the capital from the scourge that had befallen it? Would anyone here have done the same? War has left its mark on us in many ways. It has thinned our cities to desertion. It has sapped the land of its bounty, and the people of their spirit. Perhaps worst of all, it has rendered our minds rigid and stubborn. The war only lasted as long as it did because we knew no other way. It is time for that to change.

"Look at the dais. On one side, huddled and cowering, is the old guard. The blue blood of this land. Aristocrats, nobles, and the privileged and wealthy. These are the people you have taken orders from and have looked up to. Now look at the other side. Wizards and sages, yes, but also freaks, monsters, and rebels. They, along with every farmer, miner, shopkeeper, and commoner, are the red blood of this land. There are good men and women, but also scoundrels, sympathizers, and everything you have been taught to hate.

"And I gladly count myself among them. Because despite what I have said, which side contains the heroes? The red blood is the blood that is spilled. These people, these creatures, these great, wonderful heroes, risked everything because they saw what needed to be done and vowed to do it. Sacrifices were made. Lives were lost."

She turned to the others. A single seat had been left empty between them, a quiet nod to the hero who had not made it. She turned back.

"Some stories will never be told," she continued. "But because of these hated dregs of our society, the hold of war has been broken. For the first time, we turn from the conflict we have faced so bravely to the terrifying prospect of peace. Things will not be simple. The way is uncertain. But, for the sacrifices that have been made by your brothers, sons, sisters, and daughters, I don't think we have any choice but to try. We owe it to them. We must work together, as one, until the wounds left by the blade of war are healed. Red blood and blue blood. Monsters and humans. Alliance and Tressor. For our parents! For our children! For ourselves! Are you with me!?"

The crowd roared back in a single voice, leaping to its feet. It didn't die down until well after the meal had been served. With her words still burning in their veins, the guests looked to one another, then to the delegates from Tressor. Over the course of the meal, compliments, discussions, and debates began to flow in fractured Northern and fractured Tresson. Wine was poured, hands were shaken. Over such delicacies as could be offered by the broken land of the north, ancient animosities were, for the moment, set aside.

The road to a lasting peace would be a long one--but on this night, the first steps were taken.

Caya was not one to let a good celebration end, let alone one in her honor. The sun was coloring the horizon before the final celebrants staggered to their rooms. Aside from the ubiquitous servants, only the Chosen, the queen, Croyden, and the ambassador remained. The latter had been impressed with Caya's command of the language. Furthermore, Croyden had proven to be skilled in diplomacy as well.

"I thank you again, Your Excellency. I look forward to meeting with you again over the peace discussions. I would very much like to have an official treaty signed. Armistices are a bit fragile for my tastes," the queen said as a servant led him away.

"Until then, Your Majesty," he said.

When he had left, Caya turned to Croyden.

"Well, Captain Lumineblade. I must say I was *quite* impressed with how you conducted yourself today. You are quite an able diplomat. And if the tales you told about your military exploits are any indication, you are quite the soldier as well," Caya said.

"Why thank you, Your Majesty. I am honored to--" he began.

"Call me Caya," she interrupted. "If you will excuse me, though, I must have a word with the other Guardians of the Realm. I shall see you tomorrow. Over dinner, perhaps?"

"Yes, Your Maj--yes, Caya," he said, taking his leave and shutting the door behind him.

"Flirting isn't a terribly royal activity," Myranda remarked.

"Bah. Queen is just a title. Besides, it is very important to ensure the royal succession," she quipped. "Lumineblade . . . Isn't that the scoundrel Desmeres's surname?"

"Yes," Myranda replied.

"Brother or son? It is difficult to tell with elves," she mused. "Eh, regardless, it looks as though some things run in the family. Speaking of which, the Und--er, *Royal Guard* has been complaining of weapons going missing. I must look into that . . ."

Ivy, rising from her seat, made her way over to the others. She had a vaguely yellow glow about her, and an unsteady swagger to her walk. Somehow, though, she managed to make even staggering seem graceful.

"Thank you for inviting me to your party!" slurred Ivy, as she stumbled into a hug.

"Had a bit of wine, has she?" Caya asked.

"Yes. Thank heavens she is a happy drunk," said Myranda, helping to disentangle the two. "Ether, look after Ivy, would you?"

Ether's response was a stern, unmoving gaze.

Myranda sighed. "Myn, would you?"

The dragon looked up from a third cauldron of mashed potatoes and licked some errant specks of it from her nose. Ivy scrambled to Myn's back and mumbled something about going out flying as the beast lumbered out the massive entry way.

"What is next for you, shapeshifter?" Caya asked. "Now that the D'karon are gone, what will fill your days?"

Ether stared coldly at the queen for a few moments, then shifted quickly to wind and whisked away without a word.

"She still hasn't mastered the art of social discourse, it would seem," Caya said, adjusting her tousled hair.

"I am worried about her. She shows up when we need her, but mostly she spends her time at Lain's End, alone," Myranda explained.

"Lain's End? Ah, the hole in the ground in the mountains. That's right. I wish you would have allowed me to acknowledge him more properly than naming the place of his death after him. He was despicable, to be sure, but he had a role in this," said the queen.

"Lain spent his life in shadow. It seems wrong to reveal him now. Better to let him remain the legend he built for himself. It is what he would have . . ." she began, trailing off as a realization entered her mind. "No, there *is* something. Lain had spent his life trying to give the lives back to slaves, indentured servants, anyone who was forced into a life of servitude against their will, or without choice. If you could . . ."

"Consider it abolished," Caya replied. "The Alliance is going to have to be rebuilt, and we shall need every able hand to do it."

The doorway was pushed open and Deacon entered.

"The carriage is ready," he yawned.

"Leaving so soon?" Caya asked.

"I need to get back to Kenvard. There are only a few weeks left before the peace discussions resume, and there is much to be done if Kenvard is to be rebuilt. Father was not even willing to spare the time needed to join us here," she said.

"I'd wondered about him. I suppose it stands to reason he didn't want to come back to the building he'd spend so many years rotting underneath, as well. Better reasons than my family had!" Caya declared.

"What kept them away?" Myranda asked.

"Business. What with the first trade lines finally opening up, they've got their hands full filling orders at the vineyard, and at my uncle's distillery, too. At least they were kind enough to send us some of the better vintage," she said.

"Indeed." Myranda nodded. It was the first she'd heard of the family business, though it certainly explained where the funding for her prior exploits had come from--and, more importantly, where the apparently endless supply of "liquid courage" had originated.

The trio walked through the doors as the servants attempted to restore order to the banquet hall. They made their way to the entrance. The venerable castle, more ancient than memory, was scattered with signs of renewal. Cracked and damaged walls were patched, ruined tapestries were removed--but most notable were the doors. Shattered by Myn to gain entry to this place, the repaired doorway was now composed of gleaming metal and polished stone hung with glorious blue doors. Servants in attendance, only just closing them following Myn's exit, hurriedly began to open them again. A trio of other servants appeared with coats and cloaks for the travelers, and a fur wrap for the queen.

"Nice as it is to have servants, I have my concerns about being queen. I didn't think it would be easy, but I certainly didn't think it would be more difficult than running the Undermine. Do you remember how long it took to find enough diplomats that actually spoke Tresson to begin the first round of talks? Egad. And without the nearmen, frankly, we are at Tressor's mercy. I know I sought victory at any cost, but that was before they put me on the throne. I would much prefer to gain my place in history as the *greatest* queen of the Northern Alliance, not the last. It is a dicey road ahead. I just wonder . . . after one hundred and fifty some-odd years of war, is a lasting peace even possible?" Caya wondered.

Myranda looked to the gates of the castle wall as they pulled open. Beyond it, the streets were packed, even as the sun was still breaking free of the horizon. There was a feeling of life in the city that Myranda could never recall feeling before. The land had its soul back. High above, Myn wheeled in the morning air.

"The D'karon are gone. That is the important thing. Whatever happens happens. Pass or fail, win or lose, at least the shackles are broken. The people can make their own decisions. For the first time in ages, they have the freedom to make a choice. Under your guidance, I believe they shall choose well," Myranda said.

Myn touched down in the street as Myranda and Deacon entered the carriage. As the crowd parted around the creature, the heroes took their first steps along the long road ahead.

#

And so the tale is told. As I write this, a thousand different tellings exist, twisted by tricks of memory, misunderstandings, and occasionally deceit. In the years to come, the stories will no doubt pass into legend, then myth, and perhaps into obscurity. Such is the whim of fate. But you, dear reader, may count yourself lucky that you came upon this book. You, at least, know it all. You know the curse and blessing that was the Mark. You know the pain and joy that a true quest brings. You know not just the end, but the beginning and the trials between. You know the truth--and the truth is important--about what occurred in this world once upon a time.

8692492R00182

Made in the USA
San Bernardino, CA
18 February 2014